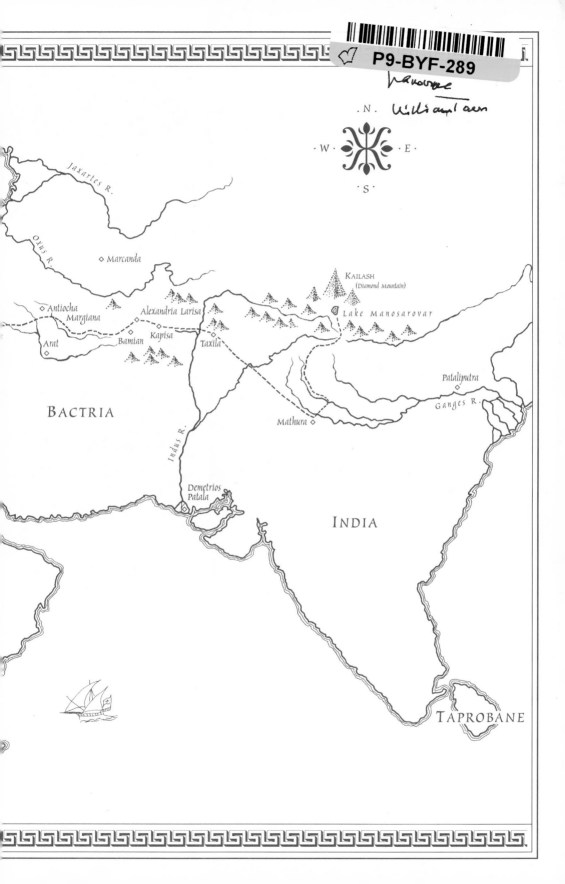

THE
GOSPEL
OF
CORAX

❦

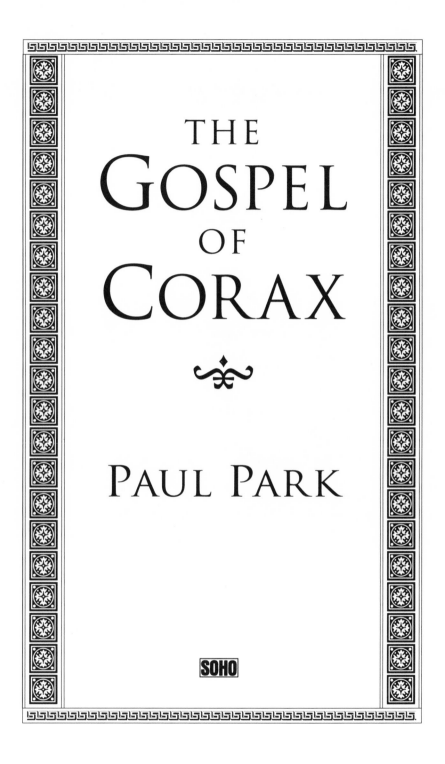

THE
GOSPEL
OF
CORAX

PAUL PARK

SOHO

Published by
Soho Press, Inc.
853 Broadway
New York, NY 10003

Library of Congress Cataloging-in-Publication Data

Park, Paul, 1954–
    The gospel of Corax : a novel / Paul Park.
        p.   cm.
    ISBN 1-56947-061-8 (alk. paper)
    1. Bible. N.T.—History of Biblical events—Fiction.   2. Jesus
Christ—Fiction.   I. Title.
PS3566.A6745G67   1996
813'.54—dc20   95–49147
                                          CIP

Book design by Lisa Govan

Manufactured in the United States of America
        10 9 8 7 6 5 4 3 2 1

For David Park and Clara Claiborne Park,
with love and gratitude

THE
GOSPEL
OF
CORAX

CHAPTER

1

IN PALESTINE

THE RIVER OF FORGETFULNESS

In the thirteenth year of the reign of the Emperor Tiberius, my
master opened his veins with a steel razor during his midday
bath, while he was resting at his house near Tusculum outside
the city walls.

I was with him. I saw him do it. I held his hands. He had a
recurring sickness in his prostate, but he was unhappy for other
reasons also. He used to confide in me—this was at the end of a
long, miserable winter in Rome. The emperor had retired to the
island of Capreae to spend his old age there. In the city he left his
affairs in the hands of the Praetorian commander, Aelius Sejanus, who had repaid him by seducing his niece and poisoning his
son. Now with the emperor gone, Sejanus conspired against the
health and character of the new heirs, the children of Prince Germanicus, and he used the emperor's dark, drunken fears to bring

3

about the downfall of many famous citizens, supporters of Germanicus's party. Among these was my master's patron, Titius Sabinus, a Roman knight, who was condemned and executed after the first of the year because of a careless overheard remark. This murder—for that's what it was—caused a despair among Germanicus's friends and those who, like my master, had served with him on the Rhine.

None of these were my thoughts. My master told me all of it. After his death I stripped the slave rings from my ears. I hid for a few days in the Subura slums, shivering in the empty lots and cellars of the potmakers, until the week before the festival of Lupercalia. In the streets they were splashing red paint on the shop fronts and putting up boughs of pine. There were musicians on the hill, and a crowd of men with painted faces staggered down from the Cybele shrine. In the confusion of preparations I slipped across the bridge and took the road down toward the port. I walked through the cold night with nothing but a bag of clothes and a few things my father had left me.

At dawn I came to Ostia, to the Augustan docks. There I spent the last of the money I had taken from my master's house to reserve passage on the first boat of dawn, almost the first of the season—a squat, two-masted merchant ship bound for Caesarea in Palestine. It was important for me to get away. For me and many others: The dock was full of citizens and Egyptians and Jews, all escaping from the new injunctions, from Sejanus's tyranny and hate.

I climbed aboard as the dawn wind came up. The boat groaned and shifted in her berth, eager as I was to be gone. The ropes were taut with frost. I stood under the torches looking over the side at the black water, and in my mind I spoke to monkey-headed Father Toth. "Oh you stupid, stupid fool," I said to him, though I was talking about myself. I had not been on a ship before.

The sailors moved around me, and I kept out of the way, hidden by their bustling disorder. Later I made a nest for myself among the casks of luxuries on the second deck. The ship was full of African liquamen, Spanish olives, pickled mushrooms, and vermouth.

I think of that journey now as if it were my passage through the darkness after death. Scholars argue over the length of that crossing, before we come again into the land of light. I don't know how long my passage took; that cold sea was my Styx, that boat my Charon's bark. I kept a single silver penny from my master's treasure and lay like a dead man. Not once did I go up on deck. There were other passengers—two families of Jews—but I kept apart from them. I wrapped myself in my blanket. My saliva and stool were full of mucus. I carried the pot to a hole in the side, and in the daylight I could see the water skimming past. At night I lay curled up, listening to the boat, the crash of the water on its thin sides, the planks groaning apart. Sometimes I wept. I was in front of the first mast and the galley was nearby; I could smell the stinking food. Sick as I was, I ate only the roasted lentils and barley I had brought with me. I drank only water and washed my burns in water. There was a place on my forehead where the burning beam had hit me. It had scabbed over, but I wrapped it every night in a strip of linen soaked in olive oil. In the morning I examined it with my small mirror, praying it wouldn't mark me.

I prayed to Aesculapius the healer. Then without speaking I touched two other powers and held one in each hand. My master had given me two images in baked clay—Mithra Tauroctonus and the Egyptian Min, or Pan, or Krishna in my father's language. I held the lord of fire in my right hand and squeezed him till he came apart. In my left hand I held Krishna, and by the end of the trip I had rubbed him down to the bare figure of a man. His flute and penis were both gone.

One night when the boat was shuddering and rolling, a sailor came and stood looking down at me. He had a lantern in one hand, and with the other he held on to an iron hook that protruded from a beam above his head. He was from Cyprus like most of the others, and his Greek was bad, even though it must have been his native tongue. Few people have my gift of languages, the useful part of foreignness. I listened to him and closed my eyes. I imagined how his words were shapes, small creatures lamed and crippled by his accent and his heavy mouth, blundering through the shadows on the inside of my lids. "What are you doing here?" he said. "Why aren't you with the others?"

"I am sick," I answered. I knew it was dangerous to speak, to give him something to remember later, but I was starved for talking. I was not accustomed to so much time alone. Before, there had always been someone to help me. Someone to serve. "I'm sick," I said, needing his sympathy. I wanted both to hold him near me and to scare him off.

The boat itself was groaning and talking, but I couldn't tell what it said. I opened my eyes. The man stood hanging over me, a lantern in his hand. He was an old man with greasy hair, and the light made streaks in it. In my weakness I imagined his presence might contain a sign. But he just stood there without speaking, and so after a few moments I turned away. Though I was drawn to him, I turned my face into my blanket.

But later when I fell asleep this man was with me, and he guided me with his lantern along a narrow track through the forest. He put his arm across my shoulder and covered me with his cloak. We crossed a muddy stream, which I took to be Lethe, the river of forgetfulness. In the morning I woke refreshed for the first time. Tusculum was far away. And I remembered nothing from my dream beyond the crossing of the river, which made me hope I had been taken to some secret place and given some small piece of secret knowledge.

Grey light was coming through the planks in the deck overhead, falling like a series of grey curtains. For the first time I was not cold. I looked through my clothes, searching for something new. There was nothing, but that was the morning the clay figure of Mithra, my master's god, came apart in my hand. The gift was given in the silent, vacant part of thought. It was given inside.

And that was the night we came to Caesarea Palestinae. Though I had recovered some of my strength, still I was frightened as the sea grew flat, as the boat turned. I crouched by a hole in the ship's side and tried to smell the land. I looked out at the foam on the water. But I couldn't keep my mind on any of these things. I was distracted by fear. I was afraid the old sailor might have said something about me to the crew. There were reasons why I'd kept myself apart. Some of the cruelest of the Roman laws, which the divine Augustus had allowed to languish, were now enforced under Sejanus once again. The markets were full of slaves with branded faces. There were new bounties for runaways, that was what scared me. I had no document of any kind. And of course my mistress could have had me whipped. She would have done it, too, out of jealousy and spite.

But it was the brand that frightened me the most. I had dreamed about it, though in a dream that contained none of the usual signs of prophecy—no birds, no rainstorms, no fish. It seemed to me I feared the thought of it more than I feared death, because my face had always been my friend, a small support for me and source of strength even after I passed through my first youth. But perhaps also it is hard to think of death, hard to think of the soul changing. In contrast, at moments I could almost feel the red brand on my cheek. At other times I felt the mark on me already, my situation was so clear. Perhaps that was the other reason I had turned away from the old sailor and hid my face. Or why I picked at the burn on my forehead, as if it were some kind of omen.

But I didn't want to appear so sick that they might speak to the quarantine authorities of the port, and so at sunset I went up on deck. First I used my master's razor and cut my hair, which is evil luck at the beginning of a voyage but good luck at the end. When everyone had left the galley, I washed myself and changed my clothes. I tied my sandals and tied a strip of cloth around my head, as I had seen on young Jews in the city. I rubbed oil into my scalp, and then I melted wax from my candle, mixed it with paper ash, and rubbed the grey ash around my eyes. At first it looked ridiculous, but then I washed and tried again, and in the mirror I could convince myself that I looked older. I rubbed wax into my earring holes, and at sunset I left my nest behind. I tied my blanket over my shoulder and went on deck.

To the east we were skirting a low, brown coast. No one paid attention to me. The Jews were gathered in the belly of the boat under some torches, and I stood by the rail in the gathering dark. I stood with my hands hanging over the rail, and to calm myself I imagined the huge curve of the earth and the land turning to greet me. I could smell the warm air off the desert full of pungent dust, and I imagined all my life until that point was wasted, gone. Behind, a continent of shame. Ahead, whole countries full of languages and hope. In front of me was the Judaean coast, beyond it Perea and the Decapolis, then the desert, and the Euphrates river and the Tigris all the way to Seleucia, where my father had been a young soldier. I had nothing but a silver penny in my belt, but I felt lucky, suddenly joyful, yet wary too when one of the passengers came to stand beside me. I turned away from him and hid my face. He asked after my health in Greek, and I answered in the language that the Jews had learned in Babylon, the Aramaean language which my father taught me, which he had learned in Ecbatana and Ctesiphon and Babylon itself, when he had been a soldier of King Phraates. Before he had been taken prisoner during the night attack at Apamea—all these names were in my memory, and these stories also. I knew how the Romans had brought him across the sea, chained and bleeding between two dead men, when Quinctilius Varus was governor of Syria.

This was the land where he had been free. This was the coast where he had embarked on that terrible journey, which had ended with his death in Rome. I stood with my hands over the rail, answering questions from the man beside me in grunts and single words, and with part of my mind I was aware of him looking at me and wondering where I was from—a Samaritan perhaps, or more likely an Egyptian. Or else he was looking with amazement at the ashes around my eyes.

This thought drew me step by step into a fear, which was that there might be soldiers waiting at the dock for me. But at the same time I was making what my father called a "shadow cloth," and I was making a pattern out of memory and my own thought, one the warp, one the weft. I thought it was right for me to have sailed in darkness and cramped misery from Ostia, and in some way my journey was subtracting from that other journey which my father had taken the other way, untying it and sealing it up into the past, so that I might become my father as I stepped free on the shore, and live the life he might have lived. In fact he died in the sixth year of Tiberius's reign, still not able to stand upright or talk to my master without flinching. That was after he had given me the sacred thread. After I had come of age.

My father had been a captain of King Phraates the Great, who had driven Marcus Antonius out of Parthia with the loss of a hundred thousand Roman soldiers. During the civil wars after the king's death, before Augustus tried to put his creature Vonones on the throne, my father fought against the Romans as they tried to intervene. The shadow cloth covered me, and as I stood leaning against the ship's rail, talking to the Jew, I could hear my voice grow loud. I could feel a new recklessness as I turned to face him under the torchlight in the warm sweet wind. I dared him to look at me. I spoke to him and did not worry that my accent might be wrong or my verbs crude. For I had a figure in my mind of my father on horseback in his leather armor with the iron rings, the bow across his back. It was a figure made of memory and imagination in equal parts, but still it was alive, moving in my mind. The Jew had a fine beard and bright strong eyes, and ridges on his cheeks that might have been from some old wound. He had his own defenses, but with my new sight I imagined I could penetrate the bone of his forehead into his mind, and see there as if written on a slate the calculations that were diminishing me, subtracting and subtracting as his face changed and became less friendly, less inquisitive. He knew I was a soft creature as miserable as Vonones had been, Phraates's catamite son, whom Augustus had corrupted in Rome and then set up on his father's throne until the people rose against him.

Like Vonones, all my skills were in the world of the muses and the pleasure world. It was not for me to take my father's place. Though like him I was twice-born of the warrior caste, I had never sat upon a horse or held a spear. And all I had to take me through the deserts and the cities was a soft body that even as I stood there was racked with sudden pains across my back and chest. A soft body and a skill at languages, and a memory as sharp and dirty and intricate as the streets of Rome near Mons Testasceus. A view of the hidden universe arranged in order like the floors of an apartment block in the Subura. But perhaps it was the burden of these secret things that made me weak.

The boat was coming into Caesarea, and as we beat around the headland I could see a house in flames. The sun had set into the clouds behind us, and the sky was dark above the burning house. In front of it small figures struggled on the beach, silhouetted by the dancing fire. I thought of my master's villa and I thought of my dream of sweet forgetfulness; yes, the timber and the palm thatch burn, but the brick walls stand forever. I felt tears on my cheek. I took from my belt the clippings of my hair, the long black hair my master loved. And as we came around the headland and caught our first glimpse of the town, I let it sink into the water and spoke a prayer to Mother Astarte, queen of Asia, goddess of my heart. A scowl passed over the face of the Jew who stood beside me. Disgusted, he turned back into the boat and went back to the others.

But the wind in the sail above me was like a whisper that had come from Rome, from the doors of Juno's temple on the Aventine Hill, from Cybele's temple on the Palatine. And perhaps it reached the ear of their sister Astarte, curled and dark and open on the Asian shore. And perhaps Astarte heard my prayer and stretched her soft arm eastward over the bulge of the world, over the ice mountains, to touch the hand of Mother Durga far away.

We human beings need so much. We cry out and who answers us? Yet there were no soldiers looking for me at the dock. The customs men were there, the tax collectors. I walked straight through the barricade, carrying my bag.

I had not thought what I would do. All my anxiousness had fixed on that one moment. When it was past I stood there looking up at the lights of the town, which rose above me on a series of low hills. I stood looking at the lights while the dockhands bustled around me. I had a sickness in my stomach. I smelt sickness on my skin, and I remember thinking I would find the public bath. I remember wondering if the baths were still open, and pretending I would go the next morning as soon as I could find the money to pay the attendant to look after my clothes. I had no money to do anything, of course, but even so I must have known in my silent heart that I had left behind forever my life of baths, of strigils and oiled sponges—unusual for such as I, and which I had cherished as a sign of differentness, a special sign of my master's favor. But my life here was not to be among the Romans and the Greeks, the easy nakedness of men. All that was done.

Aimless, I wandered into the streets and up onto the steps of the big temple at the port. I walked up to look at the statues of the goddess Rome and the divine Augustus. Small lamps flickered at their feet. Bulky and dark, they loomed above me, facing back toward the sea. They were empty, impotent, incapable of help or consolation. A hundred beggars slept on the cold stairs with me, and many children.

Caesarea had been built by Herod the king. He had built the harbor, the temple, the theater, the circus, and the baths. He had started other civic buildings too, but they still stood unfinished in the central part of the town, twenty years after Augustus banished Herod's son. The bones of one big building lay below me. Looking down on them the next morning, I thought of the stone skeleton they had found in Joppa, the lizard that had preyed on Princess Andromeda, back when giants and enormous lizards ruled the earth. Near it squatted Herod's palace, now the center of the province, where the Roman prefect lived.

I turned my back on it. On the other side beyond the synagogue lay the town itself, Syrian and Jewish and Greek mixed together, along with other tribes. It was a cold bright morning and I held out my hands, hoping to feel heat rising from a stew of love and anger, while at my back the Roman town was cold.

Later I walked down through the stone and mud-brick houses to the marketplace, comforted by the chaotic smells, the pushing crowds. I had only a silver denarius in my belt, and though men sat on the sidewalk frying eggplant in big vats and mixing chickpea paste with olive oil, I didn't let myself feel hunger. In the cold night on the steps I had coughed until my throat was raw, until something came loose in the bottom of my lung. I didn't want to spend another night like that, and so I thought about a way to make strength out of weakness, to entice the care of the compassionate gods. I had a plan. Even as the day grew warmer and my breath came easier, I did not waste my money on apricots and other strange delights. Instead, I stole things.

I made a pouch in the blanket around my shoulders and stole what nobody else wanted. There were other thieves in the crowd, marked with the sign of Mercury, which I saw clearly. Others saw it too, or something like it—the shopkeepers threatened them and warned them away. Children threw stones, and in the afternoon the thieves would slink back to the temple, clutching an old piece of bread or a pomegranate. But at the day's end I had in my pouch some straw tubes full of spices, and bundles of herbs. I had several short pieces of string and, far more precious, a length of silken thread. I had thirty-seven flat slips of wood, a few inches square, suitable for funeral cards. I had four clay tablets. I had a small, flexible piece of leather. I had nine slips of Egyptian paper. I had bought things too—some flour, some salt, a pen and a pot of ink, a brush and some small tubes of various powders for making paint.

The marketplace lay behind low, broken walls on a long slope beyond the town. There was a public well at the far end, where I had washed my face that morning. The ground was muddy in a deep ring around it. On the near side was the market for fruit and bread and meat—not a place for those Jews who still kept to their laws, but in Caesarea there were plenty of the other kind. The vendors had their stock laid out on blankets over the packed ground. A few kept wooden stalls, especially those who offered livestock, and there were some tents over the open food. It was a cold, clean day.

Beyond the well, along the slope of a low hill rose up the untouchable section of the town. During the day it seemed deserted—empty stalls and mud-brick shacks. But as evening came on, the market's center shifted up the hill as more of the vendors packed and left. Soldiers walked through the crowd carrying torches, and people followed them up into the shadow world, the world that exists on the outskirts of all towns and is to the ordinary world as dreams are to life, as dark is to light, as desire is to virtuous duty. Where everything is hidden and revealed: I meant to live in that shadow world for a few months until summer, to gather my strength and gather money also, in preparation for a journey which was still taking shape for me, but which at the end would bring me to the sacred river Ganges, and leave me whole and healed. I would say a prayer for my father, who had been born upon its banks. And during my journey I would spend whatever I had gathered or would gather, because strength and power cannot but make us weaker, as I knew from Rome.

So as the soldiers moved up the slope I followed them. They left their torches in the public stanchions and then spread out among the shacks, whose curtain doors, as darkness fell, had been hooked back to admit customers. A bucket of charcoal burned in an open circle of pounded dirt. Musicians played there after dark—small combinations of flutes and pipes and ceramic drums. Men sold wine and beer out of clay vats, and they played knucklebones and dice on low tables. They ate olives and hot nuts, and in time they got up to dance with each other or alone, and then they staggered back among the huts, searching for women or boys.

Later still, some of the women came out to watch, and some of the boys also. That first night there was a procession in honor of the god Attis. There was a crowd, and a great deal of drunken argument, for the Jewish council had protested. The prefect had sent soldiers, but he had not forbidden the procession; after midnight it took shape out of nothing. Musicians gathered around the fire, and at a certain moment there were horns blowing in the darkness from the top of the hill. "Who is here?" called out one man, and there came a new and ridiculous bleating from the horns as a crowd of boys and girls climbed down among the huts. These were the famous "spintriae" of Caesarea, modeled on the children who provided old Tiberius with his remaining pleasures. They were led by a man with a shepherd's staff, and I learned from my neighbor in the crowd that he had been with the emperor at Capreae until he got too old. If that was so, Tiberius's taste was more peculiar than I had guessed. I couldn't imagine that the man had been beautiful even as a boy, though perhaps that was my prejudice. In fact it was hard to tell anything about his natural face and body. Though much was exposed, all was painted and transformed. He wore a wig of yellow German hair, wild on his shoulders, with colored ribbons and beads woven through it. His eyes were lined with kohl and Tyrian powder, and his cheeks were painted red. He had pulled the hair from his arms and legs. He wore a strip of linen over his mouth, and his dress, though ragged, was made of fine transparent linen gauze, cut high on his thighs and barely covering him. His toes and fingernails were painted red, and the palms of his hands and the soles of his feet. His dress was cut down the middle and it lolled apart obscenely on his stomach, there was a painted symbol over his navel, which I took to be of some mystic significance, though I didn't recognize it. Finally he had blown up two pig's bladders and tied them to his chest, and painted them with nipples. I guessed he was about my age.

The others followed him down out of the dark, perhaps a dozen boys and girls. Some were dragging their drums and yawning, and the youngest boy had gashed his instep on a stone—they all looked as if they had come a long way. Many had caught colds, and the mucus flowed down freely from their noses, mixing with the paint around their lips.

The older boys dressed like their leader in wigs and veils and false breasts, which looked grotesque on their small frames. Though it was a cold night, the oldest girl was naked to the waist, and attached to her belt she wore a wooden phallos, or "lingam" in my father's language. She looked around with wide, uncertain eyes, and she was drunk or drugged. She carried cymbals, which she clashed together. At the same time one of the singers stood up near the charcoal bucket and recited in Greek the story of the god: how his mother had eaten the seed of the almond tree and had conceived him without intercourse. How he grew up beautiful as the morning, as the flowers, as the water, and as luscious as the fruit upon the branch. How Cybele—"Asheroth," they called her here—recognized herself in him, because the almond fruit had dripped out of her blood. How she loved herself in him and fell in love with his white skin, the shape of his eyes and his red mouth. And finally, because she could not have him, how she robbed him of himself, gelded him and killed him.

At that moment in the story we could hear the beast crying out in fear and rage, and three men wheeled a cart down off the slope. The calf was in it, lying on a nest of reeds, garlanded with colored ribbons and new leaves, stretched out with its hooves tied together. With it came the priest of Attis with the knife in his hands, whittling a bough of olive to test its sharpness.

But at that moment the ceremony was interrupted. Outside of Caesarea on the road toward Narbata, there lived in those days a community of Jewish fanatics and thugs called

"Essenes." They had some land on the edge of the plain, and there they lived a life of poverty, hunger, prayer, and frigid baths. Not content with this, however, they would come into the town, urging others to join them and follow their laws. They hated all gods but their god Jupiter, or Amon Re—"Jahwah" in the Hebrew language. They took to heart those verses of the poet in which Jupiter explains how, if he chooses, he can hoist into heaven all the other powers on the end of a rope, and they cannot drag him down.

These Jews were foolish enough to deny nature and the evidence of their senses. But unlike most in the town, they were not content to protest during the day and then come quietly up to the hill at night. Their only idea was to provoke fighting. That night they came over the hill just as the priest had caught the calf's testicles in his left hand. Dressed in white, they were carrying torches and chanting, and when they reached the circle of the fire they spread out among the crowd, striking people with their hands and feet. They were searching especially for the Jews, and when they found one they would spit on him and strike his head.

There were soldiers in the crowd. They were not Romans but auxiliaries from Idumea and Nabatea. They lacked the discipline of Romans, though perhaps they had received special directions from Pontius Pilate. Instead of protecting the people, they also began to set upon the Jews, punishing both the guilty and innocent, and beating them with sticks. The ceremony was ruined. The spintriae disappeared up the hill into the dark, the musicians dispersed, and the priest was chased away by a big brute of an Essene, muscular and tall, with a wild beard and wild eyes. He carried a knife. Surrounded by soldiers, he stood by the cart, daring them to approach him while he pulled back the calf's head. It was screaming and he cut its throat. Then he pushed out through the ring of soldiers, marking their faces with his bloody hands, and disappeared.

THE UNCLEAN HEALER

Soon after, I went back to the temple steps to sleep. But in the morning I was not refreshed. Since I had been on board the ship I had gone nowhere in my dreams, seen nothing and met no one. This was unusual for me. When I woke up, I sat and hugged my knees on the cold steps, looking out over the harbor.

Once in my master's house, sick and sweating with a high fever, I called out late at night in a voice not my own. I spoke some words in a strange language. Dion, the slave who was attending me, didn't recognize it. But he told me there are illnesses that attract the gods. Fevers bring them close. The smell attracts them. But on the steps I had no fever. I had a low, hard, painful cough and pains in my stomach and joints. As I sat in the cold morning, I made a list of my complaints and thought about each one. It was the cough: My coughing in the night had left me scratching on the portal of the house of sleep, though inside I could hear the guests sit down together.

Yet in another way I was pleased with my illness. It suited the part I was about to play, the unclean healer. I thought I could take the signs and spirits out of other people and let them live in me—my cough would be the advertisement for my skill. At noon I gathered all my tools and clothes, and lugged them to the marketplace again. Near where the *puja* to Attis had been performed, I rented a stall from one of the landlords. I gave him some money I had stolen in the crowd the night before, and then I sat down to prepare my business.

The landlords owned narrow strips of property that made a patchwork over the hill. People said they were related, a family of brothers. The one who rented to me was a big, sturdy man named Shimon. He had the tight hair that suggests African blood. He came and stood over me as I painted my cards and laid them out to dry.

They were crude and quickly drawn. The twelve signs of

the Zodiac. The sun and moon, the four known planets, and the unknown ones. The queen. The magus. The lover. The rose. The tower, the tempest, the crucified man, the number cards, the wheel, and then the others. Shimon stood above me with his hands on his hips, inspecting my work. "Good color blue," he grumbled. He went away and came back. "How did you make that blue?" he asked, and then he told me I would have to pay a safety fee of one hundred copper ases on the calends of every month. "Not to me," he said, by which I knew that it was for the sicarii, so called because of the hidden daggers, or "sicae," that they carried. They had been among the Essenes who had attacked the procession the night before. In the days that followed I grew accustomed to the sight of their leader, a thin man with sunburnt skin, walking openly in the marketplace. The true name of this bandit was not known, but in the marketplace they called him Bar Abbas, which means "son of the master" in the Aramaean language.

"It's the fault of the prefect," said Shimon. "Things are very bad." In the days that followed he said more, as much as he could manage in his crude Greek. He was a compulsive talker, though he always pulled back just at the point of saying anything disloyal. It didn't matter. You couldn't spend an hour in the market without hearing something. To give the prefect credit, he didn't seem to be interested in punishing seditious conversation. I heard talk in Caesarea that never would have been tolerated in Rome, where Sejanus manipulated the dark suspicions of the emperor, and every public place was full of informers and the secret Praetorian police. Where each month brought new banishments and executions, new corpses flung out on the Stairs of Mourning.

But men are seldom grateful for the softness of their commanders. The Jews of Caesarea grumbled constantly. Many of them had been to Rome, and they remembered their lives under the divine Augustus, before Tiberius had banned their festivals in the fifth year of his reign. He had forced the rabbis to burn their clothes and break apart their holy vessels. He had driven them from the city, along with the priests of Horus and the Chaldean astrologers.

Others remembered Annius Rufus and Valerius Gratus, the former prefects of Judaea. But they hated the new man. Pontius Pilate had not been in the country six months and already he had offended them. At the beginning of the previous winter, when he moved his soldiers to their winter quarters in Jerusalem, he had made them carry the medallions of the emperors through the streets. It was an insult to the laws of the Jews inside their sacred city, and he followed it immediately with a worse offense. He had stolen part of the temple treasure called the Corbonas, and used it to construct an aqueduct outside Jerusalem at Solomon's Pool. He had put blocks of stone into the Cedron river. When the Levites protested in the temple, and others at the site tried to destroy the work, he placed soldiers in the crowd dressed as Jews. They held clubs under their coats, and when the signal came they set upon the people and beat many to death. More were trampled. The fruitseller in the Caesarea marketplace put the number of the crowd at thirty thousand and said one in ten had died, which I doubted.

He was a toothless, garrulous old man. On the morning of my fifth day in the town I squatted near his blanket, looking at his pears, as he told me something new. He said the prefect had proposed new plans to the high priest and the Sanhedrin, announcing a change in the currency. Already it was an insult that the gold and silver money was stamped with the emperor's profile, but the mint for these coins was not in Palestine. Besides, no one but a Roman citizen was rich enough to use them much. But the copper money, the one and two as pieces, were minted there in Caesarea. Always before they had been unfigured in deference to the law. But these new designs included pictures of oak leaves sacred to Jupiter, and sacrificial knives. Just by using them, the fruitseller complained, he would find himself defiled in every small transaction.

The fruitseller mixed easily with foreigners, like many Jews in the town. His Greek was excellent. He ate in front of me and didn't wash his hands. He didn't follow the law himself. Perhaps for that reason he had an obstinate respect for it.

He thought the prefect was a crazy man, offending the principles of Roman justice out of arrogance and stupidity. Like many in the market, he spoke of sending an official protest to the emperor. He did not see what was obvious. He had no way of knowing, as I did, that the prefect was Sejanus's creature, selected by him over two more qualified candidates, one of whom had been my master's cousin.

He had no way of knowing that Sejanus hated Jews, as he hated Parthians and black-skinned Egyptians and Ethiopians. He detested all Africans and Asians. He thought them soft, and decadent, and subtle. In the city he tolerated the barbaric rituals of the Gauls and the Germans, whom he praised for their vigor and discipline; his own Praetorian Guard was full of them. And though he needed Egypt as a source of grain, he had actually (my master claimed) advised the emperor to withdraw from all of Asia except for Cappadocia and Asia Minor, before the sternness and honesty of the ancient Romans was infected and perverted from the east. This from a man who had seduced the grandniece of Augustus himself, and poisoned her husband, Drusus Caesar.

So what the fruitseller and Shimon interpreted as senseless insults, I thought were something different, part of a deliberate policy. Or perhaps not deliberate, for governors rarely voice what they intend, even to themselves. It is their acts that speak, and I thought there was a reason why subversive conversation was not punished in Caesarea. I thought Sejanus needed an excuse. I thought he needed some mark of defiance, something to force his lazy, cautious master to destroy Herod's temple and bring the legion down from Syria. I told this to the fruitseller and to Shimon. Perhaps I came to the attention of the sicarii that way.

But I can't tell for certain. By my fifth day in the market I was well known for other reasons. This caused me much anxiety, which could not be helped. My business depended on my reputation. But at the same time I had no wish to draw attention to myself. I was still in danger of recapture, for Palestine was under Roman law.

At first I thought I could maintain a difference between my public and private selves. In my stall at night I painted my face, but just as actors become known in Rome, by the fifth morning I was followed wherever I went by curious children. At night there were dozens of people at my stall, they milled about in front of my table. Even the ones who didn't dare to speak or look at me directly crowded close to overhear.

My stall was made out of a square frame of cedar poles with canvas curtains. I could stand up in it, and late at night I slept under the table. There was a canvas roof over the top. In time I hung a curtain from the roof's forward edge, which I would roll up after sunset and then roll down when I went to bed. I hung another curtain from the forward lip of the table. In this way I enclosed the space and added to the sense of mystery. When I pulled the curtain back and lit the three lamps, again it was like a small theater, or more especially like a Greek puppet booth which I had once seen in the Campus Martius. Like the puppeteer, I whitened my face and hands with a lead pigment mixed with clay.

From my booth I offered various services for small amounts of money. I read letters and official documents in Latin and Greek, twenty words for one as. I took dictation and made copies for double that amount. To give myself an air of separateness and power, I used no languages except those two. Even during the day I pretended to understand no others.

There were other scribes in the marketplace. Still, business was brisk. Many in the town spoke Greek, but very few spoke Latin, though it was the language of the upper court. The first few nights most of my business was in short legal translations, though that changed rapidly. I also read palms and cards, made numerological and astrological predictions. I cut hair and pulled teeth. And of course I was a healer, an infirm healer, for as time went on and my reputation grew, I took care to emphasize that part. I would interrupt a consultation to cough and spit into my hand. Sometimes I would hide some red pigment at my wrist to create the illusion I was coughing blood. Or I would overlay the white paint on my cheekbones with a hectic, painted flush.

Yet gods are different from men in their sense of fairness and the ease with which they can be fooled. Therefore men and women do become what they pretend, in their vices and virtues as well as in more ordinary matters. I felt worse and worse, and the chill that had started in the Subura changed to something else. As time went on, my illness copied my pretenses exactly. And though I didn't violate my art by reading my own stars or using my own preparations, sometimes I envied the relief I brought to others.

On my third evening in the market, they carried to my stall a woodcutter with a deep wound in his thigh. It was bleeding freely, soaking the cloth they held to it. I interrupted my translation and came out from my stall, carrying my father's kit which I had brought from Rome. I had them lay the man down on the rocks and hold his leg up straight. I called for a lantern and a lighted brazier. Then I took a length of cord and tied it tight around his upper thigh, sealing off the veins. I examined the wound to see if it had touched any of the sacred marmas, the 107 points upon the surface of the skin that, if violated, make death inescapable. But the wound threaded between them. It was in the heavy part of the thigh. The bone was untouched.

I had some time before the cord had to be released. Stagnant blood turns into pus, and the flesh starts to rot in a few hours. But first I looked at the man's palm. He was scarcely conscious, but I inquired of his wife, who was there, his date and time of birth, and made some calculations. It is important for a surgeon, before he begins, to understand the purposes of nature, for it is worse than useless to go against them. Sickness is a punishment, as my father taught me. But some punishments are meant to be fatal, and some only a warning.

All a physician can do is to help nature, to help the gods accomplish their work. So first I had to guess what they intended, and only later I laid out my tools. I had prepared a mixture of Egyptian poppy juice and "bhang," my father's recipe of cured hemp leaves crushed with oil and ginger, and now I had my patient drink some in a cup of wine. With the aid of his wife, he was strong enough to do so. Otherwise I would have had to make an enema.

In the meantime I had selected several of my father's forceps and laid them in the brazier. Then I washed out the wound, first in distilled wine and then with a confection of my own—ash from glasswort mixed with hot resin. I rubbed the wound with this until it made a froth, and washed it with water. Then I anointed my hands. Dion, my master's surgeon, would have sneered at this; he had studied at the school of Erasistratos in Alexandria and thought he knew all things. What he would have suggested was a mixture of cinnamon and perfumed lint to scent the wound. And he was right. Bad smells were our enemy, the sign of our failure. But I had always thought that it was worse to hide the truth, to fool the gods. Besides, this ointment of mine never failed to give my hands a sweet, delightful smell. It was the difference between a prostitute's perfume, which hides disease, and the clean smell of a child.

I had selected my father's heron-beak forceps and several smaller ones and laid them in the fire. Dion had showed me how the heart is a pump, with the spirit in one half and blood in the other. He had showed me how the arteries carry air, the veins blood, and he had explained how the main passages must be sealed off before the cord, in this case around the woodcutter's thigh, is released. Otherwise, blood and air will leak into the flesh, no matter how carefully the wound is bandaged or sutured. They will stagnate and turn rotten.

This was wisdom. But my father was also wise, and he had told me how a surgeon's tools also could cause ulcers. He called this the greatest crime, to spoil what you had begun to cure. He told me that steel, because it was the noblest of metals, had a memory. He told me that the memories of other wounds affixed themselves to the bare metal and could spread, just as a cold spreads between children. He told me this memory could be destroyed by using new tools with each operation, like the surgeons of the peacock kings in his own country.

But because that was impossible, he had showed me how to heat the forceps in the fire until they glowed, as if forging them anew. So that they would come to the wound with their memories childlike and fresh. I took the heron beak in my right hand, and I sang a charm to Father Toth, god of my craft. Then I searched for the artery and seized it in the hot beak, and slid the clasp to seal it and burn it shut. Then I let go. With my smaller forceps, I found the veins.

When the artery was closed, the man lost consciousness. At least he didn't kick so much. I sewed his veins shut with a silk thread. I tied off the stump of the artery as Dion had taught me. I undid my clamps and packed the wound with honey and ghee mixed with copper verdigris. Then I closed it with sticky bandages to keep its lips together. I prayed to the red sieve, the red rain, and the red gate. Then I undid the cord.

Later that night, a man complained of fever and headaches. I pulled his rotten tooth. I drained the abscess.

Later that night, they brought me a man who couldn't breathe. He sucked at the air, but it wouldn't enter in. I gave him an infusion of the herb ephedron mixed with wine.

Nature has two kinds of punishment. One is the sudden accident, the stroke of lightning, the breaking bone, the sudden fever, the slip of the axe. That is the penalty for crimes of blood or passion, and it can be fatal or not. Then there is the wasting sickness, like leprosy or malaria, or all the diseases of the lungs. These are caused by the accumulation of vices, which can be treated, as my father said. Lives can be changed, though of course that's where the physician always meets the most resistance. The asthmatic man, when he was breathing easier, I asked him several private questions, which he didn't answer. He gripped the wine cup in his fist. So I told him to say prayers and search inside himself. But I knew he wouldn't because Jews are stubborn. He gave me an evil look.

The great kings of Palestine, David and Solomon and Herod, all died of rotting genitals, from going in to unclean women. Surely they saw the correspondence. A physician can only do so much. It is for this reason that diseases often break out again, no matter how good the care. Even clean wounds rot, because the causes are not in the physician's hands. He treats symptoms only. Yet even so, people are desperate to believe in miracles, to believe the gods can be robbed and cheated. They cannot look into themselves. The word goes out they can be healed by others. On the fourth night I had a crowd of twenty men around my stall, and I interrupted my card reading to perform an operation that I knew would impress them. During the day I had seen a girl with the white blindness. I had spoken to her father and learned how the condition had crept upon her over a few years. She had not always been blind.

I asked her father to come up. He had heard of my success with the woodcutter, and so he brought her to my stall. I sat her on a bench, and after heating my needle I thrust it through the top of each of her pupils, detaching the occluded lens behind each iris and levering it down so that it lay along the inside of her eye. She was a brave girl and did not blink, though in fact the operation was quick and almost painless. And as my luck would have it, she had been shortsighted from birth. She could not tell her vision was not completely restored. She called out in amazement when she saw the lantern that her father was carrying. She could see his hand when he brought it close.

On the fifth morning I had money, and I went to the herb woman to buy hellebore to make a purgative. Elsewhere I found crushed malachite, Indian pepper, and dates. I squatted with the fruitseller and heard his grievances, and in the afternoon I left the market and walked out into the town. I had a sense I was being followed, and not just by children. There were two men dressed in white, skulking in the doorways. They were there whenever I turned around.

That night was the beginning of the Sabbath, and only a few Jews came to my stall. One was a short bald man with white skin and a drinker's face, whom Shimon had identified for me as Judas ish Kariot—a spy for Pontius Pilate. Though he was a Jew, he didn't wear the Jewish cap or the striped tallith shawl. He was disguised, I suppose, but everyone knew who he was. No one in the marketplace inspired such a mixture of fear and contempt. The children made faces behind his back, yet he could take whatever he wanted from the market without paying. It seemed ridiculous to me, a spy whom everyone recognized. But then I thought it was another example of the prefect's strange laxity. And perhaps also you can gather more information by purchasing it outright than by searching for it. When he came to my stall he didn't trouble himself to ask me any questions. I had bought a roll of paper and was copying from memory some astrological charts: the location of the planets month by month, beginning with the year of the conjunction between Mars and Jupiter, the pattern in the stars that had driven Herod mad. Rivers of blood had flowed out of Palestine that year, as Herod searched for enemies among the common folk. Women and babies had been slaughtered.

Ish Kariot watched me in silence, and I was conscious of a flush of pride. I got such pleasure from the pure mnemonic art, the mother of all the rest. I liked the admiration it brought me, and sometimes in my stall I would play tricks with it, asking long lists of numbers from the crowd and then reciting them back without a pause, doubled sometimes, or tripled.

That Sabbath night I stood with my eyes closed, my elbow leaning on the tabletop. But in my mind I stood inside the palace of the moon and stars, which rose up tier by tier into a blood-red sky. Each tier was formed out of twelve chambers, three rows of four. Each chamber carried its name in fiery letters over the lintel—the names of the months that Alexander of Macedon had brought to the Chaldeans: DYSTROS, XANTICOS, ARTEMISIOS, DAI-SIOS. . . . I entered into each in turn and read the numbers off the wall, the symbols of the planets. They were painted there like the god Marduk's words, when they appeared to Prince Belshazzar at the feast.

Ish Kariot looked over my shoulder at the line of symbols I had written. But if he was impressed, he didn't show it. In a harsh voice he asked me if I had a cure for the headaches that were driving him to madness; he had been drinking, I could tell. His clothes smelled of beer and stale sweat.

It was a dark, cold night and no one was outside. I asked him to show me his right hand. It was very white and very clean. I put my own hand upon it. I glanced at it in the light of the oil lamp, and then I rubbed my fingertips into the callused hill, the crest below the mountain which the Romans call Veneris and my father called Meru, until I felt the blood-pulse there and felt it merge with mine. Then I let my fingers slide from the slope, down the Diamond Mountain, down into Tapovan and then the valley of the Cow's Mouth, where the veins of Acheron and Phlegethon and Cocytus, cold and hot, all converge under the ice and form into the great river Ganges, the sacred stream of death and life. It comes up from the underworld and carves its channel down the palm, down from the mountains and over the great plain, past where the Jamuna comes from Kurukshetra with its message of the heart's wisdom, the innocent water mixing there with the blood of the Kurus and the Pandavas, and then flowing down past Sarnath where Lord Boddo—who had been Prince Siddhartha—once had lived, past the temples of my father's city, Pataliputra the blessed.

I murmured a charm and let my finger glide down the line of Ish Kariot's life, searching for the source of his unhappiness. I moved over his childhood, his uncle's death, his mother's marriage to an older man with three grown daughters. "I have a throbbing pain behind my eyes," he said. "Day and night," he said, and I could smell the beer on his breath. I also was prone to sudden headaches. I understood him, and I moved my hand over the rapids, the torrent of his youth, searching for the place where it went wrong. The line flowed down across the plain. Here was his marriage and his stillborn son—a boulder in the stream. After, it ran shallow in its course, easily diverted and dried up, and I could tell that he would never reach Pataliputra or the southern sea. Yes, there it was, and there it broke apart upon the shoals, and any boat traveling down it would be lost there where the line broke and ended in his catastrophic death, not far away, just a few years. And yet, what was . . . , but at that moment he snatched his hand away. "Don't touch me," he cried out. Then, "You are filthy," he said, and staggered out away into the night. After he left, I sustained a fit of coughing which brought pain to my chest.

THE LION OF TABOR

In those days, as I have said, angry talk was common among merchants in the Caesarea marketplace. My fruitseller especially would begin each conversation with a list of complaints against the Roman government. Later, often, he would lapse into a kind of wishful trance, and talk about the changes that would come once the Romans had been driven out of Palestine. At such moments he would tell me stories which I first took to be lies, about a family of bandits who were fighting for a new authority in Palestine, led by the high priest and the Sanhedrin, free from the tyranny of Rome. I thought he was lying because his stories about this family sounded like those that men tell about the gods. They had the same tone. Later, elsewhere, I would hear them again— how the bandit king, Ezekias, disgusted by the vices of King Herod, had raised an army in Galilee, had been victorious in many battles until finally he was hunted down and killed. How his son, Judah, had broken into the Roman arsenal at Sepphoris after Herod's death, had armed the countryside and had been crucified by Quinctilius Varus with two thousand of his followers. How his son's sons had been crucified outside Jerusalem when Valerius Gratus was the prefect, and how his son's grandson, Menahem, the Lion of Tabor, now lived in the Galilean hills, attacking small detachments of soldiers.

The fruitseller described this man the way old women describe Heracles when they are making stories for children. "The Lion is tall and strong, more handsome than any other," he said. He reported feats of strength and daring. He told me how Menahem the Galilean kept agents in Italy, who had managed to break down the roof of a country house in Tarracina when Tiberius was eating there. They had tried to crush the emperor under the falling stones, in revenge for the sufferings of the Jews. I doubted this story, though of course the emperor had sustained an accident of exactly that kind, just before he retired to Capreae. It was at a villa called the Cavern. Aelius Sejanus, who had been at the same table, covered the emperor's body with his own to protect him as the roof fell.

Sitting on his mat in the Caesarea marketplace, speaking in a low voice and looking around, the fruitseller gave the impression he must not be overheard. His hand fluttered in the air over my knee as I squatted down, as he proceeded to tell me stories that he must have told to hundreds of others; I was, after all, a stranger. He told me of the shadowy ropes that tied Menahem the Galilean to several other accidents in Rome. Two especially: the collapse of the amphitheater at Fidena and the fire that consumed the Caelian Hill. Thousands had died, and the houses of many senators had been destroyed.

I thought it was unlikely that the gods had chosen an obscure Jewish bandit to work their rage against Tiberius. Yet still I was fascinated by these stories. As I squatted over the mat, looking down over the figs and olives, I thought I saw how little pieces of truth could be woven into a new story, and in the pattern of the cloth you could see a need, a yearning.

One afternoon when I had been not quite two weeks in Caesarea, the fruitseller told me if I wanted to see something, I should go down to the Esdrealon Gate to watch the prefect coming in from Sebaste.

I was going to be there anyway. Pontius Pilate had not yet been inside the town since I had arrived. During his tour of the garrisons he had been chasing bandits, who were plentiful in every part of Palestine. Though doubtless these bandits were the seeds from which the stories of the Lion had grown, the reports I heard suggested they were common thieves, who squabbled with each other over money and land, and who attacked ordinary Jews more often than they bothered Roman soldiers or officials, for obvious reasons. Nevertheless, three members of the prefect's personal guard had been kidnaped near Nazareth. Their bodies had not been found.

The fruitseller told me that the prefect would be bringing in one hundred bandits, whom he had captured in Samaria. He said the prefect meant to give them grisly deaths, perhaps in the amphitheater with the wild beasts, as Gratus had once done five years before. And he hinted that the Lion of Tabor would try to free them, perhaps even would attack the cohort in the narrow street inside the gate.

This seemed unlikely. I went not because I expected it, but for another reason. I wanted to see Pilate's face. The great men of the world existed in my mind as statues, and I wanted each one's face to be clear and well carved. In Rome once I had waited many hours outside the Marcellus Theater to watch Sejanus come out in a crowd of senators, his dark mouth smiling. Once I had caught a glimpse of old Tiberius himself.

In Caesarea I had seen Claudia Procula, the prefect's wife, pass by in a litter, and I had been astonished by her youth, her beauty. She had black, sad, swollen eyes, which suggested a story to me. Now I wanted to see her husband, and so I stood with the others at the gate and watched the prefect ride through at the head of a cohort of Samaritan auxiliaries. He was a grim-faced man of middle years, a good horseman, dressed in leather armor and a red cloak. His head was bare. His hair was clipped very short in a style associated, at least in Rome, with the party of the Republic—the enemies of all the Caesars.

I stayed to watch the prisoners come in. They were guarded by a troop of horsemen, about two dozen men and boys chained together in a line. They were dressed in rags, and many had blood on their faces and open sores on their backs; they called out to us as we stood there by the roadside. But the Lion of Tabor did not come to rescue them. In fact the people near me, Jews and Gentiles both, threw stones and dirt on them, or spat.

That afternoon as I left the crowd, I was again followed to the marketplace by men dressed in white. They worried me. But I made no associations because by then I was inclined to doubt even the existence of Menahem the Galilean.

I was wrong. Days later, toward sunset, one of these same men came up to my stall. He was very thin, very gaunt, with strange patches on his head and jaw where the hair didn't grow. He was an ugly man with a big, thin, evil nose. I was afraid of him. But there is a weakness in my nature, which makes it hard for me to refuse any service that is asked. So I allowed myself to go with him. I pretended to believe his flattery when he told me how my reputation had spread throughout the town because I made the blind see and the lame walk. He was dressed almost in rags, yet I pretended to believe that he could pay me, that he was a rich man with a young son whose fever would not break. I played the part better than he, because he seemed neither agitated nor upset, even when he talked about the child. But I frowned and made grave clucking noises. I asked questions he could not answer. Then I gathered together my instruments and medicines and followed him up the hill, beyond the marketplace and up out of the town. The sun was low. Not many people were about to see me leave.

Perhaps also there was a part of me that wanted to know

something, wanted to find something out. Otherwise I can't imagine why I would have followed him so far, out into the shadows of the evening among the limestone hills. No one lived beyond the ridge; it was where the shepherds brought their flocks. We passed little boys leading goats. He walked quickly and I struggled after him, almost losing him in the mists of darkness. But I knew there was someone behind me on the path. I was terrified and I recited several rhythmic charms to calm my heart.

We were walking though a valley. To my right and to my left, small chalk cliffs rose up. In some places I could see caves and chambers that were cut into the rock, small shelters for the shepherd boys who lived there. Light glimmered in several of them.

Finally I could hear the steps of the man behind me. And there were men on either side, away from the trail. I could hear their garments catch on the thorn bushes. I could hear their sandals on the dry ground. In time they came to walk beside me, ghostly figures dressed in white. The sun was down under the hill.

"Where are you going?" asked the man on my left side, and I said nothing. I struggled onward, mouthing my chant, shaking my head when he came near me, pulling away when he reached out to touch my elbow. "You can't go this way," he said. Then we heard the whistle of the man in front, three long low notes. He had come off the path, and I could see him standing on a rock up toward the cliff face. Him or another. In the dark they were the same, and they led me uphill, finally, away from the path, up a small gully and into a hollow in the cliffs. There was the entrance to a cave. Light came from it.

Muttering my charm, I let the man behind me push me down because the entrance was low. I felt his hand upon my back. It seemed to push down into my lungs, which felt so delicate and raw. I could take only small shallow breaths, and even they scraped in my throat.

The Sicarii

There was a hemp curtain which diffused the light. Someone pulled it back for me. I stooped down and entered into a high chamber cut out of the rock.

I had been expecting a shepherd's cave. I stood up cautiously, thinking I might hit my head. I stretched out my hand but touched nothing. So then I gathered courage and looked up. At first I saw neither roof nor walls, and it was only the smell of bats and the flat pressure of new sounds that let me know I was in a contained space.

A fire burned in a pit in the middle of the sand. It gave off a small orange flame, too dim to reach out far.

People came through the hole behind me and they pushed me toward the fire. I stood there until my eyes got used to the smoke and darkness. Then I saw I was in a square chamber. Later I could see traces of paint, remnants of carving, decorating the flat walls.

When we are in a place we know, whether imaginary or real, we walk as if along a clear straight path, and we hurry or we rest. We look backward, forward. People or objects in the trail, we see them coming from a long way off.

But when it comes to a new place, the mind has room for many thoughts. They blunder up out of the dark. Now in this badly lit chamber, thoughts crowded in on me all at once, and not in any sequence or arrangement. People moved around me in the darkness. I could smell their bodies, fragrances and stenches struggling together with the smoke and the damp stone. A man squatted down to poke at the fire. Beyond him I saw another man stretched out on the sand. Asleep, I thought, or no—his arms were tied.

I thought, this cave is close to the town and they have not tried to hide it from me. No one lives here. The ground is flat and empty. They use it as a meeting place, where people gather for a few hours. They come from far away. The Romans know about it. They must. So it is a neutral space between the rival camps, and yet this man who is stretched out here, there is blood upon his head. They didn't even bother to hide the way here. They didn't blindfold me or threaten me. And then I knew as surely as if it had been whispered in my ear that the man lying on his back on the sand, with his shirt ripped away and his arms tied, and blood in his hair and brand marks on his chest, was one of the three Roman soldiers Pontius Pilate was looking for, whom the sicarii had captured near Nazareth.

They didn't care if I could find this place or lead others to it. This thought came back to me again and again. It pushed away all my other thoughts. So without thinking I moved over toward the fire and knelt down next to the hurt man. His feet were tied together at the ankle. There were six diagonal cuts above his right breast and a pattern of burns on his stomach. His mouth was swollen, and his nostrils were caked with blood.

I examined these wounds as if to read in them a clue toward my own future. I examined them as I had seen priests read the entrails of a bird. Also I needed something to occupy my mind while men gathered inside the cave. They moved around me and sat down. They came in from outside. No one hindered me and no one spoke.

I saw faces from the market when I looked up. I thought, they don't care if I recognize them. Trying to reassure myself, I thought, this is the way a dream begins. We prepare for a strange journey and we are taken to a place where we see faces that we know from the waking world. And stories gather and combine out of a chaos of anxiety, and the figures in the dream give us clues to bring back to the world of light. They threaten us but cannot hurt us.

I spoke to Sister Isis under my breath. "Compassionate lover," I said, "who washes out our wounds with fragrant tears, who sets our broken bones, who brings us up from death. . . ." I didn't mean it. These were just words I was saying to myself, hoping the sound of them would comfort me. At the same time

I had slipped my pack of medicines and tools onto the rock floor, and I was moving my hands over the hurt soldier. His jaw was broken. And the cords around his wrists and ankles were so tight that his flesh was blue; I tried to loosen them. I took my master's razor and slit the soldier's wrists apart. The fingers of his right hand were broken, and his nails had been pulled out.

"Help me as I help others," I prayed to no one in particular. I thought, was this why they had brought me here? All the while I was touching the man's body, trying to make a story from the pattern of his injuries, trying to learn something I could use and trying to help him also. I stood over him and hoisted his body up away from the fire. I pulled him by his armpits until he lay with his head against a gentle incline in the rock, his feet toward the flames, which were burning brighter now. A man had added charcoal and dry cakes of dung.

Around me I heard muttered snatches of conversation. "Bring me water," I said in Greek. "You there," I said to a young boy, and was surprised to see him get up quickly. He brought me a goatskin full of water and an empty gourd.

A man said, "Make him live." And so I took a gourd of water and washed the soldier's face. I probed the inside of his mouth. Some of his teeth had been knocked out, and there was blood on his lips. Three of his ribs were broken on the left side.

I listened to his lungs, which had fluid in them.

It is air which carries consciousness, pumped by one half of the two-chambered heart through all the arteries of the body. Consciousness will not come until the air flows freely. That was why I had cut the ropes around his wrists. Now I arranged his body so he could breathe more easily and so his broken ribs wouldn't press on him. He had been beaten without mercy, yet none of the four vessels in which the gods stored his life were ruptured. His skull was intact. I thought that if he died, it would be from despair, an injury of the will.

And as I worked over him, arranging his limbs, trying to find a position that would let the currents of his body flow without obstruction, I seemed to feel other presences around me in the dark and smoky cave. They seemed to guide my hands. Some were the projections of my fear, but others were more subtle and ambiguous. As the men crowded around me, watching me work, I seemed to feel these others hovering above them, moving through them and through me too. I felt the presence of the three old women who have names in so many languages, and who were weaving a shroud for this beautiful soldier and for me. Ancient, fragile, bent, they moved around me, touching my hair and the back of my neck. I could feel their scented breath upon my face. They were weaving a shroud for him, and it was almost done. I felt that if I let them cut it from the loom, then they would make an end to my shroud too. But if I could work faster than they— I opened up the soldier's mouth and slopped some water into it. I pushed my fingers into the back of his throat. I rubbed his hands and rubbed his fingers, trying both to soothe his pain and use it as a stimulant. I bent over him to whisper in his ear. "Apud amicis," I said, and he woke up.

He opened his eyes and made a noise. His jaw was swollen, so it wasn't much, just a little groaning, and he turned his head. His eyes had no focus, but it didn't matter. The movement was the important thing, and as if in response all the other movement in the cave stopped suddenly, and the conversation stopped too.

Then there was another voice from beyond the fire, a voice I had not heard before. It was loud and sharp and spoke in a Corinthian accent, which my master said is the most cultured and sophisticated language of the Greeks. "Your reputation is justified," he said. "You have earned the fee of one gold aureus. This man lay without moving for two days."

As I turned, I weighed the advantages of humility and pride, and chose humility. "I was lucky. And he is not yet awake."

On the other side of the fire, on a ledge of rock that had been cut out from the wall, sat a little man with long hair and a beard, whom I took to be Menahem of Galilee. The Lion of Tabor: Streaks of red ran through his mane. He wore a striped tallith over his shoulders and a white cap on his head. When he spoke, he didn't look at me, and I soon understood he was near-sighted. He could see very little of the world.

A woman sat beside him. She had a dark face, dark eye-brows, fierce eyes, and a heavy, fierce nose. Chaldean physiogno-mists would have put her in the tribe of eagles. Though many, I thought, would not have guessed her companion's surname, which perhaps was why he needed it.

On the Lion's other side stood Barabbas the bandit, thin and sunburned.

"His jaw should be reset," I said, placing my hand on the soldier's forehead. "Also his finger bones. If he lies like this, his ribs won't press into his lung."

There were nine others in the room, some standing and some sitting. My words brought laughter out of several of them. But the woman stared at me without blinking. "They would have to be rebroken," she said, in a high, clear voice. "We didn't bring you here to save his life."

I should have been quiet then. But impish Mercury, my pa-tron, goaded me to ask, "Where are his companions?"

Again the cruel, nervous laughter. Again the woman spoke. "You will keep him alive until he answers us."

She turned her head and muttered something to her com-panion. He nodded. "Come," he said to me, and then a bandit led me past the fire and made me sit down at Menahem's feet.

"They have been reborn into whatever life the one God has selected for idolaters," he said in Aramaean.

These words suggested something to me, for he spoke of death in a way that was rare in that country, as a Pharisee might have, or as my father had. The Lion was a man of education. But also he was testing me to see if I could understand his language, so I gave no sign.

37

He peered at me with his weak eyes, and then he spoke again, this time in Greek. "We will pay you fairly for what you do for us. And if we call for you again, you will come."

"Yes," I said.

"You will not speak of this. You will accept the money that we give you, and you will not try to extort more."

"Yes," I said, goaded by Mercury again. "But you must understand I am protected by the Roman laws."

The words had scarcely left my mouth when I regretted them. The Lion smiled and touched his beard. "You must think we are fools. Cornelius Celsus," he said, and when I heard the name I felt my heart pause in my chest, though again I tried to give no sign.

He said, as if reciting, "In the Roman month of February, Cornelius Celsus, the natural philosopher, was murdered in his house in Tusculum. A fire was set there, and then later in an island of apartments that he owned in the Subura district. The magistrate is searching for his boy, a slave named 'Corax' because of his dark skin. He speaks many languages and is skilled in many arts."

"I know nothing about this," I said.

"Of course not. Don't be frightened. I do not think you will betray us. We will not cheat you, and whoever harms the Romans is our friend."

He was not a friend of mine. By nature he had the mild face of a scholar, but he could make it cruel. My master had the same trick, the same cruel, weak eyes. Suddenly I wept to remember him, as I sometimes did, and turned my face to hide my tears.

"Where's the girl?" said Menahem the Lion, in Aramaean. I turned away, looking back toward the wounded soldier, looking into the face of the man who sat with him now. I remembered him, but for an instant I didn't know from where. He was a big man with powerful shoulders, a big beard and greasy hair. Then I recognized him: the Essene who had broken up the festival of Attis, who had killed the sacrificial calf. His eyes were quiet now. His hand was on the soldier's head.

But the Lion was talking to me again. "In the Caesarea marketplace you were overheard by several here to say that a disease, which we call 'Herod's plague,' comes from a certain cause. Is that true?"

I turned back. One of the figures in the rear of the cave, whom I had taken to be a boy, had now come forward. She had stripped away the shawl over her head. Now she stood revealed, a girl just past her first bleeding.

"It is a sickness of the inward part," I said.

"I understand. How does it spread?"

I couldn't look the girl in the face. "Some women," I said, "are sent by Jahwah to punish the unnatural lusts of men. They are the messengers of the god, and we know this because we can't see the sickness in them, though they carry it."

"I understand. But perhaps there is a drug, or a process, or a seed, which can bring on the sickness in a woman, so that the next man who goes in. . . ."

"There is no such drug," I interrupted him. I couldn't look into the girl's face.

"You are sure?"

"I am sure. It is the god's punishment."

"It is Satan's punishment," said the woman with the eagle's face. And then in Aramaean, to the girl, "Your cowardice disgusts me. You lie with him on every fourth night when he is in town. That is the time. Not with these slow poisons but with his own hot blood when he is drunk. As Judith did to Holofernes. Where's my knife? If I had your whore's face and body, I would do it myself gladly, now, tonight. I would thank God for the chance."

Her voice was loud, and from her breast she produced her sica, her dagger. I saw it and then turned my head, pretending I didn't understand. But Menahem put his hand on her arm to calm her. "Quiet," he said. And then the girl murmured, "I cannot. They search me."

Without looking, I could hear the sorrow in her voice. Pretending not to understand, I stared back at the Essene, who was sitting with the soldier. And I saw to my surprise that he wept with her. His eyes were luminous and bright and shining in the smoky dark.

The woman saw it too. She stood up from Menahem's side and came toward the fire. She was dressed in a long gown and a long shawl, which she threw back from her face. She held her dagger near her cheek—a long, curved blade of Indian steel.

"What are you thinking?" she asked, but the Essene shook his head.

She was the kind who, if she feels her anger thwarted in one direction, turns naturally and quickly to another. "I wonder," she said. "When we are in Jerusalem for the Passover, we depend on you to lead our brothers out. Lead them from the house of death. Barabbas says you're a strong man, but that means nothing to me. The Lion has trusted you to lead our soldiers, but I look in your eyes and I don't trust you. I think you are a coward like this girl. I think you are a coward, and not a Jew."

Menahem said something I didn't hear, because I was looking at the woman. She knelt down next to the fire so that her eyes were level with the Essene's. She reached out her knife and drew it down the inside of the soldier's arm as he lay sleeping on the rock. It made a black gash along his vein.

"Do you weep for him?" she asked. "I think you do. But this is not our way. When Judah of Galilee and Sadok the Levite fought against the Romans, they showed us . . ."

"No," said the Essene. "Not for him." His eyes were dry now, and with his big hand he seized the soldier's hair. He forced the soldier's head into the rock until he moaned. And at the same time Barabbas spoke. "Let him alone. He is a strong man and a bold one. Pilate took his cousin John near Sebaste, and he swore an oath. He is the right man to lead us. He is the right man for this work."

"I wonder," said the woman. And to the Essene, "Yet I saw your tears. Is it because you are half a Roman soldier, your own self?"

40

The Essene's face showed a sudden mixture of rage and shame. He made a movement with his hand, and Menahem saw it. "What do you mean?" he asked.

The woman went on speaking. "I told Barabbas I'd be quiet, but I know this man. He is from Nazareth. Barabbas likes him for his strength, but I think he is a weakling. I don't trust him. And he lied to you. He told you his father was a carpenter named Joseph, but I know different. I know him and his mother, Miriam. This man Joseph found a child in her already when they came together, so he divorced her. He said the boy was his own son but we knew different. It was because he pitied her. Then he married again and went to Sepphoris, where he was building houses for the Romans. But this man lived in Nazareth with his mother. We knew who his real father was. Everyone knew—a Syrian named Ben Panthera, an Arab who fought with the Twelfth Legion. They were am-haretz and she begged from the synagogue. She paid no tax. She went into the field on the Sabbath and gathered the spoiled grain. She stole from the fields. And he was arahl—uncircumcised. I don't think he made the brit milah until he ran away to Qumrun to be with the Essenes there."

Most of this was in Aramaean, and I pretended not to understand. Instead I watched the hatred and the shame burn in the man's cheeks. "You are a liar," he said finally, and he spat into the flames. His face was coarse and big like the rest of him, but saved from ugliness by his bright eyes.

JUDAS ISH KARIOT

That week many Jews left the town, traveling to Jerusalem to celebrate the Passover, to worship there in Herod's temple. They went in large groups to protect themselves from bandits.

Menahem the Lion had given me a gold coin. I held it in a

pouch around my neck, and in the night I kept my hand clasped over it.

I couldn't sleep from worrying. If the Lion knew about me, then a message must have come from Rome. Others must know. In three weeks my skill had made me famous.

I was waiting for the day of Mercury, my best day for decisions. I lay awake all night, but toward morning I fell asleep. I put myself into the gods' hands. And though I woke up without remembering what I dreamed, still I must have gone somewhere and learned something. Because as I shivered in my blanket on the hard slope, I found my mind was clear. I was resolved to cross the border into Galilee, where Herod's son, Herod Antipas, was king under the Romans.

It was the morning of the thirteenth of Nisan. At first light I went out and washed myself by the fountain. Returning just after sunrise, I met people already trudging up my hillside, sick and injured men, women, children. They had come not just from Caesarea but from neighboring towns—from Narbata, Esdrealon, and the Sharon plains. From Crocodilion, in Syria. One man, a leper, had come from Joppa on a boat.

How was I to get away? How could I have been so foolish, to have brought such attention to myself? Now I was punished for my pride, but how could I have known? In Rome my skill had been despised. Only slaves were healers there.

They stood around my stall, perhaps ten altogether. When they saw me pack my bag they started to complain, and one sank to his knees. Shimon, my landlord, stood with his hands on his hips. I paid him what I owed him and pushed out through the people, carrying my bag. "Let me go," I muttered, tears in my eyes, for they were pulling at my clothes.

That morning the sun came up strong. Then later the sky was hazy, overcast, but you could see the sun, a pale disk. And it was hot, the first hot day of spring. Flies were everywhere. They crawled out of the cracks in the ground. They had been waiting for that morning to be born.

I walked east up the ridge, away from the market and the town, hoping to circle round outside the gates to the Sepphoris road. But beyond where the stalls and houses gave out, after several stades of distance, there were still five people with me. The path divided, and a way led south down past the cave where I had met the Lion. I went north.

A woman walked backward in front of me, holding up her baby. It was healthy, or at least its lungs and voice were sound; it had a harelip, that was all, and I had seen my father work a miracle with such a case. I couldn't bear to look. I walked with my bag over my shoulder, wiping my face against my sleeve. The child was crying and I couldn't bear it.

The pattern on my shadow cloth, so dark that morning, now was fading in the muggy air. In my mind I held the cloth stretched between my fists and saw it ripped to pieces by the child's sharp cry. A wind came up. The rags flapped away. I would get nowhere like this, I thought. Along the road, on foot. Better take the boat to Alexandria.

"He made the lame girl walk. He made the blind man see," the woman said.

A swell of nausea overtook me. I must stop, I thought as I came down off the ridge. I must escape. When I reached the bottom I turned aside and stooped under the flap of a long tent, the first of an encampment of desert Arabs. Interested in some legal process, they had come from far away, and for weeks they had lived outside the town, selling wine from Thessaly, beer from Ctesiphon, while their children tended their diminished flocks.

Inside, three men in black robes sat on carpets and cushions laid out on the stony ground. They played dice at low tables. I lay down in a corner, made myself some bhang out of hemp leaves and oil, and drank it with a cup of wine. I thought it would relieve my nausea and ease the suffering in my lungs. This was against my father's rule, but I was in pain. How is it, I thought, that I can guess the fate of every man except myself?

Judas ish Kariot found me there an hour later. He bent

down in the opening of the long tent, smiling and unsure, for he was drunk already. "I looked for you," he said. "I have a message from the prefect."

"Sir," I answered when he had sat down. "Please, what can the prefect want with someone such as I?"

He sat beside me and they brought him wine. He frowned into the bottom of the cup and shrugged his shoulders.

"Sir," I said, "the prefect is not here. They told me he was in Jerusalem."

"He has left for the Antonia Fortress," conceded Judas ish Kariot. "But he got a letter. He has given me instructions."

"Sir," I said, "I can't wait. Perhaps there is a fine. I don't know your laws. But I have money." And I pulled out my wallet so that it hung outside my shirt.

Ish Kariot reached out and fingered the coins inside the bag. Then he let it go. "Buy me a drink," he said, and I motioned to the attendant, for his cup was empty.

"What are you chewing?" he asked, and I told him. I kept a wad of hemp on my right palm and I was mashing it into a paste. I offered some to him, but he wrinkled up his nose. "Not from your hands," he said. As before, his clothes and body stank of sweat, although his hands were clean. Every time he took some wine he asked for a new cup.

Soon the bhang had an effect on me. It soothed me and made me brave. I could feel a soothing mist flow through the streets of the city that was sometimes in my mind, hiding the houses from each other. I wandered until I saw in front of me the gates to the small temple on the Aventine. The door was open, so I entered in and stood before the image of monkey-headed Mercury, who is called Hanuman in my father's language. His arms were raised above his head. In one hand he held the caduceus, and in the other, a wheel.

I stared into his ancient face. Then I opened my eyes and came to Caesarea once again. "Sir," I said, "is Pontius Pilate loyal to his wife?"

Ish Kariot squinted at me. "What do you mean?"

"Please forgive me. I don't know," I said.

But I had excited him. He leaned forward. "What do you mean? Is this what you're buying with your coin?"

"Sir, not at all. A few moments of friendly conversation."

But later I felt I had to ask. He had settled back on his cushion. I tried to swallow the words down, but they came out. "Tell me where the sicarii are held, that Pontius Pilate brought in from Samaria."

He stared at me a long moment. Then he laughed. "I will show you without telling you. Where they're held—is this what you hope to buy? Idolater," he said, languidly, softly, and he reached out and tugged at the pouch around my neck. The string parted in his hand.

He held the pouch up and looked at it. "Idolaters," he said, more gently still. "Someday we will drive you out. All of you. Every one of you. And our king will come."

"Herod Antipas," I said, confused.

"Not him. But another. Whose sandals he is not fit to tie."

Ish Kariot drank until he fell asleep. I got up hoping to slip away. But there were two soldiers waiting for me outside the tent. They had chased away the woman and her child. One was standing, one was sitting on the ground in the warm wind. He had an iron cap set askew on the back of his head, an iron pike sticking up between his knees.

TULLIANUM

Once my master, Cornelius Celsus, took me to a meeting of his club outside of Tusculum, in a secret grotto in the woods. This was three years before his death. In the morning he had promised me my freedom and promised me that in the month I was free, he would stand as my sponsor in the Cult of Mithra. I know now

45

he was lying, though I don't know why. Perhaps he thought it was a kindness to delude me; the cult is for freeborn citizens of good family. Nevertheless, that day he gave me the name "Corax," the crow, whose patron was the god Mercury. It was the first level of initiation, and I imagined myself working through the ranks of those gentlemen, up through the layers of mystery, winning their grudging admiration by my wisdom and loyalty until they could accept me as an equal. Corax, Nymphus, Miles, Leo, Perses, Heliodromus, Pater. . . . My master must have been laughing at me. At any rate he took me often to the grotto, where I would wait outside the antechamber with the other servants.

I never spoke to them. I felt myself above them. I stood apart and watched the gentlemen file in—retired officers, like my master. I didn't know their names. I used to imagine what they were doing, and once when my master was in the city I went back and broke in, and stood in the central spelaeum where Mithra caught the bull and killed it.

A spring came down out of the rock into a square brick pool where they washed themselves and practiced their baptisms. Nearby stood an altar, and the ceiling above it was painted with the constellations of the Zodiac. Mithra was painted there, the god of light, with Shamash behind him. Mithra clasped the right hand of the sun, who knelt before him.

And I thought, why not me? Why can't I be baptized here and have the sacred water of the spring wash away the stain of slavery, of all I have done or been forced to do? Before his death my father had given me my sacred thread to wear, the symbol of our caste. But he did nothing for my sins. He didn't have the water, he said, and then he told me of the great sacred cleansing river that flows out of the Cow's Mouth.

I thought, why not me? I know now that my master was laughing at me and perhaps laughing at himself. But I didn't know it then and I was full of pride. Many liberti, many former slaves, had risen to important government posts.

Though Celsus had promised to free my father more than once, I, like most, couldn't make his experience my own and learn from it. My father told me, as he died, to run away and not to put my faith in Celsus, who despised us for our race, even as he admired our ancient skill and loved my beauty. I knew all that. He needed us to write his books and that was all. I knew it and didn't know it.

As always when you are loved and not loved, it opens up a crack in you. Standing underground in the spelaeum, I felt light-headed, drunk. I stared up at the statue of Mithra Tauroctonus and I couldn't see it, though my eyes were open. Bull-slaughterer, lord of the sun. When I came out into the light again, I entered into the first of the strange habits of mind that used to plague me in those days. It was part of my headaches, my heterocrania. I climbed out of the grotto, and instead of the small woods and hillocks around Tusculum, I found myself inside another place.

It was not the god who sent me there, but a trick of my own mind. As I walked back to the villa, I could see the leaves and trees and grass. But it was as if they were the painted frescoes on a wall in an imaginary city. They were less real than the cobbled streets. For two hours afterward I walked, spoke, and performed my duties at the table, yet I remembered nothing. I, who could recite all the prime numbers between one and one hundred thousand, who understood the magic ratio between the circumference and diameter of a circle, whose mind was marked with thousands of useless and trivial conversations, have no memory of those hours.

This was not a rare event. Many crises in my life transpired during these blank periods. Looking back, perhaps now I can recognize what is most important: It is what I can't remember.

So, for example, I have no memory of the soldier leading me back to Caesarea. Or else I can—it has the pale colors and fragility of a remembered dream. I imagine my hands tied in front of me. I imagine a crowd gathering, yet standing apart on some low rocks. Perhaps they cry out, but there is no sound.

And as the soldier took me back through the gate into the town, I felt I was coming in through another gate, which existed only in my thoughts. This made it easier to endure a day that otherwise would have been full of humiliation and fear. But I can't pretend I was making a choice. Certainly I had some thinking to do, and it didn't help me to imagine myself coming down the Via Appia toward the Porta Capena and the old Servian Wall, past the tomb of the Scipios, alone in my imaginary Rome. I could see the paint on the buildings as I came along New Street and into the Forum, past the Basilica with the hill in front of me. On its south crest the Temple of Jupiter Optimus, all-seeing and compassionate. To the north, the Arx, and then the roof of the Juno Moneta. At the bottom of the slope, the Tabularium. Beside it on a corner of the Clivus Argentarius, the Tullian prison. Though I could see it clearly, it was different in my mind from in my memory, a big, dark, brooding, windowless, stone building.

JOHN

There was a prison in Rome, a prison in my thoughts, but it was a different prison that they took me to that day. The prefect had gone to Jerusalem for the festival. I was to be held for his return. The duty officer told me no more than that, and then they locked me in a cell beneath the floor of Herod's amphitheater near the port. It was a damp, small room, barely long enough to lie down in, barely high enough to stand. The stones were covered with dirty straw.

Under the amphitheater, there was a secret warren of small corridors and stone compartments, separate from the magistrate's court, reached by a passage underground. As the guard led me through, I guessed it had been built for animals, for the lions and bears which Herod and the prefects used in their spectaculars. There were no animals now. The last of these circuses had taken place years before.

My fruitseller had told me Pilate's men were in the forests, gathering wild wolves, and that this was the reason why the sicarii had not yet been condemned. But I had doubted it even before my own imprisonment. Pilate was a serious man. He did not use death as a source of recreation. Already during my time in Caesarea, several thieves and criminals had been crucified outside the town. Soldiers had kept the townspeople away.

Nevertheless, no one had seen the bandits since they came inside the walls, which encouraged rumors of all kinds. I myself had thought the prefect meant to wait until the Passover was finished before punishing them. For the past several years, there had been small riots and rebellions in the week of the fourteenth, and I thought he wanted to avoid a fight. Later I assumed the opposite: By leaving Caesarea for Jerusalem, he wanted to give the sicarii a chance to try what they did try, an attack on the prison itself. Later I imagined all these events as pieces in a larger strategy, in which even I was meant to play a role.

The guard pushed me through a wooden door into my cell. I stood still until my eyes adjusted to the light, which came down obliquely through grates in the wooden ceiling. Opposite the door, the back wall of my cell was open, barred, and the light came through these bars. I stepped over to touch them and found myself looking into a much larger chamber, which was perhaps the center of the whole underground maze. Small cells like my own surrounded it, and I guessed each one of these held a single prisoner.

But the larger cell was full of men. Some were chained to the walls and some wandered unconstrained. As my eyes grew used to the grey light, I imagined I recognized the faces of these men, whom I had last seen coming through the Esdrealon Gate loaded with chains, with Pontius Pilate on horseback. I took myself back to that day and imagined myself standing in the crowd. As they came through I looked each one in the face. Under the amphitheater, as the dim light seeped down from the grate, I looked for every man and boy, trying to match them—their broken teeth, their pockmarks and sores, their wild beards. Many stood too far away or sat with their faces to the wall, and so I supplied their features in my mind. I supplied whole stories of their lives, which were based on nothing; I had nothing else to do. It was an exercise that took the place of fear.

I learned this from my father, how to drug the mind with work. When he rode the slave ship into Ostia, locked between two rotten corpses, he had kept himself alive through the dark weeks with calculations, none of which he could remember later, for fear of remembering it all. Thought, which takes us on a journey to the future or the past, or in my father's case into a world of proofs and numbers, is most useful as a way to keep ourselves from truth. For if I had been able to examine truthfully those dirty and despairing faces, if I had been able to think about their coming death for more than a few moments at a time, if through them I had allowed myself to snatch an oblique glance at my own fate (illuminated as if by the light that slanted between the bars of my cage from the main chamber), I might have hurt myself with fear. I might have jolted the foundations of the city in my mind. No one can look at his own fate. It is like staring at the sun. We snatch glances at it, and with our thinking we make clouds, and mirrors, and reflections.

But one man I did recognize, and not just in my mind. At the Esdrealon Gate he had been second to the last in line. He had been different from the others, a tall, pale, red-skinned man, thin as a skeleton. The skin was peeling on his wasted back and arms and on the top of his bald head—that was what I remembered. The way the crowd at the gate cried out when he appeared, and pelted him with stones. Jews are a fastidious people, consumed with shame for their own bodies, like many of the Asian races. These criminals, shackled and dressed in rags, had nevertheless succeeded in covering their nakedness, except for this one man.

As he came through the gate, he was hidden only by a leather breechcloth. His legs were bare and streaked with blood.

Now he came toward me across the floor of the dim chamber. Still he wore his leather breechcloth, which was ripped down the side. He was always touching himself there. He came and stood in front of me on the other side of the bars, holding himself with his right hand, while with his left he grabbed the iron bar next to my face; his hand was long and hairy. And his body was so thin, I thought he was almost thin enough to slip through the bars, which had been spaced to hold a larger, fiercer animal than he or I.

His skin was covered with orange freckles, and at that moment he reminded me of the orange ape that was presented in the Campus Martius, near the time of Prince Germanicus's murder. It had been brought by ship from the island of Taprobane, or Lanka, part of the army of monkeys that Lord Hanuman had led against the demon Ravana. It was put into a cage beside the moneylenders' tents. There it gathered crowds for several days, astounding many, until it was taken away and put to death as punishment for its indecency and impudence, by special order of the Senate.

This man, with his long belly covered with golden hair, his beard, his big teeth and protruding eyes, his expression that combined a childlike foolishness and innocence, recalled the ape to me. At the Esdrealon Gate he had been laughing as the stones hit. Now, here, he stared at me with eyes that seemed nevertheless to miss me, because he would not look me in the face. He stared at my linen shirt, absurd in that foul cell and too good anywhere for such as I. It was a luxury I had purchased in the marketplace for reasons that now seemed stupid to me, and I felt his gaze penetrate those reasons as easily as my heron lancet would have cut the cloth itself and laid bare the skin over my heart. But this was an illusion based on nothing, because he was as stupid as the ape.

I looked into his face. God is punishing me, I thought.

"I live in the desert place," he said in spotless Greek. "I eat locusts and wild honey and the bodies of vipers. I break all laws," he said, "but God makes all things clean." And he was rubbing himself inside his breechcloth until finally he pulled out his nakedness from the rip in the leather and thrust it toward me through the bars, just as the ape had done.

Though I was embarrassed and turned my eyes aside, still I could not help trying to complete my knowledge of a subject I had heard discussed, yet had not expected to examine personally. I am talking about the circumcision, the brit milah, which is both the pride and the shame of the Jewish race. It is the mark which sets them aside, yet hurts them too: Their priests mutilate the foreskins of all male children in a bloody ceremony. I had heard stories of terrible infections, stories also that too much flesh was sometimes cut away and could not be reattached. As I turned my head I saw no sign of either of these complications. Still, the mutilation was plain. Much of the prepuce had been cut away, and I wondered at the fathers who allowed this. For with the prepuce is removed all of the pleasure from copulation. It is for this reason that Jews are driven by their appetites far less than other men.

I turned my head away and raised my hand. "Ask yourself what has brought you to this place," he said. "And don't be afraid. For the axe is at the root of the tree. Are you a Jew?"

"No."

"It doesn't matter! God can change you. He can raise you up to be a son of Abraham. Yes, these are hard rocks, but they will protect us when God purges this world with fire."

"What do you mean?" I asked, hiding my eyes from his nakedness.

"I mean, be thankful for what these men have done to you. Be thankful for your suffering. For when God comes to Israel, he will gather up his grain from storehouses like this. But the chaff in the fields he will set on fire."

"When will that be?" I asked. I glanced back at him for a

moment, which was time enough to see his expression change, the pressure of his stare abate. It was replaced by a canny smile.

"Soon," he said, in a different voice. "My cousin Jeshua will come deliver us out of this place. This house of death. My cousin will do it. He can do anything. He is strong with his hands, not like me. He has the strongest hands in Galilee, and he loves me."

He had been speaking quietly. But in the chamber behind him I saw a man stir and get to his feet. I thought whatever I could learn, it would be useful. "John," I said, which was a guess. The phrase he used, "this house of death," I had heard it in a different language. But it had transported me into a different place, a cave like the dark cell, and I remembered Barabbas in the cave. He had said, "Let him alone. He is a strong man and a bold one. Pilate took his cousin John near Sebaste, and he swore an oath."

"John," I said now, and was rewarded by a knot of confusion on the man's forehead, quickly replaced by a sweet smile.

In the chamber behind him, the man who had gotten to his feet was moving toward us. "John," I said, "what day is your cousin coming for you? Is it today?"

"You know him!"

"Yes, I know him. He is a strong man and a bold one. Is it tomorrow?"

And I was rewarded by a pure sweet smile. John closed his eyes and pressed them closed. "Money disgusts me," he said.

"Can I go with you when you go?" I asked.

"Why? God can raise these stones . . . ," he said, and then he stopped, because the man behind him had put his hand on John's shoulder and pulled him from the bars.

"What are you saying to him? Idiot!" He was a coarse man, with a coarse, wicked face. "Idiot!" he said. "This man is not one of us. He is a. . . ." Such was his anger and disgust, he spat at me. He actually spat at me through the iron bars, before he pulled John back into the chamber.

A PREDICTION

The labyrinth under the amphitheater had two entrances. One, a stone ramp for the animals that led down from the street, was sealed up. It had not been used in years.

I had come the other way, through a narrow passage underground that joined the prison to the law courts outside of Herod's palace. This way was secret. Even the existence of the cells was secret, the subject of wild rumors in the town. Most people thought the sicarii were being held inside the palace. So they brought gifts of food to the palace barbican, for it was well known that the jailers provided none.

Some small portion of this food eventually found its way under the streets, and was brought into the central chamber. But there was none for me, nor did the sicarii share it. In the evening, by the light of an oil lantern, I saw them sitting together, gnawing their crusts of bread. I saw bread pass among those who were chained to the wall and could not join the rest. But no one came to me, even though I stood with my hands on the bars of my cell. I looked at John, and he glanced toward me once or twice and puffed out his cheeks.

In time I was taken back through the passage under the street, and brought into the guard room once again. I half expected it. That day when the soldiers brought me to the palace, I had felt the decurion watching me, a look that was like a touch. A kind of softness that I knew well. And even though I had been distracted with memory and sick with fear, still I had not failed to respond—an instinct. I had turned my face modestly aside.

So I was not surprised to find myself brought into a private chamber. Nor was I surprised to see this officer come in carrying a basket of bread and figs. He was a grey-faced man of middle age, with short hair and bad teeth. He was a veteran of the Armenian wars. His beard grew in grizzled patches. It was hard for me to listen to his brutish compliments. My master, after all, had been an educated man, a high-ranking officer, a camp tribune in Prince Germanicus's army.

Nevertheless, after I had eaten, and drunk a cup of wine, I let him come to me. Because I was weak and could not resist. Because I was grateful for the food. Because I had a plan. And because it is my nature to love men with power over me. I gave him what he wanted in the duty-officer's wardroom, and to tell the truth he was gentle and considerate. Though I scarcely remember, because as I was lying on the couch my mind was somewhere else, and these events seem like the lewd frescoes I saw once in an apartment chamber in Campania—unreal painted images—while in my mind I wandered through the chamber, hiding my face until I found the entrance to another suite of rooms, decorated with figures in a smoother and less vivid style. Yet still I recognized them. These were the events of the recent past, each room a day, and I walked through six rooms until I stood looking at the painted figure of the eagle in the cave, and behind her was the old blind toothless lion. But the eagle held up her foot, and her talon was as long and sharp as a curved dagger, and out of her beak came tiny marks on the plaster, as separate and precise as the marks of a sandpiper on a wet beach, scattering away in the instant before it jumps into the air, pursued by a bird of prey—Babylonian writing, which I could read because I knew what it said. WHEN WE ARE IN JERUSALEM FOR THE PASSOVER WE DEPEND ON YOU TO LEAD OUR BROTHERS OUT. LEAD THEM FROM THE HOUSE OF DEATH.

Soon I came back, and I found myself lying on the couch wrapped in a wool cloak, drinking a cup of wine. The decurion paced the floor in front of me. "I saw you in the market. A couple of times. I went to see."

As he spoke, he made small, crisp gestures with his hands. A sign of nervousness, I thought. I looked at them—broken, callused, effective. A soldier's hands.

"Sir, come sit by me," I said. And I reached out to him and

pulled him down beside me, taking his right hand in my own. I rubbed the calluses along the Hill of Mars. "Let me look at your hand."

He made a fist. "I know what you do. I don't have time. Lies and superstition."

"No," I said. And I caressed his fingers open so that he showed me his palm. "Sir, it says here you will be promoted. You are born under the sign of the crab."

He shrugged. His eyes would not meet mine. He was bored, eager to be gone, and so I said, "No. I can see it here. In this line I can see that when the sicarii attack the cells tomorrow night, you will be ready. And the prefect will be grateful."

This was my guess, my wager. Menahem of Galilee meant to attack the prison, to free his men who had been taken captive. I thought the attempt would come in the next few days, so news of it could spread to Jerusalem before the end of the Passover. And so I guessed the attack would come on the first night, when it was least expected. As in the old story: On the fourteenth of Nisan, I thought, the Israelites would be released from bondage.

"Hunh," said the decurion. "What have you heard?"

I shook my head. "It's in the lines." And I pulled his hand over toward the clay lamp on the table. Documents were scattered there, painted scraps of hide and a few scrolls.

"Hunh," he said after a moment. "They wouldn't know where to look."

"Sir, has no one ever been released?"

Embarrassed, he tried to pull his hand away. But I held tight. "I'll speak to the prefect about you," he muttered. But he would not meet my eyes.

"Three Romans were taken in the Galilean hills," I said. "Did they know the location of the cells?"

"They would die before they told."

I shrugged. "It costs you nothing to prepare."

Then I let go because he was losing interest. So I showed him something Dion had taught me, to relax him. I rubbed his chest under his shirt. He groaned, then he lay on his stomach on the couch.

But as I stood above him I was looking toward the table where the documents lay. I saw one especially—a pattern of black lines on a piece of hide. The pattern was enclosed within a circle, and I thought it was the plan for the cells under the amphitheater. I thought I recognized the line of my own journey to and from my cell. I took a chance. I needed only one look, and so I rubbed the decurion's spine under his shirt until he groaned and turned his face into the cushion. Then I stood up, sighing, and moved over to the table. I closed my eyes and made a place on a blank wall inside a building in my mind. Then I pushed the other documents away with my hand, and spread out the piece of leather and looked at it.

The decurion was there behind me. "What are you doing?" he asked as he grabbed my arm, forced me away.

But I pointed with my finger to the star-shaped chamber in the center of the maze. "That's where the attack will come," I said—unblemished idiocy, because where else? But I must have impressed him because he allowed me a few more moments before he forced me away. Again I closed my eyes. The pattern was there in the center of the whitewashed wall.

"You mean this," he said.

I shrugged.

"I have to order a new guard. What time?"

"After midnight," I guessed.

"Slave," he said, not unkindly. "Slave, dressed in your master's shirt." He held one of my arms twisted behind my back, and with his other hand he grabbed me by the ear. With the ball of his thumb he chafed at the hole in my earlobe, where in Tusculum I had worn a slave's ring. Once I thought it might heal over.

"You tell me," he said.

"I don't know. Oh sir, how could I withhold these things from you? I depend on you. You are my father and my mother."

And as Dion had taught me, I put some of the slave music into my voice to sweeten it. The decurion stared at me. I turned my eyes away, blushing with shame.

THE ATTACK

I spent most of the next day on the raw stones of my cell, drifting in and out of sleep. When the guard brought me back, he shackled my hands together. Then he ran a length of rope between my hands and tied it to the inside bars. I gnawed at it until my teeth were full of hemp, but could not loosen it. It was long enough to let me curl up on the floor.

"Oh my God," I prayed to Father Hanuman. "Save my life and I will make an offering of flowers. When I reach the sacred river I will float a crown of lilies in the water. I will make a crown of cinnamon wood. When I reach the Cow's Mouth and the Diamond Mountain, I will . . ."

I was hoping the decurion would send for me again but he did not. Instead, the guard came after sunset. When I heard him unlock the door, my mind clouded with plans because I thought he had come to take me away. Or if he stayed, that he would talk to me, say something, but he did not. He locked the door and sat down, but the key was in the lock. I saw it. I lay curled in my own dirt, but the guard wouldn't look at me. He sat down in the shadow next to the door, out of sight from the inside bars and the main chamber. In time he fell asleep and I listened to his breathing. I thought, if he slides down along the wall or if his head falls back, then he will snore.

I lay on my side, looking into the main chamber. It was dark. These cells all had wooden ceilings, for they were below the wooden floor of the amphitheater. In the old days a system of platforms and pulleys had hoisted the animals up. Light came through the drainage grates, and after sunset there was very little—just the red fire from some brazier. I could smell the coals.

I told the decurion that the attack would come after midnight. It was a guess, but when else would it come? I lay staring into the dark cell, trying to make sense out of the shadows, the slow gestures of the prisoners. They sat shackled to the walls, or they moved back and forth. I looked for John.

In time I must have dozed off, and when I woke up, it was to see a change in the light. A lamp had been put into the middle of the floor, and by its tiny flame I could see a circle of flagstones, and one was levered up. Perhaps that was what had woken me; in any case, now I heard a noise, a long low groaning, and the straight edge of the flag moved up a few inches. The hole opened away from me, and I watched the flag achieve a slow square in front of me as it came up. It was a dark, thin stone with a grain to it, different from the white limestone that formed the cells and the rest of the amphitheater.

I had a long time to watch and think about these things. As the black stone came up and made a square in front of me, I placed upon its surface the round pattern of the maze from the white wall in my imaginary room. I drew it in white lines and examined it. It had not occurred to me until that moment that the maze below the amphitheater was built of several stories underground. Yes, now I saw that the small marks on the pattern indicated stairs, and I saw the passageway from Herod's courtrooms inclined up under the street, and I saw another level in the pattern drawn in smaller, thinner lines, a level that led down toward the unused ramp for animals—I saw all this, and at the same time I was cursing myself for living in my mind and weaving these strings of memory and imagination into a webbed curtain between me and the world, because any idiot would have known from the sound of his bare foot on the flagstones that there was a level underneath. Don't think, I told myself. Watch.

Listen. Act. But as always my mind was full of shadows, and I
wandered through the curtains of shadow cloths, pushing them
aside, staggering through the rooms of an imaginary palace,
which consists at the same time of chambers from two separate
buildings, one the past and one the future. And the rooms in each
building are laid out differently if they are entered from the doors
in their west walls, which are all marked HOPE, than if they are
entered from the opposite side—each hope leads to a correspond-
ing fear, and so on, forever. Enough, I thought, and then I cried
out. And even though it was what I had meant to do, perhaps I
chose the moment less because I was watching a man climb out
of the hole than because I wanted to do something to clear away
these shadows which afflicted me and crippled me; I cried out,
and with the shackles on my hands I beat down on the iron bars
as if my arms were the hammer of a bell that I was ringing over
and over.

Light shone from the hole, and when the noise started they
passed up a torch so they could see. Perhaps a dozen men had
gathered around the hole—everyone who could move freely, except for one or two who knelt between their shackled friends.
They were kneeling down between those who were still chained
to the wall, and as I watched I understood a noise I'd been aware
of earlier, a gnawing sound that I had thought came from a rat.
But it was too rhythmic, and now it became louder as I rang my
bell—the sound of iron scraping against iron.

Everything happened at once. Torches were passed up
through the hole, and men were coming toward me across the
flagstones. They were drawn by the noise I was making. One carried a torch. Behind me the guard had come awake. He stared at
the approaching flame with eyes made wide by stupidity and
sleep and fear, but then suddenly he remembered his orders and
started up. He unlocked the door and darted through, leaving it
ajar. I moved back toward it, though I couldn't follow. The rope
between my hands and the inside bars grew taut. I stood in the
center of my tiny cell, quiet now, but the harm was done. They

knew who had raised the alarm. One of the Jews stood at the bars, cursing me and gesturing with his torch. He thrust it through the bars, and I shrank back.

The light was so bright, I couldn't see beyond it. But I heard noises—the clap of the stone as it fell back and split, a new urgency in the scraping metal, and new voices, harsh and loud. The Jew swore at me and pulled back his lips into a smile of anger. Then he turned, holding up the torch so I could see the red light move over the chamber.

Beyond his head, there hung suspended the end of a wooden ramp, which led into the amphitheater above us. I could see a movement in the ropes. Then there was a splintering crash. The ramp fell down out of the wooden ceiling until the ropes jerked and caught in their pulleys; the ramp was still halfway from the floor. But it had opened a gap, and instantly I smelt the night air cutting through the fog of smells that surrounded us: the excrement, the urine, the sweat, the bile, and everything that could be squeezed out of a man except his blood.

I felt the cold air on my face. And for a moment, there was a kind of hush, a small gap of quiet as everyone in the chamber stopped what they were doing and looked up. Perhaps the soldiers were confused when the ramp didn't drop down any farther, and it took a moment for us to see them crawling on their bellies. I want to think there was a moment when some of the prisoners seized hold of what was happening, seized hold of the time and disappeared down into the tunnel they had made. Perhaps one or two. But I don't think so. I heard no movement, nothing to disturb the hush, the bloody premonition, as we stood watching the soldiers mass in the gap, the light glinting on their helmets.

Then they squeezed through and jumped down, one after another. I stood with my hands upon the inside bars of my cell, picking at the knot of the rope. The chamber beyond me was full of shouting and the smash of metal. The torches were thrown down one by one, except somebody near me had thrust his into the joists of the roof.

We'd had no rain, and so gradually the fire held. It was a black, smoky flame, different from the oiled torches. It hurt my eyes. I coughed until blood came to my mouth, and I watched men stagger through the smoke. One, a big, long-haired, ragged Jew, was cut down right in front of the bars of my cell, under the new flame, under a spatter of black soot and resin.

The soldier hit him in the back with his sword, and he fell forward onto his hands and knees. I listened to the sounds he was making. The Jew was old, but the soldier was a young man, as young as I. He caught hold of the Jew's hair and pulled his head back as he tried to get up. The Jew lifted up his arms and staggered forward so that his whole weight was suspended by his neck, and I could see all the tendons and the muscles of his neck as the soldier pulled his head back. I could see the tendons that join the head to the shoulder, and the muscles that work the jaw; he had a beard, but it was thin and gray. Under it I could see the ringed column of his esophagus. I could see his voice box tighten from the strain, his mouth sag open to relieve it. I could see the big artery under his jaw pump up until it throbbed, and all the time the sound that he was making changed from a yell deep in his chest, changed from human words and curses into something else, a high voiceless squeal, as his larynx tightened and constricted. His legs had given out and he had sagged down to the floor. The young soldier had his foot in the Jew's back, and under his ripped clothes I could see his chest tighten as his spine bent and his skinny arms reached out to me. And all the time his squeal grew higher, softer, and sharper as the soldier forced the breath out of his lungs, and it turned into something less than human—a piglike sound. At the same time his face lost all its nature as the muscles underneath his skin were stretched too tight to move, and all his choices and his human expressions were taken away, and all the anger, all the hate, all the color, even all the fear were pulled out of his face. His eyes stretched wide. He had been looking straight at me, and all this time I had been aware that he was seeing me, that he was thinking something.

But then all the shadows of time future and time past fled out of his eyes. The pupils tightened into nothing, and they were just a beast's staring eyes, as if the soldier's cruelty had given him the touch of Circe in the song.

His own face was dark with blood. He bent the Jew's spine, and then he brought his sword around onto his throat; it was not sharp. He had to saw and hack until finally a notch in the blade caught at the artery and ruptured it, and all the blood and air spattered out of it as if released from pressure. It spattered into my cell. The heart was pumping blood, and air was blowing from the wound. His soul was bursting out of him and then away. Air was leaking from his mouth also, and now there was no noise but just the air leaking out of him. That and the blade sawing on this throat, and a small cry in the mouth of the young soldier. Saliva dripped from him as he sawed at the man's throat until the skin gave way, and I could see the throat and sinews part until the blade turned on the bone.

The soldier stood up and stood aside. His fingers were caught in the man's hair, and he made a frightened and disgusted gesture because suddenly he understood that he was touching a corpse. The man's grey hair had twisted itself around his forefinger; he shook his hand, pulled it away, and then he reached down and stabbed the Jew in the belly with the point of the sword, ripping the skin down toward his groin. The edges of the wound pulled back, and even in that smoky light I could see the packed viscera, the mottled, green intestine as clear as in one of Dion's diagrams. A smell came up from it.

"Oh my God," I prayed. "If you save my life, I will make a crown of myrtle leaves and float them in the water. I will climb up to the Cow's Mouth and Lake Manosarovar itself. . . ."

The Jew's hands still clenched and unclenched, still moved, still reached for me. I stood with my hands grasping the bar, and then I looked up from the floor and into the young soldier's flushed and puzzled face. He turned away and moved into the center of the chamber. As I looked at his back, my eyes lost focus, widened, blurred, until everything that I was watching was submerged into a pattern of dark and light. And all the voices lost their separate humanness, submerged in a pulsing roar. I watched without seeing, listened without hearing, and all that noise and movement lost its meaning until something stumbled out of it, out from the middle of it, and stumbled up against the bars of my cell. It was John.

Looking at his face then, looking at his body, I could see the skeleton inside of him, the skull inside his head. He was carrying a brand of wood.

I moved backward into my cell until the rope was taut between my hands and the bars. Then I saw he could push through. The bars were spaced for animals, and he was thin enough. "Come," I said.

His eyes were staring mad, and yet he understood. He slipped his body through, and it was only his head that caught, the bone of his skull that no diet of honey, locusts, or vipers could reduce. He dropped the brand and pressed his skinny hands against the bars, cutting his face, possessed of a god-given madness, because I could see the god was in him then, in answer to my prayer. Dionysus had blessed him and put strength into those frail hands. His head came through, and there was a long cut over the bulge of his forehead.

"Burn me loose," I said. His eyes were witless as he stood up, but I shook my hands at him and shook the rope. He saw the door ajar behind me, but again the god put some compassion in him. He bent for his torch and picked it up. The flame was still alive. He held it under the rope near my shackled hands and it flared up.

Then we were through the door, moving through the pattern. I stood inside my mind as if inside a room, and with my forefinger I traced our way along the pattern on the wall as we moved through all the false entrances and empty ends. I ran and he followed me, holding the torch, and we moved through the stone passageways toward where the line came out under the west gate of the amphitheater.

Rats scattered underfoot. And instantly I was confused as we stumbled down the stairs I thought should have led upward, and I realized we were above the level of the street. The pattern, though clear and perfect in my mind, nevertheless had not helped me understand. But it gave me a direction, a means of moving forward as we stumbled over the uncertain stones and squeezed through narrow passages that had been built for animals and slaves until we found the door. And it existed. There it was, built into the gate, a small stone entrance closed with iron bars. I went down on my knees and stared out through it at the crowd which even in the middle of the night had gathered to watch the fire, because the floor of the amphitheater was on fire. The sky was red with it.

I knelt against the bars, looking out at the people. They stood with their faces tilted toward the sky. I knocked my forehead twice against the iron bars, and then I pulled back to let John through. "Go," I said, and he dropped the torch and twisted out, as agile as a monkey, though again his head caught and again we had to force it. Then he was through, and he crawled forward a little, and he got up and ran and disappeared into the crowd.

PONTIUS PILATE

That night I was taken to a cell in another building. I lay in the dirty straw, thinking about the false pattern and the god's false help. But then after several days, the courier found Pilate on the road and he came back.

Soldiers brought me to the same room where I had met the decurion. For a moment I was there alone. The door was closed. It was the middle of the morning, and a parallelogram of light slanted down from a squat window near the ceiling. It fell across the couch where I had lain. It fell across the table, which had been moved closer to the couch so that it could serve as a kind of desk.

They had taken the shackles from my wrists. I pulled my dirty linen sleeves down over the raw skin.

The same clutter of documents was spread out on the table near the lamp. I stood rubbing my wrists. Now my anxiety had been replaced by a new helplessness, and I found myself examining the pattern on the piece of hide. It lay among the scattered cards. It was one of several. I looked at the message on the other side. And as I soothed my angry skin from a bowl of water they had brought me, I realized these drawings served a decorative purpose. They had no connection to the maze of cells. "Ah," I said, finding something restful in the thought, a restful and complete surrender. Yes, I thought. The plans of men.

Then Pontius Pilate came in through the other door. The curtain parted and he stood before me. He was shorter than I had imagined. I had seen him once before on horseback, and now he seemed diminished in this little room. He looked tired. He was a hard-faced man, and he carried on his body and his clothes the dirt and grease of travel. His voice was high but strong nevertheless. "I asked to see you," he said, "because I learned you were the first to raise the alarm the night the sicarii came into the town. In the name of the Senate and the people of Rome, I wanted to commend you."

I bowed my head. Then he continued, "What is your name? No, let me tell you. You are the servant of Cornelius Celsus whom they call 'Corax.' "

I said nothing. I looked down at the tabletop. He didn't seem to require a response. "I have received a letter, a directive that you be returned to the criminal magistrate at Tusculum, to answer questions pertaining to the death of your master."

Again I said nothing. But I bowed my head, thinking modesty and humility might still move him to compassion.

"Yet," he continued, "I have questions of my own. Tell me. Cornelius Celsus was with the Twentieth Legion under Germanicus Caesar when it revolted against the Emperor Tiberius and the authority of the Senate of Rome."

"In Pannonia," I whispered.

"Yes. And I have seen his name on a list of gentlemen, invited guests in the house of Germanicus's widow, the Princess Agrippina."

"Yes," I said.

"This was a function where the prince's children were presented to a group of senators and officers. I am talking about Drusus, Nero, and Gaius Caesar, whom they call 'Caligula.' "

"Yes," I said. "It was on the seventh of December."

"Were you there?"

"Yes," I lied. I could see where this was going. If Pilate was Sejanus's man, then he was the prince's enemy. And if he thought my master was conspiring with the prince's widow, he would not mourn his death. He might pity me and think that I had done his work. So I said, "I was with my master. I didn't see the princess. But my master showed me to Gaius Caesar, who was born with the legion. He is just a child."

"They are a family of vipers," said Pontius Pilate.

He strode over to the table and sat down. He moved his right arm with difficulty, and his right hand hung stiff from it, as if wounded or crippled. With his left hand he turned over one of the pieces of leather. It was blank. I guessed the pattern on its back was part of an official, perhaps regimental, seal.

He smoothed out the surface and then picked up a stick of sharpened charcoal. "Tell me what you saw. Was Titius Sabinus there?" he asked, naming my master's patron.

"Yes," I told him. I knew nothing about it. Celsus had gone alone. But later I heard from Dion the names of some of the other guests. Some were in the Cult of Mithra with my master.

But I didn't want to say too much, because I didn't want to contradict whatever Pilate knew. Because I didn't want to make him think that he could learn something by questioning me more closely. So I claimed to have waited in another room. Then I told him a few names and made up a half-witnessed scene, in which Titius Sabinus, my master, and one other had come out of a private meeting with the princess. "We will speak again," I made them say. And they saluted.

The prefect made some notes. "Titius Sabinus was condemned for treason in January of this year," he said. "Cornelius

Celsus is also dead, though the circumstances are unusual. He was no patriot, no friend of the Republic, and no friend of mine. Nevertheless, I am ordered to return you to Ostia."

He looked up at me. "But I wonder, why did he not free you when he died? You served him for a long time, and your father before you."

I bowed my head, looking for something to say about my master that was both a compliment and a reproach. "He was a stern man," I said finally.

"I believe it."

He wrote some more. Then he looked up again. "If you were a Roman, because of your honesty with me and because of your service to the state, I would put you on your own parole. I would trust you."

"There's more," I said. And I told him about the Lion of Tabor in the cave. I told him about Barabbas and everything that I had seen, except for one detail: I didn't mention the young girl.

When I had finished, he looked at me a long time, and I forced myself to meet his eyes. Then he stood up. "The state commends you," he said.

He fiddled with the piece of leather and then rolled it up. "There is a boat leaving for Italy at midday, six days from tomorrow," he said. "If you are a Roman and fit to be a Roman citizen, you will wait for it upon the dock. Don't be afraid. I will protect you. I will give you a letter for the magistrate.

"For six days you are free," he said. "I will see you at the dock. And if I don't, on the seventh day I'll hunt you down. Depend on it."

He gave me a smile that was half encouragement and half contempt, and I knew he expected me to run. Nor did I disappoint him. He was right to be contemptuous because on the third morning after he let me go, I crossed the border into Galilee.

CHAPTER

2

THE BEAR

SYLPHIUM

The word in the market was that Jeshua of Nazareth had sold Barabbas and the sicarii to Pontius Pilate, in return for his cousin's freedom and a treasure of gold coins. The fruitseller told me the whole story. Zakarias's son John had been seen hiding in the forest. Jeshua had disappeared.

"If he is innocent, why doesn't he come forward?" the fruitseller asked me. "Everyone knows what kind of man he is. I swear it is like him to have traded the lives of heroes for one childlike fool. His mother was a whore for the Romans."

He was talking about the Essene with the shaggy hair, who had been Menahem's captain. I had seen him in the cave outside the town, when Menahem and the woman had taken his command away. The story was that out of jealousy and spite he had betrayed them, but I knew better. I knew who the traitor was.

69

And I had no desire to stay until they found Jeshua of Nazareth and questioned him. What if John had seen his cousin and had told him the truth?

And so I ran from Caesarea pursued by a double fear. In Galilee I was still afraid, wondering if the Romans or the sicarii would be the first to find me. As soon as I could, I crossed over into Syria. Then I walked east through the desert until I left the territories of the Romans. I came to Palmyra, the city of Solomon, which the Arabs call Tadmor. And then to Dura Europos on the Euphrates river.

That town is on the western border of the Parthian kingdoms. The river runs past the ruins of Babylon into the gulf, to the port city of Spasinu Charax, and from there it is forty days by ship to Demetrios-Patala and the mouths of the Indus. Sixty days over the Indian Sea to Hippuri, on the island of Taprobane. Twice that to the straits of Cattigara, where the cinnamon trees grow.

To the north, Parthia is bounded by the Hyrcanian sea. The road runs north from Seleucia through the mountains to Bisitun. Past Ecbatana on the Median plain and through the Caspian Gates toward Nisa: It is the same road Alexander of Macedon followed north of the great salt desert. It is the road to the country of the Sericans, shy men with yellow skin and half-closed eyes who live beyond the mountains in a paradise of peach trees and apricot groves. Guarded by walls of ice and stone, they know nothing about jealousy, or pride, or hunger, or war. They never come out, never allow themselves to be seen. They speak only through messengers, but along the road they send their porcelain and silk and steel and jade, which they exchange for camel trains of olive oil, amber, pearls, wool, ostrich eggs, glass, and lapis lazuli.

The road to that country runs north and east through the Greek cities of Bactria. It was Alexander's plan to mix the blood of his people into a new race, hoping that like bronze it would prove harder and sharper than its elements. He married a Bactrian princess, and he settled his soldiers and their women along a line of cities from Hecatompylos to the Indus river. After his death Seleucus Nicator and his heirs defended the traditions of the Greeks through all that immense country. It was a battle over many lifetimes, and it was lost when the first King Arsaces rode out of the high plains. His archers' shirts were covered in small rings of the Serican steel, and they rode horses from Hyrcania, which were larger and more powerful than anyone had ever seen. He cut the road in two.

Later he made his winter court in the city of Ctesiphon, across the Tigris river from Seleucia, which had been the capital of the Greeks. My father had told me of these cities, where he had lived after the death of King Phraates, when the Italian slave girl Thea Musa ruled with her young son. She married him and bore him children, and they reigned like Jocasta and Oedipus until the people rose against them.

It was during these civil wars that my father was captured by the Romans. After Thea Musa's death, the divine Augustus sent Vonones to be king over the Parthians. But the satraps were disgusted by Vonones's softness and his Roman ways, and so they chased him northward to Armenia. When I came into Parthia the king was Artabanus, a hard, uncultured man who delighted in archery and feats of strength and hunting tigers in the Caspian mountains.

He was a strong man, yet it was a weak kind of kingship— not like Rome, where the Caesars are like gods. Between the two rivers the Greek cities had their Councils of Old Men, and elsewhere there were satraps and marzbans and arabarches and azatans, each with his own fortress, his own territory. There were Persians, Parni tribesmen, and Scythian chiefs. There were Jews. Downstream from Dura, I came to a country near the town of Nearda at the end of the royal canal. It was ruled by two brothers, Jewish bandits who had collected an army in the swamps around the town. They were like kings in that small place.

By that time I had found a new way of making money. Dura

Europos is irrigated by a system of qanats—canals—which are among the works of science in that region. But north of the city the land is still dry, and on the dry hills I found a quantity of the herb sylphium. Or at least it was a cousin of this herb. The original was from Libya, though it is now gone from there, all gathered and wasted because of its great value. The women of Rome were willing to pay as much as fifty sesterces for a small bundle, especially as the drug got rarer. But its properties, I discovered, were unknown in Mesopotamia. Nor did they have a substitute for its chief use, which is to prevent the conception of children.

I was sitting on some broken columns outside the city, looking down at my foot, when I noticed the flowers. My mind was dark with prayer. It had been a long journey from Caesarea to the river. I had come through the forests and across the thirsty, brutish sand, stealing in the caravanserais and begging in the towns, and selling what was left of my beauty. That is enough. I will say no more about it.

In oases of unconsciousness, I wandered the streets of my imaginary city, stopping often at the shrines to Mercury, and Toth, and Ganesha with his elephant head. There the stones were cool and wet. Drizzle fell from the dark sky. I groped along the streets through mists and shadows, which gave me shelter from the constant sun of the real world.

On the hill at Dura, in my mind I was sitting on a broken pillar, outside the dark wrecked temple of Trismegistos. I was muttering a prayer. Help me, Lord. . . . It was the same prayer I had chanted for weeks without result. But this time I felt a change in my body, a pounding in my head. And then the sky was clearing over me and I could see the sun. A new light burned on the façades, and a dry wind blew along the streets and buildings. The sky burned hot and white, and the wind blew away the walls and stones, and I came into the real world and felt the sun on my face as if for the first time in weeks. I knew my prayer was answered. The god's gift stretched out over the hillside—small purple flowers and the Libyan herb.

At that moment I felt alive again. Instantly, without thinking, schemes and plans occurred to me. And a sense of frustration: In Rome I could have gone down to the market with my bundles of sylphium and been a rich man in a few hours. Slave girls and their mistresses would have flocked to me.

In Asia I knew I had to be more careful. There were no freeborn women in the streets of Dura anymore. It had been a Greek city, but the Greeks were almost gone. And though rich men had many wives, they lived in secret windowless houses and never came out.

DURA

The image of the sun god Bel, a mountain of brick, still stood outside the gate of Dura at the top of a small rise. This statue was older than the Greek city, which had been built by Seleucus on an abandoned site. Its broken head and face still looked west over the dry land. Footsore and sore-handed from gathering the herb, I came past it at the end of the afternoon.

This statue gave the town its name. It had been built in imitation of a monument of the Chaldeans, one of the marvels of the world, which had stood upon the plain of Dura farther south. The Greeks had not destroyed the imitation, nor had they destroyed the ancient city gate, built at the same period after the plans of the great magus Belteshazzar—whom the Jews call Daniel—when he was governor of Persia. It towered above me now, ugly, square, and high.

The gate was through a narrow cleft along one side of that mud-brick tower. People pushed and shoved at me, and grabbed at my bag. Then I was through into the crowded streets, which were full of refuse and filth. The stones hurt my bare feet. Pigs lived in the ditches.

But when I looked farther outside myself, I could see the

streets were laid out in a careful, square design. Everything was
stone and painted brick, for wood was rare, rarer than in Palestine. The houses were dark red, dark yellow. They had flat roofs,
and in the heat the men slept out on them on mats of woven
reeds.

The great temple was to Marduk, or Bel, in the center of
the town. It was square, windowless block of stone, with a small
door, and when I looked inside I could see nothing except smoke
and shadow. Outside was the open market, lined with a Greek
colonnade. It was more pleasant; with my bag of sylphium I sat
down on the steps and watched the veiled women slip between
the piles of melons and pomegranates among the stands. Tall
bearded men glared at me fiercely, their heads wrapped in strips
of cloth under their bashliqs—conical hats that made them taller
still. They carried knives in their wide leather belts.

The herb was useless unless I could explain its properties.
But I was not in Rome, where men and women talk together as if
as friends. In Asia women are shy, and men cherish their shyness.
Ignorance has uses, and no one loves the messenger who tries to
steal it away.

So I just sat there, bored and hungry, and at dusk I stole a
melon. Sometimes I had seen Greeks in the market. Their faces
were shaved, and they wore the chiton and cloak, instead of Parthian trousers. But I saw no women of their kind, nothing but
veiled shadows flitting through the stalls, as insubstantial as
ghosts.

In this town there was no place for a penniless stranger. At
night the folk disappeared into their houses. There were no
torches or oil lanterns in the streets, nothing to guide the traveler
as he groped through the night, trying to avoid the bludgeons of
the watch. And so as darkness gathered I hoisted my bag again
and limped out of the gates, out past Bel's statue to the
caravanserai.

It was built at the crossroads; low stables for the horses and
camels surrounding an open courtyard for men. Small fires

burned in it around the central water trough. Men sat on carpets
and blankets or on the open ground, talking in low voices as I
came in.

Four iwans—three-sided, barrel-vaulted halls—opened off
the courtyard at the points of the compass, and by common con-
sent one was for lovers. I limped over to it. I dropped my bag at
my feet. Then I stood at the side and put my face against the
harsh stucco, listening to the noises of love—the high, nervous
chatter of the boys, the grunts of men. I was still hungry, and it
had been my intention to stop there. But at that moment I was
desolate. I stood there with my cheek against the wall, knowing
I was no longer a rival to these clean young boys who had come
out from the city. And to tell the truth, I had no desire to struggle
with them for the love of these stinking camel drivers. In times
past, when I served at my master's table, I had shocked the gentlemen to silence just by smiling.

Nauseated and hungry, I turned away. And as black night
fell I wandered through the courtyard, looking for a mark. I
found him drinking wine, a big Jewish oaf with tangled hair. He
looked weary, as if he had come a long way, and now he was
sitting cross-legged on the bare ground, drinking wine out of a
leather bag. But I could see a money belt wrapped in his cloak
beside his knee, and by the wandering, constant way he put his
hand over the strap, I knew there was something in it.

A man was cooking fried bread over a brazier. I could see
the Jew clearly in the charcoal glare. The red light fell on one
side of his face. It showed his big nose, his thick beard, his big,
deep-sunken eyes.

My mind was moving slowly. I stood in the shadows behind
him, thinking about his money belt. Then I recognized him. I
had seen him twice before. He was the Essene who had spoiled
the ceremony to Attis in Caesarea. Later in the cave he had wept
over the Roman soldier and been scolded for it. I closed my eyes
for a moment and the place came back to me. He had been sitting
cross-legged on the rock. And when the scolding came he had

tried to prove his strength with cruelty, as many do. He had pushed the soldier's head into the stone. His name was Jeshua of Nazareth, and the sicarii were chasing him.

He had been dressed in a white shirt. Now, opening my eyes in the red light, I could see how dirty it was. One of the seams had opened over his shoulder, and I could see his enormous arm, his dark, bulging shoulder that protruded from the rent. "He has the strongest hands in Galilee," his cousin John had said. "He is a strong man and a bold one," Barabbas had said.

But not a clever one, I hoped. He was drinking wine. I could smell it. He was drinking out of a small, baked earthenware cup, such as the water sellers use.

I stood watching him a long time. He had a leather flask of wine, and from time to time he squirted it into the cup, mumbling something as he did so, perhaps a prayer.

Like the priests from my father's country beyond the Indus, it is hard for Jews to travel without breaking their laws. I knew he wouldn't share his cup with me, and so after some minutes I picked up my bag and went out again into the darkness.

I walked among the scattered groups of men, rolled in their blankets or else sitting by small cook fires, talking in many languages. I was looking for the water seller; he was gone, but the ground where he had been, over near the wall, was scattered with broken cups. I found one that was whole, a small cone of baked clay with a flattened end.

Having no water, I washed the cup with my own urine and wiped it clean. Then I went back to where the Essene sat with his belt wrapped in his cloak and his hand poised over it.

I greeted him in the Aramaean language, and he turned his bleared eyes toward me. The red light cut across his face. He didn't say anything, but I sat down, trusting an impression of weakness, of loneliness. Not wanting to be recognized, I sat back from the light.

I felt I didn't have the skill to pretend to be one of his race. But I thought perhaps I could leave the question unanswered. I said I was from Seleucia, and I was traveling across the desert into Syria and then to Galilee. I said I thought I might have relatives there who might take me in. I said my name was Philip, a Greek name popular among the Jews.

Remembering how the woman had mocked him in the cave, the towns she had named, I asked him about the country to the west of Gennesaret. "My cousins live in Sepphoris, I think. Are you familiar with that place?"

He said nothing, but he turned to look at me. He opened his mouth. No words came out, but only a little air, and I could smell the wine. The red light shone across his teeth.

"Or they are in Tiberias," I said. "On the salt lake. Do you know that place?"

Again he opened his mouth. And I turned my head to listen, for at the limit of my ears, on that soft breath of air, I heard a sound. Words in the Hebrew language, which I couldn't understand—halting and few at first, and covered up with breath. Other words from other fires in the courtyard I heard better, though they came from many steps away. But these words: I sat right next to him, straining to hear. "Karati la me ahavai haima rimuni," he said, and then I could understand better as he lapsed into his native tongue, "God, I am wounded and my guts ache, and my heart has turned over in my body. I am gone from you and I am punished. At home death waits for me, and among the Gentiles is no place to rest. But here in the desert I sit and remember."

"Or have you been to Caesarea, in Palestine?" I asked, after a pause. "Friends have told me of that city."

He said nothing for a long time. He sat cross-legged with his chin sunk on his broad, bearlike chest. Then he raised up his head, opened his mouth, and I could hear the words escaping on the soft air, ". . . Yes, he said to me come up and come away, for the rains are gone and the cold winds are gone. And a garden of flowers has come out of the earth, and the birds sing, and the voice of the dove. And the fig tree puts out her green figs, and the vines with their soft grapes and sweet smell. . . ." Then I couldn't hear anything more, though he was still talking, still moving his lips.

"Friend," I said, when he was done, "talking of grapes, I have come a long way. I was wondering if you could spare me a mouthful of your good wine, for as you say, it smells so sweet. See, I have a cup."

I couldn't tell whether he heard me. His own cup was between us in the dust. I laid mine down beside it. In the half-light they were indistinguishable.

Again his soft, escaping voice. "Oh my dove, who hides in the cleft of the rock and the corner of the stairs, let me see your face and hear your voice. No, look for the weasels, the little weasels that spoil the vines, for the grapes are tender."

After he had spoken, he turned toward me. I now saw his eyes had been closed, for he opened them. I could see them shining, wet in the red light, fat with tears.

The wineskin was on the other side of him, near his cloak and money belt. Abruptly he lifted it and fumbled with the stopper. In the clumsiness of his movements I could see how drunk he was. He brought the wineskin over and dribbled wine into the cups, into the dust around them. I could see the skin was almost empty.

He lifted up his cup and mumbled something—again, perhaps a prayer. I copied him, mumbling some nonsense words under my breath and then choking the wine down in one gulp. It was harsh and bitter, but I swallowed it, while with my left hand I was searching in my bag for my vial of poppy gum, already dissolved in sweet red wine. More skillful and more furtive than the drunken Essene, I squeezed out twenty drops into the bottom of my cup.

In Palmyra I had made a tincture of opium for myself. The juice bleeds out of the immature buds of the poppy flower, and it forms a brown gum that is later sold as powder. I had stolen a steel knife and then traded it for some of this, which I mixed with wine. Just a few drops helped me sleep, had relieved spasms of nausea and the terrible cramping in my stomach when I rested after a day along the road.

What was it that the Jew had said? My guts ache, my heart has turned over. . . . The risk is that a man will stop breathing as he sleeps. I hesitated over the amount. Twenty drops would have been dangerous for me. But the Jew was a big man with heavy limbs.

He had put his cup down in the dust. This time when I placed mine beside it, I waited as he fiddled with the stopper, and then I put my cup down on the other side of his, closer to him. He was too drunk to notice. After a moment he brought the leather flask round again, and dribbled the last of the wine into our cups. Then he looked at me with his wet eyes. He seemed easily brought to tears.

We choked down our cups of wine again. And after that, it was a matter of waiting. Neither of us spoke. We sat staring toward the fire.

In time he slumped forward and his head nodded, and then he stretched out over his possessions, gathering them into a ball in his big arms. He lay in the dust, pillowing them under his chest and head.

All around us, men were settling down. The fires sunk down. I could still hear snatches of conversation borne to me on the dry air, and so I sat quiet, rubbing my hands together in my lap, rubbing my sore feet.

In time the Jew lay like a dead man. As the conversations hushed around me, I sat listening to him breathe. I sat listening to his faint, shallow breath. So fragile it seemed, for such a man.

And in the dark part of the night, when the fires were down, I rolled him over onto his back. I fingered his mouth and nostrils, searching for obstructions. I didn't want him to spit up his wine and then choke on it, and so when I had taken the money belt, I rolled him over onto his side and thrust the cloak under his head. Then I got up and took my bag, and walked quickly and quietly through the courtyard.

I came out through the gate. All was still. The moon was rising through some clouds. In a small clear part of the sky I could see the pattern of stars named "behemoth" by the Hebrews, the monstrous fish which swallowed Jonah, which Perseus killed at Joppa in the harbor.

And then I walked out to the slave encampment and lay down in the sand. But I couldn't sleep. I lay in my blanket, and in the cold white morning I rose up before the rest and took the road back to Dura. The stones hurt my feet. Before the sun came up, I knelt at the statue of the god Bel and stripped the coins out of the money belt. There were nineteen silver denarii, forty copper coins, and one gold aureus which I took into my hand.

I wondered, was it possible the story I had heard was true? Was it possible the Romans had paid this filthy Jewish bear to betray Barabbas? If so, Pontius Pilate had been cheap with me. If so, I deserved my share. How much had the Jew wasted on the road, while I had scavenged like a dog?

I climbed up into the lap of the god Bel and laid the golden coin into a chink in the brick, an offering to the sun. And at that moment the sun touched the head of the statue, gilding it as if with a remnant of the precious paint that had covered it in the old days.

I flung the money belt away into the stones. But I took the other coins, and then I went and stood in the crowd before the gates of Dura, waiting for them to open. It was the day of Mercury, the first of the month. And as the sun rose, the god was with me, because this was the big market day in Dura. I went among the people at the gate, buying stones and metals and spices and grease. When the doors opened we pushed forward in a crowd, down the streets to the marketplace. There I rented a stall for one day outside the great temple of Bel.

It was just a place to lay my blanket underneath a canvas

shelter. A line of merchants sat around the edges of the square, and I sat among them making potions and cosmetics out of lead, malachite, lapis, amaranth, balsam, and copper verdigris. I made sunburn oil from aloes, and from honeycomb I made a perfumed hair wax, which the Parthians love.

Other merchants had potions made of myrrh, musk, frankincense, and amber—costly things I could not afford. But the god was with me, and I made colors they had never seen. I made perfumed oils for the skin, which I packed in clay cups; I worked all day. People gathered to watch me. "This is wax from the sacred bees of Halicarnassus," I would say, even to people who had seen me mix the stuff right there. Or, "This mud is from the Jordan sea. Cleopatra washed her face with it."

And I made sylphium. I crushed it in a base of olive oil and pomegranate juice, which has some of the same properties as the herb, and which the first woman gave to the first man when they were in the garden. She gave him the pomegranate fruit. That's how old my craft was, and as I broke the herb into the seeded juice, I imagined that first moment, when men and women tried to grab their fate out of the hands of God. That garden had been near here, between these rivers. But now the people had forgotten and I didn't know how to tell them. All my customers were men, for in Mesopotamia it is the men who paint themselves. Nor is it a sign of effeminacy. I had soldiers of the guard stop by, dressed in leather trousers, steel hats, and steel mail, buying purple balm with flecks of pyrite for their eyes and lips.

In the middle of the morning my luck changed. The doors of the temple were opened. And in time some of the women came out, the temple servants. Because they had no modesty left, they could walk through the market in groups of two or three, their faces uncovered, their linen dresses low over their small breasts; they were just children, really, and some I guessed had not yet reached puberty. Outside the temple precincts they were still protected by the god. They had golden circlets around their necks and money to spend—offerings at the altar, I supposed. Many were yellow-haired or red-haired, and they spoke Greek to each other, or else barbaric northern languages.

Their loud voices and shrill laughter rang out through the market. And when they got to my blanket they knelt down, delighted. Soon I had five of them around me watching my hands, sniffing at the oil. One had a mirror, and they were laughing and playing with the ointments, and I let them play. "What's that?" they asked. "And that? And that?" they kept asking. Finally one picked up a pot of sylphium and made a face at the bitter smell. "What's this?" she asked, and I told her.

They stopped laughing and were quiet. I told them how to use it, how a spoonful could be spread into the bottom of the vagina every day and not be discovered. I told the truth about it, for it is a wonderful substance, and needs no lies to cover it. They listened to me gravely, and then without arguing they paid what I asked, nine silver tetradrachms for a small pot.

They bought twelve pots from me. With serious faces they paid their money and returned to the temple, and I went back to selling lip oil to the soldiers. But I got more pots from the water seller and made more of the sylphium—"lover's balm," I called it. And as morning gave way to afternoon, and as the afternoon wore on, I had more people come and ask for it by name—old women sometimes, and female servants, and eunuchs from the brothels. And once at the end of the afternoon, a beautiful young slave exchanged a pair of golden earrings for a large jar, and I wondered at the net that had stretched so quickly from the temple to cover all the women in the town.

All these people asked for what they wanted with serious faces and quiet voices, and they paid their money without arguing. It made me think that I had sold the stuff too cheap. But at sunset, with the help of the god, I was twenty times richer than at daybreak. So I packed up and went away. I paid my tax and went to a rooming house where I hired a boy to wash me and then wash my clothes. I bought a linen shirt. In the courtyard I sat with the other guests and ate vine leaves stuffed with walnuts, fried in oil.

I slept on a straw mattress with a cotton cover. I was tired. I was hoping to sleep soundly, but in the middle of the night I got up and stood with my eyes closed, confused and dizzy, for I had dreamt of the god Bel. A wind had passed through my dream, and then I saw the outline of his body with the light behind him, a black shadow rimmed with fire. I saw his heavy calves and thighs, his thick waist. I smelled the perfume of his beard.

Confused, I stood in front of him. But the black night was all around me, and in time he caught me in his arms and pulled me down to bed. And then pulled me down into sleep's dark kingdom underground, where I stood as if in a cleft in the rock with the cold waters of the river Lethe seeping over me. There, figures of the dead appeared to me: my grey-haired father lying on his bed, his hands hanging through the ropes. Cornelius Celsus bleeding in his bath. His blood spread through the water. When I woke up I lay unthinking on my bed until the day grew warm.

Sometimes the god gives messages that cannot be understood except as passions in the mind. I woke up afraid, knowing my luck was over. The wives and prostitutes of Dura had paid me, and now I was afraid the husbands and the priests might pay me too. When the landlord knocked at the door of my small room, I felt my heart swell in my chest; I leapt up, afraid to answer. And when he went away, I took my bag and money and hurried out the door. I spoke to no one, only accepted humbly the grass package of fava beans and lemon juice which the landlord thrust into my hands. I raised it to my forehead in a gesture I had seen my father use, then I was gone.

North and south of Dura the Euphrates river has cut a wide valley through the plain, and in some places it is lined by cliffs and hills. Most towns are on high ground out of reach of the flood waters. But Dura was set lower, and the river was a long way. With my head tied in a cloth, I passed through the gate for the last time and headed down the stone causeway toward the port. I passed through land that was irrigated with great wheels, which pulled up water from the river. On either side of the causeway I could see lines of slaves working in the beanfields, the hot light glinting on their chains. I felt burdened by the heat of the dry sun, weighed down by the silver in my bag. Often I turned to look behind me.

The fields gave out into mud flats and dirty, stagnant pools. The causeway led to a sequence of stone docks set into an embankment of raised earth. These docks were crowded with people. Still more stood on the mud flats where the poorer boats were drawn up.

I wanted to hire a boat to take me down the river. I thought I would pass along the royal canal and down to Seleucia on the Tigris. I asked the harbormaster, and he waved me contemptuously onto the shore. So I walked down through the mud beneath the embankment toward the fishing boats, past where they were cutting up some of the enormous river carp whose eggs are such a delicacy in that country.

The mud sucked at my feet. Farther on I saw a crowd of perhaps a dozen men and boys standing in a circle on a wide strand studded with mooring poles. They were throwing rocks and mud, but it was not until I heard their voices that I understood what was happening. They were shouting, "Jew! Jew! Jew!"

It was the Essene. He stood in the middle of the circle, his shirt ripped open to his waist, and his big, hairy body seemed more bearlike to me than ever, for I had seen bears persecuted in this way, during the carnival at Rome. They grimaced and threw their hands up as this man was doing, gnashing their teeth and striking out until the crowd drew back.

Someone had fetched a magistrate. I thought I recognized him by the carved wand of his appointment, which he raised up from time to time. He was a tall white-haired man, but he was powerless to stop the crowd. Already young boys with sticks had opened up wounds in the Jew's back. But then he shouted out and caught one of them, and dragged him into the center of the circle until a hail of stones forced him to let the boy go.

It was a hot day. The air seemed flat and leaden and full of nauseating echoes. I looked up at the sky and saw a cloud like a dragon, groping to embrace the world. And I imagined the god Bel was searching for me in the crowd, looking for me with his raging, sunlit eye.

My father taught me how the brain is divided into two sections or lobes. Each lobe rules different faculties. In Seleucia he asked questions of soldiers wounded in their heads on one side or the other, and he always said that every man was like a soldier under the command of two captains, and this was a trick the gods had played on us. Standing in the mud in front of the judge, listening to the anger of the crowd, I could feel the turmoil of two voices inside of me, one in the left part of my head, one in the right. In the left part was a cold room, lit with a cold even light, and the voice was telling me to go away, to take my money and hire a boat, that this was no concern of mine. It told me that the Essene was being punished by the god for his own sins, because the Jewish priests had wrecked Bel's temples and driven him out of Palestine in the old days. They had broken down the statue of the calf, which many Jews had worshiped along with their own god. So this country was not kind to Jews, and they found trouble here.

I put my hand up to the right part of my head, and I could feel the heat raging there. And that part of my mind was a hot furnace like the one in which King Nebuchadnezzar had consumed the three sorcerers—Shadrach, Meshach, and Abednego—in the old town of Dura for the sake of the god Bel. And a hot voice was shouting there, telling me the god had looked for me and found this Jew instead.

There is a hot voice and a cold one, and neither one knows

everything. One belongs to Queen Minerva in her cold high spaces, and one to Mother Kali with her altars of blood. We listen to the one that cries and threatens the loudest. And then the slighted one takes her revenge. Now on the riverbank the stone chamber in the left part of my brain was broken open and the hot voice raged through it, telling me to come forward. And in a moment I found myself in front of the magistrate, asking how much money it would take to set this story right. The Jew was my servant, I told him.

Many of the organs and limbs of the body come divided like the brain. The heart itself has two sides. We have two eyes, two ears, two testicles, two kidneys, two hands. And Minerva commands the left side, and Kali, the black goddess, commands the right. I saw it in my father's diagram: He drew a life-sized, naked figure on a roll of paper. Staring eyes, a turban, long mustaches, his split, transparent, skinny chest still circled by the sacred thread—when I was a child I was terrified of the drawing. But as I stood on the bank of the river, my bare feet sinking down into the mud, I felt myself to be that man, felt on my lips the same grimace of pain as I made my argument to the judge. He also was of two minds, and I saw him looking at my linen shirt, my scratched ankles and muddy legs. He turned away from me and walked a short distance. I followed him, and soon we stood on the dry ground a little higher up.

With his right thumb he rubbed along a crease in his left cheek as he considered my youth, my accent and bad grammar. As I spoke I listened to the curses of the Jew, the clamor of the crowd. I had put my back to them. And the sounds were quieter. Yet even so, or perhaps because of the new distance, I felt I could separate them out, and in the sounds I could see everything that was happening behind my back. There the Jew stood in the center of the circle, his hands raised to the sky.

My lips pulled away from my teeth. I was conscious of the hot wind in my breath. "Here," I said, and I pulled from my ears the golden rings I had got from the slave in Dura.

In Rome the holes in my ears had been a sign of my servitude and degradation. But here they were the fashion. And the rings also were valuable. The gold had a voice stronger and louder than my faltering Aramaean, for I imagined I could hear a stillness in the crowd behind me as the judge took the rings into his hand.

"This man has been accused of stealing a boat," he said. His voice was deep and pure and loud.

He gave his wand a shake. I looked at it, and then I saw it for what it was, a phoorbah of wrought iron. The man was not a judge of the court. He was a priest, a magus, and he held in his hand the three-sided iron dagger which the priests of that country use to cast out spirits. His white hair was shaved short upon his forehead and his temples, while in back it fell over the collar of his robe.

Then the noise of the crowd, which had flagged, rose up again, and I turned around. The Essene had broken through the circle. He had seized hold of a man who had come too close to him, and had twisted the bronze boathook from his fist. Then as I watched he leapt back, and with an immense double-handed stroke of the boathook, he laid a man out flat upon the sand. The crowd gave way before him, and I stood watching as he lifted up the hem of his ripped shirt and ran. A shallow watercourse crept down along the strand toward the river, dividing at its mouth, and with enormous agility and strength, he leapt among the scattered patches of dry ground. Then he was off, running south along the riverbank.

"Your servant has run away," said the priest beside me. With an exaggerated motion, he closed his hand over the gold earrings and swept them into a pocket of his robe.

As soon as they were gone, I felt free. It was as if they were a great stone I had carried from the city and had now set down. I took a breath, and I could feel the vessels of my body carry the air into my heart, feeding it and calming it. Almost I felt like thanking the magus, who had looked into my mind and diagnosed the trouble there. His phoorbah had exorcised my trouble. Almost I felt like kneeling down and thanking him. Only I feared to draw more attention to myself. And besides he had already turned, was already moving hastily away.

The River

But strength depends on ignorance, and the relief he gave me lasted only a few hours. When I took the boat downstream from Dura I was sick again. The strong, stupid boatmen moved around me, smiling behind their hands while I sat in the bilge. I stared out at the brown water and remembered my father.

Once I came back to the house after standing with the crowd to see the embassy of the Parthian king in Rome. Magi were there outside the Curia. They said a prayer to Ahura-Matha, the fire god. I told my father about it but he wouldn't listen. He made the sign of the evil eye, and then he told me how in Babylon they bury their dead in the mud walls of the houses. He said hands and bones reach out from the foundations until they break off or else rot away.

Why do bad men prosper? Strength depends on ignorance, he told me, because it is only through ignorance that we can escape the envy of the gods. In the West the wisest nations—the Jews, the Egyptians, and the Greeks—are broken and conquered. Rome has broken them to ashes. It rules the middle sea. The unthreatened gods allow it, because in Rome the clearest mark of a citizen is his contempt for learning, and the rich men are all blockheads. They hate all knowledge and all art.

Because of this the physicians in the city, the astronomers, the sculptors and painters, the philosophers—all of them are slaves. My master, Cornelius Celsus, collected slaves from all over the world. When I was a child I moved among them without listening, and I never so much as suffered a toothache. But when

Dion came from Alexandria, then I opened my ears, opened my eyes, opened my mouth. And through these unguarded gates came envious diseases, fevers, colds.

As I traveled eastward from Rome, I could feel a sickness traveling in my body. On the sea I felt it in my head, a sickness of memory and grief. In Caesarea on the temple steps I felt it move into my mouth and lungs. Now, heading downstream from Dura along the river, I could feel the waters open up inside of me, a bloody flux.

I had bought my place in the bottom of a narrow boat with a red, triangular sail. We stopped often, and often I was sick. I was bloated with gas. I vomited after meals, and my stool was watery and red.

We sailed down toward the royal canal. In time the hills gave out on either side, and we entered a country of marshland, of willows and high reeds. Jews lived here on both sides of the river. Their ancestors had come from Palestine during the reign of Nebuchadnezzar the Chaldaean, and even after Cyrus conquered Babylon and freed them, most had not returned. They preferred life by the great river.

The Euphrates ran broad and shallow, and many streams came into it. Oleander trees and rushes lined the banks, and on the eastern side stretched miles and miles of swamp, with towns and houses hidden in the reeds. This was the land of the brothers, Asinaeus and Anilaeus, whom I have mentioned.

These twins were so alike that no one could tell the difference even when they were together, as they almost always were. They were small men but very strong. In the boat I heard the story of how they were presented to the king of kings, Artabanus the Parthian. This was at Seleucia; he came down from his seat and offered them his open hand. When the satraps laughed at them because of their smallness, he defended them, saying their hearts were larger than themselves.

This was remarkable because they were lowborn men, who had been apprenticed to a weaver in Nibilis. Once the weaver beat them for ruining the dye-pots. In revenge they killed him and burned down his house, and escaped into the marshes near the parting of the river. There they lived for years, gathering around themselves a band of Jewish runaways and bandits, growing in strength until they could defeat whole armies.

On that part of the river they were heroes, admired for their bravery and fairness and obedience to the law. Every year they sent a treasure to the temple at Jerusalem, and though they were still young, they gave honor and privilege to the wise old men, the rabbis. They listened to them.

These brothers sent weapons and money to the sicarii, the zealots. Roman spies had been sent against them but accomplished nothing. They had survived many devious attempts against their lives. Now the king of Spasinu was preparing soldiers, because of the taxes the brothers put on river traffic.

These stories were pressed on me at every stage. They were like the legends I had heard about the Lion of Tabor. In some cases they were identical, as similar as the twins themselves. Sick and sullen from the river, I thought, what is the point of these stories? The Jewish paragon. The great Jewish king. Surely even the people who say these things know they are lying, that they are really talking about something else.

Some part of themselves. Some hope out of their bodies, out of their burdened hearts. An old man said, "When they were boys, their widowed mother took them to the desert for forty days...." It was the same story I had heard in Palestine. I couldn't listen. All those days my thoughts flowed broad and shallow as the river, and broke into the swamp. My stool was liquid as I floated down that water, sacred to black Enki, to red Anu and the ancient gods—fathers of all, for whom bright Jove is just a child. There is no sickness in the desert, that's what the old fool meant. Faith comes from there, and a corpse lasts forever. But diseases live in these watery places, and doubts breed like maggots. They rot our hearts. I found in me as I got sicker a sullen anger for these brothers, for these lies.

Close to Nibilis, I saw the Jew again. The Jew I had robbed.
I can't remember the name of the village. Sometimes the river
runs choked and narrow and deep, and sometimes broad and flat.
This was at a flat place where the stream divided around long
low islands and the water was full of broken wood.

Small ridges of hills sank toward the water on the western
side. In times of flood the river might fill the entire valley. But in
the dry season, for a sick man, the villages seem a long way back.
We landed on the eastern shore. The boat fitted into a slip of
hardened mud, and from there we walked back toward the trees.
Our feet stirred up clouds of white dust, and from far away you
could see the lingering white clouds that followed the bullock
carts as they moved down to the water. The sun was sinking
toward the hills across the river. It was the eye of Shamash, the
sun god, and the rays of light that spread out from the eye seemed
very long, very weak. They seemed to glance off objects without
penetrating them or understanding them, and even the small
stones that littered the white ground cast shadows larger than
themselves. There were four of us, and the three crewmen; they
carried oars upon their shoulders. Our shadows stumbled ahead
of us, seven long figures with long legs and tiny heads. I was carrying my bag.

I fell behind until I was the last. I let the others go ahead
and stood still under the falling sun. The light glistened on the
stones under my feet. My bag was heavy and I let it sink down.

I was waiting for something. I felt a mixture of sensations
rising in my body: anticipation, and fear, and a kind of longing.
I imagined I had been in this same place before. I knew what was
going to happen here, and it was not only because the white
strand of the river looked like the strand at Dura. It was something deeper, a feeling of delight and terror that was born from
my intestines and was rising through the vessels of my body.

A cold air was moving through my arteries, starting in my
right hand, then spreading upward. Because the parts of the body
are joined by an interior sympathy, because threads of nerves join

each organ with the others, I felt a pattern of small pressures in my glands, in the four locations of my humors. Always I have been prone to biliousness; now, suddenly, with a feeling of inevitability and recognition, I realized my complaints of the past days had not come by chance. Not chance, never chance, because sickness always flow from something, some disorder, some mistake. But in this case it flowed backward too, back to those nights when, twice a week, my master used to visit me in my chamber in Tusculum when I was just a boy.

Then I had made a study of the symptoms and I shared them with Dion. He was fascinated. He made me write them down and learn them by heart. So how was it possible that I could have forgotten, that they could have taken me, as always, unaware? Perhaps some memories are too sharp, too hard. No matter. Now, standing on the white stones under the sinking sun, watching the boatmen walk away from me with their oars on their shoulders, now I remembered. The pressure in my glands, the gas, the backwash in my throat.

Dion had named my condition "heterocrania," after the headaches that were its culmination. He claimed it was related to the falling sickness, but I doubted it. There were no convulsions, no loss of consciousness. That comes from a blockage of air, but I felt air all through me. But there were similarities in this feeling of hope, of happiness, of dread.

If I closed my eyes, almost I could hear the sound of my master's step. The god had taken hold, whether the god Bel, or some other private deity. Perhaps in this Jewish place, the great Jahwah himself. All around me the air was quiet and still. Tiny noises seemed to come from a far distance, and they were full of echoes.

My bag had sunk to the ground. Now I seized it up and hurried after the retreating boatmen. They were only a few steps away; these thoughts had not occupied more than a few moments. Soon I found the line again and followed it up into the town, which was built on higher ground. It was a village of thirty or so mud-and-wattle houses and two buildings of mud brick. We moved toward one of these, where the headman of the village was to feed us, let us sleep.

As we came into the town we crossed over a small stream, which flowed down toward the river. We passed some pens for animals. One was empty except for a man. We peered over the plaited wall. There in the mud, his big wrists tied, his shirt ripped apart, his head sunk low on his hairy chest, stood the Jew, whom in my mind I had already named "the bear."

It was if he were following me wherever I traveled, a curse and a reminder, a messenger of the gods. As soon as I saw him, I felt again a jolt of queasiness, and the pain spread from my stomach toward my mouth. I tried to swallow down some bile, but my jaw could scarcely move. The pain spread to my tongue and into the muscles of my jaw. I felt I could not speak and yet must speak. The bear just stood there in the mud, his great chest naked and exposed. I opened my mouth, and the bear raised up his head and looked at me.

Later when we were sitting in the headman's house, one of the passengers in the boat asked a question about this man. I kept quiet but I listened carefully. I stared at the bearded lips of the headman as he was speaking: The man was a thief, he said. He had been caught stealing in the village and later had been recognized as a great criminal by someone who had recently arrived from Palestine.

I had trouble listening, even though I forced myself. And I noticed also, as he spoke, our host found it difficult to form the words. Often he glanced up toward the door, as if his mind was elsewhere. But still he labored to speak, as I labored to listen, and as we waited for our food he told us a story that I knew. If it had not been for the pain in my jaw, I felt I could have told the story myself. I felt I could have shouted it out: how the man had been a member of an Essene brotherhood, how he had been a trusted captain of the Lion of Tabor, how he had been chosen to lead an attack on the Roman prison at Caesarea, how he was passed over when the Lion found out that his father was a Roman soldier and his mother lived without respect for the temple or the law.

I found myself mouthing the exact words: how in revenge he had betrayed the time of the attack to Pontius Pilate. How Pilate, to reward him, had paid him a large treasure and freed his cousin John. How, when the Lion sent to question him, he had proved his guilt by crossing the Jordan and running away. Men had died because of him, and Barabbas was a prisoner.

"What will become of him?" asked the passenger.

Our host shrugged and glanced toward the door. "He will be stoned. We have sent to Nearda for the magistrate."

I was surprised that they were talking about these things. The passengers and boatmen were all Jews, but I was not. Was I a dog, that they could talk about this in front of me? No one on the boat had spoken a word to me for more than two days. And here they had put me at a separate table by myself. They had given me separate dishes of unvarnished pottery, and I knew they would break them when I finished.

At that moment I heard a woman scream.

We were sitting in a long, low, windowless room, lit with oil lamps on the wooden tables. I was by myself. But from my separate table I felt I could see more clearly than the others the links between these people, the cords of sympathy that joined them. Our host was a grey-haired man with elegant clean hands. When the woman screamed he closed his eyes for a moment, as if in pain. But then he opened them and continued talking, answering a question in the sudden silence as if nothing had happened.

And yet surely the scream was what he had been waiting for. Now we were all waiting. She screamed again. And then a younger man came in through the door. The lamplight gleamed on his sweaty face. I took him to be the son of our host. He bent down over his father and whispered in his ear, and then the older man again closed his eyes.

Better than the others, I knew what I was listening to. I had often gone with Dion as he made his rounds among the Roman matrons; these were the screams of a woman far gone in childbirth. They sickened me. I found myself counting under my breath. I also closed my eyes. I felt I understood these things without seeing them, as I had the Essene's story. The young man was my age. The screams were his wife's screams in her first pregnancy. As we had come into the brick building where we now sat on our stools, we had glimpsed some wattle sheds behind it. I pictured the young woman there, thrashing and turning on a long table, surrounded by incompetent midwives. Perhaps she was unconscious and had just woken up; it was intolerable. Her screams now came at intervals of fifty.

We sat listening to them in the closed, stuffy room. Servants were bringing in a hot grain soup. The smell disgusted me. I felt the pressure in my head, in my right temple, and I felt my head would burst. I stood up, and in the sudden silence I cried, "How long has she been like this?"

I spoke in Greek. The men from the boat turned toward me, shocked that I would speak the question that must have been in each of their minds. I didn't care. I was looking at the young man because I knew that at this moment he would talk to anyone, even me. He was rubbing his hands together in front of his chest. And after a moment he raised his voice above the angry murmur at the table: "Oh sir, more than a day. We gave her wine to ease the pain, but. . . ."

I couldn't stand it. The cold wind flowed up toward my brain. I saw the girl thrashing on the tabletop. "Fools," I said, "don't give her wine. It will keep her closed."

Again the shocked silence, again the angry rumbling. A serving girl stood in the doorway at the opposite end of the long room, a bowl in her hands. I kicked my stool back, and it slid back through the dirt. "My name is Dion," I said, borrowing the name of my master's slave. "I am a surgeon, traveling to Ctesiphon. To the house of Tiridates Philhellene," I added, inventing a name. "I have a skill in times like this."

"Please," I almost added as the girl's scream came again, hurting me and yet relieving me, as if it were my own. I would have begged him. I would have gone down to my knees. But instead I stepped forward and let them look at me in my new linen shirt, my feet wrapped in leather sandals which I had had made for me at the previous stage along the river. "I am from Syracuse," I said, a city so distant that I hoped it might seem mythical to them.

"Wine will keep the child from coming," I insisted over the murmuring guests. They had turned back to their dishes. They wouldn't look at me. They bent low over the table, touching their beards. This was not something for a man to know about. This was for the women. And besides, I was a Gentile, a Greek.

But perhaps that was also in my favor. I stood before the young man and his father, a visitor from a far country, unclean and polluted in my habits and my flesh, but carrying with me a new knowledge. Perhaps they saw me as so strange as to be neither man nor woman. My hairless body, my hairless face. "I am from Syracuse," I said again.

I knew this much about their laws also: that they could be broken to save a life. "Please," I said, standing forward. "The child will die."

Again the shriek of pain. It seemed to paralyze them, stun them to inaction. I picked up my bag and strode toward the door. As I passed the old man he turned away from me, his eyes closed. But he said nothing, and so I pulled open the wooden door and stepped outside.

The young man was close behind me. Even with my back turned I could feel him, his cold breath on my neck, his anxious hands caressing my shoulders without touching them.

Behind the house and joined to it, as I had seen, stood a three-sided wattle structure with a low roof, which sloped up toward the fourth brick wall. I strode toward it around the corner of the house, through a yard of carefully swept earth. The sun was low. Its eye was upon me, but I turned away from it and ducked to enter the birthing shed. A woolen curtain covered the doorway. I pulled it back.

As I had already seen in my mind, the girl lay on a table set with lamps at either end. She was attended by four women, shadowy figures in grey robes who covered their faces as soon as they saw me, becoming from that moment as interchangeable to me as ghosts.

The girl was struggling and crying out, and when her contractions came she had to be restrained. One of the midwives held her feet and one held down each hand. At the moment I entered, one was holding a cup of wine to the girl's lips. "No," I said. And then over my shoulder to the young man behind me, "Bring me a brazier of charcoal and a bucket of hot water. Bring a metal dish. Bring more light," I said, though in fact I found the dimness a relief for my own pounding head. I could feel the cold air rushing through me. I blinked, and it seemed to me the dark corners of the room were full of scattered light. When I left the doorway and came forward into the room, I felt I was moving through a screen that was covered with glowing geometric figures; I pushed my hand through it. I came to the table and put my hands over the girl's belly.

Again I saw her as if through a screen, which was torn apart whenever she cried out. I put my hands through the opening to touch her belly—the child had turned in her womb. I could feel its head under her navel. And her body had not opened more than half the length of my forefinger, not one-third what was necessary. "How long has she been like this?" I asked again, and the answer came murmuring back, from which veiled mouth I could not tell, "A day and a night."

I had my hand on the girl's belly. She was small and thin-boned and very young. She was terribly swollen, yet the child had made no progress. I stood with my hands on her naked belly, waiting for the hot water, shaking my head to clear it. As if in sympathy with her, my head above my right eye seemed full of an intolerable pressure, a swollen bag of thoughts. During the intervals between contractions, I almost heard the straining of the bone, as if my skull were in danger of bursting through its sutures. As I stood there blinking, I imagined great Jove with the pain in his head, his head splitting apart to admit Minerva in full armor, shaking the aegis— God in heaven, what a thought that was!

And again, as if in sympathy, Jove seemed to give me powers. My commands were obeyed. Women brought a smoking kettle of water on a brazier. They brought me my bag. I shook my head and took out my father's kit of steel tools and also some new medicines that I had bought or made in the Dura market. I laid out on a small table a pot of glasswort ash and grease, a pot of poppy juice. I laid out my father's heron clamps, his frog clamps, his tiger clamps, his needles, and I tested the edge of my shark knife on a hair. Then I put them in the brazier until they glowed.

Dion had said that when a wound is opened, the spirits of darkness stand breathless by the surgeon's hands, waiting to get in. The spirits come out of the earth, where bodies rot. "Earth is the enemy," he said. So I laid out the hot tools on my metal plate, which first I washed in water and grease. I washed my hands as I had seen him do.

He understood, as did my father, that the surgeon also risks contamination. I mean in his spirit and his caste. It is not good to touch a wound. It is polluting and unclean. My father had shown me the purifying ceremonies of our warrior caste. The warrior before battle—I washed my hands in memory of him, and then I chose my weapons. All this time the girl was screaming and crying, her body shuddering and convulsing as the women held her down; she was a strong girl, with a strong voice and healthy teeth. It was a miracle she had not broken her heart already on this solid and unmoving lump inside her.

She would need all the strength she had. I spoke to her to calm her, but perhaps we didn't have a tongue in common, and perhaps she was too hurt to listen. Or too drunk, although the wine seemed to have no more effect on her. I wanted to give her opium as I held up the knife and watched her eyes spread with fear. But I could not until the child was out, for it would hurt the child and stop its breath.

I had to start quickly. She was bursting apart. And to stop her screaming. "Hold her arms and legs," I said. Then I showed the fourth woman how to purify herself with grease and water. "Help me," I said. "When the time comes, hold apart the wound. You," I said to the young servant who had brought the water, "stand beside me with the lamp." And all the time I was muttering prayers to Father Toth, the patron of my craft, and to Aesculapius, and to Jahwah too. Under my breath, because I did not wish to offend the people here. I wanted them to obey me without thinking. If I could not get the child out before I counted two hundred, I knew the mother would die.

"Hold her tight," I said. Then I took the shark knife and pushed it down onto her belly, cutting her from her navel to her groin, slicing through the skin and through the layer of yellow fat. Two bands of muscle run down over the belly, and I cut between them through a thin, glistening layer of gristle and meat, down to her womb.

I was counting underneath my breath. I sliced through her veins and they started to spurt blood. There was no time to close them and I pushed on. Now it was more difficult. Now the girl started to kick and scream. Her eyes rolled back in her head. I was killing her, cutting her apart. She arched her back up off the wooden table and kicked her right leg free, and I had to stand back, counting uselessly while a servant from the door behind me came and threw her body across the girl's leg; then I could go on.

When she had subsided, I pushed my hand through the cut flesh, uncovering the womb. It was a red, smooth, hard, tough bag of muscle, swollen with water over the child's head. As I touched it with my hand it spasmed and contracted, forcing the child down. I had no time to wait for it to loosen, so I forced the steel shark's tooth down into it, separating the strands of the red muscle, pushing with all my strength until it broke apart. Then water and blood spurted up into my face, drenching my clothes and blinding me; my hands were slippery with blood. But this was the moment where the gods choose death or life. I pulled the knife down over the grain of the muscle, opening a cut perpendicular to my first cut, large enough for my two hands.

The girl's back arched off the table. "Now," I cried, and the midwife grabbed hold of the lips of the wound and pulled them apart. I put down my knife and drove my hands down through the hole into the womb itself. And the girl gave out a scream of such despair and rage, I thought I had killed her after all. Every muscle tightened to its breaking point and then relaxed. Her screaming stopped, and I saw she had lost consciousness, and I praised God, for I never could have sewn her up when she was struggling like that.

The wound brimmed with water and blood. I put my hands deep inside of her; I had the child in my hands. I slid my left hand over its back to hold its head against its breast, to roll it up into a ball, and then I pulled it out, head first through the hole that I had made.

The woman was standing there to take it, and she wrapped it in a towel. I pulled out the cord, and then clamped it in two places with the heron beaks. I locked them and then cut the cord between them with the tiger jaws; the child was crying now. It was alive, and so I gave no more thought to it. I bent over the mother. I had reached 194 in my counting, and the blood was leaking from her in a wide, heavy stream down the middle of the table.

I thrust my hands into her womb once again, pulling the afterbirth loose from around the base of the cord and gathering it up—a clotted, formless mass of blood and flesh that was brimming out of my two hands. I dropped it down onto the floor.

I was still counting and I could hear myself now, the numbers falling from my mouth. The baby screamed and I paid no attention. Instead I held up a strand of silk, tied off the mother's cord next to the clamp, and released it. Then I was searching for the blood vessels and pinching them closed with the hot clamps, and burning them and tying them one by one.

Silk is made out of a magic fungus that grows on the underside of apricot leaves in the country of the Sericans. It is not perfect for work like this. The gut from an animal is better, because it disappears into the wound. The silk keeps hard places in the flesh, but I had nothing else. I strung my needle, and when the bleeding in the womb had stopped I sewed it closed. And I went on, counting out loud and searching for broken veins layer after layer, then closing them—the gristle with just a few stitches, the fat not at all. I pulled it closed and pulled the skin closed with tiny, delicate stitches. The wound disappeared, and it was done. The girl was white as a piece of clay, but she breathed.

Later I poured water out again and purified myself, and thanked the gods. I could feel the bile from my stomach rising to my mouth. My head was bursting over my right temple, and I turned away from the lantern, searching for the dark corners of the room. The young man stood in the doorway behind me, and he said nothing as I pushed past him out of doors. "Give me a room," I said, looking up toward the dark sky, for the sun had set. I stood in the swept yard, which was full of people from the village. One old man came close to me, carrying a torch, and I stretched my hand out to block the light.

I was blinded by it. But as if to make a balance, I felt my ears assailed by tiny sounds. Insects from the reeds, frogs from the river. Tiny murmurs all around me, and I searched among them for the sounds I wanted. Something from the bearlike Jew, alone in his pen. And something from the child, some little sound of crying, but I couldn't hear it. "Please," I said, "take me somewhere to lie down."

Then I have no memory until I came to myself in a dark room. I lay on a bed of knotted ropes, the crook of my elbow over my face, my body streaked with sweat. My head felt empty, as if some thought had escaped, but there was no pain in it anymore.

But still the light hurt my eyes. In time the door opened and the young man came in. I turned away from the light in the corridor. I lay there with my arm over my face, and I imagined he was going to thank me. Instead he told me that the boat had gone, and he was charging me a silver tetradrachm for the room, an absurd sum. He stood by the slatted windows and he opened them up. Light came into the room, and it was day. I sat up, stretched out my hand.

"Get your woman onto her feet as soon as she can walk," I said, to remind him of his debt to me. "Don't let her lie in bed. How is the child?"

"She dead."

With the light behind him, I couldn't see his face. Nor could I understand his voice, which seemed to have no sorrow in it, but only a small anger.

"I don't understand. The child was healthy."

"No."

The man's Greek was poor, his vocabulary small. "She blind," he continued. "Not whole. She bleeds, then dies."

Still his voice was strange, clipped, irritated. But I was angry too. "No," I said. "Let me see the body. If the women tied the cord—"

He interrupted me. "What right are you? Tell me what law? This is your fault. Your blame. Dirty hands. Please. You go."

"I heard her crying in my sleep," I said.

Then I stood. "See the mother gets up," I said. "Make her walk. Give her milk to drink. Milk mixed with blood." And then: "She will not survive another birth."

He had turned from me and was staring out the window. I could see now. His eyes were red-rimmed, his face pale. "What law tells you? Milk and blood—what dirtiness. She will have sons."

After he left I took his place by the window and stood looking out the window until the sun went down. I looked out toward the bear in his pen. Men came and went. Long robes, grey beards. Sometimes I could hear their voices as they passed under the window. Not one raised his head to meet my eyes.

I stood at the window until darkness fell. I was waiting for the moon. That night was the eighth night of the gaining moon, and I waited until it rose above the trees. In time I took my bag and crept out of my chamber, down the ladder, into the courtyard. All was still. By the light of the moon I walked down toward the river, my shark knife in my hand.

CHAPTER

3

THE MUD-WALLED FORTRESS

ESCAPE AND CAPTURE

I wanted to find where they had buried the dead child. I thought they had killed her. How did they know she was blind? Sometimes it takes months to be sure. And I thought, what right had they to destroy my work?

Under the half-moon, I walked down to the animal pens. A stream flowed down out of a wooded ravine, breaking into a net of rivulets that spread out toward the broad Euphrates. The path crossed it on the slope where it descended to the shore. The water stank, and the rocks were slippery there. The latrine for the village emptied into the stream, and a burning pit was dug along the far bank. Along the slope in that disgusting place, a row of sties.

They were woven out of strips of willow, which formed a

wall around a circular frame. One was occupied. The Jew lay in the mud with his hands and feet tied together, and for a moment I stood at the wall with my knife in my hand, watching him.

But I was searching for the burying ground or else the garbage pits. I crossed the stream and searched for a long time in the half-light. But after a while I stopped thinking about the dead child, and thought instead about the Jew. Because I found nothing, I returned again and stood outside the sty. I stood at the gate and untied the rope that held it closed.

The inside of the sty was full of garbage and filth. I moved through it warily, and when I stood above the Jew I felt no desire to go down in the mud, no desire to touch him. He lay on his side, his beard caked with dirt. He didn't move. And so I had to force myself. I leaned down and put my hand out, forced myself to run my hand over his massive shoulder, through the tufts of hair that had earned him his nickname in my mind. I could feel the ridges of the stripes and scabs where they had beat him. He didn't move.

Near him in the mud, I saw the broken leg of a goat, which surprised me. But then I thought they must have used the flesh of an unclean animal to humiliate him; I leaned over him and pried his feet apart and cut the ropes that bound his ankles. They were cruelly tight. Then I pushed him over onto his back and sawed at cords around his wrists. One by one they fell away, and he was free.

I stood up and stepped backward, and lifted up my knife. I had seen enough of him to know how dangerous he was, and I had a picture in my mind of him turning over and grabbing at my throat with his big hand. I had a picture of him pulling me down into the mud, rolling over onto me, and crushing me with his body. Almost I could feel his hairy lips around my ear and in my mind I listened to him whisper in my ear, and ask me whether it was I who had stolen his money. Whether it was I who had betrayed the sicarii to Pontius Pilate. Whether these wounds on his body were for me.

I put those thoughts out of my mind, and I leaned over him again. I pulled him onto his back, and at the same time I was fumbling in my bag for a vial of fortified wine, which I had bought in Dura.

This wine is boiled in glass pots and then drawn off and recondensed. Just the smell of it is healthful and stimulating. I thumbed open the stopper and held the vial under his nose, and then I dribbled some of the wine between his lips. I could smell it too; it is a wonderful cure-all. In time the Jew was coughing and spluttering, but he had no voice. He was as weak as a child.

I leaned down over him. "Come with me," I whispered, and he opened his eyes. I moved my face into the moonlight, hoping to reassure him. I hoped he might remember me as the surgeon who had brought the Roman soldier back to life in the cave at Caesarea. But if he recognized me then, he gave no sign.

"Come away from here," I whispered, holding up the vial. He accepted the mouth of it into his mouth, as trusting as a child. His eyes, inches from my own, were luminous and clear, and at that moment I saw him clearly also: a poor man from a small village, alone and hurt and far from home. After a moment he sat up and looked around.

We were of different tribes, he and I. But even though I was twice born, descended through my father from the court of Sandracottus and Ashok, and even though he was a peasant who had never stood, as I had, in the great places of the world, or spoken, as I had, with any of its great men, still I caught a glimpse of feeling in his eye. I squatted with him in this refuse dump, among people whose malice was lessened only by their stupidity. "Come with me," I said, because I felt a power over him. And because of the infant girl, whose life I had not saved.

In time he roused himself and stumbled to his feet. He never said a word.

I led him down the hill and out onto the white strand, searching for a boat. When I came up from the river two days before, I had noticed a row of small circular boats, overturned, fastened with stakes, but they were gone. Disappointed, I made no sign that I was looking for anything. The Jew was close behind me. I turned and walked downstream, as if with a purpose.

When it grew light, he stopped. He was still behind me but he stopped. We had come perhaps fifty stades across the open ground, the river to our right. But now we stopped near where another small stream came down out of the marsh. A silver tree trunk lay half buried in the sand. He sat down on it, and I put down my bag.

A pool of water had collected behind a sandbar. The Jew turned his back to me. And then he stripped off his shirt until he was naked, except for a small cloth that he wound over his loins. Then he stepped down into the pool and drank from it, and rubbed the water over his body while I took out my knives. "Come," I said, and he came and sat in front of me while I cut his hair and shaved his head and face. His hair was filthy. It had lice in it.

He sat still under the knife, trusting and calm, though from time to time I scraped him till he bled. I'm sure he understood the need to change his looks, though what I did meant more to him than that: I could feel it in his calmness. I was cutting his hair, shaving him perhaps for the first time in his life. His face was quiet and sad. In Egypt when a man dies, they shave his body while it is still warm.

"Tonight it is the Sabbath," he said, the first time he had spoken. I wondered whether he was telling me they would not chase us, or something else more intimate to him. I didn't ask. I took my time. I shaved his head down to the skin and cut his heavy eyebrows. When I was done, I rubbed the raw places on his scalp with oil. I rubbed oil into the cuts on his back. He crossed his palms over his breast, leaned forward and let me. He said nothing.

As I touched him I felt two sensations, which lived in separate chambers in my mind. First there was a tenderness, such as I imagine mothers feel for their young children. As the man folded his hands and leaned forward on the silver log, I felt something in the region of my heart. All my life I'd been a servant. Now this man had put himself into my care, if only for a little while.

Yet there was another sensation which was shocking and more powerful—an anger that pressed me to draw the blade of the knife across the Jew's naked scalp. At moments my hand shook.

The plans I had made were useless now. My money was useless. I had no boat. I had no food, and men were chasing me. I had made bad decisions because of this Jew. Now it was not enough to trust the gods, because of the burden of my power over him. Now my decisions became more important, at the moment when I had no good ones left.

A boat came by, four men under a narrow sail. I squatted down behind the bar. But one of the men leaned on the outrigger and pointed toward me as the boat went past. Without speaking I turned away from the river toward the east, and we followed a path along the south bank of the stream, through a thicket of willow and oleander. The Jew carried my bag.

In time the day grew hot. We were surrounded by clouds of mosquitoes which rose out of the grass. The branches whipped our faces. Yet still I pushed on with a kind of stubbornness that is unusual in me. From time to time I looked back at the Jew, and there was something in his calm face that maddened me. Surely he could see that we were getting nowhere. The path split in front of me, and split and split. I chose our way at random.

All morning and into the afternoon we wandered in this maze. The ground was marshy, and sometimes we sank up to our shins in mud. Our way was blocked time and time again by wide, overgrown canals, by stagnant ponds, by barriers of reeds that were taller than ourselves. So when after many hours we reached the river again, it was almost a relief.

We stood on the riverbank at an unusual spot, where the shifting water had carved out a bay as if along the seashore, and there was a beach. There was an inlet where another stream came down, and a flat triangle of sand between it and the river. Tall palm trees grew on it, the first I had seen in that country.

The wind made a noise in the leaves. It cooled our faces. But I stood sweating and tired looking back at the Jewish bear; he was not breathing hard. There was no sign of disappointment on his face, that we had wasted so much time for nothing. He was smiling, looking past me out into the river wind, and I watched him with a growing anger until I heard a shout from the water and turned back.

Two boats were coming upstream past the cove, and then they altered course. The bear squatted down at the water's edge and washed his arms while I looked out into the bright sun. The water gleamed around their hulls as the boats swung into the mouth of the inlet. Once they left the wide strong current of the river, they were moving fast.

They were boats of an Egyptian design, low and sleek, but with a high deck in the back behind the steering oars. Each had a single red square sail, which fluttered down as the boats came inside the point. They swung around onto the beach, and then the inside bank of oars rose up. There were shouts and cries as some of the sailors leapt out onto the shingle and dragged the boats inshore.

A man stood by the rail of the larger boat, feeding a rope out through a hole in its sharp prow. When he saw us he jumped down into the water. The sailors' chests were naked, but he was better dressed in a red tunic and a bashliq. He came toward us up the beach, brandishing a wooden stick. He shouted in a language I didn't know. Nevertheless, his meaning was clear.

The boats had canvas awnings on their high stern decks. On the larger boat the striped curtain was pulled back. Someone stood there: a tall man with his arms crossed on his chest. Above him a banner stretched out on the breeze, in the shape of an eel or a long fish.

Ignoring the man who rushed toward us up the beach, I

turned toward him and lifted up my hands. Even though he was too far away to hear, I spoke my appeal to him. I hoped he might just catch the sound of the words: "Great sir, forgive me. I am a poor iatros, a physician from the school of Herophilos in Alexandria, robbed by pirates and marooned on this unhealthy shore. I was traveling to Spasinu Charax with my servant when. . . ."

I spoke in Greek. I felt if I could spew out enough Greek, it would protect me from the charging barbarian with his stick. And in fact that is what happened. The Jew squatted by, trusting me. I raised my voice and made it plaintive, and the man stopped running. His wooden stick sagged down.

"Great sir," I said. "The boatmen took my money and then left me here to die. Yet I have no wish to disturb you or burden you with troubles. . . ."

Ten steps in front of me the man stopped. Encouraged, I stood up against him. I had seen the Thracian gladiators in Rome, only my net was made of words. I threw it over him. He was a bald man with a big chest and belly—out of breath, angry and doubtful now. But then he gathered himself together and raised up his stick, and as he did so I could feel a stiffness, a hardness in the neck and shoulders of the Jew. He squatted by my feet. Now he was rising and I put out my hand. I put my hand on his big, naked shoulder, and at that moment the man on the deck of the ship called out.

Four to a rope, the sailors hauled both boats in. Now one splashed back through the water until he stood beside the rail, and offered his bare back for the man to sit on. But instead he jumped down into the water and splashed ashore. Then he too was walking toward us up the beach.

And I could see he was a great man with a small beard and a laughing face. He was a few years older than me, but strong and beautiful, with big lips and bright eyes. If nothing else, his white grin set him apart. His was the first laughter I had heard in that whole country. And though his clothes were simple, I could see his power in the way the others treated him. The man with the wooden stick, whom I now took to be a steward of some kind, put his left hand over his heart and bent his neck. He looked down at the pebbles underneath his feet as if searching for something he had lost.

But I thought the man would reward boldness. So I stared up at his dark eyes and repeated my story until he cut me off. "Come," he said, laughing. "You know the river is full of thieves. But these at least are sparing you your baggage. Yes, no matter. If you have been treated rudely, he is sorry."

The man's Greek was muddied with the accent of the Persians. I mean his consonants were either too harsh or too soft, and he spoke in a quick monotone: "Come. He finds that he must recompense you for the rudeness of these folk. For twelve years they have kept the roads unsafe. If we had. . . . Yes, but no matter. If you are hungry, as you say, we have stopped here to dine."

The steward wore rings on his fingers and a golden chain around his neck. But the laughing man had nothing of that kind. His clothes were simple—grey shirt, dark trousers, and red leather boots. So I had to search his words for tokens of his rank. And I thought I had found it in the way he said "he" when he meant "I," for I was sure he was the master of these boats. Looking up at his face, I could imagine no one more grand than he.

"Great sir," I started, but he cut me off. "Come," he said, almost touching my shoulder with his hand. And then we were walking back the other way, almost side by side, with the steward and the Jew behind us.

The stream came down into the river, forming a point of land. On it, servants were preparing food. They took food out of baskets and set it down on a large square of cloth under the palm trees. They had built a small canopy, and under it there was a wooden chair, big-legged and luxurious, painted gold, with a seat of woven reeds. In front of it, a footstool.

"Come," said my host as we passed by the boats, which had been pulled up into the inlet. "It is Priapatius Surenas." And again I thought he was referring to himself. I thought the chair was for him and perhaps the footstool was for me. The afternoon sun was warm. My whole body felt warm because the man was still smiling as if happy for my company.

Surenas was the name of the general who had surrounded and destroyed three Roman legions, when they crossed the desert to attack the Parthians at Carrhae. That was years ago. Still, as I walked along the beach I found myself remembering the famous story. Marcus Crassus, the Roman triumvir, had been killed in the fighting. And this was how Surenas had announced his victory: He had sent the head of Crassus to an actor. During a performance of Euripides's play about the Bacchae, the man brought the dripping head onto the stage. He had held it up and then called out the verses Queen Agave sings over the body of her murdered son. King Orodes was in the audience, and when he recognized the head of his defeated enemy, he wept for joy.

But why did the image of this farcelike tragedy come into my mind? At that moment I saw it, as real as if I'd been there, though the story dated from before my father's birth. I saw the actor's hands. Perhaps as I walked along the beach, my excitement and my joy were mingled with a small anxiety. But perhaps also in the bloody head of Marcus Crassus, the gods were giving me a vision of what would come so quickly on that bloody afternoon.

The mind rebels, and there are places where the gods have snatched away my memory. I remember the food set on the ground. Servants had laid a cloth out on the ground, and on it they had set nine glass dishes full of apricots, dates, bread, damsons, pistachios, and peaches. Four gentlemen were there already, but I don't remember their names or faces. They sat cross-legged without looking at me. I stood until our smiling host sat down, not in the chair but on the sand in front of it. He reached up and almost touched my hand.

I don't remember much of our talk. We sat without eating,

which surprised me. I said nothing until my host turned to me. "I am going to Hatra to join my regiment," he said. "Tell me, have you come from there?"

"Yes," I said, which was a lie. But I was confused by his sudden use of the first person. And I couldn't imagine saying no to him or refusing him anything.

"Tell me," he said. "I want something for my father's wife, because she is in pain. It is a plant that grows in Hatra. If you are a surgeon, you have heard of it." And then he went on to tell me the story of how Heracles was wounded in his fight with the Hydra, the monster that grew two heads for each one he cut off. He lay with rotting wounds and broken bones until the god told him to walk east into the rising sun, and he would find a flower that would grow two blossoms when he broke its stalk, just as he watched.

"I have some with me," I said. It was a lie. Of course there is no flower like that. There is no flower which cures everything. But it is something that grows out of the stories of the gods and the wishes of men.

"I came through Hatra on my way," I lied. "I made a grease out of the plant." And I went on to describe its powers in any case where the flesh divides or else is joined together.

"In that country women use it when they come to child-birth," I said. At this he frowned, and for a panicked moment I thought I had insulted him. Or that he had asked me his question just to test me, because it was at Damascus, not at Hatra, that Heracles found the magic plant, as any child knows. But then he smiled again, and I would have continued, only at that moment there was a noise behind me, and we all stood up.

The sailors had strung a gangplank from the rail of the smaller boat. Now a man was coming down it to the beach, and I saw I was mistaken all this time. For this was Priapatius Surenas. He moved slowly and calmly, gliding down the ramp with small calm steps—an enormous man with a tall bashliq of polished silver, which caught the sun. He was dressed in a long robe, a cloak of golden cloth that hung down to the ground. It looked heavy, inappropriate to the heat of the day.

From his boots to the point of his bashliq he was enormous. His face was calm and noble. His complexion was dead white, altered, I thought, by a pale lotion that was spread over his cheeks, the only place where his skin was exposed. He wore leather gloves, and his chin was covered with a thick clubbed beard that had been dyed with henna until it was almost yellow.

He wore a golden chain over his shoulders. As he stepped onto the beach, a servant hoisted a parasol at the end of a long pole and followed him up the slope to the chair beneath the canopy. Then without looking at us, Surenas settled down onto his golden chair and clasped his gloved hands together in his lap.

Perfume rose from him. It made my eyes water and I could taste it in my throat. He said nothing, but after a moment he made a gesture with his hand, and we sat down. The smiling man passed out bread, and soon he and the others were talking softly, lightly. I ate a peach.

How much I wish now, when I think of that day, that I had told the truth. That there was a potion which could heal the gods, which could cure the heart when it split Hydra-like in two. Which could cure time itself. We sat under the palms with the river on one side and the inlet on the other where the boats were pulled up. Above us sat Priapatius Surenas on his throne, and above him the hot sun, made comfortable to us by a steady wind that blew away our napkins and curled the edges of our eating cloth. I sat between two gentlemen, and though they didn't speak to me, sometimes they glanced toward me. We drank wine from silver cups.

A servant stood behind me with a glass ewer. He refilled my cup several times. The wine was strong, and I felt it in my head. And in my bladder. I waited a long time, but finally I got up to relieve myself.

I had not given any thought to my own servant in all this time, but now I saw him. He was sitting by himself near the stream, drinking from the clear water. I came toward him, toward the bushes where the stream came out. I saw he had been given food. The remains of it were on the bank, heavier than what we'd had. Olives wrapped in leaves and a soft chunk of dates. A piece of meat, made from the dried flesh of swine, which he had bitten in half.

The Jew squatted by the stream. Curious, I paused to look, and he raised his eyes. I found myself staring at him, trying to understand his face: half smiling and half angry. I stood there with my head whirling and my bladder full, until I heard a noise behind me and I turned.

Soldiers were coming out of the bushes all along the beach on both sides of the stream. They were small men in leather shirts and round iron helmets.

Two men were with them, and I knew I was looking at Anilaeus and Asinaeus, the two young brothers who were rulers of this shore. They stood side by side, their tanned, wrinkled, ugly faces as alike as beans. Or not alike, for one was scowling and the other wore a gentle, puzzled face. Drunk, my belly full, I stared stupidly from one to the other. The wind off the river seemed to blow through my body and form a circle of disturbance around the bandit brothers with their Janus faces. No, it was the Hydra that stared back at me. They split the world in two. I closed my eyes and opened them, overcome by a sudden nausea. I turned away and I was looking at the boats. And then I saw the laughing man stand up. He came down out of the shadow of the palms, the sun in his black hair, his face simple and unmixed, and I thought there is Heracles himself, come down to fight the monster.

"Welcome," he said.

But I scarcely heard him because of the ringing in my ears. And in everything that followed, throughout that long afternoon, I am more sure of the images, the actions, than the words, though I was right there and heard them all. Now I am not even sure what language they were spoken in.

The brother with the gentle face stood forward. "Please," he said. "Accept our thanks. We were looking for these men. Now we will take them and leave you to your dinner."

I put my hand out and grabbed hold of the Jew's shoulder as he rose up. We stood side by side, very close, and I could smell his sweat.

The laughing man said, "Please, that is not possible. These men are the guests of Priapatius Surenas."

The scowling brother said, "No. You are wrong. Or they lied to you. They are thieves and murderers. We've been hunting them all day."

Our host looked at the Jew and me, and his expression changed. There was no trace of laughter in it. "Nevertheless," he answered. And then he turned back toward Surenas, who had risen from his chair.

The first brother said, "Please, they are beneath your notice. One is a murderer, who will be judged and convicted by the Sanhedrin of Nearda, according to our laws. The other is a thief, who stole two nights' food and housing from a man near here. His name is Dion. He is a Greek. He is from Syracuse."

Again my host looked at me, and I felt a terrible pain, which came out of the disappointment in his eye. "Then perhaps there is a mistake," he said, though I could tell he didn't think so. "This man is from Alexandria."

"No," broke in the scowling brother. He wiped his lips with his thick fingers. Then just when he might have continued, his gentle twin interrupted, "Yes, perhaps. We are less interested in him. If he agrees to pay the money, we will leave him here. But the other is a criminal of our own race. He is from Nazareth in Galilee. His name is Jeshua."

Behind us Priapatius Surenas had risen from his throne. He had taken off his golden robe, and I saw to my surprise that underneath it he was armed. He was wearing a tunic of yellow leather covered with steel rings. His hips and waist were bound by a belt made of circular steel plates.

What a great man he was, to have worn such clothing under the hot sun and to have shown no sign of it as he was sitting with us. Now he moved slowly, stiffly. Everything he did seemed practiced, like the movements of a dancer or an actor on the stage. His face was a mask without expression.

"I will speak to my father," said our host. He left us to join Surenas and I closed my eyes, not wishing to see any of the gestures that might mark their speech, describe me, bind me up, pierce me like arrows. Instead I prayed to my own fathers: Mercury, and Toth, and Hanuman the monkey, patron of travelers. "Oh my lords," I said. "I will make an offering below the Diamond Mountain, where the river rises. At Lake Manosarovar, I will. . . ."

When I opened my eyes again I thought my prayer was answered, for I saw Surenas glance up at the sun. Then he put his fists on his hips, a gesture of defiance. He frowned back at us and at the bandit twins.

The four men we had eaten with had come down from the palms to stand behind him, along with two servants. But more soldiers had now stepped out of the willows. They had long knives in their hands, and some carried bows.

Then our host was walking back toward us. No one spoke a word. We watched him coming up the beach. He stopped halfway. Mirroring his father, he also put his fist onto his hip. And he cupped his other hand around his mouth so that his voice came strong and clear: "Surenas tells me that these men are under his protection, whether they deserve it or not. Therefore let us be. We are traveling upstream to Dura, where we will turn them over to the governor. There you can apply to him."

I looked toward the two brothers. They were talking with their faces close together, one scowling and one calm. I put my hand on Jeshua's shoulder and drew him back away from the stream. Behind us servants were taking down our camp where we had eaten. Sailors were busy on the decks of the boats. They were splashing in the water. At a gesture from our host, two of them came forward to attend to us, and in the meantime Priapatius Surenas walked up toward the gangplank. At its foot he turned and struck another stiff, defiant pose, his arms crossed on his chest. Then as I watched, he raised his hand toward heaven.

To my right and to my left the soldiers had not moved. They stood silently, lining the cove, their backs to the willows. Some stood with their bows bent, arrows on string, and as I watched, whether through accident or malice, one of them, the fourth in the line away from me, let fly. I saw the streak of the arrow, and I saw it pierce under the arm of Priapatius Surenas as he stood next to the boat. The arrow struck him where his naked skin was covered with a flap of cloth between the joints of his leather armor, between the silver rings. And I knew a higher, stronger power than my three monkey-faced protectors had struck that blow, for no human archer had the skill to make that shot. And I wondered who it was, whether it was Indra, or bright Apollo, or Ahrimmon the black archer. It was not Jahwah, I was sure. For as the arrow struck I knew that it had made a mortal wound for the Jews of this marshland, for Asinaeus and his brother, and they knew it too. Because I heard a groan rise up from the Jewish line—there was a moment when they knew what had happened and the Persians did not. The arrow had sunk all the way up to its feather. And Surenas didn't speak a word. He just stood there with his arm outstretched while the sailors bustled around him. And then stiffly, slowly, like a tree that has been cut, he collapsed full length, and the ground seemed to shudder underneath his weight.

"Shit," cried out the grim-faced brother. "Son of a whore." And he moved up the line toward the unlucky bowman, not realizing he was innocent, that the god had used him for his purpose. But the gentle brother stood with an expression of pure sadness on his face as he watched the young Surenas run toward his father's body and kneel down.

The poet tells us how, before the walls of Troy, Pandaros Lykonides once shot an arrow at great Menelaos. That also was a stroke of the gods, and in it we can see the difference between true life and a song. Menelaos was only wounded, and he lived into a strong old age with Queen Helen by his side. But the events of that afternoon, no song can be made of them: Surenas was dead. And in a little while the Jews attacked us. Perhaps it was their plan to kill us all and burn the boats, so there could be no witness to their murder. Or perhaps it is just that blood follows blood, and dead men are jealous. They call for their sons to keep them company.

The Persians had no weapons. They gathered around the body of Priapatius Surenas. They lifted it up. They were still, I think, not sure he was dead when the soldiers attacked them and cut them down on the stony beach—the four men who had eaten with me, and then the laughing man. Jeshua and I had crossed the stream and run up the slope into the palm trees. A soldier caught us there, and we did not struggle. Instead we turned back to the shouting and watched the soldiers attack the boats. One was in the deeper water, and some men had cut its ropes. Now the oarsmen stood on the rail and thrust their long oars into the sand, pushing themselves away as the arrows sang around them.

Soldiers had run into the water and were hanging from the oars. But the boatmen pushed them off, and they pushed back into the current. Then the oars slid through their locks and they were free.

But the other boat was covered now with soldiers who had run up the plank from the beach. They were cutting down the sailors one by one and throwing them into the water. The two brothers were there, and when they saw the larger boat pull out into the river current, saw it turn its nose downstream, they cried out and set to work again, bloodier than ever, mad with rage, because they knew that they had lost. They must have killed twenty men.

The soldier who had taken Jeshua and me had left us and gone down toward the water. I suppose we could have run away. It was no use; Jeshua was pulling me back. We came out of the shelter of the trees and stood in the full light of the evening. The sun was sinking into a red haze.

The soldiers had pulled the boat up on the shore. It lay on its side, and we watched them pull the bodies out, break up the decks, pull out the mast. They had smashed down the curtained alcove at the stern, and there they took prisoners. Perhaps at that moment they understood some of the uselessness of death. The other boat had passed beyond the headland. Perhaps also, as the sun went down and the Sabbath approached, they remembered who they were. Or perhaps there was something about these prisoners that woke their pity. I watched the soldiers drag them up the beach, two women and a blind old man.

Anilaeus and Asinaeus stood together on the shore. One of them, the gentle one, had blood on his face. His grim brother stood with his feet planted wide, and I thought I had never seen such an expression of anger and frustration.

And then I saw it change. Soldiers had dragged up the three prisoners. The old man lay on his belly, and the grim-faced Jew stepped over him and stood over the women, who were on their knees. One was a serving girl. He ignored her. With the point of his sword he hooked back the veil over her mistress's face, and his expression changed.

I guessed the woman was Surenas's wife. She was the right age—past her second youth. Her clothes were made of pink silk embroidered with gold thread, and there were jewels sewn into her bodice and into her cuffs when she raised up her hands, which caught the light. Her long black hair was streaked with grey. And she was pregnant, as her son had hinted.

THE MAGIAN

The Jews, unlike the Gauls and Britons, are not by nature cruel. Their god has given them a code of laws, which they break often. Nevertheless, that day on that bloody beach, there were few shouts of anger and no cries of triumph to mix with the groans of wounded men. The faces of the soldiers, even as they pulled the bodies of their enemies out along the stones, were puzzled and confused.

For this reason, I think, they spoke gently to us afterwards and treated us gently—out of a sense of shame. I was afraid they would blame us and kill Jeshua outright. But instead they tied our hands and led us away.

We entered into the marshes, and as the sun went down they led us quickly along the narrow paths away from the shore. Single-file, in a long line, we marched along the tops of narrow raised embankments. On each side the swamps stretched away—stagnant pools covered with lilies and green grass, out of which rose swarms of mosquitoes and jiggling gnats. We hurried through stands of reeds taller than men, among whose roots lived snakes and frogs which sang to us in the strident voices of the dead.

Toward nightfall they made us run along a pathway of split logs, and it was almost dark before we reached our goal. It was a fortress of mud brick, built on a wooded tongue of dry land which protruded out into the middle of the marsh. Behind it a black wall of trees, and I could see the ground was higher there. In two hours we had come no more than forty stades from the river.

The walls of the fortress loomed above us in the darkness. I could see they were only half built. Inside, a square courtyard of brushed earth surrounded an enormous, square, seven-storied tower. It was the citadel of Anilaeus and Asinaeus. It was ringed with oil torches, and it had no windows except one, where the roof and wall were broken at the very top.

I didn't see the brothers on our march, nor the old man and the women they had taken from the boat. We came through the gate in the middle of a line of soldiers, and found ourselves among a crowd. For the inside of the wall was lined with tents, and in shallow pits scooped from the dirt the people had lit fires. Men, women, and children gathered around them. Smoke rose up into the black sky, and I could smell meat cooking, which disgusted me. I was still weak, and my stomach was still full of sorrow. The women hid their faces as the soldiers marched us through.

Behind the citadel the mud brick courses were still low, and there were ragged gaps where the work was still unfinished. On the far side facing the trees a group of miserable low buildings huddled against the wall, and Jeshua and I were taken into one of them. It was an airless, windowless chamber lit by a single lamp.

Jeshua had said nothing during the march, and he said nothing now. He lay down on the damp earth. He hid his face. I walked along the walls with my hand out so that I could make the dimensions clear. Our cell was rectangular, four paces by five, and I could reach the ceiling.

The bricks were damp under my hand. Still new, in some places they were already crumbling—this was not the place to build such a building. This marshland, only fools would build here. The ground was too wet. I found the thought consoling so that even in the pit of my despair, as I sat down in the stuffy dark and listened to the sound of children laughing in the courtyard, I took comfort from the knowledge that this fortress could not last, and it would fall into the swamp before it was finished. But even before that happened, the Persians would have broken it apart brick by brick.

I thought about the story of Anilaeus and Asinaeus, how they had been weavers in Nibilis who had killed their master and then run away into the swamps. How they had gathered up an army of bandits. And because they were not punished, now they imagined themselves kings. In their pride they imagined themselves kings inside a tower, forgetting it was the swamp that made them strong.

This was a story that would have pleased my old master, who delighted in stern moral tales. I remembered sitting by him at a play, a comedy of Menander's, watching some puffed-up servant get his due. In my memory I caught a glimpse of my master's sober face, and as always when I thought about those times, I felt a current of air blow through me, horror and regret, which split as it passed through my double-sided heart. In the clammy dark I felt a sweat break on my forehead and run down my ribs, though it was cold in that place and getting colder, and the air was bad. What will they do to me? I thought. They had taken all my money, which would have paid the innkeeper's charge a hundred times. Yet how could they let me go, now that they had shamed themselves so terribly to capture me?

In the dark I sweated and shivered as the lamp sank low, its blue flame clustered and trembling around the wick. And by its light I could see my companion stretched out on the bare earth, his back to me. He was asleep. How could he sleep? His naked back—the sight of it filled me with anger, except whatever they had planned for me, surely he would suffer worse, I knew. In the morning they would take him out and strangle him or else crush him with stones. Yet he lay on the damp ground as if nothing was wrong.

I felt that if my life and punishment were tangled up with his, I could expect to share some of what made him calm. We were in a terrible place. Though there was not a hole in the small cell large enough for rats to crawl through, still it was full of other vermin—roaches and flies, which chattered in the walls. They frightened me. In time I went and lay down next to the sleeping Jew, for comfort's sake. My lips were trembling with cold. I stretched out along his broad, tufted back. His scalp glowed pale and blue in the tiny lamplight, and I did feel some comfort from him. Some heat that radiated from him, from the length of his big back. So much heat, I was surprised. It dried the false sweat off my body as I lay there.

But he was not asleep. I had been wrong. Almost touching him, I perceived at the extreme limit of my hearing a low rumble of words, which seemed to push out from him like the heat along his back. They were words I couldn't understand. But still they soothed me until I almost slept. I entered into a dream, and I was kneeling by the river under the bright sun, and in front of me sat Priapatius Surenas on his throne. He was more godlike than ever, and his silver helmet shone. It hurt my eyes to look at him.

In my dream I had been taken for some crime, and I knelt waiting for judgment. But the voice of Surenas, when it came, was one I recognized—insinuating, soft and harsh. It was the voice of my old master, Cornelius Celsus the Roman, who had kept me after my father's death and treated me always with false kindness. Now I knelt at his feet, asking his forgiveness. But whereas in the past he would have beaten me with his own hand, this time he made the soldiers take me and seal me up in a dark place where there was an animal that was like a lion or a tiger or a river horse from Egypt. I couldn't see it in the darkness.

Then I woke up and the clay lamp had gone out. I lay in the darkness on my side, curled toward the Jew, feeling the heat from his body, listening to his voice, the words too soft to hear.

I thought about my dream. Now it is obvious. But then as I lay there, I couldn't understand. The images seemed full of meaning, like Jeshua's rumbling whisper, but I woke up afraid and that was all, afraid of the hidden beast, knowing that once more the gods had spoken in a language that I didn't know. Dion and my father had taught me to cure others, yet I was sick. This dream, if it had come from someone else, I would have guessed its meaning. I would have charged them money and earned it too. Their palms would have shown me the secrets of their lives, the hour of their deaths, whereas mine was just a jumble of lines. I rolled onto my back and brought my hand up to my face. I could scarcely see it in the dark.

Then Jeshua's voice came louder, and I listened to it, and it was asking me a question: "Greek. Yes. Greek boy. Tell me who you are."

I lay on my back on the wet ground. An insect passed under my neck. "I remember you," he said. "You were in the cave near the Narbata road, the day Menahem of Tabor let me go. You woke the Roman soldier who had lain sleeping for two days."

His voice was harsh and strong. I lay with my eyes closed, afraid now he would tell me that he recognized me also from the caravanserai at Dura, where I had drugged him and stolen his money. Shaken by my dream, I was afraid of him, and in the dark I listened to him turn and face me. I felt his breath on my ear. But he said nothing about Dura, and after a moment I opened my eyes.

Still, my voice died in my throat, because I was afraid. "Tell me," he said, and I heard the insects stir around me in the dark.

"I am from Rome," I whispered. "My father was a soldier of the king, from Pataliputra on the great river. He told me when I came of age to find the Cow's Mouth where the river comes out and wash myself above the temple. He told me to make a prayer for him . . ." I babbled on and on until I felt the Jew's hand come over me and seize me by the ear.

"Tonight is the Sabbath," he said. "And tomorrow. But tomorrow night they will kill me. I think they will kill you too. We have fallen among devils. Do not lie to me. What is your name?"

All the time he was squeezing the lobe of my ear between his fingers. "I don't know," I whispered. "My father called me Suryaprabha but my master called me Corax, which means . . ."

"Little crow," he breathed. "You think we are all fools but I am not. I was with the Essenes at Qumrun and Narbata, and I learned. Tell me," he continued, squeezing his thumb over the hole in my ear, "these marks mean something in Babylon and something else in Rome. Your master, you say; you are a slave. Is it not so?"

I didn't answer. "Hunh," he said. "That makes me the servant of a slave." Then as he released me I could hear his grunting laughter, out of place in our dark cell. Then he let me go and moved away, back toward the wall.

I lay frightened, and my ear was sore and thick. "Hunh, it stinks in here," he grunted, and I could hear the whisper of his body as he rose and sat. I could hear the creaking of his joints as he stretched them. "Talk to me," he said. "Are you still there?"

"Yes."

We used the Aramaean tongue. "In the cave you spoke to us in Greek," he said. "Was that another lie? Or maybe because you were a spy for Pontius Pilate. . . ."

"No," I said, for he was too close to the truth. Again I heard him stretch his arms, and then he laughed. "It doesn't matter now."

I lay on my back and listened to him as he got up. He crawled on his hands and knees to the cold lamp and fumbled with it for a moment. "The oil of Judah Maccabee," he sniffed. Then he was on his feet, and I listened to him scratching on the bricks, thumping on the wooden door.

Our jailers had left us a bucket of water and an empty pot. In time I heard Jeshua let his urine out in a long stream. It made a loud noise in the pot. Then he was splashing in the water. "The Essenes were full of rules," he said. "But one thing I miss. We used to wash before each meal. Every day we'd have clean clothes when I was at Qumrun. They gave us special trowels when we went to shit. . . . Oh, they were full of rules."

He laughed, and I could hear him scratching at the door, pressing on the hinges and the lock. "Hello," he shouted. "You there." But no one came.

And all that time I was lying there, smelling his sharp urine. At moments, images from the afternoon would come to me unwanted, as if released by that bitter smell—the red sun, the stony beach. The young Surenas with a knife at his throat. Then older memories—the girl stretched on the table and her red, uncovered womb. The attack on Pilate's prison, when the soldier hacked at the old man, spattering me with blood. And my master in his bath at Tusculum, his veins open from his wrists to his elbows.

Then I wept, and Jeshua stood over me. "Stop," he said. Later, "Be a man. These people murdered twenty men this afternoon. Do you think your tears will save you? No, but be a man."

At that moment I hated him. His coarseness, his loud voice. I sat up and sat back against the bricks. I hoped he would be quiet, and he was.

Yet as time went on, I found there was something I had to know. But it was difficult to speak without revealing myself. Finally I asked, "So is it the truth what men say about you?"

In the dark, I heard him stop and turn. When his voice came, it was soft. "It is a lie."

Then, after a moment, he said: "Who are these men that accuse me? Liars and hypocrites. Sons of whores. They say I sold Barabbas to the Romans. But where were they when Pilate's men attacked the crowd at Solomon's pool? Where were they when Barabbas and I broke through the soldiers' line with rocks and our bare hands? Do you believe them? They quibble over every word and number of the law. But in that town I saw a woman bury a living child."

In the darkness, I closed my eyes. "Where?"

"Where does it matter? From my pen, after they beat me. I watched her through the willow sticks. She dug a hole among the burning pits, and I could hear the child crying."

I was quiet for a little while. But still I had to know. "What about the money?"

Jeshua was standing over me. In the darkness, I turned away my face. I could hear him squatting down. "I robbed a man upon the Jericho road," he said. "I thought I needed it to get away. God forgive me, I didn't mean to hit him so hard."

Later I was so restless and afraid that even when I fell asleep again, I dreamt I still lay there in the cold mud, shivering on my side, unable to close my eyes while the Jew paced above me. When the gods mean to punish us, they make us dream our lives. I could not tell I was asleep until the moment of waking, when the door crashed inward. I started up, groggy and confused, my lip wet with spit and my eyes blind in the sudden light.

Two men stood at the door with torches in their fists. I couldn't see their heads or faces but I scrambled forward on my knees, reaching out my hands. "Please," I said, "please," but my mouth was full of sleep. I couldn't form the words. I couldn't think of the reasons why they shouldn't keep me here in the dark with this coarse Jew. So instead I bowed my head and reached out toward the leg of the guardsman. I grabbed hold of his leg behind his bare knee, feeling the tendons there.

But the men had not come to listen to me, even if I had been able to find words. One stood in the doorway, and with a grip that was neither hard nor gentle he reached down and pushed my hand away. At the same time another man came in with a new lamp, which he set down by the water bucket, together with some pieces of barley bread and a dish of cold beans crushed in oil. I stared down at it.

Jeshua sprawled in a corner of the cell, hiding his eyes from the glare of the torches. He looked at me and smiled and winked, and then another man led in the blind old Persian we had seen on the red beach. He tottered in, and in some small way it reassured me to see that he was still wearing his rich clothes and carrying a blanket rolled up in his arms.

Then the soldiers were gone, leaving us with the new light. The old man stood with his bundle, swaying and blinking. His eyes were the color of milk.

"Yes," said the Jew. "Father, be careful." He rose from the ground and came forward, and I could smell his body as he stepped past me. He took the old man by the elbow. "Can you see the lamp? Come this way. There are two of us here. I am Jeshua from Galilee, and the boy is Corax. He's a Greek."

He led the old man to the wall and held his elbow as he sank down. He let his breath out and sat back against the wall.

Later Jeshua divided up the food. The clay plate was lined with leaves, and he took one out and piled it with beans for me. I lay watching the lamplight, and he squatted by my shoulder. "Master," he said, smiling. He sat down with his own leaf, and together we watched the blind man eat from the plate with quick, sure, practiced movements. After every bite he closed his eyes, nodded his head, mumbled a prayer with his mouth full.

Then when his meal was still half finished, he put down his plate. He fumbled for his blanket. In the middle of the roll, in a secret, sewn-in pocket he found three small statues and one large one, which he arranged together near the lamp. There was Ahura-Matha, the great lord. Around him stood Mithra, and Shamash, and Anahita, mother of us all. The light flickered on her bronze flanks.

He took his iron phoorbah and laid it on the ground. Now he broke his chunk of bread into crumbs and scattered it among the statues. He lifted up the lamp, causing all the shadows in the room to move and sway. The four statues made a moving shadow on the wall. Among them he put down some powdered frankincense, a golden resin which flared up when he brought down the lamp, filling the chamber with sweet smoke.

We kept watching him. He swallowed, wiped his lips, and spoke again, and then we understood the words. "This I ask, who made the world? Who laid down the path of the sun and stars? And when the moon grows and shrinks ... all this I need to know. Who broke the earth and sky apart? Who made the horses of the wind and clouds?"

His Greek was pure and excellent. I raised myself up to listen, supporting myself on my elbow. "Tell me," he said. "More important than all this, who built the flawless palace of the mind?"

These words are part of a longer prayer. The magus Zarathustra spoke them first in the old days, when he explained the difference between light and dark. Anxious now to hear the prayer, I raised myself up, but the old man was silent. He had taken a stylus from his sleeve, and he was drawing patterns in the dirt around Ahura-Matha's feet.

As time spread on I grew impatient. "Father," I said. "Please tell me. Please tell me what you are doing. Tonight I am in trouble, and I need to know."

The old man turned his blind eyes toward me. Nor was he angry to be interrupted. He smiled softly and indulgently. "My dear son," he said, "come close. Come close so you can see my hands."

I crawled forward and knelt down almost beside him.

"Look," he said. And I saw the pattern of the marks he made, despite his blindness, symbols in a language that I didn't know. I saw a crude fish and a bird. "These are the marks of the Amesh Spenta," he explained. "Pure thought, this one, good speaking, and good action. And here are the rewards of pureness. Devotion, here, salvation, here, and immortality."

"Father," I said. "I am so frightened."

"Do not be. We are in the house of demons, but they cannot harm us, even if we die tomorrow. Listen," he said, and he told me a story that I knew and still found comforting, how when we die, we find our feet upon a bridge over the black abyss. It rises from the mountain in the middle of the world—Hara, or Sumeru in my father's language, the Diamond Mountain, Kailash the Great. We climb up, and in front of us, beyond the arch, there is a country full of light, shining like the stars and moon and sun together. It is the pure land. And if we step forward with devotion in our hearts, then the bridge will rise up wide and solid. But if we come holding our crimes, our eyes blind from desire, then it will narrow to a razor's edge. Mithra Tauroctonus, lord of light, will cast us down. Then we will tumble into the black pit, where black Ahrimmon rules in darkness, surrounded by his army of devils. "Only believe," said the old man. "Priapatius Surenas is on that bridge. Now as we speak. With his son Rhodaspes and his friends. And I pray that they step forward without fear. They are princes, but it is the same for you. For each of us. So when you go to sleep tonight, open your eyes."

He spoke to me as softly and simply as if to a child. But his voice was louder than it had to be, and that was partly because he was blind, partly so Jeshua might overhear. Sometimes I could see how he was staring past me with his blind eyes. And then finally he called out, "You also, my son. You also can come sit by me."

I looked up and I saw the Jew, still squatting near the wall. He smiled. But when he spoke it was to me. "If there is a god," he murmured, "then he does not bargain like a shopkeeper."

THEA BASAERTA

Nevertheless, when I went to sleep for the third time, I found myself comforted. I dreamt of the great bridge, which the Persians call Chinvato Peretav. It rose out of the snow of Kailash, out of the gash in the crystal mountainside, which my father called the stairway of Lord Shiva. It stretched above me through the darkness, a tiny endless span not more than three steps wide, without any rail or barrier. It arched up out of sight, surrounded by soft stars.

I was not in the dream. I stayed in my brick prison cell. When I awoke I watched the sunlight fall through tiny chinks between the bricks. It was like the stars in my dream. I lay on my back. The air was stuffy and the lamp burned low.

I don't know what hour it was when the guards came back. They opened up the door and let the sunlight in. They had no torches.

Jeshua lay dozing, and the blind man. He sat in the corner, his grey beard nodding on his chest. And he had not put away his statue of Ahura-Matha. The guards came in, sniffing at the remnants of the frankincense, which I no longer smelled. But when they saw the idols they were filled with a confused rage. They didn't know what to do. One was carrying a new bucket of water and he slopped it down. Another put his hand over his mouth.

The third was a big man. He let out a cry that meant nothing in any language. He raised his hand into the air and I could see his fingers trembling. Then he strode forward into the cell, and he kicked the idols over with his boot and trampled them down into the hot earth. He grabbed up the statue of Anahita and then threw it down again. His face was red and pale, and all the time he gave out little hiccoughs of rage. I lay on my side, curled into myself; there was something strange about this show of anger and disgust. What god was so jealous as to make men choose between their wisdom and their love? God has a thousand names. Anahita is just one of them. No, Jahwah was putting life into these empty soldiers just as Ahrimmon had brought life to them on the beach. They had none of their own. They swung like puppets from his fingers, stamping around the cell with an uneven, swaying tread. One grabbed up the old blind magus by his clothes and shook him until his head jerked back and forth. All the time I was thinking how men suffer when gods fight among themselves. It is the cause of evil in the world.

No, that's what I think now. Then I lay curled on my side. I turned my face into the dirt. I hoped I was beneath their notice, but I was not. They dragged me up, and Jeshua also. With furious hands they dragged us out the door into the light of day. They pulled us out into the hot courtyard. It was afternoon and the sun was beginning to sink, perhaps the tenth hour from dawn. We had been shut up in the darkness for a night and most of a day.

Our guards had not said anything and yet the news had spread. The courtyard was full of men and women outside their tents, all shouting at us, and spitting, and shaking their fists while the children shrieked and cried. I hid my face, covered my head with my crossed arms, though to tell the truth, most of the crowd's rage passed over me to fall on my companions. The old man had been the cause of a terrible blasphemy. And as for Jeshua, they loaded onto him a scorn that was more savage than anything they could have felt for a mere foreigner. They spat at him and smeared his shoulders with clay. I peered out from between my fingers and I had to admire them both. The blind magian was smiling, nodding and smiling, as if his image of the life to come, his knowledge of the littleness of his own death had covered him with a iron shield. And Jeshua was defended with a kind of pride, a power that seemed to flow from his broad back. He made no move to protect himself, but there was something in the strength of his body that robbed the blows of his attackers of their force, robbed their words of meaning. His face and eyes held nothing but contempt.

The guards pulled us to the citadel. Before its gate we

waited, and then they pulled us inside and up the stairs. And I found I had my own kind of protection, which lacked the dignity of Jeshua's or the old man's. It was a way of keeping me from myself, my own fears and reproaches. It was a way of pulling me backward, as the guards had pulled me from my cell into the bright day and then into a tower filled with tiny, airless rooms—the mind's tower. And the floors and ceilings and stairs were made of bare splintered wood, while the walls stayed white, unfigured, damp, painted with white clay already streaked with rot: It made strange patterns. No room had a purpose. They were all empty. And as we wandered up through them I could cover the walls with images that hid me and shielded me. I was safe in the past. We climbed up through rooms decorated with painted portraits in my mind. One was a painting of myself. At one time in my master's house, I had been so beautiful. My black hair curled under my ears.

Or in another room, there was Dion with the stylus in his hand. Or my father when I was a child, and he was teaching me the Charaka Samhita. Or else my mother at the limit of my memory, a veiled figure with thin hands.

We stood waiting for the sunset in an airless room, and then they lit the lamps. The anger of the crowd was muted now by the brick walls, or else they had forgotten us already. I thought the courtyard was the sunlit world, which can't prevail against the scheming of the mind. But there are chinks in the brick where light can penetrate. And the citadel is founded on a swamp.

Finally the two brothers came to us, surrounded by their court. Their Pharisees—bearded men with polished faces, who lined the walls in their long robes as if already they were figures that existed only in memory.

Shielded and distracted as I was, I didn't understand much of what followed. Much of what was said was not in Greek, or Aramaean either. The two brothers spoke little, but other men stood forward to denounce us. But there was no passion here. It was not like the anger of the crowd. Their voices were dry, their faces calm, though I knew they were talking about our lives. But after a while that was a subject that bored even me. Bored, I looked around. Or else I closed my eyes, remembering things.

"Please," said the old man. "I would like to see my mistress. I would like to see Queen Thea Basaerta, to say good-bye."

And then a soft voice: "I am here."

I opened my eyes. I was surprised for two reasons. First, because the old man spoke as if his fate had already been chosen, as if he were eager to think the worst. And second, I could not imagine the queen there in that room, together with those stiff rabbis and then all the other figures I had put in it. Now with my eyes open I was surprised to see her near the door. A lamp smoked on an iron tripod, and beside it stood two women, heavily veiled. One was the servant and the other was the queen. I recognized her by her pregnancy. And by the richness of her clothes, though she had changed the pink and yellow silk she had been wearing on the beach. Perhaps there was blood on it.

Instead she wore a heavier red gown, embroidered with gold. The backs of her hands were covered with a filigree of delicate gold chains, and her palms were painted red. And now I could smell the perfume that rose up from her; she must only that moment have stepped into the room.

Three of the Pharisees stood forward to restrain her. But she was a big woman. Besides, the loss she had suffered, together with her pregnancy, gave her a power that could not be blocked. She stepped past them toward the middle of that crowded chamber, and the Jews shrank back away from her.

Before the queen had entered, the two brothers had been the center of that room—their crisp, simple speech and their soldiers' clothes. But when the queen stood before them, they looked harmless and small. She reached out her hands. "Great lords," she said, her words unmuffled by the veil. "Lords, hear a prayer from the unhappiest of women. Lords, do not turn from me. I pray to God that he might let your hearts be softened. A day ago I sat by my husband's side, rich with the fortunes of the world. But in one stroke I have lost him and his dear son, and now my freedom too. But one comfort still remains to me, and that is this old blind man, Lysander's son, Bardesanes, who was my teacher and who raised me in my uncle's house when I was just a girl. How long ago that seems! Lords, pity me, and I will show you a sight you've never seen before. I will show you a woman who goes down to beg for mercy before the men who killed her husband. Please," she said, and at that moment she stripped back her veil and we could see her face, her black hair streaked with grey, her proud lips trembling, her black eyes full of tears. And then with one hand on her swollen stomach she collapsed down on her knees, and with the other hand she reached out.

As I watched her I was full of admiration. For I knew she was honest, and her feelings were honest. How could they not be? But I knew also she was playing a part. There was something stiff and unnatural about her too, because her words were not her own. She had taken words from the poet's song, where the king kneels before Achilles in his tent to beg for the body of his son. He reaches out to kiss the hands of his son's murderer, and Achilles weeps, not for the dead man, but for his own father, his friend, and for himself. In the mud-walled fortress, in that cramped and crowded room, I searched the brothers' faces, looking for a trace of those same tears. Tears of sympathy are soon forgotten. But tears of common feeling. . . . No, I couldn't tell. Asinaeus's cheeks were dry. But the eyes of grim-faced Anilaeus had brimmed full of tears, and yet I thought I recognized another feeling besides pity. Covetousness, I thought.

"My husband kept a vow," continued the queen. "Something he had sworn to God—never to sit down to eat without inviting some poor wretch to join him. In Persepolis he shared his table with servants and thieves. Please spare the lives also of these two men, the last tokens of his generosity. Not for their sake but for mine. Great lords show mercy where lesser men cannot. And I promise as I plead for them before you, in the same way, on my knees, will I plead for your lives before Mithridates Surenas, satrap of Drangiana, my dead husband's brother, whose heir I carry in my womb. And before the throne of my cousin, Artabanus Arsaces, in Ctesiphon."

The Prophecy

I thought it was not likely that Thea Basaerta, cousin to the king of kings, would raise her smallest finger to keep these bandits from their fate. So I thought it was not because they believed her that we were taken away and locked up again. Though perhaps a frightened man will grasp at any chance.

But it is a mistake to imagine that the powerful are more subtle and complex than the poor. The gods, who are stronger than anyone, are also the simplest in their passions and fears. Perhaps the simple truth was that Asinaeus and his brother had been moved to pity. Their double faces, grim and gentle—neither was the face of a cruel man.

This time they shut us up inside the citadel itself, in a small room on an upper floor. Again they gave us water, food, a lantern, and a urine pot, and then locked us up into the airless dark. We lay on the wooden floor—Jeshua, I, and the old magian. They had taken away his statues but left him among other things an ink pot and a leather brush, which he produced from inside his sleeve. He sat cross-legged, and as the lantern guttered down he murmured to himself and filled the surrounding boards with secret words and drawings. I watched him, fascinated and amazed that his blind eyes could allow him so much care. Or perhaps he was not blind at all, or not completely so. He drew the signs of the Zodiac around himself in a circle, and though the symbols were crude, I could recognize each one.

He drew the arch of Chinvato Peretav, the bridge into the pure land. And then in places he made marks along the span and arithmetical calculations—what could be their purpose to a blind man? Sensing my interest, he explained out loud. He pointed to a place where the bridge was still narrow, only a step across, he said. It was a dangerous place on the dark, slippery bridge, and it was where his master was tonight. The crossing takes eight days, and Priapatius Surenas still was on the slippery climb. He was sustained by hope alone, for it is only at the top of the arch that the light is visible before us, at the seventh resting place. There where the bridge thickens we meet our *daena*, the image of ourself disguised as a young virgin. In her beauty or her ugliness, we can see the mirror of our fate.

He spoke a prayer. He was concerned about one thing. The Jews had not prepared his master's body or allowed it to be prepared. They had not allowed it to be set above the ground so that it could be consumed by the elements and the wild birds according to the laws of Zarathustra. Instead they had thrown him down into a pit, together with his son, defiling the water and the sacred earth.

The old man tried to change this and correct it through his prayers. I listened for a while, and then I interrupted. "Father," I said. "Tell me about the world to come. What is that country at the end of the bridge?"

He was mumbling with his eyes closed, and then his voice came louder. "Tell me now, what god made sleep and wakefulness? What god made life and death? This I ask you, will love strengthen truth or make it weaker? And this, why is the cow the giver of prosperity? And this, who created love and made it powerful? Why is the son respectful to his father in his own heart?"

This made me quiet and I bowed my head. "Listen," he said, opening his eyes. "Tomorrow is the tenth day of the month of Garmapada. It is the solstice of midsummer, the second of the festivals that we call gahambar. Madya Sama, we call it; it is a happy time. And tonight, right now as I speak to you, Jupiter is rising. He is the great god, and by his light we must recall the oracle of Hystaspes, who was the father of our race.

"You ask me about the life to come. Listen, this is the age of the god Jupiter. Now, here, in this prison. Now you can see it, when honest men are divided from the children of lies. Now, tonight, in every city they will beg for God's mercy under the rising star. For they know this is the age when justice is despised and rightful kings are brought low. Our enemies will defile the bodies of the living and the dead, and they will not listen to the old men or pity the women or the children. They will speak out against the laws of God and nature. The earth will be pillaged and broken.

"But now tonight we must be glad. For we are among those who have set themselves apart. The godless one, Ahrimmon, is burning with anger. He will come with his soldiers to surround the place where we have camped. But when all of us have come together and we are shut in on all sides, then we will cry out with one voice. And God will send a king from the heavens who will snatch us away and free us and destroy the godless one with fire. And the name of that king will be Saoshanti, and he will be born out of a virgin from the seed of Zarathustra, when she is bathing in the water of Seistan. And Saoshanti will be called the son of man. He will raise up the dead and separate the light from darkness. And the bodies of good men he will purge with the fat of the cow, mixed with white soma. And their bodies will not rot away.

"Therefore," he said, "tonight, on the first night of Madya Sama, we must prepare ourselves."

These were stories I had not heard before. I found them powerful, but daunting too. I looked over and saw Jeshua, sitting up against the wall, a smile on his thick lips. I crawled over toward him, and together we watched the man make his preparations. He nodded and prayed, and in a little while he rose and staggered over to the urine pot. And this I was amazed to see: He squatted over it like a woman, and he took from the sleeve of his robe a little trumpet made of silver and fitted it into a crease between his legs. He was a eunuch, in fact.

Then he washed his face and hands.

"He is a wise man," I whispered.

But Jeshua shrugged. "He is an idiot. It's all the same. God will destroy the wicked. A virgin will give birth. A king will come and he will purge mankind. The Essenes used to say the same things when I was at Qumrun."

"No, but the gods move that way through men," I said. "It is the same in all places. Prince Siddhartha's mother dreamed of a white elephant, and he was born out of her side."

Jeshua leaned his head back against the wall. "You think because they all say it, then it must be true. I think it must be lies for the same reason. Stories to frighten fools, as my mother said. Laws to fill the pockets of the Levites. Along this river I heard people say these two brothers are the answer to the same prophecy. But look at them."

Then I was quiet, remembering my own doubts. I waited for Jeshua to talk again, for I was curious about him, curious about his way of thinking. Rome is full of people who have locked out all the gods and devils from inside themselves. Or else they praise them and curse them with empty words and gestures but ignore them in their thoughts. Men for whom religion is a duty only—my master was among them. It is because among the races of the world the Romans are like children, too young to know anything. Too young to feel, or to open their eyes.

But the Jews are an old race. They have an understanding of the natural world, of gods and men. So I was curious about Jeshua, and when he said nothing, then I prodded him. "These stories come from God."

He was leaning slumped up against the wall. He put his hand out, his palm parallel to the wooden floor—an odd gesture, I thought. And when he answered, his voice was burdened with a harsh intensity. "No. The lips of men. The deeds of men. The memories of men. They say God destroyed the world in a great flood. They say God spoke out of a bush. They say he built the world in seven days. He made men and women out of dirt and put them in a garden. . . . No, these stories have a truth but it is not here," he said, balling his hand together into a fist. "Not here," he said, rubbing his fist onto the floor. "Not so men and women can say, 'This is so' or 'That is so,' 'This will come' or 'That will come.' No, that is the mark of a liar." He shrugged. "These stories are like copper coins. Worthless, yet they serve the needs of men."

I was quiet, remembering my own doubts.

But then old Bardesanes took a pouch out of the inside of his robe. He pulled it open, and I scrambled over to look. It contained a plant I had never seen before. Its fat, purple stems were full of a kind of grease. When he crushed it between his fingers, a yellow grease came out, leaving behind the collapsed stem.

Its leaves were dry but I could see they had nine points. They looked a little bit like hemp. "What's that?" I said, but the old man didn't answer. He was muttering prayers and scraping the grease from his fingers into a tiny silver cup, which was also in his pouch.

The grease gave out a bitter smell.

"This is soma," he explained. "The river flows down off of the slopes of Mount Hara. It flows under the glacier and through the Cow's Mouth up into the world. It flows across the plain, into the sea that is called Vansakasha. In the middle of the sea lies an island where the white soma grows, which heals our bodies and preserves our souls."

Then he told us how the seed came from the bull that Mithra killed, how he mixed it with the milk of the cow, which drips from the moon. It is the part of God inside of us, and there are traces of it in all plants and animals. The moon fills up like a bowl. Every month the gods drink from its wet light. They empty it, and every month it makes them young. "But men and women, too," he said, "will live forever."

I looked over toward Jeshua, who was watching with a

bored smile. But I wanted that plant. The pouch was still full of the dried stems, and I thought it would not be difficult to steal a few of them from an old man. Yet perhaps not easy, because his movements seemed so sure, the motions of his hands. I thought, if this drug can open up the eyes of a blind man, then imagine what it might do for me.

And so I squatted down beside the magian, waiting for my chance. Mumbling, he lifted up the bowl and drank it off. I could see his jaw clench and his throat seize up from the bitterness. His tongue came out, and it was hard for him to pull it back into his mouth. So he used it to lick his fingers, which were trembling.

The pouch was on the floor beside him. It would have been easy to reach out my hand for it because as time went on he was no longer in this world. He sat cross-legged, his back stiff and arched, his eyes rolled back in his head, his fists on his knees, and I could see how his long fingernails were digging into the flesh below his thumbs. There was a greasy moisture on his lips.

Still I hesitated to pick up the pouch because the Jew was watching me. He lay sprawled out with his head against the wall, .watching me with a bored look; I couldn't do it. I will wait until he sleeps, I thought. So I withdrew my hand and crawled back to sit beside him, and together we watched the old man go into a dream. He sat back, rigid, stiff and trembling. The blood sank from his features, and his skin grew white as milk.

After an hour his jaw unlocked. His mouth opened and his lips curled back. And we could hear his breath, pushed out in long gasping sighs.

Then words came, distorted by the stiffness of his mouth. I could see the god was speaking through him in a strange loud airless voice that was different from his own. It seemed to buzz inside our ears, inside our teeth. The god was speaking, and his voice was sharp and raw. THESE ARE THE WORDS THAT CANNOT BE FORGOT, said the old man, and then something else I didn't understand. His blind eyes rolled upward. Scum formed in the corners of his lips. His chest inflated and then stopped.

We sat watching him, waiting for him to breathe out. Jeshua put his hand onto my arm. But when I did nothing he got up. The old man sat stiff with his back arched and his shoulders raised, and when he spoke again his voice seemed to come not from his mouth but from his nose: THESE ARE THE WORDS I . . . , and then much more in a harsh language that I didn't know.

Jeshua was kneeling beside him now. And he put his hand out to touch the face of Bardesanes. He put his fingers under the old man's nose. He was testing for breath, and when he didn't find it he started touching the man's white cheeks and forehead, searching his neck and chest with a strange patting motion that grew more and more desperate, until he seized Bardesanes by his shoulders and tried to force him down onto the floor. He put his hands into the stiff mouth, tugging on his tongue, and then he pushed him down and tried to push his hands into the man's chest until finally he sat above him, crying out and thumping on his heart. "Open the door," he shouted.

The old man's back arched off the floor. And then the guards were calling out for us to be silent, and Jeshua was pleading for me to help him. But I could do nothing. Instead I went to him and tried to pull his hands away. "It is the god," I said. "Don't touch the god." By which I meant that it was dangerous to struggle against nature, dangerous for him and me and for the old man too. The god had taken the old eunuch's body, and would not love us when we tried to chase him out. Nor would Bardesanes thank us when he returned. And even if he never came back, even if he died there in that dark chamber, then his feet were on Chinvato Peretav. His blood and mind were full of soma, which makes us live forever. When the god went away, then he would carry the old man's dry body on his head, across the bridge into the world of light.

But I felt I could not explain any of these things while the Jewish bear thumped on the man's chest and pushed ignorant fingers into his nose and mouth, as if to drag the breath out of him by force. The guards were pounding on the door now, and

I could hear their voices through the walls of mud and lath. Then the god gave me power, and I was able to pull Jeshua's hands away, though he was twice as strong. I reached out and put my hand onto the side of his shaved head, and at the same time the guards were opening the door, together with some men in robes who stood quiet and silent as the old eunuch stirred again, opened up his lips, and spewed out all his breath in one new strange excited speech. I pulled Jeshua off him, and he rose up until he sat stiff as a corpse, his eyes rolled back and his harsh voice pushing the words of the gods into our ears: THEN COME OUT OF HYSTASPES AND THE ENDLESS STREAM THAT FLOWS THROUGH DARIUS ACHAEMENES AND THROUGH GREAT PHRA-TAACES KING OF KINGS AND HIS DAUGHTER AND HIS SISTER AND HER NAME IS THEA BASAERTA AND THE CHILD IN HER WOMB IS BREAKING DOWN THE WORLD AND I WILL DIG THE PIT OF HELL FOR ALL THE JEWS AND PERSIANS AND THE GODLESS ONES FOR THIS IS THE LAST AGE AND THE KALPA WHEN THE SON OF MAN WILL RISE OUT OF. . . .

Then the soldiers were there and they were shouting "Stop!" and one of the old men in robes leaned down to put his hands over the god's mouth, to try and push the words back into his mouth. And then Bardesanes bit him on his hands, bearing down until his teeth turned on the bone itself.

THE TWO BROTHERS

Later they took me into another room. It was at the top of the citadel, and like all the rooms it was a small, cramped, low-ceil-inged place. So I thought when I first entered. But after a moment, when my eyes grew used to the new light, I saw there was a break in the roof on the far side, a rent in the middle of the outside wall that let in the night air.

I was brought out of my cell by grim-faced Anilaeus, commander of the citadel. I was led to him through tiny, crowded passages, where nevertheless the people shrank away from me and gave me space. The soldiers led me up a ladder, up into the topmost room, and there Anilaeus waited for me.

He drew me to the center of the floor. He drew me by my sleeve. He made a space around us, as if we could somehow escape the stares of the silent, watchful figures who lined the walls like painted portraits—soldiers in leather armor, bearded men with caps on their heads. Anilaeus leaned toward me and lowered his voice as if to prevent them from overhearing.

Past his shoulder, through the broken wall, I could see a square of the night sky, made yellow and red by the courtyard fires. In a moment I saw more as, still dissatisfied, Anilaeus led me farther toward the gap until I could look past him down into the courtyard itself, feel the hot wet air come off the river, and see the cook fires and the children playing games, and the men and women standing, looking up.

Anilaeus was dressed in a belted woolen shirt. He was a small man. I leaned to him so he could whisper in my ear. "The money can be repaid. But you killed a child with your dirty hands. You blinded her. And the mother: You told her to drink blood and milk, though it is against the law. Is this true?"

My head was so full of the old magian, for a moment I didn't understand what Anilaeus was saying. Then I remembered the woman whose life I had saved. But why was he talking about this? I looked out at the fires and said nothing.

"You know we heard stories about you. In Caesarea where you made the blind man see. Now with your curses, you steal a child's sight away. Yet the mother lives. She can walk. She can carry water. She can receive her husband."

This last was a horrifying thought, for it was only a few days since I had stitched her up. And I was disgusted by the hypocrisy of these men, because surely what Anilaeus had suggested was against the Jewish law. Disgusted, I tried to pull away from him, but he grabbed me by the arm. He seemed upset, and I thought he had been drinking. His voice was high and hard. "Can you do this? Can you do this again?"

Disgusted by his sour breath, I turned away. "No, you understand," he said, squeezing my arm. "You will die unless I save you."

His grim face shone in the lamplight and the flickering courtyard fires. I felt suddenly powerful, made strong and large by the ignorance of these men. They moved around me, hugging the walls as meaningless as shadows, ducking their heads as they passed in and out of the low door.

And then Asinaeus was there, the second brother, dressed in wet and dirty clothes. He came in through the door and he was talking in a language I didn't know, full of strange consonants. Then he stepped forward, and he seemed to carry with him a heavy smell, the smoky breath of the entire building. It seemed to surround him in a fog of ash and shadow. They had lit cook fires in the lower floors, and the smoke was seeping up the ladders and the stairways toward the broken wall and roof where we were standing.

The smoke gathered around him and mixed with the smell of dirt and sweat that rose from his body, and mixed also with something in my mind. It was a shadow cloud that seemed to blot away the other men in the room, hiding their faces so that the two brothers and myself seemed suddenly alone.

Asinaeus didn't look at me. Though his face was smooth and his movements graceful, there was an excitement in him that burst through his voice. "What is he doing here? I was with the soldiers breaking down the dikes along the Pumbeditha road. But I came when I heard it. And now the son of Eleazar has confirmed what they all said. Do you deny it? The devil has possessed him and spoken through his voice to curse our people and blaspheme God. Have you heard this? My God—" And he went on like this, speaking of Bardesanes, the blind magian. The words bubbled out of him without a pause, hard and very soft, so that he couldn't be overheard. "I know what the witch told you, but they all must be destroyed. Tomorrow morning. The old man is dead but alive too, cold as a corpse. He painted the floor with circles and his blasphemous devices. And now I find you with this other one, this child-killer with his unclean hands. Are you insane? These people must be put to death."

Anilaeus turned away. He looked out of the open wall, his brow and mouth twisted into an expression I couldn't read. Then he said, "The queen is innocent."

"Is she? If no more proof was necessary, look what she has done to you. In three days. Once you were a man."

"No. Remember what she said. She will plead for us before the king. Remember she is carrying the heir of Mithridates Surenas. . . ."

"No. The son of Eleazer told me: She is carrying the devil in her womb. Innocent, what do you mean? She is a Gentile, an idolater. Her mother was Thea Musa the whore, who was burned to death for her impurity. She lay with her own son. Plead for us, do you believe it? Listen. Now as we are talking, their boat is coming to Ctesiphon. Mithridates Surenas is summoning his councilors. He is gathering his soldiers. As they come they will be killing every Jewish man, woman, and child, just as they always have and always will; then who will fight for us?"

As he spoke, Asinaeus had moved into the open wall, and now he turned around, surrounded by the light of the courtyard fires, which had risen up into the sky. "Who will defend us? I'll tell you. These men who look up to this tower now and see you talking with this Greek idolater and shitting on our traditions and our laws, and lying with a pregnant woman old enough to be your mother. No, the Gentiles hate us, here and everywhere. If we have been able to resist them, it is by casting out these devils and these doubts. No, as I came up I gave the order to the guard to strangle the old man. As for this one—" Here he turned toward me.

He spoke in Aramaean, the Syrian language that was his native tongue. For all the sternness of his words, his face was still gentle, his voice calm. But not his brother, whose eyes started open. "She is innocent!" he cried. "What kind of men are we if we allow ourselves to murder women, children in the womb?" And then he shook his head as if to rid himself of scruples. "No, brother, I agree with you. The sorcerer is dead. Now if the child must be destroyed, let the Greek do it. It is not work for our hands."

I was the "Greek" they were referring to. They spoke as if I weren't there. I stood listening to them, trying to hear something in their words that I could use. My fate was in the hands of the gods, but there were words I could say, things I could do. Since I left Rome I had been feeling that the gods were setting me a puzzle to punish me for the evil I had done. They had set me down into a labyrinth of dangers, and my life hung on the path I chose. Which led to safety, which to death?

"Yes," I said. "I can do this work. I will need a steel rod."

Asinaeus looked at me, and I felt at that moment his hatred and contempt for me. It was like a cold air that flowed out of his body, out of his gentle face. It overwhelmed me, overwhelmed my tepid hopes, and as he turned and strode away he left me shivering with fear. If it was up to him, I thought, then he would kill us all.

But Anilaeus now was pulling on my arm again. I looked into his ugly face, so similar and so different from his brother's. I took courage from it, because I understood he would do anything to save the queen's life. She had a power over him, and perhaps it came from pity. But perhaps also it was from a charm. A charm that she had given him, and as he spoke I was searching his cheeks for an artificial fever, brought on by some poison that was similar, perhaps, to the ground-up shells of blister beetles, which they use during the mysteries of Aphrodite in Rome.

"This can be done?" he said. "You will not hurt her? Because I am afraid her time has come, though it is early. Our women will not touch her, because of who she is."

"It will be difficult," I answered. But there was much I

didn't understand. What was it to him whether she bore the child or not?

"I will pay you," he said. "To hide this from my brother and to take the child."

"And my servant?"

"No." He shook his head. "This is not the time for us to kill one of our own, no matter what his crime."

"That is true," I said, watching his face.

"I will put you on a boat," he said. "The three of you. But I warn you, if he comes into this country again, or to Judaea, or to any part of the land of Israel, then his life will be forfeit."

"Yes, I understand."

"That is his punishment. Never to live again among his own people."

"Yes."

"But you," he said. "You, I will pay."

SHEPSUT

I didn't believe him. I thought when the work was done, then he would put both Jeshua and me to death. But I didn't know for sure. When the soldiers returned me to the cell, I sat for a while, thinking.

The old man was gone. The Jew sat by himself, and he scarcely looked at me when I came in. In time he raised his head. His lips were broken and his face was bruised, and his eyes were big with tears.

My heart went out to him, and so I told him what Anilaeus had said, even though I didn't believe it. I wanted to reassure him, and so I told him about the two brothers at the top of the tower. Then I told him, "They want to destroy the child of Priapatius Surenas. They will free us, me and you. But they said we must keep to the east. . . ."

These words had none of the effect I wanted, either on my-self or him. He just sat there staring, as if he couldn't understand what I was saying. Then he looked down at his feet again, at the lamp that flickered near his feet. As he did so, I was conscious of a feeling in myself, which seemed at that moment to grow out of nothing—a terrible headache. It was an attack of heterocrania, but it was as sudden as if I had been struck with a stone above my left eye. I put my hand up to touch the delicate skin, and I almost expected to feel a sudden bulge. All around me in the darkness there were small flashes of light, which seemed to come together from the corners of the cell to form a pattern with its center on the lantern flame. It was a pattern as intricate and hard-edged as a leaf of frost, like those I had seen sometimes in Tuscu-lum on the surface of the water in my bucket, outside my door on January mornings.

The god had touched me with his finger above my left eye, where there is nothing but skin and blood over the bone. I pulled back away from him, and because the present now was suddenly unbearable I pulled away into the past. Not far, but I wanted to see the words the magus spoke, and so I closed my eyes and pulled back through the hours until I saw them painted in white letters as if on a wall: AND THE CHILD IN HER WOMB IS BREAKING DOWN THE WORLD.

Then I felt the pressure disappear. The change was rapid, and I thought I would open my eyes and find that no time had passed, that the finger of the god had touched me for no more than a few moments. So when I opened my eyes I was surprised to see the Jew had moved, and I myself had moved and was sit-ting in a different part of the small cell. Near me lay my bag of tools and instruments, which I had last seen on the beach when we were captured. So the guards had come and gone.

Jeshua was standing near a corner of the wall and I could hear a noise from there. It was a low, even, scraping sound.

After a while I got up and moved over toward him. I walked across the blind man's drawings, in black ink on the dry floor. And then over a litter of fragments from the pot, broken, I supposed, during the struggle. When I saw them I understood what Jeshua was doing. He had taken a sharp fragment, and he was scraping at the joints in the brick near where the inside and the outside walls came together.

But the power that had touched me had put a fear into my mind. I wanted to say something. I wanted to talk to him, and so I went to Jeshua and stood beside him. I watched him push a long curved shard from the lip of the broken pot into a space between two bricks. The mud was damp and crumbled easily, and he had already dug out a big hole.

But he spoke first. "After you'd gone, they came for the old man."

I was quiet for a moment. Then I spoke. "Yes. That's what I mean. He said the child was from the god. And now this pain. I feel I cannot do this. I have a doubt."

He stood facing the wall, working his shard of fired clay between the bricks. Dust covered his feet.

"I am afraid," I said. "When Lord Kṛishna was born in Mathura, there was a king. He tried to kill the mother of the god. He tried to kill her children one by one. And all the children in that town."

My thoughts and words were like the pot, broken into pieces. This was a story my father had told me about Kansa the demon king. The murder of the children. Now I found my hands were shaking.

Jeshua shrugged. "What about the virgin in the waters of Seistan? What happened to her? Wasn't she part of the story?" He sounded angry.

And then, "You care about the god but not the child."

Then, "Or the mother." He wouldn't look at me.

It was the truth. And I cared about myself. I had never done this work before. My mind was full of recipes, but I was afraid to bleed her, as Hippocrates advised. And Dion had once told me how to make a suppository out of wormwood and sulphur. And my father had suggested adding cardamom, from a recipe he had found in Taxila. Or else a drink made out of hellebore, spikenard, and bindweed mixed in wine, but all these were for the first months only. I would have to see. I could not tell under her robes, but I thought she was big. Too big, I hoped, to enter her, for there were dangers even if my hands had not been shaking and my mind consumed by doubt. My own mother had bled to death when I was just a child.

I had no memories of her, of anything but her thin hands. There was a dark place in my mind where those memories were meant to be. I turned away from that dark space, went and sat down again and watched Jeshua work against the bricks. And I was thinking, what if I kill her? What if it takes too long and she just bleeds and bleeds? What if she dies under my hands, as my mother died upon my father's table? He had cut her as she struggled, when she woke up from the poppy juice. He had said he wanted no more children to be born as slaves.

She had been less pregnant than the queen. I was thinking, if I killed her, what would Anilaeus do then? His brother wanted both the child and the mother destroyed. But he wanted to destroy one and save the other. I wondered, does he understand the risk? And I wondered, how could he think that she would love him after he had robbed her in this way? Because she is not a Jew, does he think she has no heart? Or does he think she is possessed by a devil which has worked its way into her body and then sprouted there? Does he think she will thank him, once it's gone?

Or did she ask to have it done?

Or was it because he could not stand the thought of sharing her? Or was it easier for him to kill the child in the womb than wait until it breathed? Was it not murder then, according to his laws?

Or I supposed he felt that something must be done. After what the magus said, he could not wait.

Yes, that was it. Yet there was something more. Something I still didn't understand. A reason that pulled back from me the more I searched for it. But not to search for it would be to give in to my fear, and so I sat puzzling it out until they came.

"Let me bring my tools," I said. So I picked up my bag. Jeshua had stopped his work when he heard the soldiers at the door. He sat down in a corner of the cell. Now he wouldn't look at me as I left. I walked past him between the two soldiers. They were tall men and said nothing, even when I told them what I wanted: hot water, a brazier, three small blunt steel rods, and some water-lily root to make a plug for the hole at the entrance to her womb, to make her body open. There is a seaweed called "mare's tail" that would have made her even larger. It would have worked quicker and better, but my guess was it could not be found.

We passed through many darkened rooms, and as before, they were all full of silent figures who hugged the walls. The ceilings were low, the walls tight together. We climbed down the ladders toward the ground floor, and then we went through to the women's quarters. I was carrying my bag, and my heart was low. These smoky rooms, filled with shadows, and there were women now, veiled and silent, dressed in somber robes. I could not see their hands or feet. I felt I had descended into some underground place, full of the captainless armies of the dead, and among them were my father and mother and even my old master, Cornelius Celsus, who had bled so hard and long.

I thought the god would strike me down, break my skull with heterocrania. Or Anilaeus would kill me when the work was done. He would be right to do so. Sometimes steel rods are placed into the hole, and then you cut the child out with the frog-mouthed knife. You cut the child in two. Would the queen struggle as my mother had struggled?

At last we came to a windowless inner chamber, lit with a blinded lantern that hung from a tripod near the door. There the soldiers left me. They turned back at the threshold. And there I was met by someone I recognized. It was the servant of the queen.

Her head was bare and I could see her face. Just to see her, my heart rose. She was a dark-skinned girl. Her thick black hair was coiled around her head. Her dark eyes and heavy lips were rimmed with kohl. And she was smiling at me and talking fast under her breath, in little birdlike whispers that I thought could not be heard by the other women in the room, the grey line of ghosts along the far wall.

"We are pleased," she said, words that astonished me. "You know we had heard about you in Dura from our sister. She gave you her earrings; that is why we sent for you now. You made the blind girl see, and then, well, you know this is difficult. My mistress's time has come, though it is a month early. The pain is hurting her, but I told my mistress at least someone is here who can take care of her. These others, even the women who are trained for it, won't help us." And here she burst into little tears which dried up almost instantly, and again she smiled.

Her name was Shepsut, after the Egyptian queen. She never stopped talking, although sometimes the noise of it subsided down below the limits of my ears. But the words were always there because her lips were always restless, and her hands never stopped from moving, from making and describing little shapes in the air in front of her mouth. And she was very bold. "Oh," she said, taking my hand, and then she led me into a dark corner of the room where Thea Basaerta lay upon a bed.

She lay covered in veils and robes from head to foot. There was no part of her skin that was uncovered. The veil over her face was so thick, I could barely see her eyes, barely guess the indentations for her mouth and nose. She lay on her back, her stomach swollen, and when I saw it I thought my heart would burst. I didn't know what to do. I put down my bag and then reached out my hand. But I felt the girl's small fingers on my wrist. "Do not touch her," she said. "She is the queen. You cannot touch her, of course. But I am here. And I will tell her."

Then Shepsut brought my hand down to her own thin stomach. Under the small shirt she wore, I could feel the hole of her navel, and she pushed the joint of my thumb into it. Her hands were strong. Then she let go and raised her right hand into the air in front of her mouth so she could talk again. "She will speak to me and I will tell you every word because it is my duty. But first I must ask you to give us something that will help her sleep. She cannot sleep at night. This is a moment when she lives in pain because of the lord of this place. I mean here," she said, touching her right temple.

"I know you have something for us," she said. "Though if you take too much it is a poison."

The bed was wide enough for two if they lay touching. Now Shepsut led me to the open side, where she lay down. "But I don't have anything I need," I told her. Then I was silent, for the queen had turned her head, and they lay with their two heads together. I could see the veil stir between their lips.

I was looking at the queen's stomach underneath her robe. Too big, I thought, too big. And I felt a gush of relief that I could not touch her, that her body was too pure and rich for my polluting hands. I felt the god inside of me, warning me not to hurt her, and I was relieved that no one had brought any of the sharp things I had desired. She was too big. I would not touch her, and it was a relief to let go of my thoughts. To turn away from the pictures in my mind, my father and mother.

But because there is a devil in us and not just a god, I found myself imagining a new plan. Something had happened when the girl spoke the word "poison." My pride suggested a new plan for me, for there is a poison that grows in the rye grass. It kills the old seed and makes a new seed that is black and soft and falls apart between the fingers. It is called the black cock's comb. When it is eaten, it can cause the vessels of the body to squeeze shut. It can cause the hands and feet to wither and turn black. It can cause dreams and visions. And it can cause the womb to push out even a child that is fully formed: I made an image in my mind. And because this poison is so terrible, even my thought of it made Thea Basaerta squirm as she lay resting. A shudder ran through her body.

Hush, I thought, and the god showed me how to clear my thoughts and clear away temptation so the queen could lie still again. I could hear her murmuring to Shepsut, though even when I bent down over her, I could not understand the words. Until the girl turned toward me. I bent down to listen, and Shepsut said, "The pain is too great and I want to die."

She spoke for the queen in a tiny, halting whisper, so different from the flow of her own words. She barely moved her lips. "It is the sin that lives in me. It is my mother's sin."

I lifted my head and looked around the room at the silent figures that still stood against the walls, almost out of sight among the shadows. Then I felt the girl take hold of my hand again and bring it down to her small belly. "This is where it hurts," she said. "This is where it lives."

Her voice was soft and she was smiling. She brought my hand across the bottom of her ribs, and I could feel her small flat stomach. She brought it lower and made me touch the bones of her narrow hips, the flat skin under her shirt. She had the boldness not of a prostitute but of a virgin, to whom all things are innocent. "I feel a terrible convulsion here," she said. "A grasping pain, though it is too soon."

"When did it start?" I whispered, touching the flat skin under her navel, and I could feel a few stray wisps of hair.

When I touched her I could see the queen squirm again, though the girl under my hand lay still.

"Last night," she murmured, words that had lost their meaning for me in these dark rooms. "After he attacked me. I fear when he stays with me, then it will hurt the child. That's when the spasm came. It is too soon."

The queen turned her face to whisper, and her words came out of the girl's mouth. I bent down over her so that my ear approached her white teeth, her dark lips. I wanted to hear each word, and I was curious also about the smell that rose from her slight body, a perfume of crushed amber that was mixed with something else, something I didn't recognize. "Tell me," I said.

"I have not had a child before. Though I am past the age. But this, it is my sin."

"Tell me." I repeated. And I moved my hand between Shepsut's high, narrow hips.

"I am the daughter of the Italian dancer, whom Augustus gave to the king of kings. Then I was happy and forgot. But this man, he is young enough to be my son. He has killed my husband and my husband's son. Now he is killing me."

I was astonished to hear these words. Yet Shepsut's tiny whisper, so close to my ear, drained them of their harshness and bitterness. Perhaps in speaking through the girl, Thea Basaerta felt she could say these things even to me. Or perhaps she thought that she must justify herself, for now I imagined I had guessed correctly, and it was she herself who blamed the child. "Only you can help me," said the girl. "I hear you have a medicine. To help me with this pain."

Shepsut had her fingers on my wrist, and she brought my hand down to her small belly. Though she lay still, I could almost feel the queen's contractions there.

I closed my eyes and let the smell from their two bodies wash my face. And I was making a shadow cloth out of the past, something to wrap these women in, so that they would not be naked in my mind. I made it from a story: The Italian whore was Thea Musa, for whose sake King Phraates gave up all his lawful wives. For her love he sent his children, Vonones and the rest, to exile in Rome. After she bore him a son, she poisoned him so that the child, Phraataces, could be king. Then she married her own son during the Aphrodite festival in Ctesiphon when he was scarcely yet a man. And they were king and queen together until the magians cursed them and the people cast them out.

She had been burned. He had been walled up alive in a stone cell. I had not heard there was a child.

"My husband put these things aside for all those years," breathed Shepsut. "He made them go away. Now they have come back."

I closed my eyes to watch the pattern on the shadow cloth, a braided line of shapes, returning symbols of impurity. A serpent devouring itself—among the families of kings the pattern is a common one, where lust is not constrained by fear. Where it is punished, as always, by the envy of the gods.

It was a chain of serpents devouring themselves, woven in strands of blue and gold. But the end of it was broken, ripped apart. And then the shape of the hole was woven back into the pattern—a ragged, dark, and empty line. What kind of man was this bandit, Anilaeus? He must have seen her not as an unfortunate and helpless woman, but as a queen only. He must have hoped that through her he could touch the blue and golden cloth, and through his violence become a part of it.

I opened my eyes again and found my face close above Shepsut's. My nose was full of her smell, and she was staring at me with her liquid and expressionless eyes. She was moving my hand over her quiet belly, so that I could feel the spasms in the womb of her unhappy mistress. They were coming quicker now.

Thea Basaerta lay on her back, and now she raised her knees and spread them apart under her thick gown. For the first time I could hear her own voice, small sobbing cries mixed with the labor of her breath. The veil shifted on her mouth.

My hand moved back and forth over the girl. Now she was squeezing my fingers, and she brought my hand up the length of her body, past her navel, through the narrow valley of her ribs. She brought my hand up to her breasts, and I was astonished to find that they were wet, that circles of moisture had soaked through the cotton of her shirt over her nipples. Now she stirred for the first time and made a little groan.

I looked over at the queen and she was quiet now. Her legs still lolled apart. But now the cloth of her gown was drenched with water, I thought perhaps in sympathy with her maid. Water spurted down beneath her, soaking the bed. Then after a little while I heard the child crying, the saoshanti whom Hystaspes had predicted and the magian had called the son of man. I realized that whatever sympathy there was, it ran the other way.

The Fire

I gave Shepsut a bottle of the poppy gum dissolved in wine. At the same time under my breath I was offering thanks for the gush of water, for I took it as a sign that the gods would watch over the child's life and over all of us. A barren mother who had given birth so easily—I thought the gods would help us, as they had protected young Lord Krishna and his companions against the evil king.

They brought me back into the cell, and I fell asleep. I must have slept a long time, and I dreamt nothing. Later I found my-self watching Jeshua scrape out the bricks along a corner of the wall, and I wondered if I deserved the gods' protection.

Because what if I had been the instrument all along, through which Ahrimmon worked to destroy the saoshanti? I wondered if those thoughts of the black cock's comb and the steel rod, those memories of my mother's death, had come from me or else from him alone. As I sat watching Jeshua raise a pile of mud dust that dribbled down the wall along his feet, I thought back over the words that Anilaeus and Asinaeus had used, both to each other and to me. In my memory I put my hands on them and moved them. Now I imagined Anilaeus had been afraid. He had been with the queen when her contractions started, and for that reason he had sent for me. Not to kill the child, that was a lie he told his brother. But to help it to be born.

Shepsut and the queen had heard of me from Dura, and they had sent for me. The miracle worker from Caesarea, to care for them when they were most in need. And Anilaeus had helped them. He had protected me and Jeshua when Asinaeus would have killed us. So was it likely he had planned the child's death? No, I thought, and I remembered his words. "To hide this from my brother and to take the child." And later, "I will put you on a boat. The three of you."

No, I thought I understood. He meant to protect the child

from his brother and perhaps the queen as well. I thought I understood: The plan to kill the saoshanti had been mine alone. And this thought made my fingers shake with fear as I reached up to touch my forehead over my eye. I didn't know what to do. Suddenly I thought that all my bursting headaches and premonitions had come out of the darkness where Ahrimmon sits among his devas, his black angels. I remembered where the heterocrania first had struck me after so long, outside the village on the river. Perhaps Ahrimmon had needed me, and he had killed the blind child in her mother's womb under my hands.

But she was not blind. And I had not killed her.

Closing my eyes, I prayed to Father Toth. But he would not answer me, and in the darkness I saw a pattern of lines. It was the pattern I had seen upon the wall in the prison at Caesarea. Then I imagined it to be the plan to the prison itself, but I had been wrong. Now for a moment I thought it was the plan to this dark tower, a gift of the gods to set me free. My heart surged and then fell, for I could not see the seven stories or the gates.

The pattern was made of silver lines, but there was a dark line weaving through it. Now I wondered if the dark line was myself, moving through the pattern of the world, drawn through by black Ahrimmon. Now I saw it was because of me that Priapatius Surenas had died, because of me that Thea Basaerta had been captured. If the Persians burned this tower and killed these brothers, that pattern also would spread out from me. And if the saoshanti died, that would also be my fault, for I had planned it.

And when I followed that dark line back into its source, all the way into the center of the pattern, I could find the square peristyle of the house in Tusculum. Beside it, my chamber and my master's bath where he had bled to death. Where he had fumbled and splashed in the bloody water.

He had cried out. His eyes had started from his head. And then from his mouth stretched that dark line, out through all the imaginary mazes and palaces of this world, as if Theseus's string led toward the minotaur and not away.

The guards brought water. Later they brought food, and then I slept again. When I woke I lay on my back with my eyes closed, listening to Jeshua scratch at the bricks. I lay there for many hours. And then I heard a different noise, a small light drumming on the door. A small, muffled voice crying, "Iatros— doctor, is that you?"

It was Shepsut. After a while the noise went away. Then it came back again, and I heard her pulling at the wooden bolt that held the door from the outside. It was a heavy block of wood, tight in its socket. I could hear it creaking as she pried it back.

Then she pulled open the door. She stood in the gap, surrounded by the grey light that pushed in from the guard room. She was veiled and dressed in a long gown. "Doctor," she said. "You must come."

As before, even when she finished speaking I could hear a faint murmur of words. When she came close I could see her lips were moving under the transparent veil. And her hands were talking also, with crisp, small, urgent gestures. She came toward me, and then she grabbed hold of my thumbs. She was pulling me forward, toward her. "Come," she said.

In the guard room she paused to coax the cell door closed again. Then using all her weight, she slammed back the bolt. I stood blinking in the light, looking for the men who had always filled this room whenever I'd passed through it. They were gone.

Then as Shepsut pulled me through the corridors and chambers, around every corner I expected to see soldiers. At every moment I expected to hear the rams' horns blowing the alarm. We moved through the empty rooms, up the ladders, and it took me a long time to realize that the mud-walled fortress was empty. It had been abandoned while I slept.

Outside it was daylight, and the light came through small chinks in the walls. The shadows were thick and dark. Wisps of smoke curled through the rooms. They thickened as we climbed the ladders to the upmost floor, where grim-faced Anilaeus lay on a bed, surrounded by the olive-oil lamps.

The light made his body glow. I paused in the doorway, and then Shepsut was pulling me across the splintered wooden floor. All the way she had been talking to herself, too softly for me to understand. And then, "You said it would kill him but he's still alive."

I pushed in through the lamps. Anilaeus lay in his shirt, with a tangled linen rag around his waist. The light shone on his wet neck and arms.

I put my hand to his mouth and felt his tiny breath. I knew what had happened. He had been poisoned with the poppy juice which I had given to the queen. His mouth was full of liquid, and his skin was wet. Sick smells came from him. His head lay to one side. His eyes were open but saw nothing when I waved my hand in front of them.

Then I heard the child screaming, loud and shrill.

The chamber was a small one with doors on three sides. We had come in from the gallery of stairs. But now I saw Thea Basaerta standing behind me in another doorway, and she had the child in her arms.

The veil was stripped back from her face, and in the lamplight I could see her black and silver hair. She had the saoshanti in her breast, but he was screaming there. He could not be comforted. Though he had come so early, he was large and strong. His voice dug into my ears, as if to punish and accuse me for conspiring against him.

And as the queen stepped forward I was astonished to see his face and neck, his tiny arms. His skin was mottled blue. He was as blue as Lord Krishna, who had also come out of a woman. And his voice was as strong as Lord Krishna's voice when he was born in the house of Nanda the shepherd among the cows and donkeys. There was a devil named Putana who was sent to suckle him with poisoned milk, only he seized hold of her breast and shouted until her heart burst from the noise.

Was I that demon? As she came toward me I could see the queen was in tears. "No, I can't," she said. "He won't take any milk. Here," she said, putting the child into Shepsut's arms, "I can't stand it. He is marked."

The child's hair was long and black. When she put her hand on his forehead, I could see what the queen meant. His eyes were closed, but there was a red mark above them in the place where the naked philosophers of India cultivate their hidden eye. "He won't eat, take him away," said the queen. "I can't bear it, I cannot. All this night." And then she was crying furious tears and pushing the child away. Shepsut clutched him in her arms, trying to stifle his shouting, which seemed to pierce into our heads and push away our thoughts.

And under it I could hear Anilaeus groaning on his bed, a soft, slow sound. Thea Basaerta heard it too. She pushed in through the lamps until she stood above his head. "God curse you," she said. "You are to blame for this. A monster. A monster."

She took a bottle made of potash-glass out of her sleeve. I had stepped backward with Shepsut and we stood next to the wall. But even at that distance I could tell what it was, and I could smell it as soon as she opened the bottle. It was a water made from tar, which in that country comes out of the ground and puddles in black pools. The Greeks make a distillate which they call "naphtha," a white liquid which burns, and which the queen was smearing now on Anilaeus's coarse hair, his face, his clothes. He was too weak to move.

"Go," I murmured to the girl. But my voice was drowned out in the child's shouting. He knew what was coming. He saw it out of his hidden eye while Shepsut and I stood dumb. He was shouting and straining, and with his tiny fists he pushed the cotton shawl back from his face so he could see.

In that place, in that mud fortress, there was a wet wind off the swamp that rotted the bricks away. But I guessed there was a dry wind too that came out of the desert, that scorched and splintered the wood floors and ceilings, the galleries and ladders of the upper stories. Now I saw that all this wood was smoking.

Smoke was curling from the doorway where the queen had come. Now she seized hold of an oil lamp and held it over the bandit's head.

I took hold of Shepsut's arm, and we stepped back into the gallery as the room filled with smoke. Then we were climbing down into the lower floors, and the smoke followed us. There was a draught that sucked it down from the pierced roof, and soon we were lost among the tiny rooms. The smoke gathered like a fog. Shepsut came behind me, coughing and wheezing while the child screamed.

Shepsut followed me, and I followed the pattern that had formed in my mind, ever since I had seen it in the officer's ward-room in the Caesarea prison. I followed my black line, lost among the smoky rooms as the ceilings creaked and whispered over our heads.

But in time we found the pit that led to the first story. Grey light was coming through an open door. The ladder dropped down into water, and when Shepsut climbed down from the gallery, the flood rose above her knees. Sticks and cinders floated on the surface of the water.

And as I watched the Egyptian girl sink down, the smoke receded from my head a little bit. A small grey watery light: Asinaeus had broken down the dikes. He had abandoned the citadel and abandoned his brother. He had taken his people back into the marsh, to wait for the army of Mithridates Surenas. I squatted at the top of the ladder, guessing at these things, guessing at what they meant for me and for Jeshua, my servant; now I remembered him. I rose and climbed again into the burning building, leaving the girl to flounder out the doorway, veiled and shrouded, her dress billowing around her in the dark water, the screaming child in her arms.

It took me a long time to find the guard room. Finally I was led to it by a sound of muffled yells and banging, but by the time I stumbled up against the door they had already stopped. The smoke was thick around my head. I could hear the fire in the floor above my head, and the smoke poured through the walls. Sometimes I went down on my hands and knees to recover my breath because the air was better near the ground. Upright, I coughed without stopping, and the tears streamed down my face.

And I could not open the door. Some damage had been done to it, just in the time I'd been away. The planks had been wrenched apart. The hinges were broken. The X-shaped beams were loose. Yet still the bolt held, jammed and swollen in its socket, and the shifting wood had changed the angle so I could not pull it straight.

But then at once the door gave way, and I dragged it open on the shattered hinge. Jeshua lay asleep on the other side.

With his usual violence and stupidity, he had thrown himself against the door until its timbers had almost given way, until he was overcome by the smoke or else he broke his head. He lay bruised and battered, and the door was smeared with blood. On the other side I could see there were marks on the outside wall where he had smashed and battered against it. None of the bricks had budged, even in the place where he had scraped them loose. They must have been many courses thick.

Inside the cell the lamp had gone out, and the air was too thick and hot to breathe. But now it was better with the door open. I crouched down over Jeshua's head, trying to wake him. I slapped at his big face, tugged at his arms. But it wasn't until I found the urine pot and poured it over him that he moved. I stripped off my shirt and soaked it in urine and wet stool, and wrapped his head with it. Coughing, I pulled him over onto his side. Then he was following me on his hands and knees. His hand was on my ankle.

As I led him through the maze I cursed myself. Why did I risk my life for him? Because out of all the evil that Ahrimmon had heaped on me, starting with my master's death, I had salvaged only the life of this one Jew.

We came to the open gallery and climbed down into the water. Then we waded from room to room until we found the door into the courtyard. It was a dark grey afternoon. We waded out through the big gate and stood looking at the marsh, the avenues of reeds stretching away.

Asinaeus had broken through the dikes. The water had risen and the peninsula was flooded. In the distance, out of sight somewhere, we could hear the saoshanti screaming at the limit of our ears. Then the sound faded away. We never saw the child again or the Egyptian girl. The world was not yet ready, for we never heard anything more about them.

CHAPTER

4

THE CATTLE
OF THE SUN

A Light over the Water

That night we slept on the hill behind the tower. We found a hollow in the sandy clay, where the Jews had been making bricks. The whole side of the hill had been cut apart.

The tower cast a light over the water. Ashes rained on us and sparks rose from the roof, which had fallen in. Squatting among the bushes, we watched the scavengers come in boats made of hollowed logs. They were small, dark, naked men with long hair down their backs. They came out of the marsh, wading alongside the boats.

In the morning we tried to find the river again, but these people found us first. We were standing on a narrow bank, sweating and wet through. All around us was the vapor from the swamp, filling our lungs with malaria and fluid. But the grey air had split apart above us, and we could see the sun. Jeshua was surrounded by a cloud of flies and gnats. His left ear was torn and swollen from where he had broken his head on the wooden door. Blood was crusted in his ear hole. But the right side of his face was unharmed, and he slapped at his cheek along that side.

Through the reeds I saw a boat, lying under a thicket of bushes not far away. Jeshua saw it too. He was looking out into the reeds where a boy was standing up in a small boat. Jeshua put his palm up, and I could see the flash of the boy's teeth. Then the boat was moving toward us.

It had some pots in it and some charred pieces of wood. It slid toward us over the water, into the mud. The boy was naked, and I could see Jeshua look at him. But then there was a movement in the bottom of the boat. It wobbled, and a girl stood out of it, holding a long, charred stick. She thrust it into the mud, and all the time she was talking in a language I didn't know.

She was naked too, except for some colored strings and ribbons in her hair, which was black and wild. She stood up in front of Jeshua, hands on her narrow hips. Her legs were streaked with mud. I saw Jeshua put his hand up to his injured ear.

But the girl was making space in the long boat. She threw the pots and sticks onto the bank while the boy paddled close. She was signaling for us to step into the boat, and Jeshua turned back to look at me. I saw an expression of surprise pass over his face, as if he had forgotten I was there. But then he stepped from the mud bank into the boat, which wavered underneath his weight when he sat down.

JESHUA

The boat took us through the reeds. Jeshua sat in the bottom, trying not to move. A sudden movement would have swamped us, for the water was a hand's breadth below the rail. Not that it would have made a difference, for the water was so shallow that

the boy and girl used their paddles to dig us forward through the
mud, and sometimes I could feel the bottom slide across a bar.
The girl ran back and forth, clambering over Jeshua's legs.

In time we came out onto a wide lake. The water was no
deeper here, at least at first, and sometimes the boy had to step
down into the red flood, to guide the boat to channels that were
deep enough. When he did this, the water never rose above his
waist.

Sometimes he would pull the boat, using a plaited cord tied
through the bow. Once when we were stuck, Jeshua and I got up
to step into the mud, to lighten the load. But the boat wobbled so
much that the girl laughed. She made him sit down. I had slipped
into the water, but she pushed him back down onto his seat with
her splayed hand against his chest.

His ear was bloody and the whole side of his face was
bruised.

The red water stained my legs. Though it was scarcely
above my thighs, nevertheless I saw it was rising through the borders of the lake, around the trunks of a thicket of small trees. The
water from the broken dikes was rising, and there was a current
on the surface as we paddled out across the lake. The eastern
shore was hidden in a mist.

In time we came to a village in the lake, a dozen houses built
on a cluster of boats and floating platforms. There we were taken
in. We were given fish and rice to eat. That night we slept in a
fisherman's house, the father of the boy and girl who found us.
We stayed there several days while Jeshua's head and shoulder
mended.

He had been knocked senseless during the fire in the mud-
walled tower. He had breathed wet smoke, which poisons the
brain. At first I thought it had made him simple, for he said nothing to me for three days. He didn't let me touch his ear, and
though I had lost my bag of tools, still I could have made him
comfortable with compresses of mud. He lay on his side under a
straw shelter on the boards. I thought perhaps he had damaged

the small bones inside his ear, so that he couldn't stand up without falling.

Sometimes when I spoke he frowned and turned his head away.

At night we lay in hammocks made of rope, pestered by clouds of insects. During the day I sat with him on the rocking platform, looking down at the water through the slats.

Our host was named Kaiooru Laraman. Every morning and evening he would go out to fish. From the platform we could see him standing with the water around his legs, and he would throw out a circular, weighted net. Or else he would check his baskets and plaited weirs, and bring back tiny fishes or else crabs. I would break open the crabs and Jeshua would suck their legs, though it was against his law.

Often Laraman sat with us. He taught me several hundred words of his strange language—I have forgotten them now, my memory has grown so bad. But Jeshua showed no interest, though our host's daughter was eager to teach him. He lay in the shade sucking crabs' legs and eating rice mixed with hot water, pounded into a kind of soup and served in wooden bowls.

But after three days his bruises were less painful. He sat up and began to speak, and I was relieved to see he was unharmed. For three days I had watched his symptoms, perhaps more closely than if I had had some means to treat them. And I noticed an odd thing. During those three days I saw a change in the language of his gestures, which reveals the soul. I remembered how he was in the cave at Caesarea, in the caravanserai at Dura, in the fortress in the swamp. He had moved like an animal, slow and powerful but hemmed in, burdened with restraints. A bear held by a chain.

But when his head was broken in the tower, then the language changed. I saw it in the way he would limp over to the side of the platform to make water, as we all did. For three days he would squat openly. But on the fourth day he went out only in the cover of darkness, and even then he turned his back and put his shirt around his hips, as if to hide from the night air the mark of his circumcision. This was in a place where boys and girls went naked until they were fully grown, and even then they never kept more than a knotted rag around their hips.

The beam had knocked him on the head. I thought perhaps for three days he forgot who he was. He let his burden rest. At night the children lay together on a raised platform in the middle of the town, and sometimes in the dark there was some laughter there. When he heard it during those first few nights, he would get up from his hammock and stand looking toward it over the flood.

In the morning our host's daughter would come back to the hut. She was the girl who had found us in the reeds. For three days he stared at her, openly and unashamed. She was aware of it, and sometimes she came to stand beside him, chattering to us and touching his arm. But as he healed he remembered his chains, and on the fourth day he turned his head and pulled away from her. The expression on his face was almost angry.

Jahwah, the Jewish god, has loaded his people down with laws, and even rebels and bandits feel the strain of breaking them. Later I came to see how every race contains a smaller group that feels the law's confinements, that fights against them. The mark of this struggle is an angry modesty, a sense of shame, and later I would come to notice it especially in people who complain, as Jeshua often did, about the injustices of governors and kings. Once on the fifth day the girl had climbed up underneath the hut to be with us. She lay on her side. She let her knees spread open. And Jeshua turned to me, his face shrouded in anger. He spoke fast and low and under his breath. "My mother told me that the Pharisees and Levites and all the old men at the synagogue were hypocrites. Now I understand."

At the time it was a puzzle to me how the sight of the girl's nakedness had led him to these words. But I had time to think and I was curious, so in my mind I went back to the cave at Caesarea. I remembered the woman there. I made a shadow cloth to wrap her in. Her words were stitched over it. I saw them in my mind.

I remembered what she had said about Jeshua: that upon their marriage his father put his mother aside, when he found she was carrying the soldier's child. I remembered how the woman said she stole from the synagogue, and broke the Sabbath, and refused to circumcize her son. Among the Jews, the Essenes were the strictest folk in Palestine, and now I thought I understood why he had run away and joined them.

Still it must have been easy for him to feel separate from his own people, for the sake of his mother and his memory. Perhaps that was the reason he had come into the sicarii, to try and touch his race's most exclusive heart. If so, how painful it must have been for him to be cast out. Once he said, "There is no word men put into God's mouth that is not a dangerous lie."

As he lay healing he was given to pronouncements of this kind. I took them as a sign of powerful intelligence not yet sharpened by education. It was the firmness of his tone that made me doubt him, because a skilled philosopher will understand that what he says is more half true than true.

For this reason I tried to listen less to his words themselves than to the unspoken thoughts. But this statement surprised me, because it was the first time I heard him speak of Jahwah in that way, as if God meant something to him. In Rome not one in ten will look into the sky and see a pattern there. I had grown used to stupid people, and at first I had thought Jeshua was just one more like them, an insect crawling on the surface of the world. Sometimes he would laugh at what he called my "superstitions." It was a laughter mixed with condescension, the clear mark of a fool, I thought.

I will describe the time. Toward evening we were looking out over the lake. I mentioned where I thought we were, how we were seeing part of the water that remained when God flooded the world. He laughed at me. "But it is your story too," I said. "All people share it."

"And Eve lived in the garden," he said, laughing angrily. "These are stories for children and old women." Then later, "There is no word that men put in the mouth of God . . ." and I sat listening to the secret reverence in his voice when he spoke Jahwah's name—itself unusual, for the Jews are given to circumlocutions of all sorts. "When we feel the truth, we know it to be the truth," he said. "But when we speak it, it becomes a lie."

Then he brooded in silence for a while. Later when I thought it would relax him, I told him part of the story of Noah. Then I told him about the hero and his friend 'Nkidu, who had traveled over this same marsh and this same lake when they traveled east to kill the dragon, but he interrupted me. "These are stories for children," he said again. And then when I persisted, he laughed. He said, "Now I understand why you are telling me. First you were a slave. Now in this story you're a hero and a king. But what am I?" And I was embarrassed because I saw what he meant. 'Nkidu was a wild creature, hairy and strong, who came out of the ignorant countryside.

We were sitting in the shade under a roof of woven reeds, feeling the shock of the boats grinding together as the wind came up. In front of us some children were splashing in the shallow water. It rose to their thighs. This was the sixth afternoon since our arrival. Jeshua got up and went to stand on the platform's edge.

His head was almost cured, and I could tell he was eager to be gone. But where? He stood looking west. I had seen how, as he healed, he told more stories about Nazareth, about the country there. Now he stood describing the Galilean lake, how beautiful it was. It frightened me because I wanted him to stay with me. Since I had worked to save him, I didn't want him to walk stupidly back toward his death. So I interrupted him to tell him what he knew. If he went back, the sicarii would hunt him down.

They would murder him or else turn him over to Caiaphas and the Sanhedrin. Or else the Romans would catch him and nail him up. I made the tale as blood-stained as I could until his eyes filled with tears.

"But in the east," I said, "there are great cities, and palaces which come down to the river. There are peacocks in the desert, and great elephants. Kings fight with their armies on the brilliant plain," I said, repeating for him some of the stories which my father told to me before he died. "There are houses of gold, with roofs of sapphires and streets of pearls. There are cakora birds which feed on moonlight. There is no sickness, nor is anyone in need. The gods live in the headache mountains," I said. I spoke to him as if he were a child. I told him about the river flowing from the Cow's Mouth. And about the Diamond Mountain, which Bardesanes had described, which stands at the border of the pure land.

"And when you see that mountain," I said, "when you step into that water, all your sins are washed away. I will make a prayer for my father, for it is the true baptism," I told him.

But I didn't say how far it was from where he stood looking out over the shallow lake.

THE ROYAL ROAD

Later he would talk about that village in the reeds and the simplicity and kindness of its people. "Because they accomplished nothing, God protected them," he said, though that was not how I remembered it. "They were like animals," he said. "Because they went naked, then God made them beautiful," and I knew he was thinking about the girl.

Later he would talk about that place as if it had been the only garden in a wilderness of desolation, though, as I have said, at the time he was eager to be gone. We left as soon as he could pick up a canvas bucket full of water without causing himself pain. Kaiooru Laraman took us two days eastward through the reeds and left us on the Tigris riverbank above Ctesiphon. It was a hot, muggy afternoon.

The river was broad and flat there, currentless and calm. Above it on the eastern shore hung the Xagros mountains, several days away. They stretched north and south as far as I could see. At first I thought they were a bank of purple clouds.

These are the ramparts of the land of Persia. The road climbs from the marshes up into the mountains, through orchards of walnuts and pistachios and almonds and pears. It climbs through the mountain gorges into a forest of oak, beech, and linden trees. Foxes live there, and leopards, and wild deer. Then the trees give out completely in the stony ground, and there are lizards and serpents, and the road winds through the peaks.

It follows the ravines for many days, and then it comes onto the high plain, where there are no towns or villages, and the desert stretches from the Erythraean ocean to the Caspian steppe. The stones are full of salt. Dust fills your nose, and the sky is like a mirror. During the summer the wind blows every day; the heat blisters your skin. But at night the wind turns cold, and lions and hyenas and wild pigs come out of the mountains, and there are rats without tails that chew the fingers of a traveler as he lies asleep among the rocks.

There is one road in this country. It is the Khorasan road, built by Darius the Persian, and it runs from Seleucia and Ctesiphon northeast through the rock walls of Bisitun, where Darius carved his images and his inscriptions. Then to the Parthian cities, Conchobar and Ecbatana on the Median plain. Then through Rhagae and the Caspian Gates, where the Elbros mountains overlook the sea. Then eastward toward Hecatompylos.

But I am moving too fast. Our journey lasted months along that road. At the beginning, near Ctesiphon, we joined the caravan of Taima, son of Taiamersh, who was arriving from the gulf.

Jeshua and I had come up from the Tigris with the clothes

on our back, some dried fish, and two blankets that Kaiooru Laraman had salvaged from the burning tower. But we had nothing else. My tools and money were all gone, except for a single golden aureus, which I had tied underneath my sex. One morning I climbed up through the trees to a bare place and made a puja to Lord Mercury and to Lord Hanuman, the monkey king. When the sun came up I jammed the coin into a cleft in the rock and put myself into the gods' hands.

We scrambled all day over the dry rocks. In the afternoon we stood above the road, on a dry slope covered with scrub juniper. We watched the dust rise into the blue sky. We followed for two days at a safe distance, and on the evening of the third day we came upon them as they rested, a crowd of men and beasts. This was near the village of Hama, ten stades from the road, where there was a spring.

I looked for the son of Taiamersh and found him sitting in the dirt, mixing camel dung with straw and pressing it into balls.

He squinted up at me. He was a small, heavy man with big hands. He was missing his front teeth. He wore leather trousers and his shirt was filthy, but he had a gold chain around his neck. And I found something impressive in the way he had taken on this dirty job. He squeezed the dung together with quick, practiced motions while his soldiers lazed around him and his boys wasted time. Nearby they were smoking meat over a fire of juniper and dung.

Most of the traders on the royal road are Arabs, and they speak either Aramaean or the mangled Greek that is the market language of the Parthian kingdoms. But Taima had been to Alexandria and Crete; he was a clever man. He understood that I had skills that he could use.

Again, I move too fast. I had prepared for this meeting. Two nights before, on the seventh night of the dark moon, Jeshua and I had slept out in the rocks. Past midnight I had gotten up and gone into the camp. I searched out the animals. The donkeys had been tethered in a group, but the camels were among the thorn trees, where they had been allowed to graze. They were guarded by two sleeping boys.

I chose a fine young mare, sitting separate from the rest. I plucked a thorn off of a bush, and in the shelter of a rock I squatted down. Instantly my stool came out. It had been watery and red for many days.

I collected some into the hollow of a stone and put my thorn in it. Then I came upon the camel from behind. They are stolid, slow creatures, not skittish in the least, and this one allowed me to come up beside her and kneel down. She didn't even turn her head. I found her hind leg folded under her, the pad turned up. I scratched her leg above her hoof until the blood ran down. Her skin was fragile there and much abraded, and she didn't even move. It was a small thorn. I pushed it up into a crevice in her flesh until the skin closed around it.

She was a strong animal, but by the evening of the second day, when I approached Taima, she was sick. They had unloaded her and kept her separate from the rest, as if her illness were infectious. Now she stood splay-footed among the rocks under the burning sun, guarded by some boys, but she wouldn't allow them to come near. She had an abscess on her leg, which was leaking pus and water.

I told the son of Taiamersh I'd seen the animal. I could help him. He squinted at me, instantly suspicious, as I knew he would be. But what could he do? Most of his camels were Arabian, but this one was from Bactria, one of only four, as I had seen when I had picked her out. Tougher and faster and more valuable, but something else. He had a name for her. She was his favorite, which was why he was making dung patties and cursing by himself. His hands moved quickly, with a nervous helplessness. He thought she had drunk bad water.

His drivers had told him to do nothing, that the fit might pass. But I told him to go look at the wound on her leg. And then if he agreed with me that something should be done, to throw a net on her and bring her down, and I would help him. He went away. And I walked over to the boys who were smoking goat meat over the fire, because I had a suspicion. The goat's legs had been cut off and hung up on a chain, supported by an iron tripod.

I thought perhaps the meat was rotten. Travelers often keep fresh meat as long as they can, and then cure it with smoke after it turns. I was right. The god was watching me, and near the tripod were the rotten pieces that the boys had cut from the corpse, scraps I couldn't identify, but which were full of worms. In fact Lord Mercury had blessed me, for behind the rocks there was some other garbage also, stinking in the heat, and some rotten bread.

I told the boys to warm some water in a bowl. Then Taima came back and told me they were doing what I wanted. He looked at me suspiciously when I picked up the meat and bread, but I said nothing. He was a clever man, and I was not going to insult him with lies. For others, I would have made a show, asked for incense and chanted prayers, but of course the gods cared nothing for this illness. I had made it. I would cure it.

They had caught the camel in a net, as I had asked them. She was struggling and crying out, and I told some of the soldiers to hold her so she would not break her legs with struggling. Five of them jumped onto her, and I stretched out her leg. I scraped away the abscess with a steel knife, which I had heated in the fire in a way I have already described. I flushed out the wound with boiling water, and at the same time I was feeling for the little thorn. I plucked it out and hid it between my fingers because Taima was watching me, squatting next to me. But when he turned aside to call for more water, then I plucked the thorn away and hid it in my robe.

I have heard doctors say that worms cause meat to rot, but this is false. Meat spoils before worms appear, and in fact their presence takes away the smell that is the sign of rottenness. Herophilos of Alexandria first used them to dress wounds, and that was by accident: In Egypt priests and scribes had long been in the habit of tying meat into a wound, to draw out the blood. Only fresh meat is useful for this purpose. But once a student, treating a soldier with a ulcer in his arm, had packed it with a lump of meat and left it tied up in a bandage for many days. When the bandage was opened, it was discovered that the worms had spread into the ulcer and that the wound was clean. The inflammation and the suppuration were both gone. After that, Herophilos often used worms in his surgery. It was Dion, my master's slave, who brought the technique first to Rome, where it was rejected by idiots because of how it looked. Cornelius Celsus rejected all our thoughts about it and refused to write them down.

Dion also used old bread and cheese to cleanse his blood, a remedy that he could never explain. Because it can't be justified, so it is better used on animals than people. The soldiers laughed at me when I called for rotten cheese, and no one moved. But I made do with the bread that I had brought from the garbage pile. I scraped off the mold and rubbed it into the wound, then packed it with maggots and bandaged it. Taima squinted at me. He was sour and suspicious, and so I made the bandage needlessly complex to reassure him with my skill. All the while I kept up a soft patter of Greek. I told him I was from Alexandria, a lie I had used so often that it sounded like the truth to me.

I knew he suspected I might be a charlatan. But I told him if he did nothing, then the beast would die, and he believed me. She was in a shivering fright, her eyes rolling in her skull. After we released her, she lay still for many minutes, but then she got up and limped away. In the morning she was able to follow the rest of the train, though her load had to be redistributed.

PHILOXENUS OF PERGAMON

That first night Taima gave us barley meal to eat. We were glad to get it because we had had nothing for two days. But Taima was sullen with us, as if he begrudged us even the little we asked in return for our services—the protection of the caravan and a small share of food. He was a rich, stingy man, a Nabataean from Petra. He owned twenty-seven camels, ten donkeys, and nine mules. They were loaded with dried fruit, dried nuts, olive oil, frankincense, animal skins, salt, grease, nard, pinecones, grapevines, silver cups, glass ingots, pearls, carpets, Tyrian dyes, and bronze statues of naked women. And food and water. He also had ten Africans from Meroë, whom he planned to sell as servants at the great market in Arat.

These treasures were guarded by a troop of horsemen, rented from the batesa of Conchobar for ten Roman denarii each day. And twenty camel boys and drivers, as well as several other travelers. It was a crowd of people, and as we walked we stirred up a torrent of white dust.

During the day we stretched out in a long line, but at night we came together at the caravanserais, which the Parthians had built along the road. These were long, roofed galleries, made of brick and sometimes wood, as we came northward to Hyrcania. The largest formed three sides around a courtyard of stamped earth, but more commonly they had two sides, or just one, set against the wind. These last were extremely miserable when, as sometimes happened, the dust blew in upon the open side.

When we were near a town, an old man would come out with a goatskin of water on his back. Or sometimes loaves of bread. Besides that we ate a soup of roasted barley, cooked in fires of camel dung. And sometimes we got meat from the drivers. They didn't share Taima's doubts. In fact we were useful, and the others accepted us soon enough. They were rough, uneducated men. They were easily impressed. In the evenings I pulled their rotten teeth and gave them free advice. I made them lotions for their cracked lips and hands and sunburned skin. For small sums I read their hands.

From these and numerous other transactions, I kept two copper pennies every day. Then I would go out and lose the rest in number games or games of dice, which the drivers played constantly whenever we stopped.

I kept myself busy, but for many days after we left the river, Jeshua was silent and submissive. I made all the decisions that concerned us. I gave him food and he ate it. He walked when I walked and sat down when I sat down. I guessed he was grieving for his home because every step took him farther from it. But the heart, like all internal organs, mends itself when the source of irritation is taken away. As we turned toward the east, he let the past recede behind him. He grew stronger.

At night sometimes, he and I would sit away from the fire. Often after midnight the wind would die for a few hours until dawn, and the dust would settle. Then in the cold thin desert air the stars hung close enough almost to touch. The night was clearer than the day. We would sit up in our blankets to watch the planets blunder slowly through the Zodiac—backward, forward. Bright Jupiter, wet Venus, burnt Mars, and in the hour before daybreak sometimes I could catch a glimpse of Mercury itself: cold and dry, male and female, doubtful as quicksilver, carrying my fate with it on its hidden and uncertain journey.

Jupiter was his planet. He was a traveler like me, but full of blood where I had bile. Especially as the air grew thin upon the high plain, blood would burst out of his nostrils for no reason. If there was a wound on his face or hand, then blood would spatter out of it. But at the same time he would heal quickly, and the cuts on his face would leave no scar.

In our time with the caravan, he achieved a reputation for feats of strength. Once on a bet I had arranged, he lifted up a donkey in the circle of his arms and set it down over a stone wall. The blood burst from his face. That night when the wind was still, just in the starlight I could see the shadow of dried blood below his nostrils, the streaks of blood that had run down into his new beard. His hair had grown back quickly since the time I'd shaved him on the river.

He sat clasping his knees, looking up into the north sky. His hair was curled short around his head. And if his lips were coarse and his nose was broken, still there was something noble in his face I hadn't seen before. His shining eyes. At first I thought it was perhaps a trick of starlight, but as I studied him I saw how the hair had grown in grey around his temples. I saw he was older than me by many years. It was something I had always known but never realized so strongly until now, when sorrow gave his face a new dignity.

In the high desert, in the cold thin air, much becomes visible that was hidden before. I looked above us into the wet eye of Jove. He was coming into the house of the bull, and I thought about that, and Jeshua saw me thinking. "Tell me," he said in his rough Greek. "These superstitions. Will I ever see the land of Israel again?"

Unwilling either to lie or tell the truth, or say I didn't know, I held my tongue. In fact these things can't always be foretold. I shook my head and smiled. "Tell me," he said. "Is my mother healthy now, and my young brother?"

Then in a little while, he spoke again: "And Miriam of Magdala. Is she . . . ?"

Again I was silent, and he looked at the stars. Then he dropped his eyes into his lap. He let his knees sink open and took his bare feet between his hands. They were cracked and dusty from the road. "Pythagoras of Samos," he said, "taught how the soul continues after death. He told of a circle of return, and every child carries the burden of evil from another life. Empedocles the Sicilian also believed this, as well as many of the Pharisees in my own land. They say when all the Jews have shaken off this burden, then our king will come."

I was amazed to hear him speak like this. It was as if a stone or a piece of clay had spoken of Pythagoras, and because of my astonishment I couldn't answer. Had I been able, I would have told him that the brahmans and naked philosophers of my father's country also talk like this. These things are well known.

But no, he was disputing them. "I wonder," he said. "It explains our fate. It explains luck when there is no other reason. But I wonder, what is hidden in the heart?" And then he told me a story.

"When Menahem sent to question me after Barabbas was captured, I was on the Jericho road. I was afraid I would not be believed, and so I ran away. I saw a man. I robbed him. I beat him with my fists and left him to die. I watched from the bushes; people passed him but did not stop. Levites. Shit-eating hypocrites. They passed by on the other side of the road. But now I wonder, has God punished me?"

I made a gesture of denial because of course if he was guilty, so was I. I had my own memories. "No, let me speak," he said. "I think about this often. I dream about it. He was a bald old man. The road from Jerusalem went through a ravine. It was sunset. God forgive me, I did not expect the man to fight me, to try and defend himself even after he had fallen from his donkey. The man struck out with his stick and must have hurt me. That is the only way I can explain it, because when I woke up I was standing over him with blood on my fists."

I said nothing, and in a little while he went on. "Sometimes I think ... There was a Samaritan on the road. I saw him as I ran away carrying the belt. He was standing in the middle of the road. Not one of my race. They worship at Mount Gezarin. But I think if this man was a good man, then he could have helped me too. He could have taken the old fellow to an inn. There was an inn not far away."

As he spoke, I remembered Anilaeus and Asinaeus on the riverbank. They had called Jeshua a murderer, and I wondered now whether he had heard or understood them. "Wishing will not make it true," I said.

At this his face took on such a sad expression that I felt I must comfort him. Jupiter had gone behind a cloud, which had been rimmed with silver. Now it came free. I pointed it out to him and showed him the sign of the bull, and explained how tomorrow was a lucky day for him, which was false. How he would meet a stranger, which was true.

In fact the day might have been lucky for Jeshua if he had acted more sensibly. This was at the start of a pattern that I came

to know, a recklessness in him. At first it puzzled me. But in time
I understood it: He was trying to seduce his god. He was making
a kind of penance, hoping to persuade the gods to let him return
home, because like all Jews he felt lost outside his own country.

It is a doubtful tactic. Man's fate cannot be changed, because
to change it is to change the world. Jeshua had robbed a traveler
on the Jericho road. But it was I who placed him there and put a
desperation in his heart, I and the Lion of Tabor. And what of
the traveler himself? Gods and men had also led him to that road.
Perhaps they were punishing him also. Who is innocent in this
world? An old man named Telephus lived in my master's house
in Rome for a short time before he was taken to the magistrate
for stealing. He told me it was a mistake to think of man's destiny
as a single cord, stretching to be cut. But it was a worse mistake
to think of it as one of a thousand cords woven together, on which
the gods will read a pattern that is hidden to us. Instead he told
me to imagine a ripped net in the bottom of a fishing boat, full
of broken strands and knots, and so tangled that the pattern is
lost, the purpose is lost, and even the fisherman himself is caught
in it, can make no sense of it, and has to cut himself free.

We rolled ourselves in our blankets and fell asleep. We were
awakened by the sand drifting over us. A wind had come up during the night. It was not strong at first, but there was something
menacing about the way the clouds scuttled above it in the opposite direction.

We got up and shook ourselves off, and walked down
among the drivers. They were muttering and cursing, pulling
canvas over their loads, and tying down the straps with special
care. The horses were nervous, they glanced up at the sky and
shook their heads. But the son of Taiamersh never stopped for
the weather. He had a schedule of hours. At dawn he blew the
big bronze whistle, and we climbed out of the ravine where we
had spent the night. We had shelter there, and a stream trickling
down between the rocks. The sky was a white shield over the
sun, and the clouds sped across it. We climbed up through the

boulders until we came onto the plain. There were mountains to the north of us, and to the south there was a line of stone towers, which the people of that country used to expose their dead. Smoke came from the top of one of them, but the wind was grabbing it away, grabbing also at the wings of the vultures circling the top of the stone pyramid, waiting to alight. They could not come down. It was a bad omen, and bad for us too, for as we passed the tower the wind beat on our faces, and it was full of grit and salt and sand.

Small stones slid over the surface of the plain, pushed by the wind. Pebbles banged around our ankles. We wrapped our faces in our blankets. The wind seemed to blow from all around us. The horsemen dismounted, and the drivers had to pull the camels forward. Cursing, they yanked them forward by the ropes cut through their nostrils, and the boys beat the mules with sticks.

Sometimes when the wind was too strong, we stopped to rest. But then the son of Taiamersh would come back down the line to urge us forward. He would shout over the rattle of the wind, telling us how we must reach the town of Xur by nightfall, how we couldn't stay up here under the wind. So we pushed forward, blind, following the stone markers that had been erected every bowshot's length along this part of the road. A boy went on ahead and he called back. When the wind sank down, Jeshua and I could see that we were in the middle of a line of men and beasts which stretched out far behind us, far in front. Our mouths were full of salt.

We came through an abandoned village of stone houses, half submerged in drifting sand. They loomed out of the driving wind. We stopped for a moment in the shelter of a broken wall. Then we heard screaming.

The Africans had been in front of us. Ordinarily they were kept together, their legs free, their hands bound with iron manacles. At night they slept apart under a guard, and during the day they marched among the soldiers. A long rope wound between them through the circle of their arms.

That day during the storm, the horsemen had dismounted. They were so blinded by the sand, they had not noticed when the rope was broken. One of the Africans had slipped away, hoping to hide in the abandoned town. But he had stumbled over the cover of a well and he had fallen in.

Two halves of a stone slab had split apart, and he, blinded by the sand, had fallen between them. When Jeshua and I came there, a crowd of men had gathered over the hole. The son of Taiamersh was there, and the soldiers and Africans. The screams out of the well had stopped. The wind clutched at our clothes. Jeshua let his blanket fall and he stepped forward, pushing the men aside. I followed him until we came up to the hole itself. Taima squatted there, and with him was an Egyptian man, a Nubian I had seen before. His hands were chained together, and he was talking to Taima in a low, soft voice. He was squatting beside him and was talking into his ear while he was staring out over the hole in another direction. His green eyes shone out of his dark face.

There were some men standing on the other side of the well. Jeshua pushed them aside and knelt down, and I looked over his shoulder. The well was dry and deep, perhaps five times the height of a man. But the African had not fallen the whole way. There was a piece of wood lodged between the stone sides of the well about halfway down. The man had fallen on top of it, and under his weight it had slid down so that it slanted at an angle into the side of the well. The man was caught in the crook of it— a precarious place, and his screaming and his struggles had made it still more precarious. Even under the rush of the wind we could hear the stones slipping down one by one.

They had brought a camel and a rope and tied an iron hook to the end of it. But whether he was stiff with fright or now asleep, the man couldn't seize the hook as it came down. I thought he was hindered by the chains around his wrists. He lay there in the crook, sagging down over the timber, a dark shadow below us.

The break in the cover of the well seemed almost too nar-row to have admitted his body, and the first thing Jeshua did was make it larger. He grabbed hold of one of the broken halves and levered it upward with just the bare strength of his back and arms. Then without speaking, without saying anything to Taima or the Egyptian, he slid down into the hole, bracing himself with his splayed legs on either side. For a moment his head was still visible in the light, and I could see the green eyes of the Egyptian had met his eyes, and he stared back, frowning. Then he ducked his head under the lip of the well, and we watched him move quickly, carelessly, almost sliding down, and we were listening to the stones come loose and fall to the bottom of the well. I had stretched out on the sand, my face over the lip, and I saw him with his legs splayed above the injured man. He let go his right hand from the wall, and he reached down with it and grabbed hold of the chain between the African's wrists, and yanked him upward.

The timber gave way. It smashed down to the bottom of the well, and then Jeshua was climbing. I saw him look up, his face angry and flushed. Then he seized hold of the rope, and he pulled up the African until the chains of his manacles slid over the iron hook.

Taima was on his feet now, and the green-eyed Egyptian. They had fastened the other end of the rope to the saddle of a two-humped camel. Now the boys whipped it with sticks. And so the man came up too hard. He struck his head on the over-hanging slab. But they pulled him over, and then Jeshua was coming up alone.

Later I wondered why he had not used the rope himself, or found another and tied it to his belt. Perhaps because there was no time. But I believe also, as I said, that he was tempting the god. The danger was important to him. By risking his life, he was asking Jahwah to forgive him.

We carried the African into one of the stone houses, a small place with a broken door, although the roof was whole. We laid him in a drift of sand. Taima unlocked his chains and squatted down, and under his suspicious eyes I reset the man's shoulder. I snapped the joint together and tied it across his body. His ribs were broken, and his left forearm, so I reset that too. I made a splint for it. He woke up under my hands, although his head was gashed and scraped above his eye, where the camel had dragged him over the cistern's lid. I picked out the bits of rock and bone and dirt.

The Sericans pay large sums for roots and herbs, and so the son of Taiamersh had packed one of his donkeys with leather pouches full of cornflower, mistletoe, sage, and German yarrow. By that time I had bought or taken what I needed, for my skill was well known. Many of the drivers were my friends. I had even pulled a molar for Taima himself, and rubbed clove oil on the wound. The men would bring me gifts of money or food, which I shared with Jeshua, though he never displayed any interest in what I was doing. Until that day—when I was working on the African, he stayed at my elbow, and everything I asked for he would bring me. A pot of water, a lamp. He said nothing, but watched me as I rubbed the bleeding wounds with water, and with marigold and lavender. I sealed them with an ointment of honey mixed with grease. And then I wrapped them in bandages while Jeshua thrust his big nose into the pouches of herbs, as if he could remember them that way.

It was hard to work in that small space. I was not used to so much staring. Taima was there, and Jeshua, and the green-eyed Egyptian. He squatted down with his hands out, his wrists chained together, and from time to time I would see Jeshua and him share a look. Especially when the African woke up: When I jolted his arm into its socket again, he screamed. Jeshua was staring at the Egyptian, and then he winced and closed his eyes. "Slave," he muttered, though he knew nothing about slavery, I thought. Over in the doorway, with the grey light across his face, Taima turned toward us. He spat into the corner of the stone room.

When I got up, the storm was less, and Taima was eager to be gone. He made the African walk, thinking he was punishing him for trying to escape. Though in fact it was the best course, for he was able to control his movement and protect his ribs; a camel or a mule would have jolted him over the stones. He was separated from the others and made to walk, tied to the girthing strap of one of the horses by a long rope. Again Taima meant to punish him, though I noticed the soldier took care to keep the rope slack between them. It was a hot day without water.

Nevertheless we made good time and came to Xur at dusk. There Taima relented. He set up his tent in the courtyard of the caravanserai, which was in an open place of large black stones. Then he gave us liquor and told us to go down into the town. Jeshua swallowed several mouthfuls of the bitter wine, but I took nothing. I had a headache above my eye in the same place where I had bandaged up the African. I suppose I guessed already at the trouble there.

Jeshua and the drivers went down into Xur, which was in a crevice in the hills. It was a small town, and in the fields outside they grew barley and dates and apricots. They had a pool of water, which came from far away through an underground canal. Greeks had built it in the old days. I went up to stand on a rock, and I could just see the flat roofs of the houses. My head was splitting apart. I paced back and forth among the boulders, and at one point I crept between the rocks to listen to the moans of the African from a place where I was hidden. The others were tending to him as well as they could, but I knew he had cracked his head coming up out of the well. I could see his bandages were soaked in new blood, and I thought perhaps some new vessel in his brain had split during the long march. In these cases there are doctors who drill open their patients' skulls above the wound. They seek to relieve the pressure when the brain swells with blood, but they are murderers and fools. The door cannot be opened into that small room.

Taima had driven him all day without stopping for water.

Now they had wrapped him in blankets and laid him in a corner of the wall. He was breathing out long shuddering moans through broken ribs—I couldn't stand it. I hid from them when they called me. I went down the path, in through the hard mud gates. The town was deserted, except for a few children. The close-packed streets were empty. But there was a noise. I reached the far gate and found Jeshua in an open space outside.

It was a dusty agora a stone's throw from the wall, where the townspeople had built a fire of thorn trees. The drivers were eating chunks of goat meat wrapped in leaves. They were drinking wine and listening to a traveling gosan tell the story of the god, how Dionysus had come to that place, had fought a devil there in Xur, had made him drunk with wine, and then ripped him apart—I couldn't listen. I felt drunk myself. My ears were ringing, and my heart was pounding in my chest. I was thinking about the African, how the wall of bone was broken above his eye.

But at the same time I didn't want the story to end, because I knew it was not for this old gosan that the men of Xur had piled up this bonfire of thorns. At moments in my heterocrania I see clearly.

A crowd of people had come into the agora, now that it was dark. The men sat in front next to the fire, eating and drinking, while the women stood behind them in the shadow of the boulders. They wore yellow veils over their faces, except for the old women and the very young. They gathered in a circle while the men sat on their heels and talked, and no one paid any attention to the gosan babbling in his wretched Greek, which not one in five there understood; he was an old man who was missing his front teeth.

I slumped down next to Jeshua. I meant to speak to him but he held up his hand. He was listening to the gosan, alone, it seemed, out of the crowd, and so I found my eyes drawn to the old man again. He was barefoot and bald, dressed in a torn shirt. His bag lay at his feet, and nearby he had placed his open hat;

there was no money in it. Now that I looked at him more closely, I could see he was not weak and frail, as at first I had assumed. He stood up straight with his legs spread apart. His eyes were bright, and there was a bristle of grey whiskers on his chin. Now he had raised his voice above the din of the crowd, and he was telling them the story of the god-man Heracles, whom the people there call Venethragna. He told us how Venethragna fought with the Ionian bull, which surprised me. I had told Jeshua the same story on the night before, to explain what it meant when Jupiter, or Jahwah, came into the bull's mansion. I glanced at my friend now, and he turned toward me for a moment. But then he looked at the old man again, and together we sat and listened to the story: how Venethragna was the son of Jupiter, and he was born from the god out of a human woman, the wife of Amphitryon the soldier. And Jupiter tested his son, loaded him with terrible burdens and sent him on twelve journeys to the ends of the earth, the mirror of his father's journey through the houses of heaven. We listened to how Jupiter punished him and broke him for his human part and burned him in a fire on Mount Oeta, until the human part of him was burnt away and the god rose to the stars.

He died naked on the mountaintop, without so much as a rag of clothing. But Heracles, because of the pains he suffered and tasks he accomplished, became a hero to the Greeks. In him they saw the sign of our godlike and human nature, especially Diogenes of Sinope and his followers, whom the Greeks called "cynic," or doglike. I sat with Jeshua listening to the story of the god, but my head was also breaking with pain, and with part of my mind I was thinking how this man might be the stranger I had predicted to Jeshua the night before. The evil bull with the red eye. He stood up and bellowed out of his broad chest. But then I thought no, he is just a dog, a barking dog, because my master had told me about these cynics. They travel the world, begging and making trouble and protesting the natural hierarchy of men.

I was thinking these thoughts as a way to distract myself,

because the African was dying on the ridge above the town. Sometimes I imagined I was hearing his cries. So I was happy to listen to the old dog; the story ended, and soon he began speaking in a high, complaining voice. He came forward to the edge of the crowd, kicking his empty hat, and when no one gave him money he began to pour abuse onto their heads, calling them idiots and fools, and scolding the rich men in the front. Taima was there, and the old dog stood barking at him, calling him a robber and mocking the gold chain around his neck. "You must know it is easier for a snake to pass through a needle's eye than for a rich man to rise up into heaven."

Beside me, Jeshua grunted. "It is Philoxenus of Pergamon," he said. He had a bronze obol in his hand, which I had given him. My head was sore. It filled me with anger to see him get up and push forward through the seated men, and put the coin into the cynic's hat. "Master Philoxenus," he said. "I have heard of you."

"What?" shouted the old man. "What have I done wrong?" And then he slapped his forehead and turned back to the crowd. "It's when others praise you, then you know you are a fool."

Some people laughed at this. But others seemed restless. This was not why the whole village had left their houses and gathered here, to see this one old clown. There was something else, some other cause that made my head ache like the dying African's, and now I could hear it starting in a murmur that spread out from the women in back of me. I could see it starting in a current of motion that spread out among the seated men. They turned around to look behind them, and I turned too, even though I felt as separate from them as if I wasn't there, as if my vision was covered by one of the yellow veils the women wore, who now thrust themselves forward from the shadow of the bushes and the rocks. A veil that was heavy, yet hid nothing. I saw everything. Six women came out into the crowd. They waded out into the circle of men, and the light burst over their ragged clothes because two small boys had piled up the bonfire with more thorns, filling the agora with a cracking, snapping noise that hurt my ears, a bitter smoke that hurt my eyes and made them swell with tears.

Now there was a young man next to the bonfire, dressed in dirty fox skins and looking like the god Dionysus in the story. His dark hair was woven in a crown of vine leaves. His face was streaked with color. Red ribbons hung down from the wooden phoorbah in his right hand, and with his left he was pouring out a fierce libation to the flames, which leapt up when the wine touched them.

This boy was dressed like nothing I had seen before, but I looked at him just once during that first moment and then never again. I raised my sleeve against the heat, and then I looked back toward the women. They had come out in the open now, fifteen or twenty naked-faced old crones. The men were rising to their feet. We were all rising, and we made a path between us, between the women and the bonfire. They came along it now, dragging someone else between them. Sometimes she stumbled and they dragged her forward. She was covered so that none of her flesh or hair was exposed, and her hands were tied behind her.

I pulled on Jeshua's shirt. "Let us leave this place," I begged him. "This is a bad place." But he couldn't hear me in the new noise. He was staring at the woman with a dull, stupid expression on his face. Couldn't he see what was happening? They dragged her out in front of the fire, and she sank down to her knees. Then the oldest and most withered of the women ripped the cloth off of her head, and her black hair spilled out. Someone else pulled it back from her scalp, and they were sawing at it with a knife until it came loose—a heavy rope of hair, which they held up and threw into the fire. The stink from it blew in our faces with the smoke.

The woman had a strong, hard face. Her eyebrows met over her nose, and her black hair was thick on her upper lip—the sign of Juno. Her teeth shone in the firelight. Her eyes rolled back until they showed only the whites, and I hoped she was drunk.

The old woman was ripping at her clothes, and she ripped them apart over her neck and breasts and pulled them down so we could see her white breasts so exposed, and her white belly underneath. Her white skin painted with sweat, and a line of hair ran down between her breasts and down into her clothes.

"Please God let us leave this place," I murmured. But Jeshua did not move. He was looking at the dirt under his feet. He wasn't looking at the woman, didn't even see her when she fell on her face in front of the fire. He stared down at his feet, and his huge shoulders didn't even move when the women came up with their stones. The heavy boulders they just lifted up onto her body. But the small ones they raised above their heads.

Ever since the woman's breasts had come uncovered, there had been a silence in the crowd. Now we could hear the crunch of every stone. The woman never cried out. We could hear her grunting as the stones fell, as the pile around her grew. And we could hear the shouts of the old fool Philoxenus. He was the only one who had stood up and pushed forward. "What are you doing?" he shouted, as if he had no eyes to see. "Stop this! What are you doing?" Men in the crowd were holding him back, but then he broke through. He was pulling stones out of the women's hands, and then he threw himself down upon the pile, shielding the broken body underneath him until they dragged him away. Even then he was not silent. "What kind of men are you?" he shouted as the stones fell.

The fire had sunk down. The women were gone now. They had disappeared into the darkness, taking their children with them. But the men came forward to examine the pile of stones and the few rags of cloth, which were all we could see. And Jeshua was with the old cynic—they had thrown him into the fire and burned his arm, and there were some bruises on his back and gashes on his head where the stones had hit him. Jeshua grunted over him, as if by tending him he could restore the woman to life. He dragged me to him, and I squatted down beside the dying embers.

Now the townspeople were gone, and all our drivers too. I

stood up giddy in the dark air. My headache was all gone. The cold air seemed to flow through me, carrying away these terrible thoughts. "Please let us go," I said. And so Jeshua threw his blanket over the man's shoulders and slung the bag across his own back, and together we brought him around the wall and up the hill until we reached our camp.

As usual Jeshua and I had kept ourselves apart. We were in the sand between some ridges of gravel and salt. It was the bed of an empty stream. I lit a fire of sticks while Jeshua laid the old man down. He neither groaned nor complained. He wasn't thinking of himself. He was a philosopher. He cared nothing for the burn along his arm, though when I came to look at it, I saw it was a bad one.

I told Jeshua to rub it with honey mixed with wine. Then I moved away from them, away from the fire, because I knew they didn't want me there. I could not have endured it to hear Jeshua say so. Instead I watched it in his movements. Then, shivering, I rolled myself into my blanket and tried to rest. I was so tired after the events of that long day, but I couldn't sleep. I couldn't lie still or find a comfortable bed among the stones, and so after two hours I sat up. I uncovered my head.

The stars were hidden in a veil of mist. It was the fourth night of the growing moon. Jeshua and the old man were lying close together.

My nose and my head were full of mucus when I got up. I moved over to the dead fire and blew it out between my fingers so it sizzled on the coals. Then I went to find the African. I climbed over the gravel ridges, and at first I stumbled and hurt my feet. But after a moment I could see the glow from the cloud-wrapped moon, which was touching all the surfaces as if with weak and feeble hands. I stumbled up out of the rocks, and then I found the open space where the Africans were camped next to a ruined wall. Two soldiers were there. They had lit a fire and sat staring into it. I could tell they weren't asleep, but they took no notice as I crept into the hollow where the Africans lay.

During the night Taima always had them loaded with more chains, to keep them from escaping. Shackles were placed upon their ankles and their wrists, which were joined together with lengths of chain, forming an **X** across their bodies. Even without the chains, a strong man would have had a hard time living in that desert alone. With them it was impossible, and so the soldiers didn't have to keep strict watch.

In the evenings sometimes you could see these slaves limp out into the sand to watch the sun go down over their own country. Then they would limp back and dig themselves a hole to sleep in. I found it sad to watch them, even though I hoped they would be well treated where they were going. Table servants, bodyguards, meat-fed, their black skin oiled and shiny—no one would pay for them to come such a long way and then work them to death in the barley fields. They had other less exotic men for that. These men were bound for the Scythian kingdoms, for Taxila and Peucelaotis, for the courts of Gondophares and Kujula Kadphises. Or perhaps if they were lucky, they would cross the mountains into the land of the Sericans, where the yellow-faced emperor lives in his palace of crystal and lapis lazuli, and even poor men wear silk, and no one dies before their time—I fooled myself this way, with these thoughts. Otherwise I couldn't stand it. Surely I of all men knew what bitter comfort these things were. Surely I of all men knew that to be treated kindly could be worst of all. Was it any wonder I hated these Africans, hated the sight of them?

They had laid the dead man out on a slab of rock. The moonlight seemed to surround him in a glowing mist. They had crossed his hands over his breast. One man squatted at his feet, another at his head, and I could hear the chains creak as he moved his hands. I could hear the two men murmur prayers in a language I didn't understand, a pulsing unison that would grow louder sometimes, then subside.

I have heard Meroë is a great city, full of all the races of the earth. These men were from different places: some of them were

Ethiopians, I knew. And some were from the Nuba tribe, the oldest and wisest race of men, who built the pyramids and the great cities of the Nile and were the fathers and the teachers of the Greeks. The green-eyed Egyptian, I knew he was from this tribe. Was it any wonder he terrified me? I crouched down in the darkness, and under my breath I made a prayer to bright Osiris, whose own brother had killed him and cut his body into pieces.

I, like my father, come from the warrior caste. We can make corpses, but we cannot touch them. It is a pollution for us. But I found myself looking at the dead man's skull, wishing I could see his wound more clearly. So at the same time I was praying to the god and piling curses onto jackal-headed Set, I was also wondering whether the man's skull would show an indentation. I thought perhaps that when he cracked his head a piece of bone had been forced down into his brain. I wondered where that indentation was. When I touched the gash above his eye, the bone was firm there; I had tested it. During the day when he was walking, there had been not a trace of red upon the bandage I had wrapped around his head. I had looked for it. Later in the evening the bandage had been soaked with blood.

Set murdered his brother and cut his brain apart. Wise Toth could not save him, nor could Isis, his queen. Wisdom and love could not save him. His body was divided into seventy-two pieces, and the Nile took them out into the sea.

I remembered picking bone out of the wound. In fact I hadn't given any thought to it, had worried more about the dislocation and the broken ribs. I had been proud of the way I had slipped the shoulder back into its joint, proud of my useless poultices. What could I have done? The man had died alone and far from home.

It was the Egyptian who sat at the man's head. Then he was talking to me. Maybe he had heard my prayer, or heard my breath, or seen me in the dark. He said in Greek, "We looked for you. You didn't come."

"I could do nothing."

I had been squatting next to the stone wall. Now I got up and crept forward. The Egyptian turned his head. I looked for his eyes but didn't see them. He was a black shape underneath the glowing sky. His head was covered with a shawl. And he said nothing more to me. I could hear the creak of his chains as he shifted his weight, and then the slow murmur of prayers again, the rise and fall.

I stood there for a moment, shamed. I thought about the woman, the hair on her lip and her white breasts and belly. Then I thought about Jeshua. All that night when I had tried to sleep, I heard them talking near the fire as Jeshua put honey on the old man's arm. They sat talking. Yet the woman and the African were dead.

And when, restless, I had gotten up, they were lying stretched out together, both asleep. How could they sleep? The African was dead, and the young woman too.

A Dog Barking

I went back and lay down. In the morning the boy came with our ration of parched barley flour in wooden cups. I got up before the sun rose and lit a fire, and made as careful a meal as I could out of what we had, which was yogurt, water, apricots, damsons, and some crusts of old bread.

At dawn Jeshua sat up in his blanket with his face puffy and his eyes full of blood. I brought his cup to him. He took it without thanks and angered me by sharing it with Philoxenus the Ionian, who had nothing of his own. Then they started talking about places in Palestine where both of them had been, excluding me as if I were a servant. As they had done the night before. In fact I could see with a kind of horror from the old man's gestures and expressions what he thought I was: a greedy servant who took half his master's food.

Jeshua said nothing to me. So I scurried about in the grey light, knowing that everything I did and everything about me added to the same impression—my race, my youth, my silent diligence, which had been meant to goad Jeshua into talking to me. Now he took the pot of honey from my bag without a word, as if it were his own. He mixed it with wine, and then he spread the thickened wine along the old man's arm as if he knew something about it, as if he understood how the wine dulls the sense, how the honey sucks the heat into itself. Honey cures everything that stings as the bee stings, but he knew nothing about that.

That morning we climbed down the dry ravine from Xur until we crossed the river. Then nine days through the desert with the mountains on our left, until we came to the Parthian town of Hecatompylos. It was their ancient capital, the birthland of the Parni tribe, the pasture where the horse that swept down to trample the empire of Alexander had been foaled.

Hecatompylos, and I had been expecting a great city with a thousand gates. In fact it was a dirty, dusty town. But as we came out of the eastern gate we passed the brick tombs of the Arsaces in a row, a place of pilgrimage. We came into the valley and the land was green. After a day, grass grew above us in the high meadows, and there were flowers and small streams.

Between Hyrcania and Nisa the land is softer, lower. There are deep wells that the Greeks built, and Greek towns in the oases. Here sometimes a traveler will leave behind the hardships of the desert and the mountains: the dry dust, the flies, the stones, the unforgiving sun. He will leave behind the wild beasts and come into dangers of another kind. The meadows are the grazing lands for cattle, sheep, and goats, and the wild tribes that tend them—the Dahae, the Xanthii, the Tochari, and the untamed Massagetae. Most barbarous of all, those creatures known to the Sericans as the Hsiungnu and to the Parthians as Hunns, who take no captives, who kill women and then suck their bones. The Serican king built a wall around his country to keep them away.

The road is made of stone slabs until Hecatompylos, and

after that it is a track of dirt and sand. It follows the route laid down by Alexander, though he was not the first Greek in this country. Heracles was the first, and then Dionysus the god, and then Dionysus the general, who crossed the Indus river with his army. Alexander found grandsons and great-grandsons of his soldiers in Nisa. And in Sogdania he found a city of Milesians, descendents of the men who sold their town to Xerxes during the great war.

After Alexander's death the Greeks ruled Bactria and Arachosia for many lifetimes, until the Scythians came. When my father was a child there was a Greek king named Hermaeus in the Paropanisadae mountains, north of Kush. And when Jeshua and I went by that way, we found Alexandria Larisa, the last trace of a kingdom that had stretched from Antiochia Margiana to the Ganges river.

Nisa is the border of this country. Farther on the land dries out again toward the Oxus river. But for a few weeks there was no dust, and the air was thick and sweet. We saw people on the road, and caravans from the opposite direction. They hurried along toward the safety of the town, guarded by troops of Parthian horsemen. Light-mounted archers like ours, but also now we saw for the first time soldiers of a different kind, cataphractii with high bashliqs and long pikes, their coats glinting with steel mail, their horses big and slow.

Once we stopped to watch a whole family of Massagetae cross the road, moving from north to south. There were about a thousand of them: men, women, and children, and perhaps ten thousand animals. The men were dressed in rough shirts and trousers, and they wore round caps on their heads. Their hair was red, their eyes were blue, and the women were unveiled. They stared at us as they hurried along, their baggage on their backs or else dragged behind the horses on wheelless wooden frames.

The Massagetae are nomads from the land of Colchis above

the Black Sea. Medea was their queen in the old days, and from her they have inherited their fierceness and wild pride. After the Greeks were gone, they spread eastward through this empty country from Colchis to India. For years they had lived above Marcanda, along the Jaxartes. Now they were moving south, driven by the bloody Hsiungnu, whose name floated like a whisper above them as they passed in front of us.

But except for the discomfort of our fears, which stayed with us after the road was clear, these were beautiful days. The desert lay behind and to the south of us. After the harsh sun and the dirty wind, which had burned our skin and then worn it away, these pastures of flowers were like heaven itself. Or would have been, except for the barking dog, Philoxenus of Pergamon, who traveled with us.

He was never quiet. He filled our ears with noise. In the towns and villages he would curse the shopkeepers and priests and tax collectors. He would make fun of any civic undertaking. More than once Jeshua had to stand in front of him, to protect him from angry folk.

Jeshua had heard of him when he was living with the Essenes at Qumrun. Philoxenus had traveled for years through Palestine and Asia Minor. He had not been in Pergamon since he was a young man, which did not surprise me—he was not someone to care for either family or friends. Nothing but himself and the sound of his own words. He was, as I have said, a deep-chested man, with a bald head and a red face, and legs that seemed too small and thin to support his weight.

He was not interested, as most philosophers were, in dialogue or argument. Instead he would speak maxims or aphorisms that he had clearly memorized, for we heard them over and over. His remark about the snake and the needle's eye, by which Jeshua had recognized him, was one of these.

Here are some others I remember. He said, "Happy I am when men hate me and reproach me, and when I go hungry.

Happy I am when they throw rocks and curse me. For if I serve the truth, I do not serve men, and if I tell the truth, then I do not tell what men most want to hear."

He said, "Do not be angry when a beggar asks you for an obol, for it is his, not yours, and you give it back to him. Do not be angry when he asks you for a drachma or a gold stater, for it is his. Crates of Thebes told us to hold our hands with the palms open, not tightfisted. And I say if a beggar asks you for your shirt, give him your trousers also."

He had a contempt for work of any kind. "Idiots and fools build houses and live in them out of the sight of God. They slave in their fields and pile up money. But I tell you life is more than food, and the body more than rich clothes. Look at the animals around us, look at the birds. Look at the flowers in the meadow, which do not dig or build, and yet great Artabanus on his throne has not a coat like theirs. Sell what you have and give it away."

In these teachings he was influenced by the brahmans of my father's country, who give up everything to walk naked on the roads. But he was different from them in the way he praised all nature. "Look at the locusts and the ants, are they poor? Look at the weasels and the crows. Look at the worms and the fishes, do they want what they have not? Look at the termites and the peacocks, are they unhappy? No, but if you want nothing, then you will lack nothing."

He mocked honor, pleasure, skill, work, and all the duties of the citizen. He cursed the temples, ridiculed the priests. "Men and women are the images of God," he said. "Especially when they eat, spit, shit, fuck, fart."

He did not believe in destiny or fortune. " 'This mad dog,' " he complained, mimicking fortune's voice. " 'He twists and turns, I cannot hit him with my arrows.' "

Once we were camped up in a meadow, in a circle of trampled earth. I was making him and Jeshua some soup, and I overheard him tell this fable as the sun went down. God did not make men, he said, neither out of clay nor out of flesh, nor did he bring them out of women. Instead he made monkeys, who lived in the forest and were happy as all animals are happy. The generations passed and the monkeys grew wise, and they learned war, desire, love, pride, pleasure, and the illusions of the world. They came out of the forests and walked on two legs, and built temples to their god. But God loves the monkeys, whom he made. He loves not women, and he loves not men.

Jeshua said, "I have heard of monkeys. Of course I have heard stories."

Philoxenus shrugged. "If you had seen them, you would not doubt they are our mothers and our fathers."

As usual I said nothing. But as I brought them their food, I was remembering the orange ape who stood in his cage in the Campus Martius. I was thinking of Sugreva, king of the red monkeys, and Lord Hanuman, who went to Lanka with Lord Ram. I remembered a friend of my mistress's in Tusculum who had kept a monkey on a chain—a nasty, spiteful, thieving, dirty beast. I thought Philoxenus was a fool. What can men and women have in common with such creatures? But Jeshua sat with his chin upon his knees. After a while he said, "Maybe it's not true they are our parents. If we live in the image of God, maybe they're our children, for our sins."

Before Philoxenus came, Jeshua and I had talked together in this same way, but without this kind of foolishness. Disgusted, I left them and climbed the hill, where I met one of the drivers who had become my friend.

No. To be fair, I cannot say it was all foolishness. Part of the reason I was angry came out of my own jealousy. For Philoxenus had been able to do what I could not. He had given Jeshua a reason to stand up in the morning and walk forward. Perhaps because he did not believe in his own fate, the old man could convince him there was something to be gained. Something to be chosen. Something to be done to change the bad luck that found him on this road. Perhaps if I had not been the source of so many of his misfortunes, I might also have been able to persuade him.

No longer did he tempt God and death with acts of stupid courage. Instead I saw tokens of a new idea: that God was giving him a chance to learn something, to see something and do something before he returned home. It was Philoxenus who gave him this idea, who was able to convince him that the world was full of questions. That God's domain was over the whole world and not just Palestine.

I had no country, and Jeshua had been cast out of his. But Philoxenus was on a journey to a distant place that he had chosen for himself. It was a land beyond the Indian Caucasus. "There is a lake beneath the mountain," he said. He was talking about the Cow's Mouth. He was talking about Lake Manosarovar. He was talking about Mount Meru, though he didn't know these names. It was a place where monkeys lived, he said. There was a forest full of monkeys. In the evenings he would speak of it. I heard him talking as I went up the hill, telling Jeshua about the Diamond Mountain underneath the pole. The gods live there. The great Lord Boddo makes his home there.

But soon I lost the sound of his voice. I went up into the cool night. This friend of mine, I cannot remember his face now. He was an old man. We lay down behind the rocks and he gave me news, because I was anxious about more than Philoxenus.

My friend said, "The son of Taiamersh was talking about you. It is not good."

I was afraid to hear. Ever since the death of the African slave, my reputation in the caravan had disappeared. No one came to me with their sicknesses anymore. No one came for readings or to play my number games, and Taima the Nabataean would not look at me.

Since the beginning when I had cured his camel, he had been suspicious. But because I had been clever and he couldn't know for sure, he did not accuse me. Still, he had begrudged us his protection, begrudged us every dry bite of food. He had used me for my skills and that was all. Once I had cured his favorite

driver of a lameness. I drilled through the nail of his toe and
drained out the blood, so he could walk again. Afterwards he did
not thank me. Nor did Taima thank me; he turned aside and spat
in the dust. The more miraculous my cures, the more he hated
me, the more convinced he was that it was I who hurt his camel
in the first place.

There was a problem with Philoxenus also. Taima hated
him ever since that first night when he had mocked him in the
agora at Xur. Taima had grown rich out of the hardness of his
life. He had no patience to be laughed at by a beggar. Especially
one who could not be silent, who every time he saw him laughed
some more and pointed his thick finger.

That night behind the boulders, my friend said to me, "In
Arat he means to sell you as a slave."

How was it possible I could not convince these camel drivers
of my value? Or perhaps I had. Valued but not loved. All of
them. Sometimes I had surrounded my treatments with false
magic and false prayers. It was a mistake. Now I could see it. A
clumsier surgeon could have been wrong more than right and
they would have forgiven him. But because I was infallible except
for that one time, now they blamed me for the African's death.
They thought I had murdered him with my potions and powders. None of them trusted me.

I lay with my hands behind my head, looking up at the stars,
and thought, of course, they meant to sell me. What else did I
expect? Why else would they have endured me for so long? And
I thought, not for the first time, how hard it is to keep your freedom on the world's stone roads, where every poor man needs
protection.

I lay comfortable and warm against the side of the old man.
As I fell asleep I thought, why not? Why not let it happen? I
calculated the rough price that Taima could ask for me—better
than for Jeshua with all his strength. Twice, three times as much
as for the cynic. Why not? Why not let them take me over the
headache mountains, through the Taklamakhan desert, and into

the country of the Sericans? As I fell asleep I thought perhaps I could find a master who was as kind to me as my old master Celsus, Cornelius Celsus, who had died so horribly, who had stirred his bath with bloody hands until the water was red.

The Hsiungnu

Beyond Nisa the road divides. It goes north toward Antiochia Margiana, south toward Alexandria Araeion, which the Parthians call Arat. The son of Taiamersh had gone the southern way. When we ran away from him, we went north and east across the trackless grass, hoping to find the Margus river.

We left the caravan the night of the full moon. There were five of us. It happened like this: The green-eyed Egyptian was named Cadmus. The night before I had gone to speak with him. I gave him a chisel that I'd stolen from my friend.

Seven of the Africans would not go with us. They had heard about the golden cities of the East. In Meroë they had been bonded workers, sold by their masters to the Arabs across the sea. Many of them bore on their shoulders the mark of the whip, which had broken their spirit and given them reasons to hope their new lives might be better than the old. They had no love for Cadmus, who was from a different tribe. And they had seen what had happened to their friend who had fallen down the well. He had planned his flight for weeks.

But Cadmus had been a free man, a wheat farmer from Opoun between the Nile and the sea. He had a wife and five children there. He didn't need to be coaxed. "Those men are cowards," he hissed when he met us behind the hill. "Their mothers were whores, their fathers were Greek slaves." He held up a length of chain, which he had used to strangle the guard.

With him was a boy from his own tribe whose name I never knew—he was the first of us to die. I had built a fire out of thorns, and after midnight we crept away from it. The soldiers were asleep. It was a beautiful night, the air black and soft. It seemed to rub against our skin. It seemed to blunt the sounds not only when we walked in the small grass, but in the dry rocks on the hills.

Cadmus and I had stolen food for us. I had a leather flask, but there was water in the meadows, I hoped. We were close to the Margus river, I hoped. I thought I could smell it in the darkness, and we walked toward it, north and east. We were close to Margiana. That was our plan, to reach the city on the tenth day.

We walked all night. And in the morning we found ourselves on a wide treeless plain. There were hills in the far distance.

We rested for a few hours in a chalk gully. Then we pushed on, though I did not think we would be followed. Taima was in a hurry, and it was dangerous to split up his soldiers. His road passed south of Margiana. He cared little for Jeshua, Philoxenus, and me, and as for the Africans, those who had come with us were the least valuable. One was too young, one was too sullen and too thin. As we rested, Cadmus complained again about the seven who had stayed behind, but I was grateful we were so few. Philoxenus shrugged. "Most men choose slavery when they can." When Jeshua questioned him, he said, "Seven out of nine," as if there were a recipe.

I mixed some barley flour with water, and rolled it into balls.

During the day we saw antelope and rabbits. We never caught them. But on the seventh night we stopped before dawn, because we felt a restlessness and a strange noise come from the valley in front of us. I knew what it was. I urged us away. Philoxenus agreed with me: He ate no meat. Hunger made him strong, he claimed. He was happy with flour and muddy water, though he had lost flesh. We all had.

But the boy was eager to find game. That day as we walked, he had made a sling out of a rock and a leather strap.

Now we lay still for a few hours until the stars grew pale. We listened to the animals and tried to guess their kind. We heard goats, cattle, horses, and sheep. But as for number, our rashest guesses were far short of the truth. We stood up astonished as the eastern sky grew pink. Below us in the valley stood more animals than we had ever seen. We had no way of counting, a million or ten million beasts. Some we had guessed, but others were strange to us—wild cattle with huge horns and a pelt like a bear. Horned sheep the size of ponies. Wild antelope with striped flanks, and they were all mixed together without any thought or order, a sea of beasts that stretched to the horizon and broke upon the slopes of the hill where we had camped.

Again I begged us to go. But the boy was already running forward, swinging his rock. A mist seemed to rise out of the packed bodies in front of us, but it was disappearing in the new light.

Jeshua pointed, and we saw two horsemen in a sea of cows. Their horses were so small, we had not noticed them. Nor could we understand how they kept to their saddles in such a press of beasts. But over the murmur of the herds we listened to them calling one another. We listened to their sharp whistles. And we saw a gap open up between the cows in front of them. They rode through, and then from the hill we watched a show of horsemanship unlike any I had ever seen. The beasts scattered and dodged as best they could in that enclosed space, and yet the two men rode through them almost at full gallop. They whistled and shouted to each other, then they were clear. Jeshua and Philoxenus ran down the hill, calling for the boy, but it was too late. Like Lampetia and Phaethusa, who preserved from bright Odysseus the cattle of the sun, these riders could not be appeased. They carried bows on their left thighs, quivers on their backs, and we saw one of them throw up his rein, string his bow at full gallop as he passed in front of us, all as quickly as the eye could grasp. He held his bow parallel to the ground and pulled the string back underneath his arm. The bow was short, but stiff and thick. The arrows were long, and we saw one of them lodge in the boy's throat, shot from the saddle of a galloping horse; it was astonishing. The boy's rock, flung in despair, did not reach half the distance. He threw his hands up and collapsed onto his face.

The other horseman had split away and come behind us, back behind the hill. We could hear his voice, and now there were more horsemen too, riding out of the herds. I watched them as they came close, especially the archer who had shot the boy. He was a short, stocky man with a big head and a flat face. He had no beard, just a thin tuft at the point of his chin and long thin mustaches. His round head was shaved smooth except for a single braid from the back of his skull, which hung down past his shoulders.

He wore a loose leather robe, open in front to his bare chest. The robe was tied with a long belt, and it was split at the sides, and I could see wide trousers, strapped tight around his leather shoes.

He wore no sign or decoration, except for some fox tails at his saddle bow, and coral earrings. But I knew he was the Hunn. I had known it ever since I heard the goats and cattle crying in the hour before dawn, in the tormented voices of the dead. Now I was ready. I had said my prayers to Toth, and Hanuman, and Mercury, and to the divine Augustus. Now I spoke to my father's ghost and told him I would burn a fire of juniper for him beside the water underneath the Cow's Mouth, if I lived. So far away. I stood on the hill with Jeshua, Cadmus, and Philoxenus the dog. I stood murmuring under my breath, watching the Hsiungnu as they walked their little horses up the hill. Their legs were strapped into their saddle girths in a way I'd never seen.

Philoxenus spoke to them. "Kind sirs, we mean no harm. You see us here because of an injustice, driven by our enemies without food or water or any kind of money into this hard land. If we have trespassed, pardon us. God loves the merciful and loves especially those who combine mercy with generosity, for we are hungry and tired. Just a little food for us. When we saw your herds we thought surely you would not miss some milk for us. God loves the poor. It is you rich men who are scoundrels and murderers. . . ." He would have gone on forever with this idiocy, though none of the Hsiungnu showed any sign of understanding. But the man with coral earrings walked his horse in front of us. In his right hand he carried his bow, unbent, but with an arrow on the string. It stuck out past his fist. He reached out and pricked Philoxenus underneath his chin with the bone tip, and made him quiet.

The horseman's robe was open. I could see his bare chest through the rent. It was hairless and brown, and bore across it a line of four round tattoos. Now one of the other men had ridden close, and I could see he had a black tattoo under his eye. His ears were strung with chunks of green turquoise, pulled through his lobes on leather cords.

I am remembering these things for two purposes. The first is to show a habit of the mind, which takes away the fear of death. But the second: Jeshua and I spent two days and nights with these folk, saw their secret homes, heard their stories, and then escaped out of their hands. Perhaps now I am the only one who can say that, who can describe them. Who can describe what all men fear. As we watched on the hill, one of them got down next to the body of the boy, and with a thin-bladed knife found the crevice in his spine, and cut through the round tunnel of his throat, and cut through the sinews and the bleeding veins, and then lifted up his head by his black curly hair.

Soon he was in the saddle again, carrying his trophy. He had taken barely four steps on the ground.

The Hsiungnu have neither art nor law. They eat nothing but flesh. They wear nothing but skins. They drink the blood of their enemies out of cups made from skulls. It is hard for me to think about, though my memory is clear. They took us to their camp. They made us walk northwest behind the hill. The goats called out to us in mournful voices as we walked away from them. Behind us rode five soldiers in a line. They didn't speak except to click and whistle with their tongues. They herded us like beasts. Others rode on ahead.

Once when Cadmus strayed too far from the rest of us and too far to one side, an arrow hit a clump of dirt near his left foot. In the air it had made a strange whirring hiss. A moment later, another arrow struck at the same place, this time from ahead of us. It too made a whirring noise, but lower, throatier. I walked past before the riders picked them up, and saw how each arrow, under its bone tip, was thickened by another piece of bone lashed to the shaft.

I thought, was this their language, their clicking tongues and whirring arrows? No one said a word to us. We walked through pastures that had been trampled and torn by the passage of the animals. We had no water but they did not let us stop, even when we passed a tiny spring. But then finally we saw their camp, which was a cluster of between thirty and forty tents.

The Hsiungnu had come there recently. The grass was still fresh under their wagon wheels, and they were still building some of the round tents. I looked at how they had been built. The walls were made of a thick wool or felt rolled down over a willow frame, and they had holes in the flat roofs to let out smoke.

People gathered round a wooden vat outside the largest of the tents. Now I know: The women make a liquor from mare's milk and fermented barley, which the men drink constantly from leather bags. They empty their bladders from their saddles, as we saw often during that first long march. They took their meals on horseback and did not allow us to stop. We were tired and hungry when we came into that camp. Philoxenus looked weak and old.

News of us had gotten back, and the people left the vat and came to meet us. They came out of the tents. The men rode away and left us in the middle of a circle of women and children, who laughed and made faces. Then, bolder, they came close, tugging at our clothes and blankets and slapping us when we pulled back. Insult led to insult, and soon we were surrounded by a crowd of brutes who pelted us with dirt and stones, who wounded our outstretched hands with daggers of blunt bone, who took everything we had, who stripped us naked and then marched in front of us, dressed in our clothes. All the time they were shouting in a language I had never heard, an evil jabbering which hurt our ears and drowned out our voices.

The children kicked and spat at us and grabbed at our bellies while the women, hanging back, laughed behind their hands. They had no pity. They shouted with delight when Philoxenus, chasing the boy who had stolen his cloak and bag, tripped over a stick that was thrust between his legs and fell onto his back. They closed their eyes and screwed up their noses. They were ugly, flat-faced, sunbeaten women, without modesty or shame. They exclaimed to each other at the size of Jeshua's penis and made lewd gestures to describe it. One of them raised her leather robe. She was naked underneath. Her wide belly and her sex were almost hairless. She had a birthmark under her breast and also a long dirty scab.

In fact many of our tormenters were unhealthy, cursed by the gods. Several of the children had twisted bones. Why had they had been kept alive? Some had crossed eyes, pocked skin, and other signs of idiocy, and several more had ulcers that were poisoning their blood. Their long hair was full of lice and flies.

I noticed these things to save myself. For when our minds are working, then we cannot feel pain. I stood without moving and took Jeshua as my model. Naked, he stood motionless and turned his back. He had not seen the women who had mocked him. Though his eyes were open, they had in them a brooding serenity, as if the boy who spat in his face, who rubbed dirt in his hair, who struck his shoulder with a cow's rib, was not there.

The boy felt something too, some cold lack of response, and he soon ran away toward Cadmus and Philoxenus. These two were shouting curses, and I could see the more they struggled, the more their suffering increased. But Jeshua stood motionless upon a rock.

Later when the Hsiungnu had gone back to their tents I found I was unharmed, while Philoxenus was so covered in wounds and bruises he could scarcely walk. Naked, Jeshua led us to a ruined cottage, which one of the horsemen pointed out to us with his spear. Philoxenus put his arm over his shoulders, and Jeshua carried him and laid him down on the bare earth near the wall. His mouth was bloody and he couldn't speak. He had lost more of his lower teeth.

There was a pond below us, down the hill. A wind came off its surface and came up into the cottage's broken side, its broken roof. We laid Philoxenus next to the wall and sat beside him without speaking. Even in the sunlight he was shivering, but in the afternoon a line of grey clouds covered the sky from east to west. Then I was afraid for him and all of us, for we were cold. We huddled together, naked and hungry, too beaten to think, while Jeshua brought us water and piled up the stones along part of the wall.

Later when he sat down I could feel the heat that thrust out from his body. I could feel it when he put his hands on me. I remembered the mud fortress in the marsh, how I had felt the fever in him when I lay by him. There it had been unhealthy. But here it was the only comfort we had, a fire that burned in him. As the sky grew dark I found I could lean against him without shame. He sat and put his arm around me and I leaned into his chest, and at the same time he had his hand on Philoxenus and was rubbing him and comforting him with small gestures and a few small words.

Cadmus stood apart, hugging his ribs.

Perhaps it was the difficulty of his journey that had hardened Jeshua and made him strong. Perhaps, sitting there with us, he remembered the times death had passed him by during these months. And perhaps those memories gave him courage and a sense of his own fate, a new hope that the gods did not intend him to die in that ruined hovel, struck down by the murdering Hsuingnu.

I had no such hope. I lay down against his thigh and tried to stop my teeth from chattering. And Philoxenus's cold skin was drenched with sweat. He said nothing this whole time, and I thought he was embarrassed by his foolishness. A man of words, now he could say nothing. We had met the monkey people he had boasted of in Taima's camp.

Cadmus stood apart. As the shadows grew around us, he began to speak, his soft voice in his dark body. And soon I could not see his chin or cheekbones or big nose, his green eyes, his bruised lips, or any of the lines of his face. His voice came to us out of the cold darkness, hesitant at first.

"No, no. I cannot stay," he said. "Since I left my house every moment has been like this. No, you think it is the worst one, here in this place. Oh but you men, what do you understand? The wind blows through me and blows toward the west. I tell you now, right now as I say these words, there is my woman somewhere in my house. Maybe it is morning there and she makes bread. Maybe it is evening and they are all there. I have five sons. I am a happy man. Five children and they all lived, because of my good woman and the happiness of God. Maybe in the dark they are there. And maybe I hope there is a little oil in the lamp and they have lit the lamp. In my mind I see them in the room. She has the baby in her arms."

And then he went on to describe each son, whose names I don't remember. But I too could see them, as we all could, straight, handsome boys, but thin and hungry in the small house—a small stone chamber like the one we crouched in, though the boys had patched the roof and filled the broken wall. The oldest two were strong enough to work. The woman he did not describe, but I thought it was because even in that place he couldn't share her. She was too dear to him. Still she was there in every word he said about the rest, and her face shone through theirs. His Greek was bad and his vocabulary small, but we could see her hidden in the words as if she wore a veil over her face. It was appropriate to her modesty, appropriate also to the mix of pride and sorrow in the Egyptian's voice: We did not want to see her features too clearly. We did not want to see her anxiousness as she waited for her husband.

Nor did he. "She does not know if I am alive," he said. "I left my house in Opoun because of a sickness in the grain. The Romans brought it to destroy us. I went down to the beach because my brother had a boat. We were looking for octopus in his string boat. We had to pay taxes to the centurion, so we went out farther, south of the port of Berenice, and we were taken by the Arabs in the gulf. They took us to Chersonesus on the Arab side and killed my brother, and now there is no one to go tell her where I am. That was the Roman month of January, when there was a storm. Now already the nights are cold. Already it is the ninth month since I saw her last. How do they live? If most people choose slavery, then you are all welcome. But I cannot."

Now it was full night, and I didn't understand what he was saying. Cadmus spoke as if there were a place to go. "You will see them again," said Jeshua. What did he mean? Cadmus was standing naked on the Bactrian plain. The wind came in through the split wall, and outside a grey light shone over the surface of the pond. Beyond it, under the hidden moon, the flat plain stretched forever north and west and east.

"There is no one here," said Cadmus. "No men or chains. We are not slaves here. But those men will come again tomorrow. They will kill us, and if they don't, we will die of hunger."

No one replied to this, though Jeshua shook his head. Cadmus had spoken all our fears. The plain outside seemed wide and dark as death. Surely in the morning or the afternoon the Hsiungnu would come to drive us naked into it. Like children, they had forgotten us for a few moments, that was all.

Something in this wind was making my heart cold, as it flowed out of the north over that endless grassland. In my mind I said a prayer to Hanuman the Great, whom the Romans call

Mercury. Who fought the bad king of the monkeys, who rescued Princess Sita from the demon's garden—Oh my God, I said, but I could say no more.

There was a wind above us that stirred the grey clouds. There was a wind over the pond, and we could hear the water lapping on the rocks. "No, tonight," continued the Egyptian. "Tonight I must go while I still have strength. North to the Margus river. To Margiana and the road. And then to Opoun," he added in a soft, wretched voice. He spoke as if his town were over the next hill. He brought his hand up to his face.

"Hush," said Jeshua, and I sat up straight. We sat listening to some shouting from the tents behind us. And there was a light coming toward us. We could see it through the wall. It was flickering and blinking, a small light coming down from the tents of the Hsiungnu. "Hush," repeated Jeshua, and he put his hand on Philoxenus's shoulder, and we watched the light come down the slope.

One man carrying a lantern, and we watched him come. We listened to his feet among the rocks. He stood for a moment outside the wall, and then he came in through the gap. He was carrying a blinded lantern in his right hand. Now he raised it and stepped in over the scattered stones. He raised up the lantern. It was a square tin box with a candle in it, and by its light we could see our own tired faces and see the stranger too, all except his face, which was hidden in a trick of shadow. He was dressed like the Hsiungnu in a leather coat, but he was not naked underneath. The gap at his neck revealed a shirt of dirty silk. The fingers that grasped the lantern's hoop were long and delicate. He wore a silk hat lined with fox skin.

He spoke, and it took me a moment to recognize the words. But when I did, my heart leapt up, for he was speaking the language of the five rivers and the Ganges plain, the old Aryan language which my father taught me, which he was speaking when he died.

I scrambled to my feet. I wanted to see the stranger's face. The others had more interest in the bundle he was carrying under his arm. He dropped it to the ground. There were some blankets and some clothes, and some meat wrapped in a basket of dried grass.

It was lamb's meat. I could smell it. And even though I hadn't eaten all that terrible long day, still what I most wanted was to see his face. Because I had heard my father mock the high, awkward voices of the Sericans and mock their tangled grammar. They are unused to speaking any language but their own.

He moved his hand, and then I saw him. He had a high forehead and long, noble features. His eyes were slitted like those of the Hsiungnu, but his face was not wide like theirs. His skin was not sunburned and dark. It was a pale gold color in the candlelight.

Cadmus had gone down on his knees and was pulling at the blankets. There were two of them, both ripped and tattered: they were the ones Jeshua and I had carried from Taima's camp. My shirt and cloak were there, and Jeshua's, and Cadmus took one of the blankets and put it around his shoulders. Jeshua took the other to wrap Philoxenus in, and when that was done he picked up the basket of meat. He had jammed his clothes down into his lap, and now he put the basket there also.

But before he did so, he looked up at the Serican and smiled. Then he raised his hand in a gesture I had seen among the Jews in Caesarea when they wanted God to bless a meal. In all the time I had known him, I had not seen him make that sign.

The Serican smiled too. Then he shook his head and let the lantern sag a little so I couldn't see his face. "No," he said in his high voice. "No talk Yavana talk," he said, using the name the Indians gave the Greeks. "Hear a little bit. You talk."

No one was listening but me. No one could understand him. Jeshua had opened up the basket and was dividing up the meat, which was cut into small burnt chunks. I was putting on my shirt.

When I was in Taima's camp, I had stolen many useful things, and now I touched the secret places underneath the arms where I had sewn them. Both purses were there.

Cadmus squatted down to chew his food. The Serican sat on a rock that had fallen through the roof. He was nodding and smiling, and he put the lantern down into the dirt around his feet. By its light I could see Philoxenus's face. He had rolled himself onto his side, and was wrapped in Jeshua's blanket. I could see the bruises on his face, but also a strange, closed expression. He would not sit up, and when Jeshua held a piece of meat down to his face, he set his lips together like a child.

"Here," said the Serican. "You take. Please."

I don't think he expected us to understand him. He was astonished when I thanked him in my father's language. "What?" he murmured. "What you say?"

"Rabbi," said Jeshua, which is what he called the old dog. "Master, take some meat." But Philoxenus turned his face into the stones. The Egyptian was pushing food into his mouth, chewing and swallowing with a brutal single-mindedness. The grease dripped down his chin. I was not hungry, and I found traces in my body of my old illness. My jaw ached, and when I opened my mouth the wind rushed into it and hurt my teeth. I could taste bile in my spit. Though it sickened me, I watched Cadmus chew and swallow, chew and swallow. I watched the meat move down his throat. To distract myself I said things. I asked questions, and my father's words lay on my tongue. The language was a kind of medicine. "Please sir," I mumbled to the Serican lord. "Who are you? What are you doing in this place?"

He opened his eyes wide. "No! I tell you," but he did not. He spoke for a long time in his odd, hesitant way, but he never said a word about himself. I thought perhaps I had been impolite. "Your pardon, lord," I said. "Where are we now?" He opened up his eyes, surprised I could ask such a thing, and instead he told me what he'd seen that night in the tents of the Hsiungnu. It was a feast for the sons of the fire tribe. The khaqan had gashed their chins to keep their beards from growing. He had gashed their cheeks to make tears of blood. Now they were drinking blood out of hollow bones—that is, if I understood him. He had to leave the tent, he said. It made him sick to watch.

Now he sat scratching the back of his neck.

But I had no desire to hear about this ceremony. "Great sir," I said. "What about your own country? Have you seen the eastern sea?"

He opened his eyes wide. "I tell you," he answered. "You fortunate person. This is king house. Tomorrow you see king. You see first son of Khe-che Khaqan, killed by Lord Cheng-tang in the old time." He scratched his chin and scratched his neck, and when I said nothing, he laughed.

We sat watching the Egyptian eat, watching the grease on his rough chin. Then, rubbing his wrinkled forehead, the Serican told me another story. And I could tell he was astonished by my ignorance, astonished I needed to be told how the emperor had given his ninth daughter to a chief of the Hsiungnu, whose name was Hu-han-ye. The emperor gave him land outside his palace in Changan. He did this to divide the tribes, and Hu-han-ye's older brother, Khe-che Khaqan, was filled with jealousy. He took his warriors and cattle and moved into the falling sun. In time he defeated all the tribes: the Wu-sun, the Chen-chu, the Kusan, and the Yueh-chih. In time he might have conquered all the world if he had not been cut down by the archers of Cheng-tang, when the emperor's army found him in the desert.

Since then the Hsiungnu had scattered west, led by the son of the khaqan. He was responsible for these choice gifts, the stranger said, indicating our blankets and our clothes. This was absurd; they were our own poor garments torn apart and then returned to us. I touched the pouches in my armpits. I touched the needle and the knife.

"My friends say the khaqan will kill us," I murmured, letting the words slide down my throat.

The Serican rolled his eyes. "No! Yavana no understand.

You fight, he kill. You not fight, he give gift. Later he give woman."

All this time, Jeshua had kept his hand on Philoxenus's shoulder, urging him to eat. "Rabbi," he said, "don't refuse it." Now he turned toward me, a question in his face.

I shrugged. Then in Greek, "He says they may kill us with stones." This was not true, but I spoke from my own fear. In my mind I made a picture of the young woman of Xur. Her white belly, her white breasts.

"No! Yavana no understand. You fight, then he kill."

Cadmus had eaten all the meat. It was because he needed it. He would need it for the days to come. Now Jeshua took the shirt out of his lap and gave it to him. He put it on, and then he stood rubbing his arms and his black legs in the shadow of the wall, beyond the trembling circle of the light.

Jeshua kept his breechcloth, which he knotted around his hips. When I saw him do this, I felt a terrible fear because at the same time the Egyptian was settling my blanket around his shoulders. But then Jeshua sat back again among the stones, his hand on Philoxenus's head.

"Come with me," whispered Cadmus.

But Jeshua smiled and shrugged and made a gesture that included both the old man and myself; I let out my breath slowly. "Will you go through Galilee?" he murmured.

Again, as if the Jordan river were close by. Not half the world away. Cadmus bent into the candlelight to look at him. Then he turned toward me, and in his thin face and his green eyes, his scrawny, greasy beard, I saw a hunger that could not be fed, that brought back an image of the house in Opoun, the patient wife surrounded by her sons. At that moment, unable to bear the strength of those green eyes, I looked toward Jeshua. His face was patient and anxious as he bent over the old man. Perhaps the rest of us were his sons too, the three of us and even the Serican lord, and then the fifth was the nameless spirit who was present in the gusting wind and in the candlelight. Who was deciding at that moment whether Cadmus's bones would dry and whiten in the desert or the grass, whether his body would be meat for the wild beasts. Or whether he would find his way. I said a prayer under my breath.

Cadmus stood up straight. He didn't speak another word to us. He put his hand out to touch the wall. Then he ducked his head and he was out the door, out in the dark, and we never saw his face or heard his name again.

All this time the Serican had been talking. His name was Feng, he said. He was a scholar. The magistrate at Kashga sent him to bring news from the Hsiungnu and all the western tribes. His high, awkward voice went on and on. But when Cadmus stepped out through the door, he wrinkled up his brow and opened his eyes wide. "He go make water?"

"No," I said. "To Opoun. To Egypt," I explained, and Lord Feng smiled and nodded, though to him the words meant nothing.

THE GREAT KHAQAN

Philoxenus had the blanket, and Jeshua sat with him after Feng had gone. I curled up in my shirt among the stones, and in the morning my skin was cold and hard. My eyes were sore. I climbed down to the pond and stripped and washed myself in the red dawn. I waded out into cleaner water away from the shore, and I drank to fill my belly. I was queasy and light-headed and my penis was stiff and hot, even in the water. I touched it with my fingers and I felt the passage open, which led from it up the middle of my spine and up into my brain. To touch it was a kind of torment, and instantly my seed leaked from the end of it, relieving the pressure in my mind. Nevertheless my jaw ached when I opened it. I turned my back to the red light and looked instead for Mercury among the clouds in the north sky. He was not there.

Then I went and lay down in the high grass until the horses came. I had no wish to see Jeshua and the old man. I undid the pouch in my left armpit and took out the knife which I had stolen from my friend, Taima's driver. It had a wooden handle and a hooked, narrow blade.

I lay back with the grass above my head. Then I slept for a few hours, because it was hot when the sun came up. When I woke for the second time, I could see the horseman above me. He had a spear in his right hand.

In the middle of the morning, six Hsiungnu warriors led us up behind the hill and into the circle of felt tents. Philoxenus was broken. All his manhood seemed to have left him. He huddled naked underneath his blanket, and from time to time a gust of air would pull up the corners and show his withered thighs. His lip was split, his face puffy with bruises, and there was a scab on his bald head.

Jeshua had only a black cloth around his waist and thighs and tied between his legs. His body was naked. His big arms, his beard, his hairy chest and back—they had not seen such hair before, I guessed. The people came down toward us and surrounded us. They laughed and pointed, but I sensed in them none of the cruelty of the previous day. The women and the boys came around us, and they touched his arms and chin. All the time they were leading us not to the tents and wagons but beyond them to a bare place in the grass. It was on the downward slope, and in the distance toward the southeast, I could see masses of cattle grazing almost to the horizon.

In the middle of the bare place sat an old man in a wooden chair. This was the khaqan, lord of the west, first son of Khe-che Khaqan. Feng never called him any names but these. He was a fat man with a fat neck, and his hair was grey. His beard grew down his chest from a tuft at the bottom of his chin. He was dressed in leather as they all were, but under it he wore a shirt. Over it he wore a mantle of grey fur, though the day was hot.

He wore a gold ring on his forefinger. In front of him on a frame of sticks near his right hand stood the aegis of the Hsiungnu, a painted leather shield trimmed in fox skin. Fox tails hung down from it.

Lord Feng stood by him with a few others. But most of the men were on horseback, as always. They seemed to come and go at random, walking their dirty, ugly ponies back and forth behind him and then riding away. As before, the crowd around us was mostly women and young boys, some of whom had fresh cuts on their faces.

There was sweat in my eyes and my head was aching, but I saw these things with a clearness that was almost painful. The pattern of cuts on the boys' cheeks. The pattern of the clouds in the sky. The pattern of the beasts in the pastures in front of us. It happened so fast. The crowd pushed us forward toward the khaqan in his chair. But we were still far away when they pushed us down onto our knees. Except for Philoxenus—he refused. He swatted at their hands. Then he staggered forward in the grass. He was muttering and complaining under his breath, a difficult old fool, and they were treating him that way. The Hsiungnu were in a pleasant mood. They laughed and smiled, and some of the children were imitating the old man's limping swagger, his toothless curses which they didn't understand. The khaqan in his chair was smiling too. He raised his hand.

"Peace," said Jeshua. He was half kneeling and half sitting, and behind us the Hsiungnu flopped down in the high grass. The women stuck their tongues out and the children shrieked, and in the meantime Philoxenus staggered foward, cursing and muttering. He pointed at the sky. He swung his arm in a circle. And because he could not keep the blanket closed around him while he made these gestures, he chose to let it drop. And he stepped forward, a naked skinny bald old man, his back covered with bruises.

Jeshua stood up. "Rabbi," he said, but Philoxenus was shouting now. He was shouting at the khaqan and the smiling warriors who paced their horses back and forth behind his chair. "Animals!" he shouted. "Animals! Murderers and pigs!" Then he was going on and on. I couldn't listen. The Hsiungnu were laughing at him. They didn't understand. I was watching them. My head was pounding and I could smell the wet stink from my own body; it was a hot day. Again in this crisis I found it difficult to think, and all I could see were the patterns in the grass when the wind found it. Patterns in the clouds. I listened to Philoxenus through the ears of the khaqan, a meaningless roar. And I could tell he was losing patience. He was still smiling, but a frown had appeared between his brows. His gold-ringed hand was raised. He spoke, but Philoxenus interrupted him.

Later I asked Jeshua what he said. All I could hear was the old cynic's barking voice and a rhythm that suggested lists of rules. I couldn't listen; he was scolding them for their bad habits, their bad smells. They were laughing at him, which he must have found intolerable. He staggered forward, waving his old arms, his voice rising higher. But then he crossed the boundary of the grass onto the bare, trampled earth. He stood in front of the kha-qan, shaking his fists. Saliva sprayed out of his toothless mouth. And, whether deliberately or by chance, he kicked the aegis with his foot, breaking the tripod of sticks. The shield fell down into the dirt.

Lord Feng and the others never moved. The women and children had fallen silent too. They were behind us. The warriors paced their horses, unconcerned, except for one. He was just a boy. His cheeks were freshly cut. He had turned his pony, whose coat was patched with black and white. Who had pieces of red ribbon in her mane. With her forelegs she danced a little pattern on the dirt. Then I heard a shout, and instantly, it seemed, within a few steps, it seemed, the pony was at a gallop, turning around the edge of the dirt circle where it met the grass. The boy had a curved stick in his hand.

Jeshua cried out. "Rabbi!" and then something else I didn't understand. I was looking at the boy. As soon as Jeshua started to run forward, I saw another of them turn—the pony was a speckled grey this time. This boy also raised his stick, which I saw now was a curved metal blade. A piece of sunlight caught it, for the clouds had split apart.

And so I ran forward too, because now there were two ponies moving. The grey came toward us through the grass. I leapt onto the back of Jeshua's leg and brought him down. He was shouting words I didn't understand. He was struggling and shouting, but I held him close around the waist, covering his body as the grey thundered by. When I raised my head, both ponies had slowed down to a walk again.

Philoxenus's body lay at the edge of the circle. But his head was in the grass. It lay face down in the grass, and a child ran to collect it. She held it up between her palms. It had been cut from the body with a single stroke through the spine. Blood flowed from the wound.

I turned my face into the grass again.

But later it was as if it had never happened. The Hsiungnu drifted away and left us. The khaqan got up and waddled away. The children and the women moved away.

Lord Feng was there. "You fortunate person. No!" he said. "You very fortunate." He was standing by the old man's body, which the Hsiungnu left where it fell.

The blood soaked the ground. It stained our feet. But they had taken the head. Jeshua looked for it a moment in the grass. He was bent over, and when he stood up I saw his face was dark. "No," he said, "no." And then he went down onto his knees beside Philoxenus's corpse. He put his hands out toward it, palms out.

But the Hsiungnu weren't done. Eight riders now came into the bare circle, boys with cut faces riding bareback. Each one was carrying an iron hook in his right hand, and one of them rode toward us. Bending down, his left hand upon his pony's neck, he thrust his hook into Philoxenus's stomach. He pulled the body up in front of him so that it fell across the pony's neck. It was as big as he was but he barely seemed to strain, because a corpse is lighter after the breath has left. He had it hooked under the rib cage, and then he cantered off.

Eight more riders gathered in a group two stades away, in another bare circle which I noticed now for the first time. One came out now to meet Philoxenus's rider at a midway point between the two circles. In a moment, from both directions the seven others followed. "Look, you see," said Lord Feng. He made a slashing gesture with his hand as if it held an iron hook.

Jeshua staggered to his feet. His face was red with blood, and he raised his fists into the air. The two riders had met in the middle of the field. Now they both had their hooks in the corpse and were pulling it apart as the others rode in from either side.

The game, Lord Feng explained, was to carry the corpse into the circle of the opposing side. There were no laws beside that. I watched for a time, but then I turned away. I had not loved the Greek, but this was too bitter a death, too bitter even for a dog. I found the tears rising to my eyes as I watched them hack the body. One would claim it and ride forward with the others around him. A knot of horsemen strugged across the field, first in one direction, then another.

Tears rose to my eyes. Feng was laughing and smiling but Jeshua was gone. After a time I turned away and walked back toward the ruined hut. When I was out of sight, I ran. But Jeshua wasn't there. He was at the pond. I saw him wading out into the water, as I had done that morning. I came down and squatted at the bank.

Jeshua stood in the water up to his thighs, and he was washing his arms, washing his hair, rubbing his wet hands over his body. He ducked his head under the surface, and the water flowed from him.

"What did he say?" I asked.

Jeshua didn't answer for a long time. He was rubbing his

shoulders and his arms. Then, "He told them not to eat meat. Not to cut meat from a living animal."

Then, "He told them not to pray to statues."

It was a hot day. Hard to be your own master on such a day. I made a gesture with my hand. I don't know what it was. But Jeshua saw it and his face took on an angry look, which hurt me. It was not a day to be apart from him, but now he turned away. He looked out over the water toward the north. "Don't laugh at him," he said.

Philoxenus had not been my friend. He had set himself up as Jeshua's teacher and kept us separate. I threw dust onto the surface of the pond. I said, "The old man thought there were choices and laws. But it was all words, and no one could understand him."

Jeshua washed his hands in the clear water. "He was a wise man."

"He talked and God didn't listen. God is like the great khaqan."

Now I could see Jeshua's face. He looked at me and then behind me up the hill.

"He died for nothing," I said.

I scattered stones onto the surface of the pond. They sank and disappeared. "It is you who are talking," replied Jeshua after a pause. "This is not a day for talk."

Then I stood up, and the blood and wind rushed through my head. "He was a hypocrite," I said, forgiving the old man nothing because he had died so terribly.

"Perhaps," Jeshua said. "But where were you when they killed the woman of Xur? Where was I? But he. . . ."

"No, he did nothing there. The woman died."

"It's true. He failed. But who are you to throw your stones at him?" Jeshua said this and was silent—shamed, I thought, because his phrase recalled the moment and the time.

Light-headed, I looked up. Above me a flock of birds flew south and west, a long straight line. I said, "We left the safety of

Taima's caravan because of me. I made us leave. That's why we're here. Because of me the old man is dead."

At first I thought Jeshua was smiling at me. But then I saw the expression on his face was closer to anger, though he had pulled his lips back to show his crooked teeth. "This is your pride," he said. "You play this game and no one else can play it."

I shook my head. But I thought nothing he had done could spread its claws into the present moment, whereas the choices I had made had hurt him many times, and he didn't know. "What about me?" he said. "What about the man on the Jericho road? Philoxenus told me what to do, what prayers to say. Now he is dead. Am I forgiven? I tell you, when my brother was born I left my mother's house because I was ashamed. The boy had no father, and I went to Qumrun because I was ashamed. I left her alone with the child and the work of the house, because I was ashamed. I was putting food into their mouths, working in the vineyard at Sepphoris, and I left her."

The water was around his thighs. The cries of the birds came to us down the hill, borne on the small wind that now troubled the surface of the pond. Jeshua raised his fists and I remembered my old master in the bath. Cornelius Celsus, his wet hands.

Jeshua turned. "Is it better?" he said. "Philoxenus gave me a prayer. Now he is dead. A fool, but tell me, are we better than that? Are we?"

When I said nothing, he brought his fists down into the water.

Later I followed him up to the house. I watched him through the door as he sat down on the fallen roof. The stone walls had supported a platform of logs, and a layer of earth and stones on top of it. Jeshua lay back against the rubble and looked out north through the open hole.

I waited outside until he said, "Come in." Then I stood in the doorway, too nervous to enter. From where he sat, he looked at me, and I saw as if reflected in his eyes how I must appear to him. I saw myself: almost a man, but small and supple as a boy, with a boy's hairless cheeks. Dark skin, dark eyes, and my black, curling hair. My ripped shirt loaded with objects I had stolen along the way.

"I wonder what to call you," Jeshua said. "Corax is your slave name, but that is far behind you. I've heard you tell people you're from Alexandria, but I think you haven't been there."

I stood in the doorway, waiting to come in. He said, "Maybe you were right to call the old man a hypocrite. Didn't he say if someone wants your cloak, give him your shirt too? Didn't he say we should come to others with our hands open and not closed? But maybe it's impossible to be so pure. Maybe if we can just forget our pride. So listen to me: My mother lives in Nazareth, where she is famous for her beauty. She washes clothes in the village, and my brother herds goats."

I stood in the doorway with my hands clasped. I thought about what others had told me about Jeshua's mother—that she was a whore. Then Jeshua said, "Come sit by me. This place is like the end of the world. It's hard to think there is a world beyond it."

I came in but I couldn't sit down. I stood in front of him, tears in my eyes: "My father was born on the riverbank in the great city where Ashok was king. The river from the Cow's Mouth."

Jeshua closed his eyes. "Yes," he murmured. "The old man told me. 'Where Boddo lives under the tree.'"

"The river flows out of a lake," I said. "There's a lake below the Diamond Mountain where we can be made clean."

A wind came through the broken wall. "Is that where you are going?" Jeshua asked.

I said nothing. "What crime have you committed," Jeshua asked, "that draws you to that lake? What have you done?"

Then I told him about the pain in my head, my heterocrania, and the cold wind in my arteries. "I want to be cured. The water takes the pain away. You know the lake is the dividing place, and everything that happens up to then is washed away."

Jeshua's eyes were closed. Perhaps he was thinking about something else. Perhaps he was thinking of Philoxenus or the old man in the dust upon the Jericho road. The man whom he had beaten and robbed, and left for the Samaritan. Or perhaps his mother, the last time he had seen her.

"My name is Suryaprabha," I went on. "After the boy in the story—it's the name my father gave me. But I am Corax, which means 'little crow,' till I reach that place. For my master's sake, but when I reach that lake I will be baptized. You know in Mithra's spelaeum, outside of Tusculum, my master never took me to the pool. He never washed me there. Now he's dead. But I will go up to the Ganges river and make a pindi for my father. I will complete my promise. I will be forgiven."

My words were senseless babbling, and I could feel tears on my cheeks. "Yes," said Jeshua, his eyes still closed. "Tell me about the lake."

Then I sat down near him among the stones. "The road goes up from the town where the rishis live. Where the river meets the mountains. Up through the wild mountains. It's a long road, but there are many pilgrims. Saints live in the caves. The river flows out of the Cow's Mouth, which is in the ice. Above it there is Tapovan, past Shiva's Penis, and the road through the snow. Then to the lake, which is the color of milk. Which is the cow that nourishes us all. Then you can see the Diamond Mountain, called Kailash. It is the navel of the world. It is Olympos, home of the gods."

Jeshua opened his eyes. "You're sure of it," he said. "You call it the dividing place. A lake in the mountains far away.

"Where God forgives," he said, "and then we can return to our own places.

"Like Cadmus the Egyptian," he said, "but what if it is simpler? What if the river, the mountain, and the lake are in our minds? What if the pure land is inside of us? And the forgiveness—nothing which exists. Nothing you can make with words or deeds. No. This is what I say, in the morning and the night, as if to someone who is there. Standing behind me. Mother, forgive me. Forgive my debt. Give me something to eat. Keep me from harm, though it is your choice."

I sat with my hands clasped together in my lap. "Maybe it's as simple as that," Jeshua continued. "Or maybe both things are true, outside and inside. Philoxenus of Pergamon was walking east. He had heard about the Diamond Mountain. He had heard about Lord Boddo underneath the tree. Who went into the desert and starved himself.

"You see?" he said. "Since I met the old man I have had such dreams. Philoxenus said I must go onward before I can go back. West shall be east, he said, weak shall be strong. Last shall be first. He told me to look among the followers of Boddo for news of my own people. Then I had a dream."

But I wasn't listening anymore. Because I could hear the sound of a man coming toward us, down the hill. I could smell the roasted meat. The man came in, the Serican lord in his fur cap, and he was carrying a basket in his hands. And he was smiling. There was meat in the basket. "Mother, forgive me. Yes, you see?" said Jeshua. "Maybe it's so simple."

CHAPTER

5

THE LAST OF
THE HELLENES

THE TALISMAN

Lord Feng brought us meat and a leather cloak made from the skin of a long-haired cow. He brought us a leather purse with a gold coin inside. I fell asleep after he'd gone. I slept a long time. In the middle of the night I woke to the sound of neighing horses and the shouts of men. I woke to my own fear. I looked up at the black sky through the broken roof until I thought I saw a flickering there, a fire under the clouds. My mind was the same way, black with a flickering across it, which was Jeshua's talisman: Please forgive me. Forgive my debts. Bring me food and drink today. Keep me from harm.

I repeated it over and over until it made a restless song. But the words never seemed right, and I knew I was changing them.

Jeshua lay near me. Even in the darkness I could tell he was dreaming. I could feel the stiffness in his body. And the noises that came from him were not gasps or snores. But they were words, although I couldn't understand them.

I slept again, and then the sky was red. When he woke up, I asked Jeshua to repeat the talisman, and he laughed. It was a long time since I'd heard him laugh, or laughed myself. "The words are not important," he said, which I doubted. I remembered the charms that my old master had taught me, talismans from the temple of Mithra. In these matters the gods are as narrow and as proud as kings. An illness can't be cured except by the specific remedy. Dion also had taught me charms to say over a wound and struck me on the hand if I made a mistake. These incantations must be found and tested, and every word must be in place. It is a patient wisdom. I told all this to Jeshua, and he laughed again.

"You see how quickly it happens," he said. "Thinking turns into belief. It hardens and grows stiff."

He refused to tell me the right words. But perhaps in my sleepy fumbling I had struck the formula. Perhaps also it was Jeshua who caused the miracle, as he had the night before. Then food had come when we were hungry. Now we went out into the day. The Hsiungnu were gone.

I thought, are we forgiven also? Out of politeness to the god, I imagined how our enemy had been defeated by an awful power. It had rolled them up and crushed them into dust, but Jeshua said nothing about that. When we were on the hill he pointed to the marks the wagons made. At first light the Hsiungnu had broken camp.

It was a curious, grey day, and though there was no mist in the air, it was impossible to see any great distance even on the endless plain. I went to where the tents had been to see if I could scavenge something from the cook fires. But there was nothing, just garbage and hot bones and some scraps of smoldering wood. I stood in the circles of torn earth and yellow grass, looking north, and I could see a disturbance in the air. At first I took it to be a mass of beasts and men, covering the plain at the limit of my eyesight. But then it rose up toward us through the air, a sudden wind. It swept over the high grass. It circled around us, pushing from all sides at once.

Then as I watched, the western sky was broken by a thunderbolt out of a grey cloud. The rain came. At first I was glad, and I stripped off my shirt to let the rain wash me. I imagined the rain washing the ground where the Hsiungnu had stayed, washing their filth away. I stood with my teeth chattering as the thunder burst around me and the rain fell in stinging drops.

But then Jeshua was there. He was wearing the skin that Lord Feng had left us, but now he stripped it off and wrapped me in it. He led me back to the stone hut. Against the wall there was some shelter.

The night before, Lord Feng had sat there. He had talked and laughed, and I had worked to understand him. "You fortunate person," he said. At the time I thought he was referring to the gifts he'd brought us—the thigh of a sheep, roasted in the fire, too much for one night. The gold coin, which carried on one side the portrait of a beardless king. On the other a tower of stones and under it the word BODDO in Greek letters.

The fur cloak and blanket. We huddled in them until the rain broke.

Then toward mid-morning, under a grey mist, we set off toward the southeast, away from the track the Hsiungnu had left. Away also from our small plans, away from Margiana. Nor did we retrace our way. Taima had gone south along the road to Araeion, so to avoid him and the Hsiungnu, we struck south and east across the rising plain. We had the rest of the meat, three tubes of barley flour which I had hidden in my shirt, and water from the pond. I cut a patch of leather from the skin to make a bottle. I sewed it and then caulked the seams with clay and hair, but it always leaked.

This was the beginning of a terrible march, which took us from the plain into the mountains. It was our thought to leave behind the watered pastures, because of the tribes who lived there. It was too dangerous a place for lonely travelers. Soon we left the grasslands and came onto the dry steppe, which stretched east toward the Margus river and beyond it.

After the golden grass, the stones hurt our feet. We suffered from thirst in the hot sun. When the water had all leaked away, we lived on what we found. We were lucky, for the storm had passed before us. For three days we found pockets of water among the boulders.

On the fourth day we crossed the river. It was a small stream through a barren valley, and we followed it up toward its source. We had wanted to go east but feared there was no water. So instead we turned toward the south and followed the stream into mountains east of Araeion, toward the Bamian valley and Kapisa, a long, weary way. During the afternoons the sun burned our shoulders and our necks. At night we rolled up in our blankets and pressed between the roots of dead trees, which were common.

We had hoped to find towns along the river. We had hoped to find food. But it was all empty. The Hsiungnu had passed that way. One town we came to as we climbed up off the plain—it had been burned. The autumn barley had been set on fire. The wall was broken. Every house was empty.

"Keep me from harm," I murmured. "Keep me from harm." Jeshua led me, and I followed.

Once my old master had shown me a cave in Tuscany, one of the caves his ancestors had lived in before Aeneas came to Rome. He had a torch in his hand. He showed me painted pictures on the wall. Horses and cattle and men, and I followed him back into the cold earth, out of reach of the grasping sun. Water flowed out of a crack in the rock.

Now in the Margus valley, sometimes it was as if I closed my burning eyes. I followed Jeshua into the dark. He led me as if underground, sheltered from the sun, and the words of the talisman were like the figures on the wall, leading me back and back into a dark, cool land. Jeshua was my guide, and I surrendered to him as he led me between pockets of water in the scorched rock, and then up the sandy stream. Underground, I thought, the world might still be fresh. Underground. I climbed back into the cave in my mind and hid there in the dark until my eyes changed and I saw a light far up ahead. It flickered like the torch my old master had held up. He had gone ahead and I had stumbled after him, holding out my hand. He was looking at the paintings. Now I saw beyond him there was a light set into the rock, set into a window in the rock. A house had been carved into the cliff, and the light burned in it. I entered in and saw there was a bed laid out for me along the wall, a rope bed with a feather mattress and a feather quilt. Nearby stood a wooden table, and on it were a bowl of hot water and a bowl of oil, a sponge and pumice stone for washing, and a candle on a silver spike, which showed a whole feast laid out for me. It was like one of the dinners I had served for my master in Tusculum. In fact now I saw many of the dishes were the same—the rice-stuffed partridges, the sardines in lemon oil and liquamen, the honey custards and sweet ices, the artichokes from Lugdunum in Gaul. The table was a long one. It stretched back and back. There was a pike fish, and there were silver plates of mussels in pepper sauce and fried squid. There was the roast leg of a pig. There was a pitcher of wine for me, and new clothes were on the bed, made of the white cotton that Cornelius Celsus liked.

But my feet were splashed with blood. I sat down to wash them. "Master," I said, "I can't walk anymore."

So we rested between two dry hills. Jeshua's lips were cracked and bleeding. The meat we carried was full of flies now. He cut off a piece of it and held it out to me. I closed my eyes and shook my head.

Then I felt his hand. I was leaning back against a rock, and his hand took me by the mouth and forced it open. My throat was trying to close, but he pushed the chunk of meat behind my tongue. He had already bitten it in two so that it wouldn't choke me. Then he sealed my mouth with his big hand. He pushed my head back against the rock until I stopped struggling and I swallowed.

He hadn't spoken in days, or else I hadn't heard him. Now he said, "This is a game of yours. A child's game. The way you play at sickness. I've played it with you for some days, but now I've lost patience. Do not count on my debt to you. You go on a journey in your mind. But this land, this place, this time—nothing takes us away from it."

Then he said, "You think you are cunning and strong. Yes, except when strength is most required. Open your eyes now. What use is it to travel the whole day, except for the last hour? Look for yourself. I will not take you any farther."

In the open air I saw the sun had settled down behind us into a layer of dust. An orange light painted the rocks. "Master, forgive me," I breathed. "Forgive my sins. Give me food to eat, water to drink."

But Jeshua's words dripped away like water. That night it was cold, and the next day we were climbing among the rocks. The river came down next to us, a fast stream now. The water crashed over the stones.

In my mind I was in the house at Tusculum where I was born. I was standing in the dark corridor when Dion the Egyptian came out of the room. "Your father asks for you," he said. His hands were wet. It was a question of time.

There was no window, just a lamp. I sat down on the dirt floor by my father's head. He was lying on his stomach, and his fingers curled through the ropes of his low bed.

My father was a drunkard after my mother's death. She bled to death under his hands, and after that he rarely spoke to me. I thought it was because I looked like her. I thought my face was a reproach to him, but perhaps I'm wrong. Perhaps it's natural for fathers to lose interest in their sons when they come of age.

When I was a child he was my teacher. He sat with me hour

after hour. But a boy as he grows older is like plaster as it sets, harder to form, except with grunts and blows. After my mother's death he left me to Dion of Alexandria and Cornelius Celsus.

Now he was close to death. He was laughing when I came in. There was a bowl of vomit that had spilled into the dirt, and a clay cup of wine. "Your man is an ignorant fool," he sputtered, as his laughter turned into a cough deep in his lungs. Then later in the Aryan language that Lord Feng had spoken, "He is not a true vaidya. He is not a true surgeon. He does not know one word of the surgical mantras. He does not know one word of the Atharva Veda, the Charaka, or the Sushruta Samhita. He knows nothing of the 3 doshas or the 107 marmas. How can he hope to treat me? And his hands are black, as black as yours. Unclean. I didn't let him touch me."

He had lighter skin than I—a disappointment, as he never tired of reminding me. The oil lamp shone over his thick white hair, which fell down on his forehead. Moisture bubbled on his lips. "Give me some wine," he said, and when I handed him the cup he fell back on his side.

"Well, this is ridiculous," he said, laughing again. "The last son of Udayana, who was captain of the elephant guard. Here he is, finally dying among these casteless vagabonds. My father made me promise that wherever I went, at the end I would come back to the holy city. The river that flows out of the Cow's Mouth, what has become of that? I promised him. Yet here I am in this filthy room, dying by myself. No, except for my dark child out of the Italian whore, who never understood a single thing I taught him. Who has no notion of the laws of dharma or the duties of his caste. Who is a catamite for the degenerate Romans— oh my son. Celsus will never let you go. But will you carry my bones to the great river and say a prayer for me?"

And later, "Will you step into the water, and with a seven-metal cup pour out a stream that catches the dawn light and the last light of evening? Will you speak my name, my father's name? Will you make the pinda offering? Will you take my bones and scatter them into the water?"

Later he told me a story. As I listened, tears came to my eyes, for I could not but remember the long afternoons when I was a boy. After I had made my recitation of a hundred verses from the Sushruta Samhita, after I had made my practice cuts upon a melon rind, upon the leg of an animal, upon a doll, then he would sit with me in the courtyard and tell me stories. Now I remembered how much I had loved him. This was a man who I had seen make a new nose for a leper by cutting a flap out of his forehead, twisting it to keep the vessels alive, and bringing it down over new nostrils he had constructed out of clay. Now his hands shook so badly that he couldn't hold his cup.

When I was young, the stories he had told me were all alike: how a poor boy from the warrior caste would leave his home and walk across the world, and come at last into the city of Pataliputra, ruled by Priyavaraman the Just. Along his way he would outwit demons and shopkeepers and whores. He would marry a spotless virgin. "Listen," said my father on that last day. "There once lived in the village of Brahmasthalaka on the Hydaspes river, a young man named Suryaprabha. His skin was fair and white, not like the sun but like the moon, so much so that the cakora birds, who eat moonbeams for food, would perch in the evenings on his balcony, waiting for their supper. Now one year when the elephant of winter was still stirring with his tusks the lotus pools, and the lion of spring had not yet come out of the jungle to challenge him, in that year Suryaprabha's father left this life to embark on another. Now the old man was a drunken fool, but if duty toward a good father is a virtue, how much more virtuous is duty toward a wicked one, in which there is no self-interest. . . ."

Then he told me the story of how the good son loaded his father's bones onto his back and walked across the five rivers toward the Cow's Mouth, where the Ganges flows down from Kailash out of Shiva's hair. He was tormented by a demon who followed him from the cremation ground, who stole away the bones over and over again and would not return them until Suryaprabha had answered some riddle or performed some task. But he would not be discouraged, for "harder than diamonds," said my father, "more precious than gold, is the constancy of a good man."

I came to myself next to a rockfall on the banks of a small stream. We were coming into the high mountains now, and in the distance I could see the ice peaks. And still the valley was deserted. Jeshua stood beside a broken wall. Flies drifted around me.

I could hear flies buzzing near me. Jeshua came back and I saw what he had been looking at: a pile of skulls and bones next to the wall. The Hsiungnu had built a tower of skulls, and then it had collapsed.

"Stop your crying," Jeshua said. "Stop your sniveling before I beat it out of you. Here," he said, and he sat down beside me. His body had lost flesh. His skin was dark and blistered from the sun. His lips were bleeding. "Shut up. God curse you. Here," he said, and he squatted down. He had found grasshoppers to eat, which lived among the bones. He had mixed them to a paste with water and barley flour.

My feet were torn upon the rocks. But he didn't let us stay. In the morning he unwrapped me from the bed that he had made, and we continued up the path. "Look around you," he said. "Don't let me lead you like an animal." In the morning I did what he said. I looked up as the way got steeper. We climbed up a dry ravine where the boulders were as big as giants' fists. Above us loomed sharp peaks covered with snow.

Behind us the valley and the plain had sunk down into a burnt mist. I looked back as we came into the mountains and left behind us the last trace of men. How can I say what I thought? We were going to die in that wilderness.

The gods want men and women to live together, which is why they collect into towns all of their temptations and delights. Outside they put wild beasts and the harsh lands. My heart sank with every step we took.

But again I took refuge inside the caves of my own thoughts, beyond the reach of the grasping wind, the hammering sun. I crawled into the crack that always leads to the past. But this time I felt no comfort there. My head ached, and I could tell with a sick feeling where I was. I knew the time and place. I saw the stain of palms and fingers along the plaster wall. And there was something about the grease of the fingers, the coarse grain of the wall, the crack in the shape of a rooster's head that opened up again no matter how often it was repaired—something about these clear small things that made me understand there was no refuge here. I could feel the skin move between my shoulder blades, exactly as it had when I stood in the storeroom in Tusculum with my ear pressed to the wall, listening to the sounds Cornelius Celsus made with the new boy he had brought from Epiros, a boy so young he had no hair on his body.

Cornelius Celsus was a stingy, fat, filthy old man, and my father was right. He had no intention to let me go, even after he had cast me aside, out of his heart. In Rome men freed their servants after five years or ten years. There were liberti high up in the administration of Tiberius, but no, I was too valuable, and after Celsus died his young wife would keep me just for the pleasure of watching me grow bald and toothless, cleaning the chamber pots or carrying bags of grain. These thoughts made a storm inside my head, a mist before my eyes that whole fateful day as I pursued my duties in my room, copying and correcting one of Celsus's idiotic manuscripts on the flow of blood. Now as I watched myself, I read the text for the second time through the veil both of memory and that old emotion—in the afternoon I took the heated towel to my master's bath. When we were alone I reproached him and accused him in words that could not be forgiven or taken away. He laughed. "I've had enough of your jealousy," he said. "You've become like an old woman," he said, which stunned me and amazed me.

Now I saw myself kick over the brazier of scented water so the coals spread over the threshold. From the bath he cursed me for my clumsiness. He stood up with the water around his knees, and in his hand was his steel razor, for he had been shaving his face when I came in. Now he put down his mirror and tried to get up out of the bath, but I pushed him and he slipped. He cracked his bald head, and the razor slid across the tile, and I reached for it. For a moment he lay dazed in the water, and as the smoke started to move across the wall I stepped down into the bath. His arms lay stretched out on the surface of the water, so with the razor I uncovered his veins from the inside of his elbow to his wrist, following the diagram that I had just revised in his stupid book. Then he woke up from the pain and started to flail his arms so that banners of blood spread out through the water from the cuts. I clambered out of the bath and stood over him as the flames from the red coals started to spread, and he never cried out. He never cried out.

There are some things that should not be remembered. They must be transformed underground. I scrambled up into the light and found myself alone. I was sitting on a rock, looking back toward the valley of the Margus. I had no sense of how much time I had spent in these thoughts. I had no sense of how many hours I had spent laboring to give form to these images. My head ached and my stomach ached.

Always I had had this skill, to leave the world and find a sweeter place inside my head. A shadow landscape made of memory and desire. But this time there was no refuge. I climbed back gratefully into the world, and I was sitting on an old blanket in a wilderness of stones. Above me the trail climbed up through the ravine. One side was in shadow, and the afternoon sun burned on the other, on the dusty walls of rock.

And then I saw Jeshua above me on the trail. He was at the limit of my eyesight, a small ragged figure toiling up the slope. I cried out but he didn't turn, and perhaps he couldn't hear me because my voice was just a croaking in the bottom of my throat. I waved my arm, but he didn't see me, and I felt a cold wind blow through me up the ravine. Jeshua had left me some food, some dry flour without water, and in my haste I too left it there, an offering for the cruel gods who lived in that place. "Forgive me my sins," I croaked, and then I hurried up after Jeshua, who had disappeared among the shadows of the rocks.

There was a pass between two dry hills. I could see it when I came out of the ravine, and I could see the trail, which was less steep now. There were cairns among the rocks, and when I came into the pass itself, I saw a spire of stones twice as high as a man, rising up out of the trampled earth. As I had seen on the gold coin. It was a shrine to the god my father called Siddhartha and Jeshua called Boddo, the Greek form of an Aryan word.

Jeshua was there.

LIONS

I speak about this time as if dreams were more important than the world. It is the way I remember it, a measureless distance of stony wasteland. My head ached, and I saw everything as if through a curtain of light and shadow. I suffered much from heterocrania. At night I lay awake on the cold ground.

We were hungry. We had no food for this journey. The meat was long gone. Jeshua carried the bag of barley which I had stolen from the son of Taiamersh. I had hidden it in the seams of my old shirt. But there was not enough to feed us for those endless days. I knew it, but I didn't ask myself how it happened. How night after night there was always a little bit left. I would watch as Jeshua unrolled the old cloth bag.

He was skilled at finding water among the stones. Whether a tiny pool of old rain or else a tiny spring, he sat cross-legged next to it. He unrolled the worn fabric, and in some fold or crease of it he found just enough of the grey powder to make a cheerless meal. Night after night he rolled up the bag and there was nothing in it.

Sometimes our way was blocked by landslides to the right and to the left. Yet Jeshua could always find a trail. Not once did he seem in doubt, even when the valleys came together.

Once when we had come into a high pass, and there was ice around us in the shadow of the rocks, Jeshua found the entrance to a cave. My fingers and joints were numb, but inside Jeshua found some brambles, which he lit on fire. I don't know how. Once a great stone slid down from the mountain toward us. He lifted up his hand as if to ward off a blow. The rock slowed and stopped.

I was too tired and feverish to think about these things. But now I look back and it seems clear. Many times in that desert I made prayers to Father Toth, to Hanuman the Great. When the sun rose I would pray to Indra or to my master's god. Now I can see how Jeshua had been given strength in answer to these prayers, to help me and protect me. Or else I would have died there in those places and never reached the Diamond Mountain. I would have never—no. Perhaps I still don't understand why my life was spared or for what purpose.

Once we lay down in a flat place in a circle of stones. It was an airless night under a full-moon. We ate water mixed with barley flour, and then Jeshua stretched out on his blanket.

I sat up for a while longer, looking at the stars, watching Jeshua as he slept. Often now his dreams were violent. Often he would cry out and throw up his arms. Or else he would sit or even stand up—fast asleep, his black eyes open.

I looked up at the stars. There was no wind. Only I saw a movement in the shadows beyond the rocks. Two long black shapes came out from behind the boulders. They made no sound.

At first, I'm sure, I felt no fear. My hunger and exhaustion had made me weak in some ways. But in other ways they had made me strong, or else I could not have endured these visions of my father and Cornelius Celsus. Now I thought for a moment that these shapes were demons out of hell, sent by black Ahrimmon to punish me for what I'd done, for what I had not done.

I felt no fear, and my prayer to Hanuman was small and wistful. I was so tired and sore. "God, my God," I said. But perhaps that is enough. I was too tired to move.

But at the moment when the shapes came clear, I could see them for what they were: two monstrous cats, hungry in that dry land. At the moment when I first could smell the dirt from their bodies, at the moment when the sound of their huge paws among the rocks first came to me, then Jeshua started awake. Or not awake—he had been dreaming, muttering to himself, clasping and unclasping his hands. Now he struggled to his knees, froth in his beard, dirt on his wasted face. Blood burst from his nose and dropped onto the sand. "No," he shouted, his eyes bright, and the lions shied away. He labored up onto his feet, his arms stretched wide. And perhaps those beasts recognized in him some spirit of Venethragna, or Heracles, who killed the lion and wore its skin.

He remembered nothing in the morning. That was the day we climbed up the pass where we saw the stupa to Lord Boddo. It was a column of thirteen round disks—the spheres of heaven, as I discovered later. It was built onto a boulder. At the top, a token of the sun and moon.

We sat underneath it. And in the afternoon light Jeshua prepared the last of our food. There was a pocket of rain water among the rocks. He sat down cross-legged and unrolled the bag. He searched in it a long time until finally he found a seam of flour, which he scraped out with his fingernail onto his palm. Then he mixed the grey dust with water and rubbed it carefully into a ball. Then he split the ball into equal parts and laid them out for me to make a choice, which was his custom.

First I had to drink some water from the rock. My head was throbbing, and it was hard for me to stand. I crawled over to the pocket of water and then crawled back, and I saw him turn the bag of barley inside out and shake it. No dust drifted from it. It was empty.

I took the ball of food onto my tongue. I was too weak to feel hunger or despair or fear. I sat back against the boulder below the spire of rocks, closed my eyes, and let the barley dust turn into a thick layer on my tongue. I was sure I was too weak to swallow, but when I opened my eyes, my mouth was empty.

We had come over a pass between brown hills, the lowest place on a high ridge. In the distance on either side, a line of white-faced peaks. And below us the land changed. It sank down more gently into the valley. There were trees with silver bark, and some of their branches had leaves on them. Silver branches, a few silver leaves. They were a welcome sight.

Jeshua combed his hand through the pebbles underneath his knee. He cleared his throat and spat onto the ground. His voice, when it came out, was low and harsh—unused. "Rabbi Philoxenus told me he was not afraid to die because the soul lives on. He said we'd meet him again here in the land of Boddo. That is why we've come."

He spoke. "The night before the rabbi died, he told me not to fear death. Then the next day he stood up and cursed the great khaqan. But I think he was wrong because our lives are a costless gift. To love God we must love his gifts. But not be frightened when we let them go."

Then he was quiet for a little while. "Look," he said, and raised his hand. I saw there were people among the trees. I forced my eyes to see them. They were far away.

Below us to the east the valley was in shadow. Shadows lay over the sunken land. They lay over the silver grass that licked up toward us, and in the middle of that tongue of grass, under the trees, there stood a car.

It had spoked wooden wheels of a Parthian design. Iron scythes protruded from the hubs. Four horses, unyoked, grazed around the car, which was empty. Its long shaft slanted down into the grass.

Then I saw men coming out from the trees. They carried javelins and bows. One had a long spear, and I saw it had a crossbar below the long point. It was a hunting spear.

My heart leapt up. I saw their naked legs. These were not bashliqed, long-trousered Parthians. Their heads were bare. One carried a cloak over his shoulder. Now they laid their spears inside the chariot and unstrapped their bows.

Alexandria Larisa

They had been hunting for lions but found none. They took us to their camp in the next valley, where we slept. We filled our bellies with water mixed with wine, which they served in silver cups. They roasted an antelope over the fire, but that night our stomachs were too empty to eat.

Demetrius Soter was their king. He was a boy younger than me, but tall and strong. This was the story he told us the next day as he led us down the mountainside into the town: Alexandria Larisa had been built and settled by horse soldiers from one of the companion regiments, forty men from the same village in Macedon. Something about these valleys reminded them of home. They built the rock fort above the town during the reign of Stasanor, who was satrap of Bactria after Alexander died.

We sat in the car because I was too tired to walk, and I drank water constantly. Once I vomited it up. I was too tired to listen well, especially because the king was hard to understand. He spoke a Macedonian dialect that I guessed had scarcely changed since Alexander's day. In it he recited the names of the Greek sovereigns of Bactria: Diodotus, Eucratides, and Menander, who had brought the one true faith out of the east. Others named Demetrius and Euthydemus, whose name and face were on the worn coin that Feng had given us. And many others whom I do not now remember. The king was eager to tell us. "Margiana and Marcanda and Taxila and Araeion and Arachaton—all have fallen to the barbarians," he said. "Only Larisa remains. We have hidden from them," he said as we bumped along, drawn by four horses and followed by a score of riders. I had a sickness in my stomach, and it was a hot day.

By barbarians he meant Scythians, or anyone who wasn't Greek. I told him I was from Alexandria itself, as I had so often on my journey. The great city on the middle sea, as distant from us now as if it never had existed. "My name is Dion," I said, as I had so often.

The king was eager to talk to us. "Listen," he said as we came down the gorge along the rough stone track. "You know King Alexander married Roxana, daughter of Oxyartes, who was a satrap in the Kush."

"Sir, I'd heard," I murmured, as if we were talking of events only a few years past. Flies buzzed around my face.

"But in the last year of his life, he took Stateira, daughter of Darius Codomanus."

"Yes," I murmured. Jeshua said nothing.

"After Alexander died, Oxyartes had the new queen poisoned—you knew that."

The wooden wheels were rimmed with iron which grated on the rocks. Insects buzzed around me. "Yes," continued Demetrius Soter. "The queen was on her childbed when she died. Lord Bessus was there. He took the child from her body."

These stories are all lies, I think. They are as old as dust and time. "It was Alexander's son out of the queen of Persia," said the king. "Bessus wrapped him in a blanket and stole him from that place. He had another child killed to show to Oxyartes, and they stole the boy away."

"Sir, I'd always thought there was a child," I murmured. We were coming down beside a dry riverbed. The rough rock walls loomed above us on either side. Once we heard the sound of a rockfall, and once we came upon some boulders that had slid across the road. It took four men to lever them down into the ravine.

"When Oxyartes found he had been tricked," said Demetrius Soter, "he killed all the children between the two rivers who

246

had been born that year. But Lord Bessus came by night over the Khorasan road. A goddess went before him, a winged daevi. She flew before him in the darkness, carrying a lamp. She led him to this place."

I thought it was a rare thing to see travelers here. Greek-speaking travelers. Perhaps we were the only people he had ever seen who might not know these stories. He was hurrying to be the first to tell us. Otherwise it was hard to understand. We lay in the car and I could scarcely move. In my mind I gave my thanks to great Lord Hanuman the monkey, who crossed the desert and the headache mountains. I lay in the car giving thanks, and the words of the king drifted around my head.

But I sat up when we came into Larisa. The stream flowed through a crack of shattered rock that rose on either side up to the sky. The road passed by seven towers of rock and mud and then climbed through the crack next to the stream. We came through a wall of piled rocks as thick as it was tall. Then another, of finished stones with soldiers on top of it. We came in through two enormous wooden doors.

In front of us was a small valley, sealed in by cliffs and the high mountains. The stream ran toward us through the middle, and the ditches made a pattern of colored squares lined with poplar trees. The harvest was all in. The fields were empty.

The car bumped down along the road. On either side, slaves worked in the ditches or the fields, preparing them for the cold weather. Naked children stood in the doorways of the tiny houses. Women drew wagons of brushwood toward the town. They stood aside to let us pass.

In the center of the valley rose a small hill. On top of it, a stupa painted with white clay. It was a column of painted stones—water, earth, and sky, and then the thirteen layers of ether.

This was the tradition of the Yavana Greeks. They built towers of stone to Lord Boddo, who was a saint who lived before the reign of Alexander. Now I know the story better than my own: He was from the warrior caste, born out of his mother's side without the help of copulation. This is common when gods and women lie together. In our minds we think of gods as men, but they are not.

Like the Jews and the Parthians, the followers of Boddo look to the coming of a king, a saoshanti named Mayatreia. They worship Ahura-Matha, or Amitayus in their language, the lord of everlasting light. Bright Apollo, they called Avlokitto—a name I'd never heard.

They make no offerings or sacrifices. They pray for many hours at a time, sitting by themselves. These customs had been brought into the town by King Menander, whom the Indians called Melinda. He built the wall around Larisa at the valley's head, where the stream came down out of the mountains.

It was a stone wall with wooden gates in its three sides, and the fourth side was the cliff behind the town. Like all Greek towns it was divided into quarters, four square blocks of flat-roofed, whitewashed, square stone houses, each built around a courtyard. Streets led from the gates to the gymnasium in the center. Facing it, an agora, a thermal bath, and one small civic building.

Behind the town the road continued up the cliff along a series of cuts that drew the eye upward. There another cluster of white houses hung suspended from the mountain like a wasp's nest on a wall. This was the acropolis, where we spent the winter months until the Scythians came. We were too weak, and it was too cold to go on until spring. We were the guests of King Demetrius and his sister.

There was a walkway on the acropolis that stretched from the old temple of Artemis to the palace steps. From it I could see the valley spread in front of me. Below me I could see the square roofs loaded with their piles of wood. I could see the women in the courtyards and the men in the streets. I came to distinguish them, to recognize the way they walked.

Over the next months I spent many hours on that walkway,

leaning over the stone parapet. From it I could see how the town was put together. The first horse-soldiers had each been given a piece of land: square tracts now joined together into larger holdings, which belonged to the separate Greek tribes. Slaves farmed them, a dark-skinned race who lived in villages outside the walls. I could see their cook fires among the poplar trees.

The Yavana Greeks rarely troubled themselves with planting or harvesting. They left that to their slaves. Instead they spent their time in the mountains, hunting, or else in the gymnasium or bath. They argued among themselves in the assembly and the other councils. Each council had its officers and magistrates, some appointed, some elected; it was these elections that took time. On sunny days I could see the men sitting in the agora. I could hear their shouting borne on the cold wind, and sometimes they would hit each other with their fists. Later when they moved indoors, sometimes I could still hear their drunken muffled shrieks of rage. Then the fights would spill into the streets.

Jeshua and I took up a strange position among these men. They were an angry, proud, distrustful, ignorant lot, and their loneliness had made them worse. They imagined themselves the last stronghold of Alexander and Darius, the last storehouse of the Yavana tradition, the shield of the world against the Scythians and Hsiungnu and all the other tribes. They made no distinctions. All barbarians were the same to them. Though their own language was guttural and strange, though their own blood was perfumed and diluted by the races of the east, still they were Greeks, and all the rest of us were slaves.

On the third night after our arrival, we sat with the Council of Old Men to answer their questions. At first they were curious and respectful, because there was not one of them who had so much as glimpsed the waters of the middle sea. But at the same time they were suspicious of our faces. And when they came to understand that we ourselves had no hellenic blood, they lost interest in what we had to say. This was in spite of all the lies I told them. They had seen people from my father's race before. They recognized the string I wore around my body, the cord of three-fold yajnopavita and cotton, which my father gave me when I came of age.

After that night they left us alone, as if they had forgotten us. Except they gave us a place to live, a storeroom behind the old temple of Artemis—a windowless, boxlike room. The walls were made of whitewashed stone and mud. It was a cold place when the weather changed, heated by a charcoal pit in the middle of the stone floor.

Jeshua and I stayed there together. We were like servants with no duties. I lay for hours on my rope bed or stood for hours on the parapet. It took me a long time to feel well again.

As for Jeshua, his time in the wilderness had changed him. Though he still kept the strength of his chest and arms, he had lost flesh in his face and thighs. He never regained it, though in Larisa they gave us meat to eat, and bread, red wine, and barley soup.

I had time to watch him now. He rearranged the beds in our square room so that we slept close together, his head close to mine. When we were alone he would talk about the world and the track we had made across it. He would ask me about the cities and the lands beyond the Indus. I would lie to him, making stories about things I'd never seen. But he listened. "Behind me there is nothing," he said, "nothing but my own death." Then sometimes he would tell me the story of the man on the Jericho road, whom he had beaten and left for dead. Or once he described a prostitute he had seen at her window in Magdala. He was like a child in so many ways.

Barabbas and the others had gone into the town looking for women, but Jeshua had hung back, ashamed. Then later he had run to catch up and had stood in the gutter, watching this prostitute at her window. Her red hair was thick with perfumed oil, and it shone in the lantern light, and he could smell it from across the street. He had not spoken to her.

I thought how in the wilderness, memories of my father and

Cornelius Celsus had seemed more real than life. I wondered what he had seen, what he had remembered, walking in the same valleys. Once I asked him about his mother, and he told me a story about when he was a boy and she had beaten him for breaking a pot. He was smiling as he told me, as if made happy by the memory. But listening to him I caught a glimpse of a fierce woman, quick to slap him, quick to raise her voice. Whatever Jeshua told himself, I thought it might not have been shame alone that made him leave her when his brother was born.

Often when he spoke about these things his voice was slow and unwilling. He would frown and scratch his beard. But sometimes his mood was anxious and bright. Then he would talk about his journey eastward to the river. He would talk about Omphalos, the Diamond Mountain. He would ask me questions.

When I remember Jeshua and our journey together, I think this was the happiest time. It didn't last. Jeshua was curious about the teachings of Lord Boddo, and I knew nothing about that. Now it is strange to remember my ignorance, my lack of interest, but Jeshua was eager to learn. I suppose during their long march together Philoxenus had made him curious. I suppose that's what they'd talked about during the nights when they had kept apart. Certainly there was nothing else in that old dog to make a friendship, I thought. God, how I hated his memory. I was glad he was dead. The more so after I found myself excluded once again, after Jeshua came to the attention of Queen Agathocleia and her counselor, Nagasena.

Let me describe these people. Agathocleia was the king's older sister, the first child of their dead parents. I guessed she was my age or a little younger, perhaps eighteen years. She was a dark-skinned woman with a birthmark on her face. It was a red stripe across her cheek, passed down in her family since the days of Darius Codomanus. At least that was what people said. Whatever the truth, in that valley it was a mark of authority. I thought it ruined her beauty, though Jeshua disagreed.

Because in that valley no man had power over her, she was

able to do what she pleased. She hunted from horseback with a bow. Her hair was cut short like a man's. To my mind there was nothing womanly or soft about her. She had big hands. Her voice was not pleasing or musical. Like Hippolyta she had made herself into her own image of manhood. And like an actor playing a part, she overstated it so that the whole audience might understand.

Nagasena was her opposite, which explained his power, I thought. He was a man whose male part had been scraped away. I don't mean he was like Jeshua, circumcised, damaged in his sex, for men can be crippled there and still maintain their strength, as Jeshua was the proof. I mean in a deeper way. His body was both thin and soft, his skin both dark and white, as if dusted with white powder over a dark base. His step was mincing and his hands were long, his gestures like a girl's. His voice was soft. I had to strain to understand him.

Everything about him seemed false to me. Even his name was not his own. The real Nagasena had been King Melinda's teacher. His tomb was at Mathura, a place of worship for generations of pilgrims. But this man in Alexandria Larisa had no connection to the saint. I thought he had no education at all, but with his glib tongue and smooth hands he had come into this mountain wilderness to fool these ignorant Yavanas.

Nagasena

Once Jeshua went alone to Lord Boddo's temple. The next day a man came to our room, to bring us before Nagasena. This was at the end of our second week in the town.

It was a cold day. We walked along the parapet and then went in through a courtyard of the palace. There was ice on the small surface of the pool.

Demetrius Soter had given us new woolen shirts and leather slippers. That morning, even inside the king's house you could see your breath. We shuffled into a long room, and at the end of it was Nagasena, squatting down before a clay statue he had made. For a while he pretended not to see us. In his hands he held a pot of perfumed coals, which he moved back and forth.

I had thought the followers of Boddo did not worship statues. My father told me that, but he was wrong. Later when I crossed the country of five rivers, I saw many. But I think this was the first of the god's statues in Alexandria Larisa, and when I saw it I turned to look at Jeshua.

I knew what he was thinking. Of all men in the world he was the worst at hiding what he thought. Not just from me, because I had been with him so long and knew him so well. Anyone could have seen the trouble in his face.

The Jews make no images of God. But it was more than that. Jeshua would have been just as awkward in the temple at Jerusalem, watching the priests at Jahwah's altar. His frown would have been just as deep, his cheeks just as red. He cared nothing for the laws of his people, but still he hated ceremonies of all kinds. He said this was how people turned their backs on God while still pretending to praise him. In this way he was like Philoxenus, who had never given up a chance to mock at the hypocrisy of priests.

There were five others in the hall, and the queen was among them, dressed for hunting. She sat down, and then Jeshua and the rest sat down behind her. He looked down at his feet. This was not just to show her honor and respect. Scowling, he bowed his head to Nagasena.

Once Jeshua had said to me, "Only a fool can learn nothing from a fool." At the time these words had made me angry, for I saw in them an attempt to reduce experience into maxims, which had annoyed me so much in the old man, Philoxenus. How could it be true? Wisdom is different from stupidity.

I myself could learn nothing there. I detested Nagasena, his mincing voice. If Jeshua's face showed only what he thought, Nagasena's was made for lying. There were seven of us sitting there, yet still he pretended not to see us. He knelt before the statue. His eyes were closed, his lids were fluttering, as if through an effort of holiness. He made small movements with his fingers.

Then finally he turned to us and sat down in the same cross-legged position as Lord Boddo. He crooned and chanted for a moment in an unknown and perhaps invented language. He gave us no greeting before he started to speak. If Philoxenus had been irritating, this man was four times worse, because at least with Philoxenus you could understand him, and his lessons were short and to the point. But Nagasena went on forever in a voice almost too soft to hear. Nor did he speak simply, though his Greek was bad. Everything he said was a puzzle, a parable, like these that I remember:

"This I am telling you—who is it who walks upon the mountaintop with bare feet and a bare head and with money in his hand? What kind of blockhead is it who puts a new strip of cotton into an old shirt? Who pours new wine into old cups?"

Or, "These men who call themselves teachers, do not trust them. This I am saying—a wise man made a feast for the brahmans and invited them all. But they could not come. Because of serving the fire and their lessons, they were busy men.

"Then the wise man sent his servants to the lord of that place, inviting him to come. But he could not. Because of his lands and gardens, he and his soldiers, they could not come.

"So the wise man said someone must be eating this food, for it is growing cold. Then he sent his servants out into the city, and asked them to bring all the poor men and the cripples and the fools.

"They did this, but there was still room at the table. So then the wise man told them now go out into the world, to send him everyone that they could find. Therefore you are here with me."

Then he opened his eyes and smiled. But there was nothing warm or friendly in his face, only a look that I found venomous. He smiled at the others, but they didn't see what I saw. This was the hour for questions and they all had some. The queen spoke for some time. I didn't listen until Jeshua said, "Rabbi?"

Nagasena turned to him and shook his head.

"Rabbi, tell us about the pure land. Tell us about God's kingdom."

I couldn't listen. Nagasena went on forever in his soft voice. "Listen, my son. Listen to what I am telling you. Meru is the mountain that lies between the worlds. It shines like a fire without smoke or ash. The stars turn around its head. At its foot it has four sides, and the one closest to our world is made of sapphires, which is why the sky is blue. The other sides are made of rubies and emeralds, and then diamonds on the side of the pure land. It is round at its peak, and rises to the height of eighty thousand yojana, half of which is underneath the earth.

"Rivers of sweet water flow from it," he said. Then he went on to describe the golden houses of the devas, the gandharvas, the apsaras, and the guardians of the world. He described the lake Manasa and the mountain passes full of jewels.

"Rabbi," said Jeshua. "What you describe, is this a true place in the world?"

Nagasena smiled but didn't answer. Instead he spoke of the great mountains around Meru, made of gold and silver. Nishada where the nagas live. Nila of many colors. The path wound through them one after another until it reached Kailash and Lake Manosarovar, which is the source of the Ganges river.

"Rabbi," interrupted Jeshua, but Nagasena made a gesture with his hand. "Listen to me," he said. "These things are both unreal and real. There is one being that contains all opposites. Therefore listen to me. A lady asked her servant to prepare her bed for the king who was to marry her. So she prepared the bed. The lady asked her servant to put flowers in the bedroom, and baskets of apricots and grapes. So the servant did these things. Then the lady told her to wake her when her bridegroom came, and went to her own room.

"And then when the king came, he made no noise. He did not pound on the door. He had no servants or trumpets or elephants. But he stood there and he asked the servant, who is it who prepared this bed? When she answered, he said, who is it who prepared these flowers? When she answered, he said, who is it who waited up for me? And she said, lord, it was I. So he took her into the bedroom and sealed the doors.

"Therefore," continued Nagasena, "you must be vigilant, for you do not know the hour or the day. But when it comes, you will be awakened as if from a sleep, and you will see the world for what it is, a maze of sorrow and illusion. But it will have no power to harm you...."

I couldn't listen. His language was so coarse. This talk of bedrooms—this man was not a brahman or a warrior. He had not been instructed, as my father had, in the vedas or the art of understanding. He was a sramana, a wandering beggar, growing fat here among these stupid Yavanas. I raised my hand and spoke to him in the Aryan language. "Why do you tell us these stories? Why can't you speak clearly to us?" All this time my head was aching, and there was a patterned mist before my eyes, otherwise I would not have dared to challenge him before the queen.

He smiled. His face was cold and poisonous and insulting. He answered me in his coarse Greek. "But it is clear. Twice-born," he said, referring to the string around my body, the symbol of my caste, "twice-born, these stories mean you are not welcome here. I speak in riddles to you because you are not fit to know the mystery of the pure land. But to him," he said, indicating Jeshua with his thin, smooth hand, "to him my words are plain."

Jeshua's Dream

Later Jeshua told me again: "Even a fool can share his wisdom with others."

By this time he had had several conversations with Naga-sena. After one of them he dragged the rope beds together in our little room, and we lay among the blankets. It was evening. There was a small grease lamp.

He was telling me about the relics Nagasena carried with him—part of Lord Boddo's fingerbone. Also a tooth from the great saint Ananda, and some bones from Vipasyin and Konakamana, Boddo's ancestors in the world.

"What is left of these saints," I asked, "if every beggar in the world carries a piece of them? All these bones would fill a warehouse."

Jeshua laughed. Encouraged, I went on. "This man Nagasena is a liar," I said. "He cares nothing for Lord Boddo, but he uses him. He has everything he wants. Food and drink. Kings and queens obey him."

Jeshua lay on his back, his big nose in the air. I could see the profile of his face. His big nose and jaw.

"You don't understand," he said. "Listen. A man comes, a teacher. He says you must do this and that. You must live this way. Think these thoughts. You must not be distracted."

Jeshua stopped, then started, "A great teacher comes, a simple man. He says you must give up all things. You must do no harm to living creatures. You must bring your mind into your hands and gather it up. Then you will learn the path out of the world, into the pure land where God lives.

"These things are easy to understand, hard to accomplish. Too hard for most. So another generation comes to tell us no, there is a second way. Follow these rules. Use these words. Bow down to the floor. Make an offering of fruits and herbs to empty statues. The pure land will come to you. You do not have to search for it. Feed us and admire us, for we are the guardians of the bones. Listen while we explain forever. These mysteries are easy to accomplish, hard to understand."

He said, "To worship something is to destroy it. For Nagasena, Boddo is a god. Born from his mother's side. Tempted by devils. No one can be like him. No one can follow him. It is useless to try. But you can worship his bones."

"Yet you listen to them. Nagasena and the rest."

Jeshua grunted. "Moses is dead, and Boddo too. Only these fools are left."

And then, "You of all men and women should be patient. You should not blame others for your own mistakes."

It was cold in the little room. The cold stone walls. But as always I could feel the heat from Jeshua's body. I lay near him and I felt it on my skin. After he had gone to sleep, I lay thinking about him, wondering about the source of that strange heat. Was it in his brain, his stomach, or his heart? That is the purpose of the blood: It pushes through the cold flesh and warms it into life. The heart pumps it. But where is the fire that makes it hot? Is it in the anus, as the Egyptians claim?

Late that night I woke to the sound of Jeshua's dream. Or I couldn't tell—he was muttering in his sleep and moving his big hands. He had thrown off his blanket. The air in the room was hot and stifling.

Groggy, I sat up on my bed. In a moment he rose also. His eyes were open, but he couldn't see me. I called out to him but he couldn't hear. He strode over to the door and unbarred it. He tugged open the panel, and the cold air washed in. And the moonlight also—it was two days before the full moon. The light washed through the door. Jeshua knelt down into it and raised his fists above his head.

GONDOPHARES

My memory is bad now. But I believe it was the next day that Demetrius Soter called for us, because of the embassy which had come into the town.

No, I don't know. It must have been later, or else why would the king have sent for us? Already Jeshua must have taken his place among the leaders of these people. Try as I might, I can't remember him. I can't remember where he sat.

But I remember the Scythians. Kujula Kadphises was their king, a young man who had brought the tribes together. He ruled the five rivers from Peucelaotis and Taxila.

He was too great a king to make the journey to Alexandria Larisa. Gondophares was the captain he had sent, a chief of the Tochari tribe, which the Sericans call the Yuehchi.

It had snowed during the night. And then the wind had blown the snow away. The fields were bare, but the snow had blown into the lines of trees. It had blown into the corners of the walls.

But in the morning the sun was bright. From the parapet I watched the Scythians ride their small horses up the middle of the valley. They paused before Lord Boddo's stupa. Then they rode on through the open gates.

Demetrius Soter had come down from the acropolis, and the men met together in the agora. The Yavana Greeks sat according to their tribes, with the magistrates and archates in front. Everyone was dressed for fighting, though the Scythians were unarmed.

We swept the frost from our seats and admired the gifts the Scythians had brought. They had piled them up on the bare stones, the skins of lions and leopards and wolves. A silver bowl and one carved out of a single piece of lapis lazuli, the stone of heaven.

The Scythians wore sheepskin coats and leather hats and boots. We recognized Gondophares from the red cloth on his head, weighted in place by a circle of gold. Under it we could see his coarse grey hair, his unlined face. His long mustache was grey. His chin was shaved. He had rings of bronze over his gloves and a bronze buckle on his belt, a circle as big as my hand.

He stepped forward over the icy stones among the seated ranks of Yavanas. No one rose to greet him, an insult that I felt with him. He stood up straight with his legs spread, his gloves clasped behind his back, and in the language of the five rivers he asked Vipasyin and Amitayus and the rest to bless this meeting, which took place under the blue sky and the all-seeing eyes of Boddo. Then he went on for several minutes, loading praises onto the race of Alexander and the assembled company, several of whom he knew by name. He praised their wisdom in consenting to meet with him and suggested that if they were able to come to an understanding, it would be pleasing to Avlokitto, who at that moment was looking down from the clouds.

Then there was silence for some time until Nagasena got up to translate. He had tied a strip of wool around his head and pulled a blanket around his shoulders. His lips were dark with cold. Still I admit that he spoke well, and if anything his words were softer and more gracious even than the Scythian's. But when he was finished, the Greeks sat without speaking, wrapped in their skins and robes.

The third man to get up was an old chieftain of the Kushans, Adzes, the son of Spalirises. His hair was tied behind him and he wore a wolfskin coat. He talked a long time. He began by praising the firmness of his hosts, how they had defended the Larisa valley since the time of proud Alexander. How they had stood against their enemies. He compared them to an old oak tree, grown from a strong sapling, though the acorn had arrived from far away.

But, he said, now there was a wind come over the mountains, a storm out of the northern desert. And, he said, sometimes in a storm the tree standing by itself might fall, regardless of its strength. Often, he said, after a storm, morning would find the outlying trees blown down, while those in the grove still stood. Then he described how farmers plant a row of willow trees against the wind, trees more flexible than oaks and stronger for that reason.

The son of Spalirises was no great orator. Still, there was a direction to his language that made it restful to listen to. We knew where it was flowing. Nagasena translated after every few phrases, and the Greeks listened in cold stillness as the Kushan told them how farmers had been known to weave a barrier of willow shoots between a line of trees so that the dirt from their fields would not blow away.

Then after a pause he talked about Kujula Kadphises, his young king. He described several feats of strength and horsemanship. He described how, by his fierceness and cunning and virtue, he had brought all the tribes together into a kingdom that was now the greatest in the world and included in its army many Yavanas from the old cities of Margiana and Qandahar. It was this mixture that made Kujula Kadphises invincible, because his mother was a Greek on her mother's side. In this way he was like Ashok, whose grandfather had married a daughter of Seleucus. But in other ways he was the rightful heir of Alexander himself.

Then the son of Spalirises began to talk about the Hsiungnu. This was the reason King Demetrius had agreed to meet with the barbarians. He had heard rumors that a family of Hsiungnu had crossed the passes into Bamian, walking their horses through the deep snow. They had attacked several villages and burned them to the ground.

The son of Spalirises called the Hsiungnu the Hunns. This was the news he brought: On the morning of the first day the Hunns had come under a rose-colored flag to talk. And they refused to be goaded, even after the defenders shot at them from the walls. Their interpreter explained how if the gates were opened during that day, then the people would not be killed. The Hunns would enter and take what they wanted. Then they would go.

But if the gates stayed closed, then on the second day the Hunns would attack the town. Their flags would be yellow. If the gates were opened or the walls were breached during that day, then the soldiers would be killed and their skulls would be piled into a tower. But the old men, the children, and the women would be spared. The town would be left standing.

But if the men resisted until the third day, the Hunns would come under a white flag. Then it would make no difference if they opened the gates or not. Because when the Hunns threw down the walls, they would slaughter the soldiers, the old men, the women, and the children. They would take what they wanted. They would burn the town.

The Hunns had seemed so ragged, so starved and desperate, the soldiers had laughed at them from the walls. But now the town was gone. On the third day the Hunns had found the water supply. They had broken through into the underground canal. The water had run clear. Then it was thick with blood, whether a man's or an animal's, no one could tell.

As I listened, I thought there was a shape to this story that did not fit the Hsiungnu as I remembered them. It seemed too formal, too clear a tragedy. And the Yavanas also had their doubts, which seemed to rise from them as they sat on the cold stones. But I didn't think their thoughts came as mine did from experience. Rather out of pride. They did not think the Hsiung-nu could defeat them. Not in three days or three hundred.

And that's what they said. Several shouted out, interrupting one another, and then one stood up. He didn't give his name, but I recognized him as Zoilus, the son of Amyntas, whose land was on the east bank of the stream. He asked, what could be expected when barbarians fight among themselves? No, what he said was, "Gentlemen, these are animals, not men. Why are we listening to them? Why are we not driving them away with kicks in the backside? I am freezing while I listen to these pigs. My dinner is getting cold. Which reminds me, what is it they eat that makes them smell so disgusting? How is it that they dare to bruise the name of Avlokitto with their foul mouths?"

Then other men got up to shout out this or worse, which Nagasena found difficult to translate. He was frightened, I could tell. Perhaps he'd been impressed by the story of the Hsiungnu. Perhaps he couldn't bear to drive the Scythians away. Or else he didn't want to translate such rudeness, particularly to men who had been so courteous and soft. So he made slippery speeches,

which were contradicted by shouts and the gestures of the Yavanas—the Scythians would have been fools to listen to him. And
in fact they were not fools. Gondophares's face was tight and red.
He held up his fist. He spoke a few sentences in faultless Greek,
which shamed the Yavanas to silence. Or perhaps just surprised
them; they had no shame. To them it was as if an animal had
spoken.

JESHUA AND THE QUEEN

I can't remember where Jeshua sat during these ceremonies. But
I don't think it was with me. By this time he had made a reputation in Alexandria Larisa.

Distrusted by the ordinary Yavanas, Jeshua had become a
favorite among the group of courtiers who lived on the acropolis.
It was because of who he was, a man from the middle sea. And
because of his strength and size. Like all backward people they
were fascinated by these things. There was not one of them or of
the Scythians either, who came up to his shoulder.

He was stronger than any of them. It didn't matter; because
they were Greeks, they challenged him constantly to wrestling
matches and footraces. They mocked him and insulted him when
he refused, but he could not be baited. He had no interest in
games of any kind. He hated the gymnasium, hated the nakedness of the Yavanas. Their oiled skins, the way they used to grab
at his genitals—everything about it insulted his modesty, his
sense of shame, which I have often described.

That winter he was more interested in sitting by himself
and taking walks on the mountain, where he had found some
caves. The heat from his body kept him warm. Sometimes he
would come back, exhausted by a story or a new idea. But in the
morning when he showed himself, men from the town spat on
the stones in front of his feet. They shouted and threw stones.

I told him they were cowards and fools, but he was troubled, I could tell.

Philoxenus of Pergamon thrived on the disdain of others, but Jeshua was proud in his own way. He could be tempted. And he was skilled with his hands: In Palestine he had been a soldier for the sicarii. One morning he was coming back through the town, and a fat hulk of a fool named Apollodotus slapped him in the face. He grabbed hold of his penis, trying to see how large it was. He spat on his shirt, and then Jeshua almost killed him.

I didn't see it. I wasn't there. I heard about it later as did everybody. But I understood without seeing—there were moments in those days when Jeshua seemed a figure made of glass, with a fire burning inside. A fire from the god, and people said it was as if Dionysus himself had come alive in his wild shouts and glaring eyes, his tangled hair, which by this time had grown long. Four men had to drag him away from Apollodotus's blood-smeared and unconscious body.

But when the god left him, he was horrified by what he had done. He awoke from these moments as if from a bloody dream, frightened and confused. Because he believed that men are masters of themselves. He believed the path to the pure land led through a wilderness of discipline and self-correction. And he knew the gods punish us for our mistakes. Now he was horrified because for him the journey of this past year, which had taken him so far from home and taught him so much, had started from the same kind of accident. When he had beaten the old man to death upon the Jericho road.

It was not Dionysus, but a devil, whom Jeshua blamed for the destruction of Apollodotus. As if that fat bully didn't have his own fate to wrestle with, and as if the road to God leads always the same way. That night I came back to our small room and found him standing on the floor, stroking his naked shoulders with the rope from his belt. Sweat and blood ran down his back. When I tried to stop him he pushed me away, and I could see the rage of Dionysus in his eye. "Only the pure," he told me later. "If your fingers hurt you, cut them off. This road is easier for cripples than whole men."

But the gods have many ways to show us our weaknesses. Because of this event, as I have said, Jeshua became the frequent guest of Demetrius Soter and the queen. "It's because of my sins that they admire me," said Jeshua. Apollodotus had been a champion in the games.

It was not just because of his sins. It was for a mixture of qualities. At that time Jeshua carried with him the power of the wandering philosopher, who has turned his back on money and love and all the desires and illusions of this world. Beside that he was bold and strong. Even worthless, casteless fools like Naga-sena could use empty powers to move into the house of kings; how much easier for Jeshua. In this way he was like Daniel, who was made a lord in Mesopotamia.

Or no, because Alexandria Larisa was not Babylon. The acropolis consisted of eleven houses and the old temple. When King Demetrius had dinner with his family, they could be served around a single table. His father and mother were dead. Of the rest, several were weak-boned and feebleminded, because they had tried to keep the blood of Darius and Alexander among themselves. In the same way the Egyptian kings were frugal with the blood of Amon Re, and with the same result. The gods spill their seed upon the earth in order to enrich it. They destroy those who try to hoard their ancestry, as they do those who are too greedy for gold or food or love or any other of their gifts. Desire has a sickness hidden in it, as Lord Boddo knew, as Jeshua taught me. That fat cow Cornelius Celsus . . . No, but that was different. I can't claim he got what he deserved.

These children of the mighty Achaemenids and divine Alexander, they were a pitiful lot. I could see it in their yellow faces and their nervous hands—too much bile. Their teeth were small, their faces thin. Demetrius Soter and his sister were the only ones who could sit up and take a cup of wine without spilling half of it out on the stones.

In fact King Demetrius was a beautiful boy. It was as if an old and rotten vine had gathered up its strength and brought out one last beautiful flower. His hair was dark, but his skin was so pale, it was almost white. His eyes were grey, and his brows grew straight across over a proud nose. Though he was subject to all kinds of colds, skin rashes, and fevers, still his body was well knit and strong. Often he went down to the gymnasium to wrestle or play games.

After the victory over Apollodotus, Jeshua was his guest at dinner. I went with him the first time. I stood next to the wall with two other servants while Jeshua lay down on a low couch. With him around the table were the king and two other men, and they ate and drank wine for several hours. They asked Jeshua questions and made fun of his answers, which were awkward and crude. A man from the countryside, he did not know how to behave in such company, and after a while, as the Yavanas grew drunk, they began to laugh at the grease in his beard and the coarseness of his hands, the way he wiped his fingers on his wrist. It was a damp, cold, airless room.

They were eating a stew made of rabbits and apricots, and drinking wine from silver cups. I stood next to the wall of white-washed stone, looking at the smudges, the patterns of the streaks of dirt. From time to time I came forward to refill Jeshua's cup, and he would look at me, his eyes troubled by a mix of feelings. But among them was laughter, especially as the hours wore on. By the seventh cup I saw him wink at me, and it was not through drunkenness but rather the reverse. The excess of blood in him diluted the wine. But the young king could not stay with him, and in time he fell asleep, snoring like a peasant on his couch.

The other men were nodding also. Servants brought them packed snow from the mountainside, scented with a syrup of mixed fruits. But they were too drunk to eat. The snow melted in the silver bowls. Jeshua looked at me, and I could tell he was asking himself whether we should go or stay. But at that moment Queen Agathocleia came into the room, dressed in a man's short chiton and a woolen cloak. She sat down in a chair next to the smoking brazier.

Jeshua got to his feet. The others lay on their couches, but he stood, his big hands clasped in front of him. A servant brought her a cup of wine, and she raised it up. "I heard about your victory in the games," she said. "Lord Nagasena also commends you. He has told me about some of your conversations."

Her face was hidden in the shadows. But then she leaned forward, and by the dim light of the brazier we could see the birthmark on her cheek. Without drinking from it, she put the cup of wine onto the table. Then she leaned forward with her elbow on the curved arm of her chair, resting her face against her hand. I thought for the first time how young she was. I thought how her birthmark, the sign of her descent from the immortal gods, might be a source of pain to her. I thought also how her mannishness might be a sign of her despair. There was no king in this valley to marry her. The Yavana princes of Margiana and Taxila were all dead. Perhaps that explained her devotion to Lord Boddo, who had given up his wife and child for another kind of happiness.

I stood against the cold stone wall. Agathocleia took no notice of me. But she asked Jeshua questions about his own country, about his village. She asked whether he had a wife or children there. She asked whether his mother and father still lived, still waited for his return. She asked what had brought him on this road across the world.

"God has brought me here," he said, standing up among the sleeping guests, the sleeping king. "But it was not my choice," he said, which made Agathocleia smile.

His hands were clasped together. He stared down at them and would not meet her eyes. I wondered what he felt for her, wondered whether he was at the point where shame, fear, and desire join together and become pity.

To the Yavanas of Alexandria Larisa, I was Jeshua's servant. It was impossible for them to treat me otherwise, because of my race. That was the last night I was inside the king's house, though Jeshua went back several times. He was eager to attend because the queen was there. I never saw any more of these dinners. But I knew they were a source of rumor in the acropolis. Servants told me Agathocleia would come down to dinner dressed as a man, and would drink and talk with the other guests. She had a cruel tongue, they said, after she had drunk her wine. She would mock her guests to their faces. Jeshua was not spared, they said. She mocked him for his clumsy manners and big face. She called him a bear, as I once had. Now I was surprised to hear the word, my thinking had so changed.

The servants said she was especially cruel to him. Which he bore calmly, they said, but I knew differently. At night he would come back smelling of wine, and he would lie on his rope bed and tell me stories of the land of Israel, the country around Gennesaret, and the whore in Magdala, whom he had not so much as talked to but had seen across the road, her red hair braided and oiled and falling down her back.

Once I came in from a walk in the cold night when I was looking at the stars. It was early morning. I was looking for my planet, Mercury, which I had not seen for months. I came in without warning and saw Jeshua beside the lamp, standing naked in the middle of the room. He had his back to me but I could see what he was doing. He was finding consolation with his hands, stroking himself until the seed burst from his body. The room smelled of it, and of his tears also. I could see the movement in his shoulders and the muscles of his back before I turned my head and left him. I don't think he heard me. When I returned, he was asleep. His mouth was open.

This was a sign of his misery, and I was used to it. His shoulders carried wounds where he had hit himself. And sometimes he would spend the entire night sitting by the lamp, or in the dark, or on his knees. Muttering the words of the talisman: "Mother forgive me. Father forgive me. Give me food to eat, water to drink. Keep me from harm. Forgive my sins and I will forgive them. Do not tempt me. Not my will, but yours." Each time it was different.

In those days I rarely spoke to him. I also spent much time alone, until the Scythians came. Near the calends of February, when it was still winter, they attacked the town. It was a year since I had left my master's house.

THE WHITE FLAG

When they spoke of the Hsiungnu and blamed their cruelty, the Scythians were speaking of themselves. This is often true when men accuse others. It was they who attacked under a red flag.

The Yavanas kept the mountain passes around Larisa, which were still deep in snow. But in the cleft where the river ran out, Lord Gondophares sent his men against the walls again and again. When they died, shot down from the towers above the gate, he cut their heads off and sent them over the wall, thrown from catapults that he had brought from Taxila. He cut their bodies apart and sent them over piece by piece, hoping to sicken and disgust us. And to daunt the Yavanas from coming out to fight him. In time he brought elephants to break down the door.

All this was told to me. I didn't see it. Because we were not Greeks, Jeshua and I weren't asked to defend the walls, for which I gave thanks. Nor were the other slaves, but only citizens, the members of the tribes. I spoke to old Lysias, and he allowed me a corner of the temple to prepare my art—something I hadn't done since our night in Xur, when Set had crushed the skull of the Egyptian and I had not saved him. When the women from the town had broken the adulteress with stones. I had felt my hands were cursed. My sins had overwhelmed me. Blood flowed from my fingers.

For a long time my headaches had been bad. Often I saw the curtain of white squares that separated me out from the world. Often I heard the roaring in my ears or felt the wind rush through my arteries. Often I felt a sickness in me, which made me pity the young men and the boys who came back from the wall. It was they who told me how the fight was raging, after I had drawn out the arrows or the broken stumps of spears, depending on whether they were anuloma or pratiloma, as my father taught me. After I had washed their wounds with vinegar, then wine, then distilled wine, and bound them closed with honey mixed with ghee. After I had tied off the bursting veins. After I had picked away the scabs.

When the wounds were rotten, I let maggots clean them, hiding the worms in bandages so Lysias couldn't see.

Lysias had a poppy garden out of which he made a potion called nepenthe. It was the name Helen gave it in the song, and it cured the deepest sorrows as she said it would. But beyond that he was useless, all thinking and no learning, which is the curse of our poor art. He would recite the lessons of Hippocrates, that miserable fool who thought the world existed in his mind. Content with his mind's eye, he forgot sight, sound, taste, smell, touch. As a result, many thousands have been bled to death or poisoned. Lysias killed dozens with his blind stupidity, taking blood from men who had already lost too much, starving the hungry and pushing his fingers down their throats. I had better fortune, and when Jeshua saw it he came to me. "Teach me," he said. Like me he was moved to pity by the wounded soldiers.

This was the time when I was closest to him, sleeping beside him during the nights, working with him during the days. On the ninth day of the attack the Scythians came again, and this time their flags were white.

Throughout the month of February the Yavanas brought their men and boys up to the acropolis and laid them in the old temple. In the evening from the parapet I watched the carts come back, and sometimes Queen Agathocleia rode with them. The gate itself was out of sight around a shoulder of the hill. As the sky got dark I could see the red glow.

But in the whitewashed sanctuary I offered prayers to Aesculapius and Toth, at night when Lysias couldn't see. He spoke to Avlokitto every morning. But I thought Lord Boddo did not hate death as much as Father Toth, who fought against it at the beginning of the world.

In the third week of the attack, after the round tower had fallen, after Gondophares had taken the first salient, he sent men upon the walls with grappling hooks. After that fight, we had many soldiers burned with the Greek fire. Their skin was charred. The fire was in their lungs. We could do nothing. I made a salve of wool lint and ghee and gave them enemas of nepenthe. But they died after the first day or the second.

There was a white-haired man who had been a soldier on the wall. His right hand was burned away. But he carried his friend up from the valley, up the pathway from the town. He carried him on his broad back and laid him down past midnight on the square stones—a young man from his tribe, from his own cleros.

The Scythians had crawled under a culvert where the stream ran out. They had exploded their fire; the young man was close to death. His yellow hair was burned, and yet his eyes and half his face were still beautiful. I put straws into his nose so he could breathe. I washed him in wine, and Jeshua helped me. Under my breath I was muttering prayers, and then the white-haired man seized hold of my hands. "Say it," he commanded, and he led me in the old hymn to Artemis, who had been the protector of that town before Lord Boddo came: "Mother of the arrow, mother of the silver bow," and then the rest.

"We had seven towers that have stood since Alexander's day," he said. "Four are taken, and the barbarians are on the wall. Tomorrow Gondophares will bring his elephants against the door. He is carrying the white flag—it doesn't matter. We are already dead. We died when the statue of our lady was removed."

With his one hand he held the two of mine. "You with your prayers to bright Aesculapius. You with your potions that bring back the dead. Come help me now and we will light the lamp for these dead men. For my dead friend. My grandfather was a priest in this same temple."

He brought me to the back of the old shrine, which was built against the cliff. There were small stones piled up, a wall of them. He pulled them down until he found the surface of the living rock. "Here," he said. "Bring a light," for it was dark and we could scarcely see.

There was an alcove hidden in the rock. And the statue was there, broken, on its side, the virgin mother with her helmet and spear, her rows of breasts. They covered her stone belly. "Help me," he said, and we pulled the statue from its place and set it on its feet.

"Look," said the old man. And he drew the lantern flame across a crack in the rock wall. A blue flame followed it, still flickering when he pulled the lamp away.

"My grandfather was a priest here," he repeated. "But we've forgotten. No, it was the tower of the moon that fell today."

There were rows of men laid out in the temple where the people had come in the old days. We were in the shrine, separate from them. But I raised the lamp, and its light fell through the open door onto their empty eyes, their empty faces.

Jeshua was sitting with the wounded soldier. He was bathing his burned face. I had brought snow from the mountain and mixed it in wine. Jeshua sat with the cold wine in a shallow dish, and with a towel he rubbed the burned man's cheek and shoulder. He put his fingers into the man's mouth to open up his throat, as I had taught him.

His hands were gentle and correct. I stood with the old man in the doorway, holding up the lamp. The soldier would die, I thought, and I could tell the old man knew it too. I could tell it from the hardness of his face. He stood beside me almost without breathing, his arms covered with dust, and there was dust in his white hair.

We watched Jeshua prepare a salve of olive oil as I had

taught him. But then the young man's breathing must have failed. We watched Jeshua kneel over him, watched him pluck the straws out of the soldier's burned nose and put his big hand over it. Then he bent down to kiss him, to force the air into his burned lungs; the old man turned away. "I must go back," he murmured, which I didn't understand. At midnight the gate to the acropolis was closed. There was no other way of descending to the town.

I thought he meant to wake the guard. But instead of going out the door into the night, he went back into the shrine where we had placed the goddess. Back into the alcove cut into the rock, where the blue fire still flickered. "Here," he said. "Give me the lantern."

When I made no motion, he stepped into the alcove. And when his shadow shifted I could see there was a hole, which had been hidden by the statue and the piled-up stones. "This was the temple's secret," he said. "My father showed me."

Then he took the lamp. "The priests of the temple," he said, "could light the fire here and in Larisa at the same moment. At the temple of Artemis in the old town. They could go back and forth, and no one saw them. They said the goddess hid their footsteps. This cleft was protected by a curtain, but it doesn't matter now."

He was telling me these things to keep from weeping. Except there were no tears in his eyes. But in his voice I could detect a breathy softness. Perhaps inside him there was still a secret corridor, I thought. He bent down almost to the floor and slipped inside. The light shone on the wall, and then it disappeared. I stepped back. Behind the statue the rock face flickered with a blue and sacred fire.

I said a prayer to Artemis the virgin. And when I went back to Jeshua, the soldier lived. The goddess had restored his breath. I brought another lantern from the door, and together we tended him until I fell asleep.

Nagasena Murdered

On the next day Gondophares brought his elephants to the gate. But he had no success. The timbers were studded with bronze spikes, and the elephants could not put their foreheads or their shoulders against them. The defenders raised a storm of arrows from the walls. So many Scythians were killed that Gondophares used their slaughtered bodies as a kind of pad, which he tied over the heads of the elephants to protect them. But still they were not able to break down the door, especially when the soldiers shot at them with burning arrows. They stampeded back, and many Scythians were crushed.

That morning Demetrius Soter led the Yavanas down from the mountainside by a secret way. He attacked the Scythian camp and pushed them back. They ran before his spear as if he were Alexander himself, come out of the pure land to punish them.

For three days our soldiers fought over the door. When finally the Scythians broke through, it was because of treachery. Because at night the slaves inside Larisa opened up the gates.

In the morning I stood on the parapet of the acropolis and watched the Scythians come in. The elephants, and Gondophares on his yellow horse—he rode up through the middle of the valley, pausing only at Lord Boddo's tower. He carried the white flag.

The first defenses of Larisa were the seven towers at the valley's mouth, where the river ran out, where the cliffs were filled with stonework and joined with the wooden doors. Those gates, out of sight beyond the shoulder of the mountain, defended the entire valley. After they had fallen, the people closed the portals to the town itself, which huddled below us at the bottom of the cliff. But there were no soldiers for its long walls.

Many of the women climbed up the last slope to the acropolis, which was now filled with them and with their children. But the rest—that day the town below us surrendered. The old men came out. The old women came out. And in the open space before the gate Lord Gondophares slaughtered all of them, as he had promised. The slaves he spared. But every Yavana, all the citizens and their women, he killed, and put their bodies in a pile. I didn't see it. I will not describe it. He made them lie down on their stomachs. The soldiers pulled their heads back by their hair and cut their throats until the ground was stained in a great circle. The women watched from the acropolis. In the temple of Artemis we listened to them scream.

That night the Scythians set the town on fire, and the smoke from it rose and stung our eyes. Gondophares rode up to the last gate, which guarded the steep climb to the acropolis. He threw down from his saddle the body of Demetrius Soter, next to the bonfires which burned against the wall.

But in the temple of Artemis, Jeshua and I carried the young soldier into the recess of the shrine and laid him at the statue's feet. He had made a strange improvement. In that evening of cold death, his life was a flame for us to warm ourselves. He lived as if inside our cupped hands. Piece by piece I cut away his charred skin. Underneath, his scars were red and clean.

He took soft shallow breaths with his burnt lungs. But his eyes were open. He stared up at Jeshua, always at Jeshua, as if there were something in Jeshua's face that commanded him to live. He followed Jeshua's hands as he washed him with oil and wine, his big careful hands.

That night Queen Agathocleia came into the temple and stood alone inside the door. She had put away her leather shirt, which she had worn during the siege. She was dressed in a blue robe. Her hair was covered with a veil which she had thrown back.

It was the first time I had seen her dressed in women's clothes. I went toward her thinking she was someone else. I was going to tell her to go, because that was no place for a woman among the rows of dying men. But I recognized her height and the mark of Alexander and Darius on her cheek. She stood next to the door with her hand on the post. She stepped past me without a word. The hem of her silk robe brushed the stones.

In the old days no women were allowed into the shrine of Artemis. But she stood on the threshold of the inner door. I came up behind her, and beyond her shoulder I could see Jeshua under the lamp, washing the burnt soldier. He lifted his head.

"You there. You there, slave." Her voice was harsh and soft at the same time. I smelled her as she passed. She smelled of wine.

I didn't listen. I turned back into the temple. I walked out through the wounded men. Lysias was with them. But I went through the door into the night, into the crowd. The stone walls of the temple had blocked out most of the sounds, most of the light. But in the tiny streets of the acropolis, men and women pushed against each other like penned animals.

The sky was red, the air was full of smoke. I was suffocating in the hot press of bodies. My ears were broken with the shouting until I pushed through to the parapet above the burning town. There I stood sweating in the cold air, watching the people murder Nagasena.

He stood in a torchlit circle. I found myself behind him in the crowd. They held him by his arms, twisted behind his shoulder blades. They had ripped his shirt apart, and now they pulled his head back by his long hair.

Three boys stood in front of him, slapping his face and chest. They accused him. They blamed him for the rage of Gondophares.

They said he had insulted him when he had come to talk, goaded him in languages that no Greek understood. This was stupidity to anyone who had been there. But I was frightened because I knew it was his foreignness they hated, and their own unprotected shame.

Now they were beating him with long clubs. I turned away, but found myself caught in the circle of the crowd that pressed around me like a solid wall. I had no wish to draw attention to myself, so I turned back and watch them beat Nagasena until his face and shoulders were streaked with blood. They dragged him to the parapet and pitched him over the roofs of the burning town.

The air was full of smoke and noise. And something else,

some odd mist that stung my eyes. I pushed out through the crowd and I saw soldiers. Agathocleia had put her guard into the streets. There were soldiers on the road into the town, which was so narrow and so steep. One man, people said, could hold it against Gondophares's army.

I doubted it. We had no food. I went into the temple again. And it was quiet inside. No one called to me among the wounded men. One lay with his arm out over the stones, and I squatted down to look.

In the evening Lysias had given them all draughts of nepenthe according to his custom. But this night as they slept he had moved among them, opening their veins. Now I understood what he was doing when I left the temple, only I had been too blind to see. I wondered if Agathocleia had seen.

He had murdered ten men as they slept. They were still warm. I moved among them, and among the cold corpses which we had not moved—the blankets and bedding were wet. Blood flowed on the stone floor. But in the shrine the burnt soldier was breathing deep and slow. Jeshua sat by him. "Listen," I said. He looked up at me but I said nothing. Instead I went to rummage in a corner of the wall, where we had stripped off the armor of the soldiers as they came in. I remembered there were some leather caps, which the Yavanas had taken from the bodies of their enemies.

I remembered what the Scythians had worn, who had come with Gondophares to the meeting place. I took a leather shirt with iron scales. I took a red cloth for my head. Then I went into the alcove and stood next to the flickering blue light. My cap dangled from my hand. "Come," I said.

I didn't have to speak. Jeshua knelt over the soldier. And I could see he understood. The Yavanas would kill us if we stayed. They would throw us over the parapet like Nagasena. Or else Gondophares would kill us when he broke the gate. But if we went down by the secret way into the town, then something could be done. I spoke the Aryan language. Our foreignness would be our strength.

With his towel Jeshua was washing the man's neck. And his

breath came out; I was astonished. What had begun as a burned rattle was now clean, a soft flow through blistered lips. The soldier's eyes were open too.

Jeshua shook his head.

We had to go quickly before Lysias came. Or someone else. I could hear the shouting in the street. "Come," I said, and gestured with my hand.

He shook his head, stubborn as a bear. "I cannot leave. Not now."

He meant he could not leave the queen. Where was she? I had not seen her in the temple or the street.

How foolish he was! He must have known her life was coming to an end. He must have known she did not think of him. She was like the whore in Magdala that he saw from across the street. Where was his faithfulness to me?

As if he read my thoughts, he said, "She is nothing to me."

He didn't move. I admit I was relieved. I confess it now. I thought he was too big to go down through the rocks. I thought he was too big to escape and not be seen. He did not have my gift of language.

But I felt a burden of sadness. It was too heavy to carry and be free. Too heavy to carry and escape. So before I left I tried to put it down. "I was to blame," I said, and told him how I had betrayed the sicarii to Pontius Pilate.

He turned his head away. He dipped his towel in the bowl. He was washing the soldier's head with it and pressing his eyes closed.

"No, you don't understand," I said, angry now because I felt no better. I told him how I had tricked him in the caravanserai in Dura Europos and stolen his money. I felt my anger rise as I described it. How stupid he had been!

His hands were gentle on the soldier's face. Jeshua looked up. "That money was a curse to me." Then, "I knew you from the cave, when you healed the Roman soldier. How could I not remember you, in Dura and afterward?"

Then he said, "So it was you who freed my cousin John."

His hands moved down the soldier's chest, rubbing at the charred skin. Between the cracks I could see the soft pink flesh. "You say you are to blame for what has happened. Yet you saved my life three times. Now you must go, and God will save me."

Then, "A man lives as he can according to God's laws. Where is the profit if he doesn't understand? You made me give up everything and put me on this road. That was the beginning."

For a moment the crowd's noise was gone. It was quiet in the shrine under the statue of bright Artemis. I knelt at her feet to pick up an oil lamp. Several had been left there by the faithful.

Jeshua put the soldier aside. He laid him on his back and came to me. My head was weak and I was weak when I got up. He touched me on the head with his big hand.

THE WAY DOWN

I pulled the leather cap onto my head. I bound the red cloth around it. With the lamp in my hand I bent down in the alcove under the flickering blue light. There was a fissure in the rock and I crept into it. The walls were rough and crumbling. The steps led down.

All was quiet in the pure dark. Yet there was a roaring in my ears. I held the lantern at my cheek. The flame burned straight and sure.

There were words of a small prayer to the goddess, which I was mumbling over and over until the sense was lost. The steps were small but carefully made, and I thought perhaps the distance was not far. The temple was built into the cliff face above the town. With another part of my mind I counted the steps.

I found the place where I could not go through. The stone had shifted over the years since this had been a pathway for the priests. Or else there was another hole that led down to the ground and I had passed it, choosing the larger way. Or else this was the puzzle that could not be undone except by the true worshipers of Artemis. The man with the burned hand, the old man had come this way. He was a bigger man than I.

The pathway ended in a pit where the rocks came together, and I could not go down. But high up on the wall in front of me, there was another hole which seemed to lead upward. It was beyond my reach. I couldn't find the place to climb. I tried, and slid back down inside a patter of small stones.

Now I had failed, and the sweat flowed under my leather hat and metal shirt. The air seemed hot and hard to breathe. My lungs closed around it. "Forgive me," I said, and then I whispered the words of Jeshua's talisman, which was a mistake. Because after a little while the lamp burned less. Then it went out.

I felt my life had burned out like the fire. There were no words in me, no thoughts. I crouched down at the bottom of the pit and tried to breathe.

But most dangers are not real. I was no worse off than I had been. Without light I could still climb back. And surely God intended me to find my way to Manosarovar below the Diamond Mountain. To say a prayer for my poor father who had died so far from home.

Still I crouched there in the luminous dark. The silence filled my ears. I stared up at the wall of stones, though I could not see it. Or anything except a pattern in the air, which seemed huge and far away from me or else as tiny as a coin suspended just before my eyes. White lines in the darkness. It was the pattern that first I'd seen in Pilate's prison when I was in Caesarea. Then I had seen it in my cell in the mud fortress, a pattern that went nowhere, for the ends of it were lost.

There are explanations which explain nothing. I put my hand out toward the knotted line. It gleamed in the darkness, meaningless, without substance, but for me it was the thread which Ariadne left for Theseus, which brought him from the maze. So I climbed up to my starting place again.

How long could it have been? Everything was different when I reached the top. I stood in the darkness behind the statue of Artemis, hidden in the cleft of the rock. The blue flame burned lower now. It was almost gone.

I peered out into the alcove, and I saw Queen Agathocleia kneeling down before the statue of Artemis, a few paces from where I hid. She knelt in her blue gown. Had she been there all along, when I said good-bye to Jeshua?

Near her the young soldier lay asleep. And at the entrance to the temple where the bodies of the Greeks lay in rows, Jeshua stood facing me, although he couldn't see me.

I was listening to Agathocleia, her low voice. She murmured a prayer, and I caught only a few words. She bowed down to the virgin goddess, then she turned. Still on her knees, she was facing Jeshua, and I admired the silk cloth between her shoulder blades, lit by the flickering blue fire. "Tonight is the last night," she said. "For all of us."

Jeshua spoke, but I couldn't hear him. There was a roaring in my ears, a pain like a cold wind in my mouth. Agathocleia got to her feet. "Look at me," she said. "I've made my peace with the Virgin. I prayed to her for strength. But I'm still afraid."

Perhaps my eyes, starved in the darkness, could not at first make sense of what they saw. Agathocleia held a knife in her right hand. Heterocrania cannot hide the truth; I knew what I was seeing. Now there was a roaring in the streets outside. However long I was in the dark pit, it had been time enough for Gondophares to break down the gate. There were Scythians in the acropolis.

"Slave, look at me," said Agathocleia. But Jeshua was staring at his hands, which were clasped in front of him.

"I share the weakness of my sex," said the queen. "But you are a strong man."

She held the knife out toward him. "You brought him back to life," she said, meaning the young soldier by her feet. "What good is that?" She turned the blade until it pointed toward herself.

Jeshua looked at her, dry-eyed, an expression almost of anger on his face. "I cannot."

"If you can't, others will. No man has looked at me until tonight."

Blue light flickered on her skin, on the silk between her shoulder blades. There was a crash at the door, and the smell of burning. Jeshua stepped forward, grabbing at the knife. But Queen Agathocleia was too quick. She hid the blade behind her back, and, laughing, she pushed past him into the belly of the temple, where the dead men lay. She disappeared. After a moment, Jeshua followed her.

"Great mother, defend me," I said. "If you spare my life, then I will bless your name beside the lake. And when I see the Diamond Mountain I will go down on my knees. . . ." I went on and on, mumbling this nonsense, and then in my Scythian armor I ran for the entrance, between the rows of corpses. My eyes, veiled with sickness, could see nothing.

Outside there was a roaring and a crying, for the Scythians were in the streets. I didn't stop to look. I ran down through the crowd along the parapet, where soldiers dressed like me were throwing children to the rocks, choosing only the boys; it was a game for them. Women were screaming and crawling over the stones. I couldn't hear. My ears were full of a strange silence, as if the men and women around me had no substance. They couldn't touch me. They were like figures painted on a wall.

I ran toward the gate. No one could touch me. No one could harm me. Only one man—he pushed through until he reached me and grabbed hold of my arm. "You!" he shouted.

He had been a slave, a servant of Demetrius Soter. I had seen him many times in the acropolis. Now he was grabbing at my cap and trying to pull it off. I put my hands out. Scythian soldiers were there.

"You," he said. "You were with them. You were with the stranger. They took him to the king's house."

I answered in the Aryan tongue. "I don't know what you mean."

"Yes!" he shouted. "The barbarian who defeated great Apollodotus. You were with him. Now. Just now."

But I answered, "I don't know him." God gave me strength. I pushed his hands away, and then the Scythians came and threw him down upon the stones. One had a club and beat him on the shoulders and the head.

I didn't stop. I ran down to the gate. And then the rest, it's like a dream to me. Now after so many years, it's like a dream inside a dream. Yes, there were angry faces, but I passed through them, through the burning town and through the valley all that night, crouching in the ditches beside the road, stumbling along the lines of willow trees. I crouched in the shadows and climbed by the ruined towers. I followed the stream, and followed it east for many hours. When I could go no farther, I found a shelter in the rocks and wrapped myself in an old blanket, which I had stolen in the town. In my fist I had the gold coin with Lord Boddo's name on it. I would have given it to anyone who'd asked.

In the morning when I woke, I crawled down to the stream and washed my face in the icy water. But I could not offer thanks to God.

Jeshua went into the street, where the soldiers tied his hands in front of him. The sky was red and full of soot. He stood in a crowd of people in the cold air, testing the rope until his wrists were sore.

No, he thought, I will not break these ropes. Not mine but yours, he thought, in the middle of his prayer. He prayed without stopping. Father, forgive me. Father, forgive me.

With many others he was taken to a storehouse and locked

inside. There were no windows but a small crack in the wall. Because there was no room to sit, he stood. Around him men were whispering and crying.

All night he stood there. Toward morning he spoke aloud. "Hatzilayni mi poalei ah ven umesh anshei damim hoshi ayni." When they led him out, he said, "Nafshi b'tokh le va im."

So the soldiers might understand, he said, "My soul is with the lions, and I lie with those whose bodies have been set on fire. Their teeth are arrows and their tongue is a sharp sword. But oh my God, you are above the sky, and your strength is above the earth."

One of the soldiers asked him, "What is the god you cry to?"

He answered, "There is only one."

Then the soldier asked him, "What is the language that you speak?"

He answered, "It is the language of the Jews."

He was standing in a line of prisoners behind the temple, waiting to climb down into the town. But the soldier separated him out and took him to his captain, who was waiting in a corner of the wall. He said, "This is no Yavana, but someone else."

The captain questioned him. When he was done, he sent word to Gondophares, saying, "This is no weakling or dirty Greek, but a man from the western ocean. He is a strong man, as you will see."

But Gondophares did not come. Jeshua stood near the parapet, dressed in his shirt as the snow trickled down. "Shim ah Elohim rinati hakshivah tefillati. From the end of the world I will cry to you," he said, as the Greeks were stretched out on the rocks and killed with their young sons and daughters. "Va ani ashir uzeh kha. I will speak aloud of your forgiveness on this day," he said, as the gutters filled with the red snow. He did not weep, but blood dripped from his face.

In the afternoon the women were taken away. The soldier cut the ropes from Jeshua's wrists and led him down from the acropolis, into an open space beyond the walls. He told him, "When you come before Lord Gondophares, kneel in front of him and put your head into the dust." But where they were, the ground was wet with blood.

"I will not kneel to him," said Jeshua. When they brought him food and water, still he did not eat or drink.

That night they locked him by himself in a cold room, in a house they had not burned. He lay on the floor and dreamed this dream: There was a mountain that was separate from the rest, a tower of snow and ice. The sunlight fell on it, and the ice glittered like a jewel. A voice out of the mountaintop was loud and yet could not be understood. In his sleep, Jeshua put his hands up to his ears.

The Scythians brought him barley and water in the morning, but he took neither. He sat by himself on the cold floor. Then in the afternoon he dreamed again: He saw the walls of Jerusalem with the sunlight on them. He saw the Hasmonaean palace and the fortress of Antonia. And away from the wall in a bare place of stones—it was the hill where criminals were put to death. The Romans had put up three heavy poles, and Philoxenus of Pergamon was nailed to the top of the right-hand pole. Nagasena was nailed to the pole on the left hand, but the middle pole was empty.

"You cried out in your sleep," said the soldier when he came in. In the evening they brought him bread, but for the third time he refused it. And that night he dreamed of his mother's house in Nazareth. There was a crowd of people, dressed in festival clothes as if for the Passover. But there had been no guests like that in his mother's house, and the room had never been so richly prepared. There was a table with a feast spread across it, with bread and meat and wine. "Come," said his mother, and she brought him a bowl of water. He washed his hands and washed his face until the water was black and red, and then she dressed him in a new shirt and led him to the head of the table. "All is forgiven now," she said. To others she said, "Bring out his father's robe and put it on him. Put shoes on his feet. Bring the calf and kill it, and let us eat. For my son was lost, yet here he is. He was dead and now he is alive."

He looked down the length of the board. And in the crowd of faces he picked out his cousin and his uncle and his little brother. He picked out his friend Barabbas and Menahem of Galilee, and beside him stood Joseph the carpenter, who had put his mother aside when she was with child, who had never before been to that house, but who was smiling now and saying, "This is my son."

When Jeshua woke, his eyes were dry as stones. Philoxenus and Nagasena were in his mind. Had they already been reborn, cast out into the bloody world once again? Or had God taken them home into the pure land?

He sat remembering Nagasena and their hours of talk. How they had talked together in the king's house, and Nagasena had sat cross-legged on the bare stones. Once he had said, "Jeshua, when the spring comes to this valley, where will you go?"

Jeshua told him what he had learned from Corax the slave about the golden cities of the east. Where men and women live forever because of their wisdom. Where there are no rich and poor. Where there are a thousand temples by the riverbank, and Nagasena said, "To you and me, all cities are the same."

Jeshua told him what the slave had said about the great river that takes away our sins. Which flows out of the Cow's Mouth and across the plain. And Nagasena said, "To you and me, all rivers are the same."

Then Jeshua told him what the slave had said about the lake, about the Diamond Mountain where God lives. And Nagasena said, "To you and me, all mountains are the same."

He said: "These places, they are not for you. Now you want to go. You want to see. You want to learn. But a man without desire, only he can understand. Only he can love."

He said: "As for the pure land, you can find it inside every fool and beggar."

And he said: "There is another stream that runs from Alexandria Larisa. It is a small stream, and it runs south and east through the mountains until it reaches the city of Taxila. There it joins a larger river called Vitasta, or Hydaspes in the Greek tongue. This river flows south until it joins the Indus as it runs through the Gandara. And at the mouth of this river where it comes into the gulf stands the city of Patala. There you can find the ships that sail to Spasinu, and Berenice, and even to the town of Elath on the borders of your own country."

As he spoke, Jeshua moved on ahead to streams he hadn't named. In Bethabara, beyond Jordan, he had gone with his cousin when they were both children. As Nagasena spoke, and now in Gondophares's cell as he remembered it, he saw an image of his cousin John standing in the water up to his knees.

Now Jeshua closed his eyes. "God if you choose, deliver me," he said, and in his mind he saw the water brown and clear, its surface specked with gold. John stood with the water dripping from his two hands. He looked up in the morning sunlight, and Jeshua was coming over the hill, and he was dusty and dirty and thirsty from his long road.

6

THE DIAMOND MOUNTAIN

LOOKING BACK

Now I am at the end of my story. Now I have time to think while the bronze is heated and the mold is prepared. A week ago, all night I lay unsleeping on my little bed. In the morning I left the dormitory and stood outside in the cold air, watching the sky grow pink over the ice mountains.

Then I went back into the courtyard where the students of the temple were bustling and stirring and carrying water. I went up the steps and looked in at the door, where old Pemba was lighting a fire of juniper in front of the statue, offering prayers in his reedy voice. I breathed in, filling my lungs with smoke and the sweet smell of the butter candles. Light glistened on the bronze thighs.

This is Mayatreia, Lord Boddo who is to come. He is twice the height of a tall man, cast in pieces out of seven-metal bronze.

Though it is forbidden, my pleasure at his shining face is mixed with leaden pride—I made him. No one else could have done the work.

The previous night it was the first night of the growing moon. It rose, a tiny sliver, and we sat in the courtyard under its tiny light, saying together the words of the pratimoksha, the rule that governs our lives in this place. And I renewed my promise not to steal, not to lie, not to kill, not to drink beer mixed with poppy gum or hemp, not to spill my seed. Then afterwards we spoke our faults aloud. It was not my turn, for which I thanked Lord Hanuman the monkey, because I had no wish to confess my pride. Our teachers are strict men. They might have stopped the work on the new statue. Already they argue about it in their debates, which are interminable.

Some of the old men reject God and all his names. Others worship every natural power and demon. I am a servant here. No one asks for my opinion.

At first I worked in the kitchen. But one of the old men came to ask me about the places I had been, and I told him stories. Later I made a drawing of the pattern as a gift for him, because he asked me about it many times. I drew it on a sheet of cloth, using colors I made myself—the pattern of lines I had seen at first in Caesarea, in Pontius Pilate's cell, and then many times inside my mind. Now it is painted on the wall beside the statue of Lord Mayatreia. Now it is complete—the floor of an imaginary building painted on a blue circle, which is the circle of our lives. And I can see now that the lines are not ways of escaping but of going in. If you sit and stare at it, as many do, then when you close your eyes you can walk into it room by room, and up each stair into the topmost chamber, which is empty, but has a door in each of its four sides.

In fact I never reach that chamber, though I know it's there. Others climb farther, because they don't have as much to think about as I do. Memories clog the rooms and stairs, and I get tired.

But I stood in the doorway looking at the round pattern on

the wall. I am not allowed to enter in, if the students are there. So I came in the early morning. As the first students took their seats, I turned my back and wandered out past the dormitory.

The new statue was cast over many days. I went out to the shop to look. No one else was there. The men were all working in the fields. I had given orders to wait, to let me alone, so I could see the finished head before the rest of the bronze was melted and poured.

This was because of some changes in the process since I had cast the head of Mayatreia. Some ideas I had borrowed from the Romans. I had built my head in layers on a wooden frame. First a matting of straw, and then a model of rough clay. Then on the clay I carved the head out of a layer of beeswax.

Then sixteen layers of clay of different grades. The first was the purest I could find, which I had strained and kneaded over many weeks. Each layer was painted on. But all of them together made up a thickness, so I put in many holes, so that the wax and air would come out easily.

I had built the mold inside a furnace at the bottom of a hole. Then when the wax was melted and the clay was hard, I took the furnace apart brick by brick. I had it lifted out. Then I covered my mold with a wooden frame and let the men fill in the hole so that the earth was level and the mold was under it. All the time I was enlarging the vents which had drawn off the hot wax. I made tubes of baked clay and ran them through the earth, especially at the bottom of the mold—the neck and chin. The air collects and can't be driven out.

I stood over the place. Others had poured the metal while I rested, then I let it cool for several days. I stood with my shovel, looking at the sun, remembering Jeshua, my friend and helper, whom I had left to die in Alexandria Larisa.

The dirt around the mold was loose, and I began to dig, even though I am not made for that work—my hands have never been strong. But on the night of the new moon I had thought about my sins and about my penance. As I began to dig I thought about Jeshua and the last part of the story. Which was the longest but also the shortest—it took me four years to reach the Cow's Mouth where the river comes out.

Along the way I practiced my art in Kapisa and Taxila and Mathura, on the Jamuna river. And I grew sicker all the time. It was the burden of a sadness that made me take to my bed. In my memory I recognized the sadness that had killed my father, for as time went on I ate more and more of the hemp gum, the bhang that was his recipe. I did this to relieve the aching in my head, to let me sleep.

Once in Mathura I was living on a mat in the temple court-yard. In the mornings I went to the market, where there was al-ways a crowd around me while I worked. They seemed to crush me with their presence. I could not remember, could not think, though as always these miseries did not affect my skill. My hands seemed to live apart from me. I could not stand it, and in the evening I pushed out through the grateful people and walked down to the water. There where the filth washed out of the town, I watched some men and children on the funeral ground, burn-ing their dead. Once again I thought of my poor father and the promise I had made, which I had put off so often because of my sickness and unworthiness. That night, as I watched the fire burn down and listened to the laughter of the children, I told myself how I would reach the mountain even if I died there.

In those days I was driven mad by heterocrania and regrets. At times I thought my brain would burst out of my skull. I made a list of my complaints: loose and bloody stool, boils on my back and arms, a rash on my head, which made my hair thin over my left ear. My lungs were full of water. Sometimes I coughed and coughed until I tasted blood in my mouth.

I had an ache in my stomach and my heart. And always a pain in my head that filled the air with light. I had terrible fevers, which burned my skin from the inside, which made me drink and drink and not be satisfied—From Mathura northward stretches a vast plain. It is a country less of the world than of the mind, and I think of this process of my body as the important one as I walked through the endless fields, over the endless roads. It was wintertime, dusty and dry.

The rivers of the underworld, cold and hot, stretch northward through the dry ground. They are the arteries and veins, and one river carries wakefulness to every part of the body. The other carries heat, for when the blood stops moving, the flesh begins to cool.

The rivers of the underworld come to the surface underneath the ice. In that country, wakefulness was coming up from underground. Beset as I was by constant pain, I had no interest in the world. Nor do I want to speak of it. This was a meaningless journey, though it took many months. But at last I came into the mountains, and I climbed up from the town of the rishis, up the river to the Cow's Mouth.

There is a mass of ice and dust and rock that fills the valley. And the river comes from underneath it through a tunnel in the ice. It is the throat of the cow, and the water bursts out through lips of shattered rock and falls into a pool.

There is a constant froth over the pool, made of ice and air. The water is white as milk. Piers of rock fall into it where I climbed down. I splashed in the water between the ice boulders, and in the last light of evening, the first light of morning, I said prayers.

This is the way of pilgrims, and there are many on the road. Others stood with me on the bank, huddled in their blankets or else washing their clothes with icy fingers. Women had made this journey. Some were carrying children. Downstream there was a temple at the first waterfall. Brahmans lived there. Little towns had gathered there among the trees.

But above the Cow's Mouth the road is harder. There is a valley with cliffs on either side. The sun comes late and soon it goes away. Pine trees grow in the shadows. In the spring the rocks are wet. The cliffs are lined with waterfalls, which fill the air with spray.

As you climb up, noises in your body spread outside your-self. The pounding of your heart, the sucking cough that comes out of your lungs, the rumbling inside your head turns outward into a thunder of rocks falling and water flowing. In the thin air you can hear everything. The ice above the river is full of sounds. And above the cliffs the ice peaks rise forever into the pure land, and you can hear the clouds of sliding snow. Above them, in the middle of the day, the sky is almost black.

The river flows out of the ice and falls steep into the valley. The road follows it down. But above the Cow's Mouth the valley is wider, and it is filled from edge to edge with ice and shattered rock. The road climbs up over it, an unsure way, and sometimes men are killed. The ice splits and changes as night freezes it, and then the sun makes it soft.

But after a day we came up to the field of Tapovan. No trees grew here. The air was thin and hard to breathe. The grass was covered with small flowers.

I slept for two nights in a small cave, trying to recover my strength. But when I stood up I felt sick and dizzy and could only take a few steps. I sat against the rocks, watching the light move over the ice walls of Shiva's Penis, which is the mountain that rises over Tapovan. Patterns of light hung suspended in the air. They hurt my eyes.

I sat with my back against the rocks. The clear sunlight seemed to push against my face. My skin felt thick and burned. My lips were burned, and I drank ice water constantly. At night I rolled up in my blanket, chattering with cold. I couldn't eat. Nevertheless, on the second morning I woke up refreshed, and we set off again over the rocks—a train of mules and men.

No one travels by himself in that country. But these men, the sun shone so bright, I could barely see their faces. At every step the light seemed to hit me on the head. And there was noth-ing to think about in that wilderness of rock, water, dust, ice, air, and light, except the working of my body. The thin air cutting in through my burnt lungs. The pain in my head and my bruised hands and feet. But in time even these things disappeared as we came up onto the high plain that is the center of the world.

At night the stars circled above us, around the pole. During the day the wind blew unimpeded from its source, the cave of winds beneath the Diamond Mountain. It filled our ears and eyes with dust. It made us bleed out of our noses and our gums. I put my hand over my face as if warding off a blow.

Pilgrims had made cairns among the rocks. And sometimes we could see men in the distance, and shaggy cows grazing on the tiny grass. Black-skinned men rode by on ponies. They were the inhabitants of that place. They waved their arms when they saw us and made strange, joyful cries.

Our faces and our hands were burned and cold. I wrapped rags around my fingers, over my cheeks and mouth. I felt weak. Yet at the same time I had no urge to pause or stop or sleep or eat. Walking seemed effortless. We passed under a gate. It was two towers of piled stones, and a rope strung between them lined with red and yellow flags. They made a flapping like a thunder, which we heard from far away.

In time we came to the shores of Lake Manosarovar, which is the largest lake. Through caverns underneath the rocks the sea comes up, stripped of its salt, distilled out of the fires underneath the earth. Sometimes you can see the skeletons of sea creatures printed on the rocks. The water pours up like a fountain, up to the high middle of the world. And from the plain it flows off to the east and west, south and north: the Rhine, the Tigris, the Euphrates, the Indus, the Ganges, the Yalung, and the Serican rivers also, which run out to the circling waters of the sea.

As we came down to the shore, the wind was still. The water was still. It was the color of milk. We shouted with joy and waded into it, throwing fistfuls of water into the air, where the light caught it. Then we made fires. It was evening, and the sun glowed red.

But in the morning I got up before dawn and went down to the water. There was dust, and clay, and iron, and sand. The sand was full of ice. And then finally I came to the water, where I knelt down and said a prayer for my father. And because I had not brought his bones, his body, his ashes, or any part of him, I made an image out of clay. It was an image of his face, the first I ever built out of any material. Though later I learned this art and became skilled in it, that morning I could not make the lines of his face come clear.

The ice melted in the sand. The sky grew light, but the sun never rose. After weeks and weeks without a cloud, the sky above me was now filled with a fine mist. It drifted over the lake.

I went up to the layer of clay again, and when I came back I saw the water had washed over the image I had made. So I left it and walked back toward where I had left the others, but I couldn't find them. The mist had covered them, had covered their yawns and whispers and the grunting of the mules. It had covered the cairns and flags and fires. I walked along the shore, wondering how it might feel if they were swallowed up, if I were alone in that high space. And I was thinking also of the jouney I had made from Tusculum, where I had murdered Cornelius Celsus and left him bleeding in his bath, four years before. I stood there with the water of Lake Manosarovar around my feet, making the calculations in several languages. As near as I could guess, now in Palestine it was the second week of Nisan. The week of the Passover. Now, perhaps, four years ago, it was the evening when I saw Jeshua of Nazareth in the cave outside of Caesarea.

Then at the moment I conceived of this, I saw a man walking away from me along the shore. There was something about him. I saw his back, his big, broad back. I saw his hair, part of his beard. His shoulders bent. I saw him walking like a strong man carrying a stone. "Master," I said. "Rabbi."

Then he turned, and I saw I was mistaken. All these things were the same in him, and yet it was not he. How could it be? I had left him to die in Alexandria Larisa. His coarse hair, his beard, his broken nose. It was like the image I had made in clay of my father's face. Every detail, and yet I could not recognize him.

I thought perhaps he was a ghost. Yet after a moment he blew his nose on his hand and stooped to wash it in the water. Then he smiled, and spoke in a language I had not heard before. But I did not approach him.

THE DREAM

And after that, there is nothing to tell. Only a dream. In the afternoon the mist burned away. I climbed up to a hill, and between the clouds I saw the Diamond Mountain rising above a bank of clouds, a flawless triangle. The sunlight caught the edges of its adamantine sides. I could not look. It hurt my eyes. But through my beaded lashes I saw the crease of Shiva's ladder, which rises to the peak. No one can look at it. I fell down to my knees, seeing not with my eyes but with my body, my mouth, my ears. God, I thought. That is the pure land.

I curled up on the rock. Out of the wind, the sun was hot. Almost at once I fell asleep. I had a dream, and he was there, complete in my memory. Every mark of his face. "Rabbi," I said, "where are you? I left you in the town."

In the dream he showed me the prison where he was held. But Gondophares had let him go. And God had showed him a stream of water, which led back to his own country.

"Rabbi," I said, "what then? Did the Sanhedrin condemn you? Did Pilate nail you up?"

When he didn't answer, I said, "Rabbi, what shall I do now? Where shall I go?" And in my dream he took me to the lake. He made me step into the water and wash the tears out of my eyes. Then he showed me an image of the place where I now live, a village to the west of the high Himalaya, in the country of Kashmir, in a willow grove on the banks of a loud stream. Hemis is the name of the village. Go-Tsang is the name of the house.

These were the thoughts I was imagining as I dug in the

loose dirt around the mold. My hands were covered in blisters, which bled water mixed with blood. But I knew I had nothing to fear from these small wounds. There was no salve or ointment I could put on them. Soon they would be dry and clean, because from that day to this I have had no fever, sickness, ulcer, or abscess. When it comes to the knowledge of these things and all the rules that Dion taught me, I have told nobody. I have forgotten much, and the rest will die with me when I die. The skill in my hands is gone, replaced by this new skill. With my shovel I broke through the clay spouts, full of weak bronze and air. Then I broke through the top of the mold itself, chopping it down until I could see the face. It is Lord Boddo who heals all sicknesses, the first of eight statues I have planned. But the face is big, with a big nose and lips—perhaps the teachers will be angry. Because there is something in the face that is not the calmness of Lord Boddo, that belongs instead to my master, Jeshua of Nazareth, who first put my feet upon these stones. If he escaped to his own country, if he died there without a single man or woman learning his name, if he is forgotten now as if he never lived, then let this image I have made remember him so he will live, like it, forever.

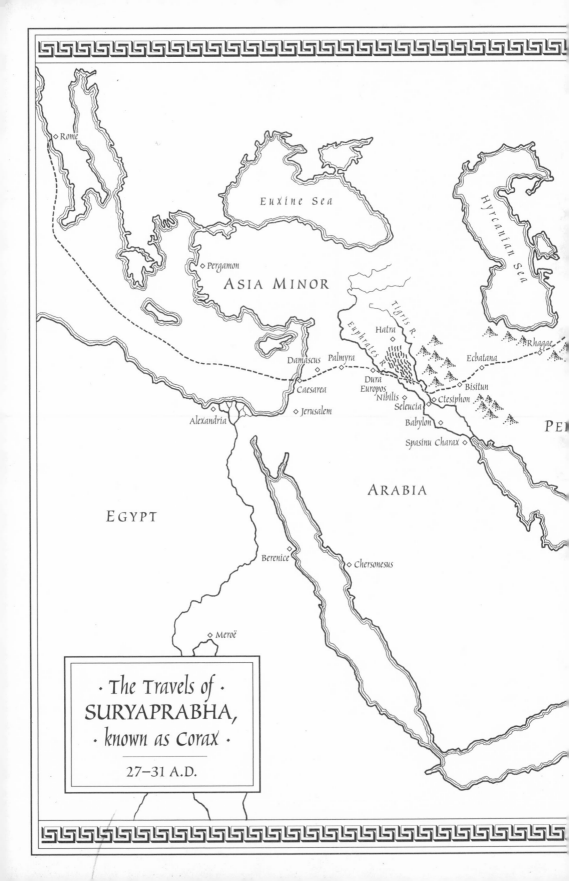

Rome

Euxine Sea

Hyrcanian Sea

Pergamon

ASIA MINOR

Tigris R.

Euphrates R.

Hatra

Rhagae

Ecbatana

Damascus   Palmyra

Dura
Europos
Caesarea   Nibilis   Bisitun

Seleucia   Ctesiphon

Jerusalem

Alexandria   Babylon

Spasinu Charax   PE

ARABIA

EGYPT

Berenice   Chersonesus

Meroë

· The Travels of ·
SURYAPRABHA,
· known as Corax ·

27–31 A.D.